Of MYTHS & Muses

A DARK FATES NOVEL

T.C. KRAVEN

DIVERSION
BOOKS

Diversion Books
A division of Diversion Publishing Corp. www.diversionbooks.com

Diversion Books and colophon are registered trademarks of Diversion Publishing Corp.

For more information, email info@diversionbooks.com

First Diversion Books Edition: July 2026
Trade paperback ISBN: 9798895150634
e-ISBN: 9798895150641

Design by Neuwirth & Associates, Inc.
Cover design by T.C. Kraven
Chapter header illustrations by Artywings
Interior cover illustrations by Snow_WI

Printed in the United States of America
1 3 5 7 9 10 8 6 4 2

Diversion books are available at special discounts for bulk purchases in the US by corporations, institutions, and other organizations. For more information, please contact admin@diversionbooks.com.

To those who've yet to tell their stories
but carry on anyway.
For Nessa

The Divine

OF THE DARK FATES

PROMETHEUS

TITAN OF
KNOWLEDGE

ZARENA

DAUGHTER
OF THE MUSE
OF HISTORY

HADES

GOD OF THE
UNDERWORLD,
BORN OF OLYMPIAN
ESSENCE

PERSEPHONE

GODDESS OF SPRING,
BORN OF
DEMETER + ZEUS

HEPHAESTUS

GOD OF THE FORGE,
BORN OF HERA,
BONDED TO
APHRODITE

APHRODITE

GODDESS OF LOVE,
BORN OF
OLYMPIAN ESSENCE,
BONDED TO ARES +
HEPHAESTUS

ARES

GOD OF WAR,
BORN OF ZEUS,
BONDED TO
APHRODITE

HERMES

MESSENGER GOD
OF THIEVES,
BORN OF ZEUS +
A MORTAL LOVER

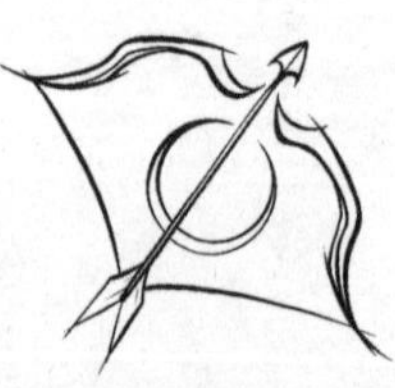

ARTEMIS

GODDESS OF
THE HUNT,
BORN OF
ZEUS + LETO

NICK

WOODLAND NYMPH

HELIOS

TITAN OF THE SUN,
BORN OF
HYPERION + THEIA

ZEUS

GOD OF GODS,
BORN OF OLYMPIAN
ESSENCE,
BONDED TO HERA

DIONYSUS

GOD OF WINE,
BORN OF
ZEUS + SEMELE

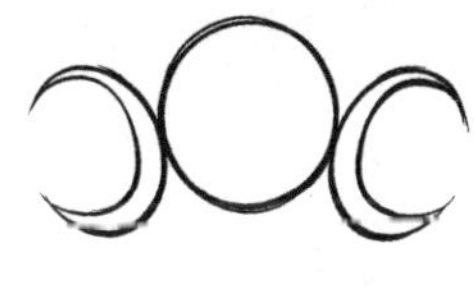

HECATE

GODDESS OF
WITCHCRAFT,
BORN OF
ASTERIA + PERSES

THANATOS

GOD OF DEATH,
BORN OF
NYX + EREBUS

HERA

GODDESS OF
MARRIAGE + BONDS,
BORN OF OLYMPIAN
ESSENCE, BONDED
TO ZEUS

POSEIDON

GOD OF THE SEA,
BORN OF OLYMPIAN
ESSENCE,
BONDED TO ATHENA

ATHENA

GODDESS OF
WISDOM,
BORN OF ZEUS,
BONDED TO POSEIDON

Playlist

1. *Possum Kingdom*—The Toadies

2. *No Safe Place*—Party at the Moontower

3. *Marked For Death*—Emma Ruth Rundle

4. *Colorblind*—Counting Crows

5. *Wires*—Athlete

6. *Hurt*—Nine Inch Nails

7. *Terrible Thing*—AG

8. *Running Up That Hill*—Placebo

9. *Hearing Damage*—Thom Yorke

10. *Wicked Game*—Giant Drag

11. *Cruel Melody*—Black Light Burns

12. *The Earth Isn't Humming*—Thrice

13. *Moving Mountains*—Thrice

14. *The Man Who Sold the World*—Nirvana

15. *Come a Little Closer*—Cage The Elephant

Scan the QR code
to access the Spotify playlist:

AUTHOR'S NOTE

The next books in the Dark Fates will take us to all manner of places, but I would be remiss if I didn't take a moment to touch on New Orleans, where the majority of the books reside, and the importance of the representation in these pages. Louisiana is a mecca of culture, people and languages, and you will see that reflected in the characters, in the city itself throughout the series.

I grew up in diverse circles because of my city, and because I lean so heavily on my own experience when writing, I couldn't fathom not including those voices. As they are not always my own, I have endeavored at every turn to employ an extensive and trusted group of sensitivity and inclusion readers.

Of Myths & Muses has us branching out into the city more, with Zarena, Tatiana, and Andros born and raised in the N.O. In Myths, we are introduced more thoroughly to the LOA, Vodou spirits revered and respected in our city, even from those who do not practice. It is important to note that Root Work, and many other spiritual practices rooted in RW in Louisiana are CLOSED PRACTICES. We do not, in any way, invoke those closed practices or show them depicted in the Dark Fates. That is *not* our story to tell, and for me, personally, no amount of sensitivity readers in the world would make it so.

But telling the story of gods in the city and not paying homage to the LOA felt inauthentic, so after careful consultation with three active practitioners (in addition to the returning Black and

BIPOC sensitivity readers we are blessed to have), I decided to slightly alter the origins and certain aspects of the gods, in efforts to not tread on active practices, or exploit gods brought to this country on the back of Black pain. We do not in any way, shy away from the horrors inflicted on the people stolen and brought to this land for greed and cruelty, but with respect to the many sects of gods, I have altered a sliver of their origins here, guided by hands more skilled and knowledgeable than I on the subject. I tell you this, so that any readers who practice will understand why the origins read a little differently in these pages. I would like to thank Avena, Stella, and Chels for your patience, diligence and wealth of knowledge in your sensitivity reading for the LOA.

To Rowe, Malcom, Tatiana Shondrell, Ashley, Diana, Mattiew, Kiana, and Shane, thank you for your continued efforts, expertise and insight for the Dark Fates and of course, *Of Myths & Muses*.

The Dark Fates explores many themes, including kink and BDSM, the complexities of trauma, a myriad of relationship dynamics, sexuality and fluidity, and the deep effects of misogyny and its permeation through society. Intersectionality, racial inequality, and class warfare are all part of the real struggles and lives in the Crescent City. You'll find them in this series. I am extremely proud to work with the people I do, and to be blessed with their honesty, integrity, and patience. With that being said, if there is ever a moment that an own voice feels the need to raise an issue, I welcome that contact. I can only move with open intention and be ready to listen, for conversation, and learning.

I know that best intentions do not negate unintentional harm.

Thank you for entering my world.

Welcome back to my New Orleans.

CONTENT WARNING

Our fourth installment finds us telling the stories of those deeply affected by Zeus and his abuse. Most of those stories aren't pleasant, because Zeus is the actual worst. There are mentions throughout the book that allude to SA done by him, and one chapter in particular recounts the act through memory, and it is explicit, told as respectfully as possible. When you see the italics in Chapter 52, please proceed with caution if this is a trigger for you.

Other content that could be triggering are adoption/identity turbulence, suicide, imprisonment, death of a parent, death of a spouse/child, PTSD and flashbacks.

In addition, this novel contains several themes within the BDSM sphere including but not limited to: Hard Dom/Brat/Sub dynamics, impact play, marking, soaking, praise/degradation, informed consent, rough sex, bondage, DP, anal, exhibitionism, breath play, and more. If you have questions about a particular kink, you can contact me, and I will be happy to provide any insight I am able.

Prologue

Following his victory in the Titanomachy, the unimaginable weight of Zeus's oppressive cruelty went unchallenged for centuries.

He shackled the divine not with open war but by whispers and oaths, by favors promised and debts collected. He unmade rebellion with a kiss to the brow and a knife in the dark.

Cruelty cloaked under the guise of justice, his tyranny sanctioned in the name of reason. And when the other gods trembled, he smiled, for their trembling was proof of his order.

Of their supplication to his will.

Murderer. Adulterer. Tyrant. His sins could fill the heavens and still overflow.

In his jealousy, he tore mortals from their other halves, splitting shade from shade to keep them yearning. In his wrath, he shrouded them in darkness. He was cunning, the God of Gods, imaginative in his punishments. Those aware of his trespasses feared the wrath and retribution of his ire far too much to speak against him and with the Bond of Hera to keep the well of his power infinite, who could stand against the rule of Olympus?

It was Prometheus, Titan of Knowledge, who dared defy him. Out of love for humankind, he stole the flame horded by the Olympians and placed it in mortal hands. For that mercy, he was chained to the bones of the earth, the desolate mountain between realms, condemned to an endless death.

His punishment became legend, his agony a warning to all who might dare to care too deeply.

But that was long ago, and the world is not what it once was. Empires built upon fear cannot silence Fate forever, and for the God of Gods, the tides are turning. Zeus does not yet see the shape of his undoing, but the Titan of Knowledge seeks the path, finding the tiniest spark of hope in the depths of Tartarus.

A purpose.

The lost Library of Alexandria, where the only weapon capable of breaking Zeus's reign of terror lies hidden, and the half muse whose life he will have to upend to get it. Zarena doesn't know yet how stained Zeus's hands are with the blood of her own, but she'll learn. In her, Prometheus sees something nearly as terrifying as his millennia chained to that rock—a tenacity that rivals his own. Compass to map, lock to key. A tyrant formed the chains of this realm, but the time has come for their breaking.

Spark to fire, titan to muse.

And Zeus will learn, as they will remind, vengeance is a flame that never dies.

Zarena

CHAPTER 1

MARCH 1996

"I just think that there's a reason the so-called 'gender wage gap' exists," my date, Gregory, drawled on from across the table.

The wine I was swallowing stalled in my throat as my eyes narrowed into slits. *The fuck did he just say?*

Gregory was my third blind date this week, and I made a mental note to smack the piss out of Becky, the newest member of the Local History department who set this up. Gregory, *not Greg*, had been quick to point out when I showed up at Antoine's, my go-to first date spot.

I studied him, mentally shutting out whatever idiotic notions I'm sure followed his flippant comment. He was a meteorologist and worked at WDSU with Becky's boyfriend, Alex. Gregory-not-Greg talked with his hands, brandishing his silverware around, and though those green eyes were deep and beautiful, the mind behind it was as shallow as a sink. His dark, sandy blond hair sat perfectly coiffed on his head and impeccably straight teeth sat behind a nice set of lips. He knew he was conventionally attractive, making him even more insufferable.

If he had just eaten dinner and talked less, I probably would have brought him home, gone a few rounds, then sent him on his way. As it stood now, he'd be lucky to make it out of Antoine's without a fork in his thigh.

For over an hour, he'd barely shut up long enough to ask me anything about myself. What was more, his "hot takes" were some of the most delusional and uninformed pieces of regurgitated rhetoric I'd ever heard.

"For example, take your job." He surveyed. "You're a librarian, which is great, but you wouldn't make as much as say, my job. You don't have as many responsibilities, and to be frank"—he spoke between bits of his well-done-but-not-overcooked steak—"the government jobs in lower-tiered and nonessential services are really pushing us toward a recession."

The blood in my veins cooled to ice. I could overlook a lot of things, but library slander was a mile too far.

I set my fork and knife down gently and placed my hands on either side of my plate, splaying my fingers over the white tablecloth. The candle between us burned low, almost to extinction. Perfect symbolism for this neanderthal. He hadn't noticed my demeanor shift, hadn't even taken a moment to stem his tirade to spare me a glance. "Ahem, Greg?" I cleared my throat. "Can I call you Greg?"

He stopped mid-sentence to survey me with a look clearly thinking me rude for interrupting. "Actually, it's *Gregory*—"

"I actually don't care," I cut him off. His eyes bulged. "I just gotta stop you right there. I'm not going to put too much into this, because frankly, this has gone about—" I checked my watch, "forty-five minutes too long. But have you ever been told before that you're completely insufferable? Wage gaps between men and women are *very* real. As for my job at the library, I am an *archivist*.

I have a *master's degree* from one of the best schools in the country. And you have, what? A bachelor's degree from a state school? Don't get me wrong, there is nothing wrong with a state school, but acting as though you have some moral superiority because you don't value public services is horrendous behavior. You're a meteorologist for a local news station, let's not act like you're out here saving *lives*. And as for your dig at public libraries? I'm not even going to get into that because I don't think your bird brain could comprehend how unfathomably classist you're being. So, you should go. *Now*." I sat back, folding my arms over my chest.

Gregory-not-Greg went red from the embarrassment my verbal lashing had given him. His fork clattered against the plate. I licked the pad of my forefinger and thumb before leaning forward to snuff out the dying flame dancing between us. A signal to Mattias, our server, to get this dude gone.

"I can't believe you just fucking said that! My job *does* save lives," he hissed, leaning over his plate. A vein in his neck strained as I chuckled, a feigned innocent tone, pressing my hand to my chest. "Greg, why are you getting emotional? I'm just being *frank*, and facts don't care about your feelings."

"*You fucking bitch*." The words left perfect lips curled in a snarl, showing me the ugly living just below his shallow surface. I braced myself as he puffed out his chest. "I shouldn't even *be* here. You're lucky I even agreed to go out with someone like you," he snapped, discarding his napkin onto his plate, sitting back in disgust. His gaze felt like slime on my skin as he looked me up and down, and for the first time, I wished I'd worn something with sleeves, anything to act as a barrier between us, but I refused to show him that. Instead, I raised an eyebrow, daring him to go on.

"I should have turned right around when I saw you were a fat chick. But I thought, nice tits, probably an easy lay." His green eyes raked over the tops of my breasts. I suppressed a shudder, and instead, leaned in. He was baiting me, going for an obvious dig because I had curves and full breasts and hips. He thought he could tear women down. It was what men like him did for sport. He wouldn't get the satisfaction, not today.

I laughed.

Loudly.

His brow furrowed in confusion. "Greg, Greg, *Greggggg*," I drawled. "You thought I'd let those grubby, second-rate hands touch me? That you'd get the *honor* of seeing how perfect my tits are when they bounce? You think someone like you deserves that?" I ran a dark purple nail over the swell of my cleavage, saw his lizard brain kick in, watched him trace the trail hungrily, tongue darting out to wet his lips. I smirked.

"You think for *one hot second* I'd let your limp, pencil dick near my vagina? I wouldn't let you touch me with someone *else's* cock. You think I'm fat? Alright cool, I am. So what? I'm a 'fat bitch' that *still* won't fuck you. Enjoy that," I scoffed and stood, tossing my napkin down.

He stood as well and his large hand came up to grip my arm as he glanced around nervously, my words causing a scene for the folks around us. Too smooth fingers squeezed, not painfully, not quite, but close enough to have my hackles rising.

I shot daggers at him through the curtain of red curl whirling around me. "Remove that hand or I'll do it for you," I snapped, rage building in my chest. With a wrench, I jerked my elbow free, watched him take in my fully standing body through his beady little eyes. They roamed, unwanted and hungry, making it clear he regretted how badly he'd fucked this up.

"Listen—maybe we just need to take a beat. There's clearly been a misunderstanding." He shot me his best panty-melting smile, one I'm sure worked on many women over the years. My lip curled at the insult, at the implication his looks would excuse his shitty behavior, enough for him to get his dick wet. He stepped into my space, pressing his body closer, all hard planes and defined muscles under his sharp black suit.

What a shame he was such a sack of shit.

"I didn't mean that earlier. You're beautiful, so sexy," he murmured, sucking his teeth, "I do like a little extra cushion for the pushin.'"

The fucking nerve of this man.

His fingers brushed against my nipple, and it took everything in my power not to vomit all over him. Instead, I slid my hand down his chest, gifted his answering smile, his eyes lowered over the silky tops of my breasts. So confident he'd smoothed over his horrific behavior and my resulting reaction.

Wrong, bitch.

My hand snaked down the front of his slacks, wrapping deftly around the mediocre cock already pulling a chub behind the cheap fabric. I massaged just a little and he bit out a small groan. "You like that, baby?" I asked, and he nodded, slightly breathless.

The rest of the room's patrons forgotten, I leaned a little closer. "I think this is *exactly* who you are, and I can guarantee it's *exactly* who I am." With sudden and considerable force, I clamped my hand down, stretching my fingers to make sure the uncomfortable pressure applied to his balls too.

"You're a fucking pig," I hissed as he yelped like a kicked dog, knees buckling. Tears welled in his eyes, but I refused to let go. "Fucking pathetic little man with a below-average dick. Don't *ever* call me again," I spat, and released him, disgusted. He looked murderously up at me, hunched over with his hands cradling his crotch and a small part of me hoped he'd push it, take it just a little too far. My hand twitched; I *itched* for a fight, for any excuse to wipe the floor with this maggot.

Instead, Mattias and my six-foot-four Marine brother, Andros, stepped from the shadows, flanking me. Mattias was tall and lean, but Andros was the size of a small mountain, with hard lines and dark brown skin rippling with rage. His chef's coat fought for its life under the strain of his muscles, threads pulled taut.

"Get the fuck out of here," Andros snarled.

Gregory-not-Greg looked between us, considering. With a sigh, he threw up his hands and backed away. The coward was several feet away before he spun on his heels and high-tailed it past the host's stand and into the muggy New Orleans night.

I grabbed my purse, fishing out some cash, but Mattias held a hand up in protest. I pressed it to his palm anyway.

"This is why we have the first date here," Andros reminded me as he gave me a once-over. Overprotective. As always.

I nodded, rolling my eyes. "I could have taken him."

He chuckled, satisfied I was unharmed. "Sis, I have no doubt. But I'd prefer to be in the area just in case." Andros turned, heading back to the kitchen, pausing briefly by our table. Deft fingers scooted the napkin off Gregory-not-Greg's unfinished steak, lips lifted in disgust. "Of course, he was the well-done cover."

The patrons around us continued to eat, ignoring the scene that just unfolded.

Welcome to the Big Easy.

Zarena

CHAPTER 2

"He said *WHAT*?!" Becky whisper-yelled, fury written into her kind face as I recounted the events from the night before.

I grimaced and leaned back in my chair behind the half-moon circulation desk, smoothing down the front of my dark green cardigan. "It was an entire shitshow."

She leaned forward, looking mortified. "I swear I had *no* idea, and I know Alex doesn't either. He's a total golden retriever, he's going to be livid when he hears about that jackass," she promised. I squeezed her hand with a soft smile. Becky shook with indignation on my behalf, and I loved her for it.

Becky *looked* like what stereotypes portrayed our profession as: small and fragile, straitlaced and proper. I'd also seen her toss grown men out onto the streets by their ear for disrupting the peace. She spoke lightly but carried a big stick.

I scanned the library once from our perch and relaxed into the familiar routine of the space. This place was home. It was comfort and warmth, a sanctuary in a cold world. A library built a hundred years ago off the generosity of a Creole slave-turned-socialite, elevated through her wits and deep ability to charm those in power. It was sort of a local legend, the way she commanded the attention of those around her at her slightest whim.

Some even said she was a witch, a queen of the dark arts, Mrs. Sillah De LaFleur. Though she lived a century before me, a feeling of reverence overwhelmed me when I walked these shelves. I admired her, from the perseverance and the tenacity she showed in a time where women, let alone a Black woman, held little to no authority. She used her status to fight for justice. Elevated her own mind and ensured that knowledge was available to *all*. Even through segregation, her will and trust guaranteed that all could enter, and all could borrow.

The high ceilings arched above me, soft light emanating from the chandeliers that adorned it. Silver stars lay painted on the ceiling, a design ordered by Sillah herself, lending a magical appeal to the space. The stacks of sturdy oak, felled by the hands of the freedmen hired to build them, stretched along the aisles, strong and proud. Smoothed and polished with the sweat from the stolen who made their own work, their own way. No masters, no whips or dogs.

When the Klan burned it down six months after completion, Sillah had it rebuilt on the same ground, by those same hands as a fuck you.

This library was filled with more than just books—it was legacy.

A legacy that would never belong to me, but I could help protect it. Uphold it, and do my part, even if I could never understand the type of burden my brother and sisters felt, being Black in America. It was a luxury I never took for granted. I was dropped on my parent's doorstep twenty-five years ago, and whoever abandoned me didn't bother to leave a note. Just a baby, bundled up and sat on the steps of the dark green house in the middle of the Ninth Ward. My parents took me in, and if they ever thought twice about it, they'd never let me know.

And up I grew, with red, unruly curls and a spattering of freckles over pale skin that all but shriveled in the sun; a stark contrast to the varying rich shades of browns of my siblings, but it didn't matter to us. I was theirs and they were mine, and biology didn't negate that.

If only it stopped with us.

Segregation ended years ago, but I saw the way they had to fight every day for the right to simply exist. It made me angry for them, mad enough to protest with them, fight for injustices they endured. But it was their pain, and I could only stand by with open ears and an aching heart while they grieved. And the Sillah. I worked here, preserving history the white-washed versions taught in schools never told.

My feet traced the familiar path of the Sillah on their own, guiding me to the very back of the library. The lush rugs stifled the sound of my flats over the floor, until I found myself standing outside of the Jewel. A room thus named because it was a hidden treasure trove of untouched history, discovered by our head librarian just days after I started here. Originally a circulation clerk, Letta Clarke changed our lives that day, helping me find a book on the bottom floor that unveiled a secret chamber hidden behind the bookcase.

Inside were genealogy charts, slave registries, diaries of slavers and captains. Three thousand feet of floor-to-ceiling bookshelves, lined with tomes so old they required the utmost care to even open, completely hidden from any official plans of record. We held each other and cried at the discovery. Hurricanes, floods, rioting, and fires had torn through this land since its inception, but Orleans Parish survived, and against all odds, so had this room.

The Board wanted to keep the discovery of the Jewel on the low until we'd properly cataloged, and the timing of onboarding an archivist seemed fortuitous. They gave me a timeline of five years to work my way through the records and properly catalog them for inspection.

It was job security if nothing else.

Though I'd never give Greg the satisfaction, his words last night sliced deep. I *was* supposed to be doing more. Not that archiving work wasn't important, it was, but it wasn't what I'd imagined for myself. Being in the field was always more my speed, and knowing that I'd had, and lost it, was a sore spot for me.

Still. The Jewel was an incredible pocket of history. When the restlessness became unbearable, I could imagine I'd stumbled into my own miniature version of the Library of Alexandria. This was a once-in-a-lifetime opportunity, but being cooped up set my teeth on edge. I wanted *more*. I missed fieldwork, craved the adventure, the shock of electricity that thrummed through my bones like an undercurrent so close to a discovery.

I'd had that, not long ago, but it had been stolen from beneath my feet and now I was listless, back in the N.O. crashing with my older brother and avoiding my parents' worried calls while I figured my shit out.

I would start a new shelf today, and I wasn't sure what these books held, but it was better than throwing myself a pity party over my shitty dating life and stalled career. I grabbed a pair of white gloves and slipped them over my fingers. I selected a faded indigo tome, cracked open its spine, and let the pages wash over me. My eyes scanned the yellowed parchment and faded ink, and I lost myself in translations and cataloging before recording my own notes of the secrets the pages held. It was important, methodical work. In it, there was order and magic and knowledge.

There was purpose.

Prometheus

CHAPTER 3

"This is bullshit," Grumbling, Ares slashed through the thick overgrowth on the rotten path with a giant machete. I shot him an annoyed look.

Hermes turned, the soft glow of Hecate's moon torch illuminating Ares's scowl, his thick eyebrows pinched together in annoyance. "We're almost there. We'd get there sooner if you'd quit complaining," he joked.

Ares's scowl deepened, eyes narrowing at his brother's ribbing before attacking a vine that snaked up toward Hermes's foot. It squelched under his blade, falling limply back to the ground in a spray of black goo. Hermes shuddered, giving the God of War a terse nod.

"Thanks."

Ares ticked his chin up for us to move on. "I'd much rather be at home, with my wife and husband, than gallivanting through the bowels of Tartarus with you two." Ares spoke, his timbre simultaneously a hybrid of bitterness and admiration—the latter most apparent when he mentioned Hephaestus and Aphrodite.

"How did Hephaestus take it when you told him he couldn't come?" Hermes asked, curiously.

Ares scoffed, swiping lazily at another vine, this one barbed and leaking some sort of black ichor smelling of sulfur. "How do you think? Telling him what to do doesn't end well for anyone involved, normally. Telling him I had to come to Tartarus *without* him? Let's just say we had our first fight as a Bonded unit. It didn't help that Aphrodite was completely on his side, which was a disadvantage. She doesn't fight fair, to say the least. Eventually he understood, but he wore me out after." He said the last bit with a suggestive wink.

"*Dude.*" Hermes shuddered. "Too much information."

"You asked." Ares shook his head, chuckling.

Meanwhile Hermes raised the moon torch and led the way through a deep cavern. Water trickled down the stalactites' luminescent teeth hanging from the ceiling. Hecate's moon torch seared the cold light of the full moon into the darkness with us, and I crowded slightly closer. Tartarus was the deepest, blackest void in the cosmos, the realm under all others. Very few among our kin could travel freely here.

"Tell me again why you're here instead of Hecate?" I struck down a tentacle-like tendril unfurling menacingly from the shadows.

Hermes ducked under the overhanging vines swinging into our path. "Hecate was summoned by the LOA to attend to pressing matters. They're on an island with the other Afro-Caribbean deities. I can travel through here, so it made sense to send me. I would have been useless there."

I let out a low whistle. "Lucky us," I grumbled. Ares snorted up ahead.

The walls and ceiling of the cavern tapered down, shrinking in on itself. I bristled; I'd never been this far in before.

Sensing my hesitation, Ares turned to look at me.

"You sure you can handle this?" His eyes pierced through mine, searching for any sign of hesitation. I dipped my head once, holding his stare. He waited a beat more before deciding I was telling the truth. The God of War traversed Tartarus more than almost anyone else, and we'd been lucky his hatred of Zeus nearly rivaled my own. It was the only thing that had him back down here, in the Pits.

"When was the last time you saw him?" he asked as we made our way through a shrinking passageway of surrounding stone close enough to touch.

I shrugged. "The Titanomachy."

The passageway opened again to a small cavern—sigils carved into the surrounding rock face, a giant pool of dark water overtaking the floor. The water sat unnaturally still, drawing me closer to examine the glowing sigils. Titanic marks for locking and impenetrability shone back at me, foreign and jagged in my mind, even though it was the first language I understood. I hardly partook in the reading of my native tongue, and after the Titanomachy, it became forbidden to speak aloud.

Ares lifted the hilt end of his blade to me. I took it gingerly as he reached into his boot and produced a much smaller knife, one wickedly sharp and glinting in the moon torch's light. The metal sliced deeply into his palm, his rich blood freely flowing from the slit skin, dripping down his arm.

Muttering, Ares walked to a far corner of the wall, leaning close to the marked stone. When his eyes landed on whatever he'd searched for, he let out a soft grunt, pressing his ravaged hand to the illuminated sigil. He smeared torn flesh over the lines etched into the stone and his blood began to glow, magic rippling from the mess of it. Satisfied with his handiwork, he turned back to us, reaching for his rucksack and slinging it on his back.

The God of War spent his entire existence in a military of some sort— this century for the United States. When he'd been forced to return to the Underworld to save Aphrodite, the persona he'd crafted had been killed in action. There was no shortage of need for his skills, and though I knew it had been hard for him to burn this identity, he'd done it for love. I looked him over.

He was dressed for this; tough canvas pants tucked into his now muddy boots, only it wasn't mud. It was the very deepest depravity of the cosmos—the wretchedness leached from all things dark and despicable—that lay splashed across the tops of his boots. My eyes lingered there for only a moment before I forced myself to focus on what was to come next.

Ares's blood flowed out from the sigil he'd chosen in small veins carved into the thick stone. The crimson drew deep into the rock, winding up to connect with other intricate parts of stone. A violent tapestry revealed itself to us, creeping along the walls until the offering of god-blood connected with itself in a full circle.

"What now?" Hermes asked.

Ares's hand flew up defensively to silence him, the God of War's head cocked slightly, like he was listening. Waiting for instruction, or for some unknown signal. Ares remained still, a statue among the decaying stone.

A soft ticking floated over the stagnant air, faint at first, but quickly rising in a crescendo. The sounds of cogs turning and clicking into place resounded through the chamber and the smooth surface of the lake rippled with movement.

Ares stepped away from the wall, eyes on the dark pool before us; Hermes and I followed suit.

Several glowing Titanic runes appeared, stark in contrast to the black water, crossing the surface in dashes and geometric circles loosely resembling a clock. The ticking was louder now, echoing around us. I resisted the urge to cover my ears, instead concentrating on the patterns moving in front of me.

Without warning, everything ceased.

Prometheus

CHAPTER 4

"Theo, hand me that bag." Ares's voice ripped me back to reality. I reached for the satchel slung across my shoulders, tossing it over to Ares. He caught it easily before laying it at his feet, shuffling around inside until he straightened with a thin rope clutched between his fingers.

"I don't know what you're into," I cocked an eyebrow, "But I think I'll pass."

"Suit yourself. But for the record, the restraints we use are generally leather or metal anyway, so you're safe." Ares winked, just as Hermes let out another groan. "No, this is to keep us together."

He unraveled the rope and tethered himself around the waist in a bowline knot. Ares lifted one end out to me and the other to Hermes. "Tie it around yourselves, tightly. The last thing we need is to be separated."

I took the rope and fastened it around me, pulling it snugly around my torso. Hermes quickly mirrored the action on himself, and we stood there in awkward silence, tethered together in the Pits of Tartarus while Ares took a deep, calming breath.

"Okay, so here's how this is going to go: When I say, we're going to fall into the pool. *We're* going to go on my count and break the surface *together*," Ares instructed, gesturing with outstretched fingers punctuated by a knife hand, stressing the importance of his instructions. I nodded in understanding.

"Then, against every instinct that you have, we're gonna swim down—all the way," he said. "No matter what you hear, no matter what you *see*, you keep swimming and following me. If you get into trouble, you tug this rope twice," he yanked the rope slightly between us with quick thrusts in demonstration.

"What kind of trouble are we talking?" Hermes secured the moon torch to his arm with a leather strap.

"There are safeguards to ensure that only those with access can get in and get out. Since you two have no such clearance for the cells we're going to, we need to move together through the doorway. In theory, crossing together should trick the system." Ares swiped his bloody hand over my neck. The slick lay against my skin like warpaint. He reached for Hermes, who jumped back in disgust.

"In *theory*?" Hermes asked.

In response, Ares grabbed his arm, sliding his bloody hand over Hermes's forehead. "Yeah." He nodded. "There's only one door, and if you want access to the prisoners in this part of the Pit, you gotta be on the list. Since we're keeping this from the old bastard, it's the only option we have."

Taking a few steps, Ares tiptoed right up to the smooth water's edge. Its glowing runes still glistened atop the dark water and he turned, placing his heels to the waterline before he offered a hand for both of us to take.

"Remember, bend your knees, fall back like a dive. Swim straight down. On one." He looked between us.

"Got it," Hermes answered.

"WILCO," I replied. *Will comply*. Ares grinned slightly at the jargon and steadied his breath.

"Three." The strong hand holding mine tightened.

"Two." A tic in his jaw.

"One."

A sharp sensation pulled from where we were joined, and I found myself falling backward into what I was sure would be too-shallow water with Ares and Hermes. My back rolled through the air, spurred by gravity, and I watched in wonder as we passed through a forcefield-like barrier, shimmering and rippling around us at the intrusion.

We crashed into the darkness with such force the air knocked from my lungs. The light from the cavern ceiling obfuscated under a raging tidal wave, clear and dark and menacing. The bone-chilling water stung, a thousand needles jabbing into each inch of my skin. Every instinct in my body rebelled against the weight dragging me to the depths like an anchor.

I stretched my fingers toward the fading light above, desperate to break the surface, to free myself from the oppressive cold. The distance grew wide, a great chasm the farther I was pulled. Despair settled over me. This water was colder and far more deadly than the Styx; all the warnings given by Ares washed from my mind as it swallowed me whole, pulled with unyielding cruelty into its trenches to ensure I was forgotten forever. What little air I had left in my lungs expelled in a sigh from my lips, tiny bubbles of hope that left me hollowed and drowning with clouded vision.

A sharp grip on my face, searing hot, pulled me from the recesses of my own mind. My eyes flew open, irises stinging from the freezing water, but Ares held on to my chin forcefully, shaking me to look at him, to *remember* where we were.

I pulled free of his sharp grip as a light behind him caught my eye. Hermes floated, unconscious but tethered by the rope around his waist to Ares. The moon torch on his arm remained lit, roughly illuminating a twenty-foot radius in the abyss. Ares glanced over his shoulder, catching a glimpse of his younger brother knocked out, then back to me, rolling his eyes. His hand drifted in front of my line of sight, thumb and pointer finger pressed together, the remaining three fingers fanned behind it—the diving sign language for *all good*.

I nodded and mirrored his hand sign.

The warring sensations of being painfully cold and blissfully numb surged through me, but adrenaline pumped through my veins in worry at the glimpse of Hermes's lilting body. As deities, we didn't *need* to breathe so I wasn't sure he could actually drown, but we were a man down, floating in the limbo between Tartarus and the Pits of Despair.

Ares pointed down before bowing his body in a graceful arc and slicing into the darkness. I followed his dive. We glided through the water in sure, steady strokes but it felt like being suspended in slow motion. Hermes floated along behind Ares as we delved deeper into the vast emptiness, his beacon of light the only sentry against the encroaching darkness. Stroke after stroke, we sank like stones until my bones ached from the cold, or the damp, or the sheer weight of cubic pressure. My muscles strained in protest from the crushing compression, but we swam on.

Time ceased to exist; the sound of my own lazy blood slowing in my ears in an almost hypnotic effect. My mind drifted, body mirroring Ares through mechanical response, as I contemplated what it would mean to simply *stop*. Intrusive thoughts crept through my conscious mind even as I propelled myself deeper. My own voice pushed through my mental wards, slithering through cracks in walls I'd spent centuries fortifying. The voice echoed, far off and everywhere all at once, giving agency to rogue thoughts better locked away.

What is the point of all of this? To kill Zeus.

It's getting old, fighting this fight. Aren't you tired? I can rest when he's dead.

Do you really think after all this time you'll be able to make him pay? He has to.

He's stronger than you. Faster, more powerful. I'll find a way.

Are you sure? He's outsmarted you before. I've learned.

Still, the voice was persistent, drilling into my consciousness and cracking open the tiny crevice to my darkest memories.

Have you learned? It's all I've thought about for three thousand years.

Ah, but while you were atoning for your sins, did you ever consider you deserved to be there? He must pay for what he did to her. To them.

What he did? Or what you did? I—

The words died on my tongue like acid, necrotic and corrosive, as I stifled the bile in my throat threatening to rise.

It was my fault. It was *my* actions that had landed me on that mountain; I'd known the risks. *None of them would have ever been there if not for me . . .*

Guilt was a stone in my chest, and I stilled, slowing my arms and legs.

My fault, my responsibility.

The water closed in around, crushing me under its weight, the pressure. I wanted to stay here, to die—

A sharp tug, delivered twice, dug the rope at my hips into my skin, a single sensation cutting past the biting cold. Ares treaded water at a glowing barrier in front of us. It looked like the surface we'd left behind moments or maybe hours ago, I couldn't recall. He gathered the rope holding Hermes behind and pulled, wrapping his arms across his brother's chest. Ares lifted his chin, beckoning me closer as I tried to shake free of the frost clouding my mind. I cut through the water toward him slowly.

Ares positioned Hermes between our bodies, an arm draped over each of our shoulders. He held his hands up, three fingers extended, and then pointed to the barrier. I nodded. His fingers began to drop.

Three.

Two.

One.

We lunged forward, breaking the surface of the water in a tandem thrust. Tumbling out of the abyss face down toward the earth, we landed in a heap on the lifeless ground with a wet smack that reverberated through every bone in my body. Ares took the brunt of the fall, still cradling Hermes's limp form to his chest. I sprawled out, chest heaving as the God of War lifted his head to make sure I was still alive.

My teeth chattered, but Hermes had yet to wake up. Worry spurred me into action, and I pushed to my elbows, the better to look him over. The Messenger God's lips were blue, his chest rising and falling in shallow pants as beneath delicate skin, his eyes darted back and forth. A whimper broke past his lips that had both Ares and I sitting up fully in alarm, bending over him.

Ares swore, delivering a few quick smacks to either side of his brother's face. Hermes bolted into consciousness after the second hit, but Ares finished tapping both cheeks, even as his eyes opened.

Hermes pushed away from him and levelled an indignant look. "I was awake after the second one, arsehole," he mumbled, massaging his smarting cheek, still looking a little shaken. His golden radiance returned slowly. "What happened?"

Ares blew out a breath using his god-power, and the air around us warmed, drying our clothes and bone-chilled bodies thoroughly. It was a power I'd never known him to possess. "You weren't used to the gravity pull. Someone like you travels often without obeying the laws, but here, the laws of the cosmos are strict. The barometric pressure and the cold seized you up. I knew you'd be fine, hence the rope." Ares stood to his feet, stretching his muscles.

Vertigo had my head spinning, the pressure in my skull enough to make me nauseous. I put my head in my hands, tucking between my knees and willing the splitting headache to subside, still wrung out over the words from earlier.

What he did? Or what you did?

Ares's hand came down in front of my face, outstretched with an understanding grimace on his face. I took the offering and he dragged me to my feet, checking the rope was secure.

"Whatever you heard wasn't real. You did real good, Theo," he said, staring at me knowingly. "Whatever is heard in the Sea of Sorrows is just a manifestation of your own guilt. It isn't real. So, whoever you heard, or whatever was said, it was meant to make you give up. You didn't. Leave that shit where it's at." Ares clapped me on the back and turned back to Hermes.

"You good?" His tone held a hint of concern I'd rarely heard Ares display. He'd never been particularly fond of others except for Aphrodite, but Hermes and Ares had an *especially* aggressive approach to one another, one that seemed to be mending since his Bonding to the God of the Forge.

Hermes dipped his head a few times and Ares squeezed his shoulder. "Alright then, better beat feet. It's time for the real unpleasant part," Ares announced.

Hermes and I shared a look. "It gets worse than being roofied by the Sea of Sorrows?" he asked, skeptically.

Ares nodded. "Oh yeah. Have you ever had a conversation with a trapped titan? Real fucking nightmare," he said before setting off down the blackened path.

Hermes and I followed in silence, unease crawling over every inch of my exposed skin.

Prometheus

CHAPTER 5

The jagged stone protruding along the wall kept the corridor tight before opening in an upward slope. Ares stopped us just before he crossed a threshold.

"Not a word until I get us into the right cell," he whispered, "No need to risk waking the others."

We nodded our understanding. He turned back to the open doorway and stepped through quietly. I followed, Hermes right behind me.

As we entered the final circle of the Hells, I had to stifle the urge to cry out from the buckling onslaught of despair gripping me. Hopelessness slammed into my chest, binding my heart in a vice, squeezing with a barbed grip.

The cavern was vast, *endless*, the size of a coliseum and circular. The ceiling above appeared to be a replica—as surely this realm was buried deep beneath the realms, it couldn't possibly be real—of the night sky. The illusion sky was deep blue, a cruel false heaven of cruel beauty, peppered with stars and constellations that constantly moved and shifted.

Ares's footsteps ghosted over the uneven, cobbled gray stone. The glow from the stars illuminated our way, bathing everything in cold moonlight. It was beautiful in a desolate way, but the stench of despair and loneliness crept over us, leaving the taste of ash on my tongue.

Great, dilapidated pillars as tall as a petrified forest stood between prisons of my kinsfolk. Floor-to-ceiling heavy bars blocked the way into each cell, dripping with impenetrable power. Darkness shrouded the inhabitants inside, and if they sensed us or heard us, they made no commotion or effort to approach the bars of their cells.

Ares walked through on instinct, never stopping to look around. He'd been here more than almost any other god. In the beginning, the God of War guarded them personally on Zeus's orders, before he'd been recalled to the field. He stopped outside of what looked to be the most fortified and intricate gate and pressed his bleeding palm against the mouth of a boar carved into the metal. Just as before, where his blood touched flared and flowed with power, glowing crimson against the filth of the flagstones. The gate cracked a few inches, enough that Ares was able to shoulder through. He waited until we were all inside before closing the gate and sealing it with another swipe of his bloody hand.

Trapping us inside.

This prison was shaped differently from the rest. The floor sank into a shallow recess, an octagon carved neatly into the stone, dripping three feet deep like the mouth of the Pits. At each point, a cracked pillar jutted upward, reaching into the night above. Black vines coiled around them, pulsing faintly, the same parasitic growth that infested the upper levels of Tartarus we'd traveled through. Iron rings nestled into each pillar; chains threaded through and drawn tight at the center. There, they converged on the stone effigy of a man. *Of a titan.* Kneeling, bound, head bent in eternal supplication with a crown of thistle on his head, brittle and gray from eons of decay.

My heart faltered in my chest. This was the prison of Iapetus, brother of Cronus, Titan of Mortality. He held the timeline of every mortal life within his consciousness.

Ares stepped into the pit, approaching the statue, coming to a stop in front of the mighty stone. He glanced back only once and I followed him down, but I didn't move as close as he was. I couldn't make my feet close the distance, but from where I was rooted, I studied the statue. The face. The features. The proud brow, bent. The laugh lines eternally etched in the stone subdued in a painful grimace.

I've never been allowed here. As a titan, Zeus deemed it unsavory that I should visit, *"Lest the temptation to free my kinsman overtake common sense."*

Ares reached into his satchel and pulled a small container free. He popped the lid and the sweet smell of Ambrosia wafted through the air.

My mouth watered, just the hint of the sweet nectar on the air enough to draw me closer. Ambrosia could bolster our powers in the right quantities, but it was also addicting. *Destructive.*

Ares dug two fingers into the container and scooped out a generous handful. One last glance at me—met with a nod of confirmation. He smeared the Ambrosia into the open mouth of the statue. Stepping back just as quickly, Ares took his place to my left, licking the remnants of the golden liquid from his fingers as we waited.

Hermes and Ares flanked behind me, a safeguard if this all went to shit, but my palms were sweaty anyway. Their presence was a comfort but didn't stop the uptick in my pulse or the nerves that twisted my stomach into knots over what I was about to do.

The Ambrosia dripped down the statue's chin in languid drops, staining the stone with a molten sheen. Where it touched, a crack, minuscule in its might, resounded through the open air; a tremor nearly deafening in the cavern's silence. Another, then another. It fractured in tiny, webbed fissures drifting up the face and down the neck and torso, defacing the stone beneath. The statue's shoulders flexed, sending cascades of dust and shattered fragments tumbling to the floor as the golden shimmer seeped deeper, flooding the crumbling stone as the glow spread.

I watched in fascination as it all gave way, and Iapetus appeared beneath it, revealing flesh that once had been stone. Skin pale, scarred and faintly stained with the Ambrosia, shook loose the last remnants of broken mineral as his eyelids cracked open warily. His gaze found mine, slow and reluctant, until twin eyes of silver liquid pinned me in place. I couldn't breathe under their weight.

I willed my body to remain calm, to show no emotion through Iapetus's transformation.

He rolled his shoulders back, stretching his muscles there, and cracked his head to the side, eyeing me with curiosity. The rusted chains rattled as he moved, jostling over his frame. He was still massive, twice my size and three times as wide. Even in this position, bent and bowed, he struck an imposing figure.

Silently, we assessed one another. Hermes and Ares stood motionless at my sides, waiting for my instruction, but they could have not even been here, for all the attention we gave them. The titan settled back on his knees, large, manacled hands resting on his thighs. He let out a long, deep sigh, clearing the cobwebs from his throat.

"Prometheus?"

The sound of that voice was a javelin through my chest. Emotions buried long ago surged to the surface of my mind, even as I struggled to keep them locked tight. I sucked in a breath, squaring my shoulders, my gaze never faltering from his.

"Hello, Father."

Prometheus

CHAPTER 6

A slight crinkle at the corners of Iapetus's eyes creased as a broad smile cracked over his lips. He sat back on his haunches and let out a hearty bark of laughter.

My jaw tightened, biting back every foul insult I could throw at him. He waited for me to speak, relaxed even as the chains grated and groaned at his slightest shift in posture. They must have been heavy, but that was a burden he deserved to bear after his betrayal.

During the Titanomachy, he turned on us. Few titans sided with Zeus, but the ones who did understood that the cruelty of Cronus couldn't be allowed to continue. He was charismatic, a strong leader when the world had begun, but as his power grew so had the paranoia. His cruelty increased tenfold. Cronus became obsessed with the prophecy his father, Ouranos, cursed him with. Even though Cronus used Ouranos's imprisonment of the Cyclopes and the Hecatonchires to condemn his father, he'd turned around and eaten his young himself.

The creatures of the world suffered under his rule, as did many of the other titans. When Rhea hid Zeus, saving him from the jaws of Cronus, it had been at my father's direction. But in the hour of judgment, my Iapetus faltered and instead warned Cronus of the impending coup. Zeus was able to band together with the rest of the newly freed Olympians, the few titan allies, and along with the Cyclopes and Hecatonchires, secure a bloody victory, but there was a price for his betrayal.

My father's interference nearly cost us the war, and while I could see now that he understood the threat Zeus would become, it was the act of his betrayal that caused a death I couldn't forgive. He pushed us into a war, propped Zeus up as the golden beacon, and in the end, it was for *nothing*. The tidal wave of brutality from the war washed over the world and all creatures of the mortal realm were destroyed; my mother lost her life, and Iapetus was cast into the depths with the rest of the titans. He hadn't trusted me with his fears of Zeus, had left us woefully unprepared for the tyrant he would become, and I never stopped paying for that. His hands were as stained as Cronus's with the blood of my mother.

I hated him for that, the most.

He studied me, drinking in my form hungrily, like he could etch each detail of my face into his memory. Zeus denied him my presence for thousands of years, but I wouldn't have allowed him the privilege now if we had any other options. Patiently, he waited.

I ground my teeth together, willing no emotion in my voice. "We've come for your help."

Iapetus bobbed his head, pursing his lips. "Yes, I expect you did. Tell me, has he proven to be just as wretched as his father?" he asked, raising his chin to look at me thoughtfully. I stepped closer, but Hermes's hand flew out to stop me. "He's dangerous," he warned. A thrum of nervous energy danced across his skin. Hermes was on high alert here, practically vibrating with anxiety.

Iapetus scoffed incredulously. "I am no danger to Prometheus. He is my son." Pain radiated through his words, as though the mere implication he could harm one of his own was the deepest insult.

I folded my arms and bit out, "Your sons are off limits, but your wife was fair game? Interesting take from the Titan of Mortality." I couldn't help the bitterness lacing my tone.

Iapetus's face fell. "Your mother wasn't supposed to be there. It should have been just Zeus," he whispered, eyes cast down.

"Well, she was. Cronus ran his spear through her chest, cracked it wide open," I replied bitterly, but once I started speaking, I couldn't stop. I never got to take my pound of flesh, and I wanted it now. "She bled out in my arms. Because you betrayed us all." He flinched, the clang of disturbed metal, of chain on chain, echoing loudly. "So, you're going to tell me what I need to know, because you owe me that much."

I moved slowly past Hermes's outstretched arm, nodding my thanks for his caution as I went. I stopped in front of my father, close enough to see the subtle ravages of time upon his face, but far enough that if he tried anything I'd have time to react.

He brought his silver eyes up to meet mine. "What is it that you need my assistance with?" he asked, though I was sure he already knew.

"I need to know how to kill Zeus," I answered, matter-of-factly.

Iapetus cocked his head. "What makes you think I know how?"

"Save that for someone who doesn't know who you are. You see *every* angle of *all* situations. Zeus took your council before the Titanomachy, and I know you told him how to make himself invulnerable. I want to know what he did, and I want to know how to undo it."

Iapetus rolled his lip between his teeth, lifting his ironclad arms. "If I tell you, I want something in return."

I shook my head, amazed at how predictable he was. "Your freedom from the Pits, I'd guess?"

Iapetus opened his mouth to speak but was cut off.

"Absolutely *fucking* not." Ares stepped forward, Hermes hot on his heels. "That was never part of the deal. If we free him, we risk alerting Zeus to what we're up to here. As it is, he may already know."

Iapetus chuckled and turned to face Ares, who had taken up residence near my right arm. "Ares, Ares," he admonished, an elder scolding a child, "I'm disappointed in you. God of War, bred as a blunt object for your father's designs. You think the thing I desire most is my *freedom*? Whatever would I do with it? Dwell topside amongst mortals in a land rife with corruption? Press my company upon sons who can't stand to look at me and endure the memory of a wife who died because of my miscalculations?" He let out a bitter laugh. "I'll politely decline."

Ares and Hermes eyed him with a mix of shock and disbelief at his admission, but I heard something *more* in the undertone of his voice—my father was telling the truth. It was that knowledge alone that had me moving close enough that I could see the constellations reflecting in the silver glow of his eyes.

"Then what do you want in return?"

He stared right through me. "I wish to tell you a story, and after, I'd like you to kill me."

I balked as Hermes shifted uncomfortably and said, "We can't just kill you. There are rules. *Balances*. It isn't like you're a minor Olympian or even an Otherworlder. You're a titan, Iapetus." Hermes looked between Ares and me, waiting for backup.

Iapetus's eyes never left mine. "Consequences can be circumvented. Everything has a check and balance, this is true, but it runs more like an unwavering flow. If one knows where to apply pressure, one can redirect the attention and power *elsewhere*." My heart dropped through my stomach and out of my asshole.

It was true that I had a complicated relationship with my father. In my childhood, he was good, just, and kind. He taught me to take care of those around me, to support and provide for them. This empathy had been my ultimate downfall, which set me off on this path with Zeus, and for that, I supposed, I had a lot of complicated thoughts too. It was my love for my father, my unfaltering loyalty and faith in his ability to make the right decisions that shattered and scattered into the stratosphere at his betrayal. If he was susceptible to folly, then what hope did the rest of us stand?

But did I want him to *die*? To be the one to kill him over it? No.

"I'll hear you out, but I make no promise of action. This is all I can offer." I swallowed around the words. *He wanted to die.* What would he gain from dishonesty at this point?

Iapetus bowed his head. "Very well, I accept your terms. You may want to have a seat," he said. "I'm afraid it is quite a tale." I sat down on the hard stone floor. Hermes and Ares stood a beat more before trading uneasy glances and doing the same.

"In the beginning, our father, Ouranos, was cruel. There were no moments of kindness, just an unwavering pursuit of power. He took what he wanted when he wanted it, but he was also insanely paranoid about losing that control. He claimed that he threw the Cyclopes and the Hecatonchires under the mountains for vanity, but in truth, he was threatened by the power they possessed when together. He knew if anyone *ever* realized the weight of their might and weaponized it, they could overthrow him. A fact I pointed out to Zeus early on. Their freedom from the mountains wasn't benevolence—it was necessity.

"I'd been orchestrating the fall of Cronus for centuries before Rhea produced Zeus. I knew when he was born with lightning in his veins, he was the one prophesied by Ouranos. So, I had a little birdie plant the seeds into Rhea's mind about saving Zeus, and then, from the shadows I orchestrated the series of events leading to his being allowed to grow and thrive.

"I worked for years, carefully pulling each piece into place. You can't possibly know how precarious a time it was. I played the dutiful lieutenant to Cronus, all the while setting up a series of checks and balances that tested for any chink in his defenses. It turned out there wasn't anything particularly special needed to dethrone him, complacency and laziness did it for us. With his progeny out of the way, Cronus had no reason to fear, as nothing else was named in the prophecy that could threaten him. When Zeus's full power matured, we struck."

I leaned in curiously. "If you orchestrated it all, then *why* betray us in the end?"

Iapetus raised a hand to stay my questions as he answered. "Because as Zeus grew, I saw his father's cruelty reflected in him. He was as charismatic as Cronus, sweet like honey when in pursuit of his agenda but that sweet soured into acid as his whim shifted. His very nature swayed with his mood. I knew that we would be trading one dictator for another and that was not something I could be responsible for."

Hermes and Ares exchanged uneasy glances, but I soaked up my father's words, my mind reconciling what I thought I knew from his version of events. He *had* seen it all.

"I began to assess the new threat and formulated a way to have them both destroy each other so that we could live in harmony. For ten years, I arranged and nudged and whispered in the shadows during the Titanomachy, awaiting the full Blood Moon. Only Atlas knew of my plans; I needed him to be in a position of power among Cronus's ranks, so we had control over battle strategy."

I jumped to my feet at this new revelation, blood ice in my veins. "Atlas wasn't on our side. He stayed loyal to Cronus to the end," I spat, pacing as panic clawed at me. Every word my father spoke struck against the facts I'd known to be true, truths I'd lived and died a thousand lifetimes for.

"He was there because I *needed* him to be there. Just as you knew *I* had designs to remove Cronus but had to fight alongside him to gain the advantage. Atlas never told you? I was going to send you, but Atlas insisted it be him." Iapetus looked confused, then his brow softened in understanding. "Ah. He wanted to protect you. After my betrayal, if you showed him loyalty or love in any way, Zeus would have cast you into the Pits with me." Sadness etched through the lines of his face. It was the face that had shown me so much love and hope growing up. One I cursed every time I'd died at Zeus's command.

Uncomfortable needles pricked at the back of my eyes. I'd publicly denounced my father and Atlas following the Titanomachy. Hated them for fighting on the side of Cronus, and for Cronus killing my mother.

I cleared my throat. "So, Atlas played both sides as well. Why didn't *you* tell me?" I accused, trying as best I could to keep my voice level and steady when all I wanted to do was rage. *Had he not trusted me?*

"Your brother insisted he had to be the one because he was the oldest. It made sense that he would lead. He wouldn't put that carnage on your head. Atlas carried the burden without complaint, and he was happy to do it to keep your mother, you, and Epimetheus safe."

I flinched at the mention of my only remaining brother. Iapetus spoke about our family with such deep-seated sorrow I had to flex my hands into fists to keep my head focused.

"The day of the Reckoning, I arranged for Atlas to lure Cronus to the sacred valley on Mount Othrys. I convinced Zeus to meet me there to secure vital plans Cronus had for the next battle. Cronus and Zeus were to meet and fight, as neither of them could be seen as a coward who fled from close combat. I arranged for a prison to be fashioned beneath the stone. Once the moon was full, the cell would be charged and the mountain was to crack wide, trapping them both inside. I knew that once this happened, it would show my hand. It had to work." He paused, and I leaned closer.

"It happened *exactly* as I had foreseen. I watched from the shadows as they fought mercilessly and bolt after bolt of lightning rocked the skies. They were mountains of power, colliding with each other, like the very cosmos was breaking apart. As the moon rose high in the sky, the ground below us charged with anticipation. Cronus and Zeus were both growing weary but unwilling to submit to the other. All was going to plan. Then Themis was there, and it all fell apart." My father's words dropped to a whisper that carried over to us and a chill ran down my spine. I remembered this part too well.

"She came riding on the waves, the rain fueling her fury. She thought Zeus needed help, and though Cronus was distracted, he was still one of the deadliest beings to ever live. Maybe he saw her reflection mirrored in Zeus's eyes, or perhaps the look of triumph on the Olympian's face gave it away, but whatever the case, he knew she was coming . . . She wasn't supposed to be there. *None of you were.*"

Pain ricocheted through my chest as I watched the memory match his words, the earth-shattering loss clawing at my insides.

"I saw the moment he decided she became a threat. He turned on Zeus, for only a moment, to hurl his spear at her chest, but it was enough to give Zeus the upper hand. I ran across the pitch, desperate to reach her. I saw you running from the other side. The mountain cracked, and Zeus pushed him into the depths. If I hadn't sealed it when I did, both you and your mother's body would have been swallowed as well. I knew that it would be for the greater good. I knew that the sacrifice of two was worth more than the suffering of all he would rule over, but I faltered. I couldn't let my son die for my hubris, Prometheus. I made the wrong choice, failed in my morals, and Zeus read it on my face from a mile away." Iapetus's head hung low, defeated, as he cracked open his shade and poured out his deepest, darkest secret.

I shook with rage.

All this time, I blamed him for turning on us and having never heard the truth of that day. Now, I knew everything that happened was because my father failed to make the hard choice.

The suffering of so many had started with me.

"You chose me over them? Over *everyone*?"

He nodded. "And I would have made that choice a thousand times over again. I've run every possible outcome of those events through my mind. In every one, I couldn't make the choice to sacrifice you. I convinced Zeus that I acted alone, and he punished me, Atlas, and the rest of our kin. But he let the few who fought with him live. He poisoned the rest of our names, made us the monsters that went bump in the night. But I'd been his mentor for his entire life. As time passed, he'd visit."

"Why?" Hermes asked, hanging on to my father's every word.

"I'm not sure. At first, it was to gloat, and then, to plot. Over the years, he confided in me his secrets, his paranoia, his delusions. Don't forget that I helped raise him, and I think in many ways, Zeus saw me as a father of sorts. He wanted advice." Iapetus leaned back, rolling his stiff neck. The chains groaned.

"Why would he tell you all of that if you could use it against him?" Hermes asked.

Ares, who'd stayed quiet so far, perked up. "I can answer that. I was the only one with access here. Even Hecate can't get this far. Just he and I. It took two to build the blood locks," he explained, shuffling slightly.

Iapetus nodded. "Indeed. His paranoia grew, and as you made humans and your brother made animals, he feared they would worship you above him. You had already become so powerful, Prometheus. You were righteous, and kind. They loved you. Zeus saw a reflection of me in you, and it scared him. The way you protected them. The way you cared about mortals and all others. When you stole the fire and gave it to humans, he finally had his opportunity to imprison you. I'm so sorry about what happened to your—"

I cut him off with a strangled noise. "We're not going to talk about that. Move on," I snapped.

"He came to me in search of a way to make himself unkillable. He wanted an unlimited power source to pull from. Said that if I didn't find one, he would kill you and your brothers. The True Death. I said no at first, and he slew Atlas. In front of me. It was so quick, the way he crushed him. My boy. My oldest son. I had no choice. I'd failed Themis and Atlas, and I couldn't fail you again. I plotted and thought. And because I loved my remaining sons, I obliged."

Sorrow laced every word that fell from his lips.

"I found the way for his wellspring of power to never run dry, was to pull from other Olympians. Hera is the Goddess of Bonds, and she derives power from every Bond she creates. By Bonding with her, he would always have that power to pull from. He courted Hera. He tricked her into falling in love with him, and the things he put that poor girl through—even I couldn't have predicted *that* level of barbarism. I had no idea he wouldn't be satisfied with just being Bonded, the lengths he would go to keep her tethered to him. As long as they are together, try as you might to take him down, he will never tire."

Ares's jaw tightened. This wasn't what we'd wanted to hear.

"So, there's no hope?" Hermes asked.

My father's mouth quirked into a grin. "It is ironic that you mention hope."

Hermes

CHAPTER 7

I watched Theo do all he could to create a cold distance between his father and himself, but it was plain in his posture. He *wanted* to believe Iapetus, *needed* to. More than anything, we all needed this information to yield something promising, but for Prometheus, this was more.

A pang of jealousy swept through me. Family units in our world didn't truly exist, not in a human sense. We didn't share DNA that would bond us as family, the magic that created each of us went deeper than that. Athena sprang into creation as a zit on Zeus's forehead, for Hells' sake. No, for our kind, family was a construct used to manipulate and shatter. There were some exceptions, but there were *so* few in our world. Thanatos and his brother Hypnos, and the children of Death Gods were fiercely protective of each other, but outside of that, familial bonds were unheard of. The gods were too wrapped up in selfish worship, gluttonous of our own power.

It was different for Prometheus, even then. For Theo, his parents had truly been partners, had very much loved each other and their children. Even Atlas and Epimetheus, who were from

Iapetus's first wife, was loved by Themis, or so I'd been told. All accounts of Iapetus were that before the Titanomachy, he'd been a fair and wise titan. It was before my time, but I'd spoken with Helios about it over the years. Seeing Iapetus laid so low now shifted something uncomfortably in my chest as I took in his words.

In all respects, I *was* him. The plotter. The tactician. Every move I made was with purpose, and oftentimes those motivations couldn't be made known. It had put me at the opposite end of a sword more times in my life than I cared to recall.

It almost cost me Hecate.

Listening to Iapetus was like looking into a mirror at what I would have turned into if any *one* of my many schemes had gone wrong. If Minthe had killed Artemis and Helios. If Hecate hadn't forgiven me for the truth serum. I shuddered at the near misses—in our world, even the best laid plans could go to shit.

"I think there is a way to break Zeus's Bond to Hera." Iapetus said, looking only at Theo, pleading with him for forgiveness.

I understood the need for redemption. He lost everything because of one executed plan that fell short. His wife. His children. His freedom. But more importantly, he'd put a tyrant on the throne and unleashed thousands of years of pain and misery at the hands of Zeus. I'd have stayed here in chains, too, rather than witness the destruction I'd wrought.

"Bonds can't be broken. Trust me, we tried," Ares answered flatly.

Iapetus's eyes flicked to the two golden rings circling Ares's fourth finger with a raised eyebrow. "Well, *no*, I'm sure the Bond you were trying to unmake couldn't be undone, but it could be transformed. Unless your much-improved demeanor means you've just returned from a battlefield and not from marital bliss?"

Theo let out a bitter grunt. "This is Ares with a much-improved demeanor? Yikes."

"Speaking of, can we wrap this up? I'd like to get home to my husband and wife before Zeus finds out we've been here. As it is, we're on borrowed time." Ares turned to Iapetus, who regarded him with respect. I suppose there was a particular camaraderie between captive and jailer, and Ares had spent the most time down here of anyone.

Iapetus nodded, pressing on with his tale. "When Hera was born, she was the Goddess of Marriage, but it was a closely regarded secret she also held the power of *Dissolution*. She had the power to make or break Bonds. When Zeus courted and wed her, he wanted to make sure she could never leave him. Using a tool fashioned from the very marrow of Tartarus, he cleaved her power from her, locking away the part of her that could un-work a Bond. He kept her down here for ages and ages. Her screams . . ." The titan took a deep breath before continuing, "It was slow, agonizing work, you understand. It should have been done with finesse, with precision. But Zeus was a butcher, and he flayed her alive in his attempt to pull the power from her bones. You all thought they were on their honeymoon, but they were here. He brutalized her."

My mouth hung slack. Hera had always been a cold shrew to me and those around her, but this shone a new light on her mental state. Hells, the state of her shade. Suddenly, the see-sawing between extreme kindness and unabashed cruelty on the slightest whim made perfect sense peppered in with bouts of mania and rage. Knowing this came from trauma, not petty jealously or wounded pride, twisted my guts.

"Why didn't she ever tell anyone? Even us? She knew we were coming here, she could have told us this," Confusion furrowed Theo's brow.

"She doesn't remember."

Iapetus cast his eyes down "After each extraction, he'd force her to drink from the River Lethe. Each sip cost her a little more of herself, of her *goodness*. She used to be such a happy girl." His words were a miserable whisper.

Rage ignited beneath my bones.

Ares stiffened, that same anger etched into every feature of his face. "He did *what*?" he hissed, stepping forward. Theo reached to stop him, but Ares shook him off, rage rippling from the God of War. "*It's forbidden*. Hades would never have allowed it," he snapped.

Iapetus nodded solemnly. "Hades *would* have forbidden it, had he known. But this realm is far below his domain, and at the time, Zeus created a . . . *distraction* to ensure he could get what he needed from the Underworld unnoticed. In the beginning, the world was destroyed after the wars. The first humans you made, son. The first sickness. Nothing like a little mass death to rock the boat."

Theo's hands fisted by his sides, but beyond that, he kept his emotions in check. I felt violently ill at the easy way I could see it all come together. It was simple in its depravity; beyond any stretch of cruelty a normal person could fathom. But Zeus was and is a monster, expecting morality from a creature incapable of it was a barrier I hadn't considered before.

It was all too clear now.

"He violated her, stole her memories, and poisoned her shade? There's a reason Hades forbids using the Lethe without permission. It's a mercy for shades to survive the guilt they carry, but it also corrodes them within. Most become addicts until they fade away to nothingness. But because Hera is an Olympian, her power corrupted her instead," I mused, disgusted as I put the pieces together like lock to key.

It's how I would have done it, if I was a megalomaniac with a torture kink.

"Indeed, he did. At the end, he brought her to see me. She looked . . . *ravaged*. A ghost of the vibrant, happy goddess I'd once known. He stripped Hera of half of her identity, then filled the gap with worship of him so she'd never stray, be completely reliant upon his love and affections," Iapetus replied.

"Then, he left her there to rot and turned her into a gnarled, miserable version of herself so she could fuck up the rest of our lives?" Ares asked. Again, Iapetus confirmed with a nod.

I never thought, in *any* world, I'd feel anything other than disdain and begrudging respect for Hera, but here we were. The abuse doesn't excuse the part she played in damaging others, but abused people tended to perpetuate that circle of violence. I wondered, briefly, what she could have been if Zeus hadn't mutilated her.

Suddenly, her push to take Zeus down made sense. She may not have remembered this part of her abuse, but she surely remembered *something* to spur this on. We were here because of her. *She* had suggested Iapetus.

"So how does this help?" Theo asked.

Iapetus regarded him with softness in his eyes. "When Zeus cut her spirit from her, he had to put it somewhere. A box, fashioned from the strongest ore in the cosmos. Then, he gave it to a woman—*the first woman*, made from the clay of the Earth by Hephaestus. Bestowed the spark of Life by Prometheus. Given beauty from Aphrodite. This woman was then gifted to your brother as a wife and instructed to guard the box. Which she did dutifully for many years."

The tumblers fell into place and my mind—already understanding where this was going—raced.

"One day, as Zeus knew it would, curiosity got the better of her, thanks to subtle hints he'd placed around her to encourage her to take a peek. When she did, the evil he created from the shadows of Tartarus unleashed on the world." Iapetus's recollection sent a chill sliding down my spine. He knew because Zeus told him. There was no other explanation, as he'd been in captivity for centuries by then.

"He told the world that only hope remained, and for it to endure, it would have to stay locked up tight. He took the box and hid it, moving it around the world for many centuries; until one day, he locked it deep within a library and destroyed it."

"Pandora," Theo and I said together. My heart raced, bones thrumming with purpose. This was the first solid lead we'd had, and suddenly, I felt useful as the first threads of a plan formulated in my racing mind.

"I assume you mean Alexandria? It's been gone for centuries." Ares added, nervously. "Completely wiped off the face of the planet."

I studied him closely, trying to decipher what he knew, because the God of War looked suddenly stressed. I put it together as he glanced between us, eyes falling.

"I set it ablaze myself, under Zeus's orders. It was completely razed," he confessed. I slowly blinked as my stomach dropped.

"Ares, how *could* you? All that history? Clio hasn't been seen since that fire, Ares. The *knowledge*? *Just gone*," Theo cried, throwing his hands up. He had been particularly devastated by the loss of Alexandria, at the destruction of knowledge and disappearance of Clio, the Muse of History.

Ares looked hollow and ashamed. "I was following orders. Ever the good soldier."

Iapetus cleared his throat and shuffled under the weight of his chains. "You didn't burn the *actual* library, Ares."

My head shot up, searching the titan.

"It was a smoke screen. Zeus had the entire enterprise moved, with the help of Poseidon, to a small island near Greece. He did eventually sink it, though. I believe the mortals called it . . . Atlantis? And as for Clio, she isn't *missing*, Prometheus. He took her. With you locked up on a mountainside, and me in the Pits, he became obsessed with finding another to keep his secrets, became obsessed with *her*. Clio's defiance of him, her denial of his advances put him on the hunt, and he enslaved her for it. Built her into the keys to his city. She found a way to escape him, in the end. Not even he can stop death." Iapetus whispered softly, in a chilling blow.

Prometheus went pale at the news about Clio. Knowledge of her death cracked a chasm in my chest, but I compartmentalized my emotions to unpack later. Iapetus could have cut through most of this to get us the information half an hour ago, and every moment we spent here put us at increased risk.

"If she's dead, then how do we find the Lost City of Atlantis?" I pressed.

"There was a compass, of sorts, that acts as a map and can only be read by Clio's blood . . . which Zeus thinks there is no more of. But Clio was a clever woman, far cleverer than many I can recall. He kept her locked up for ages, and that was plenty of time for plotting. She was the keeper of his Atlantis, and when she died, took his most obvious path to the Library with her. It's been lost to him since, but once you have the compass, it'll pull toward the key. Use the map to find Atlantis, and in turn, the Library."

"And where is the compass, Father?" Theo asked, tentatively.

Iapetus lifted his eyes to give him a sad smile, before pushing the tattered fabric away from his chest and patting a spot right over his heart. "It's right here. You'll have to kill me to get it out."

Prometheus

CHAPTER 8

"If you've had the compass inside of you, why hasn't Zeus just killed you to get it out?" Hermes snapped while I stood frozen in front of my father, shock and grief blasted across my face.

"Because I convinced him to hide it there. You must understand, Zeus thinks she was the key, and now that she's gone, the compass doesn't' matter, but I had faith Clio would find a way to outsmart him. I just needed to wait for the right time to collect it. That time, as it seems, has come."

My denial choked my tongue even as I tried to say the words: *I can't. We'll find another way.* But I knew we wouldn't. If my father had played this long game, surely, he thought of every loophole, every mistake, or thing that could go wrong. If he said this is the way, he'd be right. And, if we wanted to move forward, we'd have to sacrifice him to find the Library.

"What about the consequences?" Ares asked, from beside me. His tension was clear from the way he held himself, and I wondered just how close he and my father had become while he was down here. Close enough to have Ares feel a responsibility for him, undoubtedly.

"Zeus set up a protocol. In the event of my death, as long as it happens here, my shade will be caught in my cell. I won't receive the rest of oblivion, but the river of power will stay connected. You have to do this, son." Iapetus turned to me, pleading. "For your mother. You have to do it for Themis. And Atlas."

My jaw set. "Tell me what I have to do," I whispered, kneeling before him.

Ares made a noise of protest, but Hermes stopped him. He knew, just as I did, that my father wouldn't have given us this option if it weren't the only way.

"Take a blade and cut here," he instructed, gesturing to the expanse of his muscle just over his sternum.

I reached into my boot and grabbed my blade, sharp and heavy, in trembling hands. He regarded me as I took a steadying breath, then pressed the tip just above his breastbone and sliced. Blue ichor slid down in fat droplets from the wound, yet my father showed no reservations. No fear. I pulled the blade back and swiped it over my pants, cleaning away thick swaths of blood.

"You're going to need to press through the bone, crack it. Wrap your fingers around my heart and pull. When you do, you'll only have a few minutes to get outside of my cell before the shade lock snaps into place. The compass will lead you, Prometheus. I am at peace with what you must do. Trust it and finish this."

I stared into his eyes, a thousand unspoken words passing between us. Heat burned against my nose, choked my throat, but I nodded and pressed my hand against the split flesh, commanding them not to shake or betray the chaotic conflict roiling through me. They paused against thick muscle and seeping blood. I held onto disappointment and hate for him for so long, but underneath all that pain was *love*. Betrayal at who I knew him to be. Now shame and guilt mixed with that, with the truth finally laid bare. Rage ignited inside of me.

Ares moved around us, reaching for the shackles that held my father at bay. He began unlocking them with blood that flowed freely from a new gash he'd opened on the God of War's hand.

"What are you doing?" Iapetus asked.

Ares let out a grunt. "You're not dying shackled to the ground with indignity. You deserve more than that." The chains fell to the stone ground, banging loudly and echoing through the chamber.

I helped Iapetus rid himself of the weight crossing his torso and back with my free hand. Ares reached past me and unshackled the metal collar. It, too, cascaded to the floor.

"Thank you, old friend." My father dipped his head low in respect to Ares, who reached his arm out. Iapetus clasped it in a final goodbye before the God of War stepped away, leaving just the two of us and a pile of broken chains.

"Father, I—" The words died on my tongue.

He pulled me close in a crushing hug. My chest cracked at the feel of him, at the comfort and love in his arms, it took all the will in the cosmos to keep my tears at bay. My father looked at me with such warmth, such *pride*. I didn't deserve any of it. I'd spent so long in my anger and hatred for him. "Please forgive me," was all I managed.

He shook his head, running his hands over my face, gently pushing back the long strands of my hair that fell as my head hung in shame. "Son, no. You must forgive *me*. I failed you all before. Let me do something meaningful. *Please*."

My chest shook as I struggled to keep my composure, but time pressed in around us, all of us knowing we'd lingered far longer than we had intended. Zeus could be on his way at any moment. My father let me loose as I shifted back, his blue blood smeared across our chests.

Reluctantly, I dug my fingers into the torn flesh of his chest, into the wound made by my own blade. Warmth greeted me in another gush of blood, and I *hated* it, hated the way his muscle and tissue gave way under my grip. He was so weakened, so old now, that I glided through the viscera of him like a hot knife through butter.

When I got to his breastplate, I hesitated. He only gave me an encouraging smile and urged me on. My father threw his head back, those constellations above us swimming in his eyes as he found his peace. Maybe he was seeing my mother, some memory of her better than the last he had. I separated myself from the moment, from the actions my hands were carrying out. Dissociating, as cold washed through me, numbing the reality of patricide. A sharp crack signified the breach in his core. I plunged my hand deeper into his chest cavity. My fingers wrapped around the beating muscle as he looked back at me. Unchecked tears trickled down his cheeks.

He smiled. "I love you, Prometheus. You're a good boy. It's okay, son. Let me go," he encouraged, and with a grunt, I ripped the last vestiges of life from my father's bones. His body sagged unceremoniously against me, as Hermes and Ares rushed to help me guide him to the ground.

The cavern shook around us.

The world around me went silent except for the ringing in my ears as I watched his body sag against the flagstones. We had mere moments before we were trapped here, but I bent down to kiss his forehead anyway. To close his lifeless eyes, still dancing with the stars above.

His stilled heart remained clutched in my hands, and suddenly, I was filled with a singular focus: I was going to kill Zeus. Not imprison. Not trap. I was going to rip the shade from his bones and discard him into oblivion. It was the only way to repay this debt.

The thought consumed me down to the marrow.

I let Hermes and Ares pull me from the chamber just as the gates swung shut, but I was no longer in my body as a cage of blue light erupted around my father's lifeless corpse. As we watched his shade rise from his broken body, bouncing off the barrier above him like a trapped butterfly. Blood pooled around him, seeping into the stone ground. The first sprigs of poisoned Ambrosia burst through the cracks, deadly and brutal and solemnly beautiful. Like the rest of his body was now doing in the center of that cage, the heart in my hands turned from flesh to dried clay.

I crushed it between my fingers until my hands came to rest around a circular object buried deep within. I heard Hermes and Ares speaking around me, felt their hands on my body urging me to move again as I brushed the dirt from the gold, and turned the compass over a few times in my palm. A deep weight anchored in my chest, and I felt a pull—*outward*. Upward.

The compass was guiding me to the map.

I intended to make good on my father's dying wish.

Zarena

CHAPTER 9

I glanced up at the clock on my desk and bit back a curse. It was well past six, and I was going to be late if I didn't get my shit together.

Quickly, *but carefully*, I placed the volume I'd been working on back into its protective sheeting then gathered up my notes, sliding them into a manila folder; I'd type them up later in a full report. I slipped my white cloth gloves from my hands and threw them into the hamper before scooping up my purse and heading for the door. Turning down the gaslight knob on the wall, the sconces dimmed all the way to darkness before I stepped out onto the main floor of the Sillah.

The lights were low in the mezzanine in the late hour and as I rounded the corner, my best friend, Tati, came into view. She was hopped up on the circulation desk, dressed in her usual gothic attire, every inch of her stunning. Her hair fell in dark sheets around her, laid flat as she leaned in, flirting with one of the new clerks. Mark, maybe? He was enraptured by her attention, not that I could blame him. Tati was hot, with a banging silhouette and larger than life personality that took no shit from anyone. Her plaid skirt rode up her thighs, exposing brown skin that always seemed to be glowing, something she chalked up to a good moisturizer, but it made her look angelic. Her black platform boots buckled all the way up her legs, stopping about mid-thigh; the hardware glinting in the low light as she crossed one leg over the other. The woman oozed effortless confidence, always snaring whoever she set her sights on, and Mark? With that dopey look in his eyes and wolfish grin plastered across his face, she could have asked for his wallet and the keys to his car, and he'd have handed them over without question.

Yeah, Mark was a goner.

"Cool, so, can I call you sometime?" he asked, a little too eager. He was cute, in a shy way, and though she smiled, I knew well enough he wasn't her type. There was no way he could keep up with a woman like Tatiana. She'd tear him apart.

Tati leaned in, looking up at him through her lashes in that completely natural confident way of hers. "Maybe," she teased. Her eyes flitted past him to me, where I stood arms crossed and amused. Her face lit up instantly. She hopped off the circ desk, all thoughts of Mark gone as she brushed past him to get to me.

"Damn girl, you lookin' *fine* today, can I get that number?" she cooed, slinging her arm over my shoulder and steering us toward the light of the stained-glass doors. Tati was normally three inches shorter than me, but the boots she was rocking made me look up at her for once.

"You all done for the day?" she asked, and I nodded. "Let's get the hell outta here then, it's tequila time. Later, Mark, call me!" she quipped over her shoulder, dragging me toward the exit.

"But you didn't give me your number!" he called, distressed as he scrambled to grab a pen and held it up, looking flustered.

I turned back to him, shooting a sympathetic smile. "She'll eat you alive, my guy. Better move on," I suggested before turning back with Tati to head out the double doors.

"Do you need to change?"

I appraised my cardigan and flats. "Yeah, I guess, we can stop at the house on the way. What band is playing again?" I asked as we weaved through the tourists and local folks milling around.

"The GorgonKnots, the band I was telling you about. Very Pussy Riot. Mostly all-girl lineup and very punk rock. My cousin turned me onto them, and they only ever play that one spot, Electric Delphi."

I made a face at her verbiage. "Ugh, you know I hate that word. Can't we just call it cunt like everyone else?"

She laughed. "Babes, some people hate the word *cunt* just as much, so we're all gonna have to just find a way to move past it, not everyone can be pleased."

"I get that, it just seems—I don't know. Maybe because when men say it, it's always followed by the cringiest shit they can think of," I replied, eyes wandering to the tops of the buildings along each side of us. We cut down toward the Lower Quarter just as the heat started to ease up; the sun sinking lower over the iron balconies and chipped shutters of the colorful houses on Commons.

We took a left on Dauphine, making our way to Andros's and my home, a small shotgun style pressed shoulder to shoulder with the others, the pastel purple paint darkened by the remnants of the three P.M. storm. Living close to work was a major bonus in a city where having a car was a bigger pain in the ass than it was worth.

"Hey, as long as I'm wet and getting mine, I don't give a damn what it's being called," Tati said with a shrug. "If men are really wearing that thin, you could bounce on over the line a time or two." She wiggled her eyebrows suggestively.

I rolled my eyes, laughing. "T, if I could make myself magically attracted to women out of nowhere, all my problems would be solved because you and I would just get married."

Tati eyed me thoughtfully, tapping her chin. "You know, that's not a terrible idea. I mean, we would obviously seek outside sexual fulfillment, but I'd be down to live together as life partners. Whatcha think? Be my wifey?" she asked, dropping to her knees on the cracked sidewalk.

People around stopped, startled, thinking she was actually proposing as Tatiana dramatically reached for my hand. Brown eyes wide and glistening with laughter, she stared up at me, raising her voice, "C'mon, baby, I don't care that you're completely obsessed with me on a stalker-like level, I'll love you forever!"

"Get the fuck up!" I hissed, practically bowled over with laughter. "You're ridiculous." Helping her onto her feet, she clung to me as she slung her arm over my shoulder. "You know, I think my level of obsession with you is completely justified," I replied. We reached the gate to the house and pushed through onto the cobbled path.

"True, I'm amazing. Come to think of it, you could be *more* obsessed. Also, since we're engaged now, can I choose your outfit for tonight? It is my *birthdayyy*," she sang.

I shot her a look. Knowing Tatiana, I'd wear a nightie for a dress if it was left up to her. But it *was* her night, at least starting at midnight. I sighed. "*Tomorrow* is your birthday, but yes, I suppose that you can. *Within reason.* All the important shit needs to be covered."

"Oh, this is about to be fun!" Delighted, she disappeared through the front door like she owned the place. As much time as we spent together, she practically did.

Prometheus

CHAPTER 10

ionysus's club was packed, and I was in Hells.

Two weeks. It'd been two weeks since we'd returned from Tartarus and I was no closer to finding the map than I'd been before I'd taken my father's life. I winced, a sharp bolt of pain spearing into my chest at the memory.

This was the only thing he'd asked of me, what he'd given his life for. And I couldn't find a fucking map.

We'd reemerged in New Orleans, a fact Hermes found most interesting. The pull brought me back to *this* city, but other than that, nothing.

The cord in my chest led me all around town, pushing and pulling me without my consent. It fucking hurt, the *weight* of the tether. Sometimes it felt like I was being ripped apart. I told myself that it was the magic of the compass, and not the increased guilt I'd been carrying around since we'd returned topside, but that was bullshit and I knew it.

The good thing about divinity was that it shone brightly for others to see, an armor of sorts. An aura that hung around each of us like a flashing sign saying, *God of Lightning, do not fuck with*. This served us well, allowing the Otherworlders around us to know who it was we were dealing with. But Iapetus was sure Clio would have hidden the map well, and I didn't expect to just find it out in the open. Muting was difficult to do. Cloaking it completely was harder. Hermes even had Hecate try to spell a pair of eyeglasses so I could see past enchantments, but so far, I'd only managed to see through petty glamours and minor warding. No map.

I should have been out canvasing the city, but Hermes and Ares *insisted* we take the night off. Hephaestus and Hecate both played in the band performing at Electric Delphi, their first show since Persephone and Hades had their little one, and though it set me on edge, I'd let them drag me along.

As if summoned from the stormy recess of my thoughts, Hermes flashed past, stopping next to my seat at the bar. Dressed in black slacks and a nice shirt, his eyebrow arched as he looked me up and down, letting out a low whistle. "You really showed up to show out tonight, Theo. It'll be fine, though. Grunge is very popular right now."

I swiped my beer off the bar, giving myself a quick once-over. I looked fine. Maybe a bit dressed down in my flannel and jeans, but it was a bar. I didn't know there was a dress code.

I shot him an annoyed look. "I didn't even want to *be* here tonight, so why would I care how I look?" I grumbled, tipping my bottle to my lips, swallowing down the last of the wheat ale I'd been nursing for a half an hour.

Hermes grabbed the empty from me before I could set it down and ordered another round over my shoulder. "Listen, I know you've been on your own for a long time, and you've suffered a huge loss, but you're safe here. As safe as anywhere, honestly. Zeus wouldn't dare step foot in the N.O., and the amulet you're wearing wards you from others being able to pick up on your divinity. Frankly, you need to let loose a little bit."

I tightened my jaw. "Just because he's not here doesn't mean he doesn't have cronies watching. You think he gives a shit that this is Hades's domain? He doesn't perceive *anything* as a threat to him. I have one job; find that map. I should be out there putting in work."

"Tough shit. In pairs only, that's the rule, and everyone is here. Besides, you're especially vulnerable at night, you can't be out there by yourself. That seems more reckless than taking a single night off to reset, right?" Frustration rose in Hermes's tone, my bullheadedness an obvious grate on his nerves.

"It's not the same for me as it is for you. You and Ares have people. You have a life outside of this. I don't and with good reason. Drinking together, making small talk, building bridges and relationships doesn't ever bode well with me," I replied honestly, leaving out the "or for anyone else." I knew I was being a dick—Hermes was trying, but I couldn't help it. Connections and attachments were dangerous. I couldn't afford the weakness, not when I was the closest I'd ever been. Sort of.

Hermes sighed. "I get that. I know *some* parts of what you've been through—" he started, but I cut him off.

"You don't know shit about me or what I've lost, so let's just leave it at that," I barked defensively. I needed to cool down, *needed* to get out of here. There were too many variables involved that I couldn't mitigate, and it had my hackles up, but even I could tell my attitude was fucking foul.

Hermes lifted the tray the bartender sat down and swung it under my nose. "I'm not saying I know everything, Theo, just some things. And the thing I know the most? You need to blow off some steam. You're dangerous if you're too wound up to think clearly. Grab one of these drinks. Whatever you need, they're designed to provide you with. If it's a good buzz, you'll get that. If it's calming, you'll get that. If it's a good fuck—*which I think would highly improve your morale*—you'll get that. Pick one, find someone to blow your load, and let's get back to it in the morning. What do you say?" Hermes shimmied the tray gently, offering me first pick.

I eyed the many colored concoctions warily, unsure of which to choose. A short tumbler full of hot red liquid caught my eye. I picked it up from the back of the tray. "Tomorrow we're back on the hunt?"

He nodded. "First thing. I promise."

I shot him another look before tipping the liquid back and letting it slide over my tongue. It was warm, all cinnamon and cloves with a hint of whiskey. I jolted as the magic spread down my throat, tingling to my fingertips and rolling over my skin.

"Feels good, doesn't it?" Hermes grinned.

"It doesn't suck. But I don't know what I drank, Hermes."

He nudged my shoulder encouragingly. "It's fine. Stick to us and we'll keep an eye on you." He jerked his head to the front of the stage where Ares, Aphrodite, Hades, Thanatos, Dionysus, Helios, and a few others I didn't recognize waited. With a sigh and throat still burning from the rye, I grabbed another beer off the bar and followed behind Hermes, weaving through the crowd with his precarious tower of libations.

Helios extended a hand as we approached, and I took it with ease. The knot taking up residence in my chest since I'd touched the compass lessened as the liquid courage spread through me, and I felt lighter than I had in ages. Maybe Hermes was right. Maybe I needed to loosen up for a night.

"Holy Hells, Theo, I can't believe you're here!" the titan boomed, eyes crinkling with happiness as he pulled a tall, slender man against his side, and pressed a kiss to his cheek. The man in his arms was stunning, soft and delicate with white-blond hair. Helios towered over him, a protective bear as his accent thickened with the drink. "This is my husband, Nick. You didn't get to meet at the wedding; he had to rush off. Baby things."

I dropped Helios's hand but couldn't help but notice how *normal* he looked. I couldn't read his aura or his partners'. Helios's husband offered his hand and I took it. His touch was featherlight as he lowered his striking eyes. Helios's words registered.

I turned, shocked, to look at Helios. "Did you say *baby*? You had a kid?"

Helios grinned wide. "*We did.* Little boy, named him Aero." Nick pulled out his wallet and slid a small square photo from inside, handing it over. A smiling, blond baby boy sat in Nick's arms with Helios behind, holding them both closely.

"He's beautiful. Congratulations, man." I clapped him on the back. Nick tucked the photo back into his wallet before turning and grabbing a drink off the tray from Hermes. "So, you adopted? That's really amazing."

Helios shot me a wild smile and leaned in. "Actually, he's *ours.* Both mine and Nick's. Happened before we were mortal."

I choked on my beer, recovering with as much grace as possible before turning to fully face him. "I *knew* something was up! Helios, what the Hells happened?"

The titan—well, former titan, apparently—cocked his head to the side slightly, surprised. "You could tell? How? Nick and I are both glamoured," he said, shifting uncomfortably.

I put a hand up to stop him; maybe it was the compass. "I'm sure the glamor is fine. I've been kind of wired differently lately. Picking up on subtle things no one else would look for. You know, old habits." I shrugged. Helios relaxed just a bit. "Tell me about your boy. How did this"—I gestured between him and Nick—"happen?"

"Well, the thing is, there was this threesome with a nymph, and you know, they are kind of amorphous. We weren't careful that evening, and when she found out something had taken root, she asked if we wanted it. We'd just become mortal, everything was a mess, but we both *knew* we wanted him. She agreed to carry Aero for us and make sure that he was only made up of our essences. He's all ours. Think of Senna as a surrogate, one that can see him anytime she wants. But he's not of her in any way, so there's no obligation on her end. She's actually watching him tonight, though, so Nick and I could have a night out." He brought his cocktail to his lips and drank deeply. Even without his divinity, I could see how much joy radiated from Helios and his husband. He deserved it, after everything.

"That's amazing, man. Is he showing any signs of divinity? How old is he now?" I asked, leaning in to shout above the sound check happening on the stage. Hecate, Persephone, and Artemis tuned their guitars and bass, as Heph set up his drumkit. It shocked me how interested in this development I actually was, now that the initial shock of Helios's mortality processed. Perhaps it was a little nosy, but, also, what a fascinating circumvention of the conformed process of procreation.

Helios barked a laugh. "The sun shines outta his ass. Little dude is sunlight incarnate, litcrally and figuratively. Aero's eight months, just a little older than Hades and Seph's daughter. She keeps joking they're going to grow up and fall in love, so we'll be in-laws forever."

Hades whipped around with a scowl. "Absolutely not," he shot back, but there was no venom in his tone.

Old animosities seemed long forgotten as Helios roared with laughter and threw his arm over Hades's shoulders. "Oh, come on, now. Afraid your little storm cloud's gonna fall in love with a golden boy? Just think of the holidays. They'd cause tsunamis and hurricanes!" Helios, clearly a little tipsy, roared but Hades laughed along good-naturedly.

His wife, Persephone, approached the edge of the stage as Hades tilted his chin up to her, adoration clear in his gaze. She was everything to him and anyone could see it. The Queen of the Underworld looked like the juxtaposition she was—open and inviting with her pastel high-waisted pants and crop top, but black flowers and thorny accessories that shouted, "Back up, I bite," adorned her as well. She popped some bright pink bubble gum between her lips before leaning down, sliding a purple bass behind her.

Hades broke free of Helios and pressed closer to the stage, hands roaming to the backs of her thighs. He gave her a sharp tug, reeling her body against his chest. Persephone let out a small shriek of startled laughter as she steadied herself on his shoulders.

"Little Flower," Hades growled. She bent down, tangling her fingers in his hair as she kissed him deeply. What started as a sweet kiss quickly devolved into something much more heated, nearly obscene as their tongues danced. Thanatos and Dionysus shouted catcalls while Ares and Helios whooped and hollered. Hades shoved his middle finger in the air toward them, all the while wrapping Persephone's hair around his fists and devouring her. When he finally released her, his wife stumbled back, slightly dazed with kiss-swollen lips. Hades blew a bubble with the gum he'd stolen from her mouth.

"I'm coming back for that later," she promised.

The God of the Dead planted his hands on the stage, stretching forward as she retreated and pulled her bass across her front. "I've got something you'd enjoy putting in your mouth even more," he teased, bold as brass. My eyebrows shot up at his brazen suggestion, but Persephone's breath hitched where she stood.

Thanatos cocked his head sideways at Hades in disbelief. "Oi, mate, this is a bar not a brothel."

Hecate slipped forward, reaching her hand down to Hermes. He took it in his own and turned it palm up to plant a kiss there. "Hey, boyfran. You on your best behavior tonight?"

He shot her a mischievous grin. "If I told you, I wouldn't be very good at mischief, would I, darling?"

Fucking Fates, they were all so in love. *All of them*, living out loud, loving freely. My chest tightened, anxiety warring with the drink, my thoughts dangerous and clouded at how easy it would be to get swept up in the safety and comfort they had here, as a unit. A family. My palms itched, ears buzzing as thoughts waged war inside my head.

Medusa walked out as the lights dimmed, looking impressive and commanding when she took her place at the microphone. The crowd ramped up, pushing toward the stage to get a better view, pressing us slightly in on stage. Snakes coiled high on her head, indecipherable to mortals, who'd just see a petite Black woman with impressive locks twisted up, but I could see in all her glory. Her oversized sunglasses sat in place, her armor, bright red frames that looked like blood against her dark complexion. The red jumpsuit, with a black anarchy sigil spray-painted across the front and side matched perfectly, down to the red-painted combat boots.

"I'm Medusa, and we are the GorgonKnots! Are you ready to set the patriarchy on *firrreeeeeeeeee*?!" she roared, working the crowd into a frenzy around us.

Heph snapped three clicks on his snare rim preceding their launch into a series of songs about politics, equality, and my personal favorite, feminine rage. The music pumped through my body, causing my blood to rush, adrenaline to flood with every beat of Hephaestus's drums, every scream of Artemis's guitar.

I loved it.

The feral lyrics, the ferocity of the conviction in Medusa's voice. From the beginning, women had gotten a raw deal. I'd tried to make them superior, giving them the ability to create life, but instead of revering and worshiping them, mortal men oppressed them, under Zeus's supervision.

I zeroed into Heph's stare as he smashed and struck his drum set with rhythmic precision. He shook his head once, jaw set, in clear warning. I glanced sideways, following his line of sight and let out a laugh. Ares had Aphrodite's back pressed to his front, hands roaming up and down her body. I looked away quickly, careful to school my features in case either of them saw me. I didn't feel like taking a punch to the gut tonight. Sexual tension swallowed up the air around me, and I was reminded that I was surrounded by Bonded or *practically* Bonded partners. Medusa and Artemis were still unattached, but they did no good as buffers all the way up on the stage.

The crowd surged against my back, sloshing my beer, and I suddenly needed to be anywhere *but* here. I pushed my way to the back, separating from the crowd and headed to a far wall, desperate for a little peace to finish my beer.

Sure, I felt loose, the usual knot in my chest free, but that didn't make it any easier to be surrounded by so much *love*. They got to wear it proudly, openly even. It sounded great in theory, but it also made me wary. Such weakness on display, for anyone to see the way to make Hades crumble was to go after his wife.

It worked before.

Same for Hermes and Hecate; or Aphrodite, Heph, and Ares. Even Nick and Helios were playing it fast and loose as mortals. Zeus could and would exploit any weaknesses he could suss out.

I leaned against the back wall to take in the rest of the show, but a soft moan caught my attention from the shadows, coming from under the stairs. The lights of the club danced and pulsed with the music, but I could still see *her*, pale skin and fire-red hair. Beautiful face thrown back, eyes screwed shut as the dark figure of a man moved sloppily in front of her. I wasn't trying to eavesdrop, though the little sounds she was making shot through me, down my spine straight to my cock. Without my permission, my ears trained onto her frequency, desperate to hear more of those breathy little moans.

"You're so hot." A nasally male voice shot from the darkness, his hands roaming without purpose over her like she was a lamp and he was trying to pull a genie out. He traced mouth breather kisses up her neck, and though muscles were tight with tension, she seemed to be inexplicably making the best of it. Mystery girl turned her head away from him, her body screaming that he was doing it all wrong. I watched like a voyeur, partly out of bizarre curiosity as to why this angel was even letting this cretin near her and partly in rapt fascination at the way *she* moved. Then I heard it, the words that finally broke her completely from whatever fantasy she was living inside.

"Tell me how you want it. You want me to French kiss your pussy?" nasally guy asked, and I couldn't help the laugh that worked up my throat. I almost choked on my beer at his words, and mystery girl froze completely under him, pushing herself as far into the wall as she could get.

"Hey, umm, actually could you back up? This is moving a bit fast; I think we should take a beat." Her voice firm, but placating. Mr. Nasally pressed the issue, trying to put his lips on her again. She braced her arm across his chest. "Hey, I said back the fuck up. It wasn't a request."

Her anger, *that fire*, pulled me closer and I pushed off the wall, ready to end this fucking guy if he didn't comply immediately.

"What the fuck? I thought you wanted to do this. Don't try and back out now." His voice turned darker, meaner. Mystery girl heard the shift, too, and she moved subtly into a defensive position, still maintaining the frame of her arms against him.

"Yeah, well, that was before you licked my neck like a dog. I don't owe you anything, now back the fuck up," she demanded.

I had enough. I sat my beer on the small mahogany ledge next to me and stalked over, invading their space. "Hey baby, there you are. Who's this?" I asked, blocking the exit.

Her eyes locked to mine, and I willed her to understand that I was on her side, not a threat. Ole throat licker stepped back a hair in confusion, and she took advantage of the opening, dropping her defensive position and slipping from behind him. I offered my hand, which she took like a lifeline. I pulled her closer to me, tucking her against my side, but maintaining a respectful hold on her arm instead of her body. Fates, she smelled amazing, and rather than fear, she trembled with anger. Strong muscles tensed against me, solid biceps and thick thighs honed from athletic work lent a smooth transition from the softer parts of her. I hadn't saved her; this woman was a fighter, through and through, and I had probably saved *his* life by stepping in.

Zarena

CHAPTER 11

oly Hell was this man *hot.*

I had no idea how I'd gotten here. When Tom or Tim, whatever his name was, pulled me to the back, I thought, "Well, he's not the brightest, but he'll do as long as he keeps his mouth shut." Unfortunately for him, he hadn't, and unfortunately for me, making out with him felt a lot like being slobbered on by a hound dog. The gargantuan next to me pulled me closer to him and I melted into his large frame. He kept his hands over my elbow, not copping the feel I knew he could.

"What the fuck is this?" Tim or Tom demanded, hands on his hips.

Big guy next to me shrugged. "Just a little game me and my girl like to play." He sent me a wink. "She picks a total tool off the dance floor, makes out with him a bit. I like to watch until she's had enough, then we send said tool on his way and fuck all night. It's pretty straightforward."

The bulge of his bicep pressed into me, and I had to resist the urge to sink my teeth into it. I tilted my head up to look at him, which was a big mistake. My body set itself on fire with want at what I saw. He was quite possibly the most beautiful man I'd ever seen. Tall, sure, but I never really cared about that. No, he was tall—in stature *and* presence. This man took up all the air in a room, and I was responding to it in all the right ways. He had a sharp, chiseled jaw covered in only an inch or so of dark beard. His hair was longer on top but sheared short on the sides, and his eyes were deep green and dissecting with a pair of slutty little glasses perched on the bridge of his nose. The casual way he held me to him, oozing confidence, set off waterworks between my thighs.

Yeah, this was working for me.

"That's bullshit. She was ready to hop on my dick just seconds ago. What the fuck is this really?" Beady little eyes darted back and forth between us. "She a hooker? Is that what this is? Because I'll pay for it, hell, I'll let you watch if you want. A whore's a whore to me."

Wrong fucking answer, Tim.

I was seconds away from lunging at this asshole, but the growl that reverberated from this man's chest turned my legs to jelly. He started forward and Tim took a step back, but I reached for his hand and brought him back to me before he committed murder under the stairs of this club. Most men wouldn't have heeded my protests, but as soon as my fingers tightened over his bicep and yanked, this monster of a man stopped, a beast waiting my instruction.

Okay, that was also fucking hot.

I needed to get this under control if I hoped to salvage any part of this evening.

"Tim, I wouldn't fuck you for all the money in the world. Now, I suggest you crawl back out onto the dance floor and see if you can convince someone else to touch your dick. Because if you stay here, I'm gonna let my man beat the shit out of you, then fuck me against the wall over your unconscious body." I informed him, using my most saccharine voice to soften the blow. Tim didn't move, just narrowed his eyes like he didn't believe for a second a man like this was into me, and that pissed me off too.

I turned to the Adonis in front of me, ready to make a point, hoping he'd be okay with it. His green eyes searched mine for a split second before I launched myself at him, pressing my entire body against a wall of muscle. He wasted no time returning my efforts, tenfold and holy mother of hell, I knew immediately I was in over my head. His hands, they were everywhere, warm and commanding as he backed me up against the wall, eradicating any air between us. One of those big hands reached behind my thigh and wrenched my leg up with ease, hooking it over his hip. He let his full weight sink into the cradle of my thighs, and I was engulfed in the smell of him, the scent earthy and woodsy with a hint of fresh parchment, like my favorite book I'd yet to read. His mouth, hot on mine, commanding. Stars burst in the blacks behind my eyelids, the blood beneath my skin rushing to the surface as he stole the breath from my lungs. Something told me nothing about him asked for permission.

I moaned into his mouth as his teeth scraped over my bottom lip, his grip on my throat possessive, commanding, *fuck*.

He broke away from my mouth and traced his lips across my jaw, down my throat, scenting me in the most primal way. He took turns nipping down the column of my throat and laving his tongue to soothe the sting after each bite, erasing any trace of the cretin earlier.

Take notes, Tim.

I was consumed by him, his aura, his confidence. His hands slowly stilled, and he moved back just a fraction, enough to give me space to breathe. His hand still had my thigh gripped over him, fingers rubbing small circles on the exposed flesh beneath this barely-there dress Tati picked out. We were both breathing hard, his eyes roaming over me, startling green.

"I think he's gone," he whispered, inches from my face. "Are you okay?"

My brain short-circuited. A million years had passed for me since I'd removed myself from Tim's grubby hands and felt the white-hot touch of this man. I nodded, blinking several times, clearing my throat. "Thank you," I managed to choke out, keenly aware that our hips were still pressed together. I could feel every inch of him beneath his jeans, so close to where I'd like him to be.

"Of course," he whispered like it was a prayer, a song on his lips. "It's lovely to meet you." His hands roamed over my body, taking liberties he'd abstained from before, the longer we stared at one another. Every graze of his fingertips sent a jolt through me and my cunt throbbed with want as I struggled to breathe. "Tell me why you let that idiot touch you," he demanded, voice low, gruff. Hungry.

I shrugged, closing my eyes as his nose grazed my jaw again, ghosting over my skin. He left trails of sparks in his wake. I let out a soft moan.

"I just—I needed to . . ." My words died in my throat. I didn't owe this stranger any explanation for why I did what I did. The truth was that I'd gone quite a while without touch, having had a real string of terrible dates lately.

He brought his hand up to my throat, cradling my neck and chin with his massive grip. "You needed what?"

I hummed, clenching around air, painfully empty. "I needed to come. It's been . . . longer than I'd like," I admitted, and he pushed his lips into the soft flesh of my neck, pinning my throat back to the wall with his hold. He shifted, caging me farther with his hips, so my weight rested on his muscled thigh. His now-free hand slid up my leg, pushing under my dress, skating down even farther to the soft flesh above my clit. He hovered there, circling his thumb, and I moaned, the sensation sending me into sweet oblivion.

"Give me permission then, Red. It's not polite to keep a lady waiting, but I need your words," he whispered into the shell of my ear. I bucked forward into his touch.

"Yes, you have it, just *move*," I whined. He pressed a kiss to my lips, deep and crushing.

"I'm not going to ask you how you want it or what you want me to do to you. Any man who needs you to draw a roadmap doesn't deserve the privilege of tasting you. I intend to feast."

Zarena

CHAPTER 12

Those words leaving his mouth should have been illegal. He slid the pad of his finger over my clit, and I let out a harsh cry as he moved against me, shifting his thigh up for me to ride. The hand pinning my throat slipped up and clamped over my lips with force, just enough pressure to let me know he was in charge. I was soaked, no doubt through the thin silk fabric of my dress, and I couldn't imagine the mess I was making of his jeans.

My mind shut off, and this, *this* was what I needed. The type of dominance that couldn't be manufactured or faked, the natural charisma and command of a man who knew how to quiet my mind. A shadow fell over us that reminded me we weren't alone. The stranger stilled his movements, shifting back slightly to give me my space. His eyes, green pools of emeralds, burned fire into mine. He'd read my body language and immediately stopped, something I found incredibly hot.

"You okay, sweetheart?"

I flicked my gaze behind him where a few guys gathered to wait in line for the bathroom. We weren't exactly hidden, but his massive frame covered most of me, save for the bare leg he had slung over his hip. He turned to follow my gaze and let out a grunt, understanding dawning on his face.

"You got somewhere we could take this that's a little more private?" he asked, and I pushed down my annoyance at the men over my shoulder.

"Don't you?" I countered, and he smiled.

"Just in town for a few days and I'm staying with friends. Trust me when I tell you that we don't wanna be anywhere near there when they get done here tonight."

Anxiety welled up inside of me as I battled with my baser instincts. I *never* brought men back to my house. It was safety, first and foremost. The dating scene was one big dumpster fire, and the last thing I needed was a one-night stand knowing where I lived. Then, there was Dro. He'd likely rip apart any dude I brought back he didn't deem worthy of his little sister. On the other hand, this man barely had his hands on me, and I needed him so badly I was tempted to let him fuck me right here against these stairs.

"Do you have a condom?" I blurted. He raised an eyebrow at me, but I didn't have time to be ashamed or embarrassed at my straightforwardness, I just needed answers. His face fell slightly, but he gave me a sweet smile before unhooking my leg and setting me gently back on my feet. The hot air of the club felt cold against me without his warmth, my body on fire as he carefully straightened my dress and ran his thumb over my lip.

"I don't, I'm sorry. I wasn't expecting this. But you know what, this was amazing. You're beautiful and I got to spend a little bit of time touching the divine. Let me walk you out to the floor at least?"

He was disappointed but doing all he could to make sure I didn't feel pressured. He wasn't trying to change my mind. I knew the bar was in Hell, but my body was practically vibrating with the need for him to put his hands on me after that.

Instead, he grabbed my hand gently, carefully entwining our fingers, and led me toward the crowded club. It was a bad idea; warred against every survival instinct I had, but I pulled back, gripping his wrist with both of my hands. He turned to me, eyebrow raised.

"Promise you're not a crazy stalker that you won't try to rob or kill me," I said, and he let out an amused laugh.

"If I *were* a stalker or murderer or thief, I don't think making me promise I wasn't would actually do anything. But if you need the reassurance, I promise that I'm only in town on business, and the only thing I would intend to steal from you would be orgasms. If you die from that, I can't be held responsible, Red." His eyes darkened as he leaned down, gaze catching on the rise and fall of my chest, the flush of my cheeks. I wanted him even more.

"No names. One night. And if I die by orgasm, that's completely on me," I whispered, and he nodded, wasting no time pulling me through the club.

I scanned the room, looking for Tatiana. I'd need to let her know what was up before I let this man break me in half, and I found her grinding and winding her body between two guys, one in a dark maroon suit and the other more punk-looking with tattoos and a mohawk. She glanced up and caught my stare, eyes flitting between the man hauling me out of the club and our joined hands. She raised her eyebrows and I gave her a thumbs-up, which made her throw her head back and laugh, as the one with the mohawk buried his face in her neck. Tatiana waved me off with the hand flung over his shoulder and blew me a kiss. She was fine, and with luck, would be in the middle of her own dicking down before the night was over.

As he pulled me through the throng of people, my eyes roamed over his broad shoulders. I wanted to strip him out of that flannel so I could run my hands under the hard muscles I'd felt beneath, but there was an excitement to this, a tension in the wait. He pushed through the doors and the hot, wet Louisiana night slammed into us as he turned, pulling me against his chest.

"Cab?" he asked, and I nodded, pulling him in for a searing kiss. We lived close enough to walk, but the cab offered another level of caution. A walk was easy to retrace steps, but in the back of this cab, I made for one hell of a distraction. His lips were demanding, no hesitation to be found in the strokes of his tongue against mine. I broke our connection and leaned back, breathless. Those fingers traced and roamed over me, outlining each curve. He raised a hand, signaling one of the waiting drivers along the curb with their light still on. I followed as he led us off the curb and opened the door of the yellow cab, ushering me inside.

"Where to, folks?" the cabbie asked as we folded ourselves into the back seat. Mystery man pressed right up against my side, his large hand rubbing up my thigh gently. I ached for him to touch me higher, fill me full.

"Dauphine and Commons, please." I answered, the words nearly a pant.

The cabbie tipped his head and flipped up the rearview mirror, giving us a bit of privacy. It was obvious what this was, and if he drove regularly in the N.O. this wouldn't be the first or last hookup he'd helped get started. He turned the radio up, blasting "Wicked Game" through the speakers as the tires rolled beneath us, carrying us through the city.

In the darkness, my handsome stranger moved against me slowly, situating us so my back was against his chest with one hand grazing over my shoulder, down my torso. He splayed his hot hand over my thigh, and with the other, cupped my neck as lips trailed softly down my throat, his teeth nipping at the flesh of my earlobe, sending shivers down my spine as I melted for him. I leaned back, granting him a little more access. The hand on my thigh pushed higher, scooting the bunched fabric of my dress up, fingers demanding and patient all at once. His hands were rough, slightly calloused, fingernails scraping lightly over the flesh of my inner thigh, and my chest rose and fell rapidly as I struggled to maintain normal breathing.

"Spread for me," he commanded against the shell of my ear, pushing my thighs apart with his slow and steady grip. I complied, every inch of my body on fire while the occasional marquee lights flashed above us as we drove.

His fingers brushed over my lace panties, slipping easily over my cunt. "So ready," he mused, almost moaning. He jerked the fabric to the side and slid his fingers through my core, gliding gracefully through the moisture gathered there. His thumb and forefinger latched gently around my clit, rolling it between them with sure, lazy strokes. A soft whimper escaped my lips, and he clamped the hand on my throat over my mouth.

"*Shh, shh*, or he'll hear you." He moved faster, circling my clit with more purpose. "Do you think he knows what I'm doing to you, Red?" His finger slipped down, teasing my entrance, the touch too light, the pressure not enough. "Think he can tell how wet you are for me? I want him to know, but he doesn't get to hear your moans, those are only for *me*. You gonna be a good girl for me and keep quiet?"

I nodded frantically, rolling my hips against him, desperate to feel his fingers inside me. The music swirled around us, drowning out the world outside. I had to give it to the cabbie—he never once checked that mirror.

"That's what I want to hear."

He plunged his finger inside, deep, curling, and I saw stars. My body bowed, but he kept me close to his chest, strong arms binding me to thick muscles. He pumped his fingers in and out, agonizingly slow, stretching along my walls, alternating between two and one with his thumb over my clit. I was lost to bliss, eyes rolling backward as I relaxed into him. The hand over my mouth never relented, and I breathed heavily out of my nose while he worked. The wet sounds coming from the back seat were so obvious, there was no way what we were doing was discreet, and that turned me on more.

I clenched around his fingers as he talked to me, whispering affirmations in my ear the entire time he stroked me. "That's it, Red. Take what you need because I certainly fucking will. You're tight. We're gonna need to stretch you out a little more, sweetheart, get you nice and ready." His words ramped me up, and I was there, right on the edge when he dropped the hand on my mouth to my breast and gave my nipple a pinch.

It was over for me. I bucked as he returned his hold on my throat, securing me flush to his body as pleasure flooded down to my toes. He used his grip to tilt my head back to him, swallowing breathy moans with his mouth. I was a panting, disheveled mess by the time he let me go, only slightly loosening the pressure. The fingers inside me stilled slowly and he lifted them carefully from me, straightening my panties, pulling my dress down as he retreated. His fingers came up to my mouth, soaked with my arousal, smearing the hot liquid over my lips and chin before bringing them to his mouth and licking them clean.

"I want this here for later, so I can taste you while I fuck you," he whispered, and my body tightened under his gaze.

The cab came to a stop at the intersection near my house. He reached into his pocket and pulled out a hundred-dollar bill, handing it to the cabbie. "Thanks for the ride, keep the change," he said before grabbing me and lifting me from the back seat. I pushed the door shut with my hip and led him by the hand to my front door, legs shaking, steps wobbling, desperate to have him inside me again.

I wasn't sure who he was, but if he fucked like he did foreplay, *I was so fucking in.*

We stumbled up the porch, his hands and mouth back on me as I struggled to get my key in the door. I fumbled for the light, dropping my bag, and he turned me around, grabbing the backs of my thighs to lift me up. I wrapped my legs around his waist, marveling at his strength. I'd never had a man toss me around like this. I was tall, thick, and curvy. A lot of men were intimidated by my height alone, and I'd struggled with body issues when I was younger, but now, I embraced myself. Moments of doubt still crept in, but I worked hard to keep those thoughts from consuming me. I wrapped my arms around his neck, and he buried his face in the valley between my breasts.

"Where?" he demanded.

I pointed to the hallway that led to my room. He carried me to it, and I pushed open my door. Tingles ramped up my spine as he walked us inside, kicking the door shut behind him. Moonlight streamed in from the large bay window, bathing my room in a pale glow. He tossed me onto my bed and crawled up from between my spread legs, crowding my space as my bed groaned under our combined weights. His face, inches from mine, hovered, giving me a final chance to stop this.

I ran a hand through his hair and pulled his face closer to mine. "Feast," I commanded.

And he *did*.

Prometheus

CHAPTER 13

Her body lay spread out below me, bright blue eyes shining like oceans in the moonlight. "Feast," she commanded, and I closed the short distance between us, desperate to feel her body pliant beneath mine.

Whatever concoction I'd drank at Dio's club spurred me on, silencing every thought of how bad an idea this was. The only thing that mattered was worshiping the woman beneath my body, hearing her little moans as she came on my tongue. I kissed her once, sucking her full bottom lip between my teeth before moving down her torso, trailing my tongue between the valley of her breasts. The night air clung to her skin in a soft sheen, embedding into the very marrow of my bones as I licked the sweat from her skin. She smelled of meadowsweet and lazy days by the riverbanks, and I wanted to taste, to devour. Her breasts, so full, heavy and perfectly on display as she arched her back, seeking my touch. I ran my palm over the silk fabric, massaging her firmly, relishing in the way her nipples hardened under my caresses. Red's hands flew up past her face, pushing through her fiery locks, as she grinded her core against me with need.

I chuckled, moving lower. "So impatient. Don't worry, I'm gonna give you what you need, Red." I slipped off the end of the bed, grabbing her hips and hoisting her down to the edge. She bent for me, and I ran my nose along the inside of her thigh, fingers digging into the crease where her hip met, pushing her open for me.

My arms wrapped underneath each of her thick thighs and I pressed my palm flat over her soft belly, applying enough pressure to keep her grounded and present. My breath hitched slightly at the sheer ecstasy that was her body, her scent, when I brought my face down and licked over the lace. Soaked, the fabric tasted like sin, like her, and I breathed hot and heavy over it, laving my tongue against the barrier keeping me from feasting on her flesh.

"Please," she whined, wanton and desperate as I felt.

I hooked a finger around the scrap of fabric and yanked it to the side before pressing my tongue flat against her clit. She rocketed off the bed, bucking her hips while I devoured her, slid through her lips and speared my tongue inside of her. She tasted *divine*, like pure Ambrosia that burst in my mouth with every swipe of my tongue. The sounds of her moans filled the room, and I ground my hips into the bedside, eager for some relief of my own but unable to take my hands off her body to get it. Red's hands fisted my hair and I suctioned to her, claiming her in ways I hadn't let myself touch a woman in years.

I didn't do this. I didn't come home with random women, but there was nothing random about this. It felt grounding, rooted, like the Fates had spun this web just for me.

She came hard, a shaking, writhing spectacle, and I grinned, lapping up her release. Cheeks flushed, she sat up on her elbows, looking down at me with glazed-over blue eyes. Red stretched an arm over toward her bedside table, twisting her body as best she could with my grip still holding her, where I kissed and nipped and licked her through the comedown. The drawer creaked open, the bed jostling as she rooted inside frantically, moaning and whimpering all while pulling out a golden foil packet.

I released her to stand straight, unbuttoning my flannel shirt and tossing it aside, then grabbed the hem of my T-shirt and shed it too. Red tossed the condom to me, and I caught it in midair, undoing my belt with my free hand. Her eyes fixated on the motion, biting her lip as I pulled it free, sliding the leather through the denim loops with ease. I popped the button of my jeans and slid my zipper down, fascinated by the way this goddess devoured me unapologetically. Her gaze was fire across my skin, and I preened under her approving perusal. She was still wearing that dress, and skimpy and lovely as it was, it needed to go.

"The dress—take it off."

She flushed, a deep crimson blooming over her cheeks and neck as I scanned her body hungrily. The bed dipped under my weight as I crawled between her thighs on my knees, leaned back on my heels and pulled my jeans and boxers down, fisting my cock while I drank her in. Red's gaze traveled down my torso, over the bulges of my chest until they came to rest on my hand, stroking for her. I gripped the edge of the foil packet with my teeth and tore it free, then positioned the rubber over my tip before rolling it down my length and pinching the tip.

Her eyes bulged, taking in the size. "Whoa, whoa," she cautioned, backing up just a fraction. "That's, umm, quite a piece you're rockin' cowboy. I don't think it'll f—"

"It'll fit, Red. I've done the work, you can take it," I promised, sliding my fingers over the tip and back down again. My voice came out rough and broken with want, one I hadn't heard fall from my lips in *so*, so long. Just being this near to her, tasting her on my tongue had me straining against my base desires to consume, *to devour*. She let out a nervous laugh, still eyeing my cock with apprehension. I rested my weight over her on my hand, released my thick shaft and caressed over her clit, coaxing small figure eights across it. She hummed, inching closer, relaxing under my touch as she chased the pleasure.

"You can take it because you *need* it. How long has it been since someone fucked you like the divinity you are?" I asked, and her eyes flew open, her blue orbs trained on mine. I retracted my fingers and she let out a small huff of frustration, but I just pushed up the hem of her dress over her hips, exposing her to me. Trapped breath expelled from my chest as I grabbed my shaft and slid it through her slick lips, watching her body react to the touch. She was hot and silken and I needed *more, more, more*. Her stomach rolled, clenching. I smirked.

"I'm not going to ask you how you want it, Red," I reminded, and she brought her hand up to grab my wrist next to her head. "Relax for me," I instructed, pressing a kiss to her lips as I pushed the crown of my cock into her tight warmth, fighting the bolt of lightning shooting down the backs of my legs at her fit. "*So tight,* sweetheart, you're doing so well," I murmured, voice strained as I peppered her neck with kisses. My head dropped between us, panting, unable to resist watching her swallow me. Her walls pulsed and fluttered around my cock, squeezing and gripping as I lifted my head to look into her eyes. "You okay, Red?"

She moaned, body shaking as she nodded her head. "Deeper, I want more," she choked. I rocked my hips up more, giving her another few inches. The pressure was insane, the pleasure intense to the point of pain and I wasn't even inside of her fully. Red's mouth opened, head arching back as she pulsed around me, walls gripping with every shallow thrust as I fed her more, deeper, out of my mind with need. She enveloped me and every nerve in my body exploded. Red rolled her hips to meet my thrust, and I sank fully inside of her, buried to the hilt.

"Fuck, *fuck*," she panted, her nails scratching into my neck, marking me, drawing blood from the sharp tips and fuck if that didn't make me harder.

I flexed inside her, testing her pain level. "Does it hurt? I can back up," I asked, voice serious, but choked with the iron grip she had me in. It would be the greatest test of my self-control to pull out of her, but if she wasn't ready for it, I would. I brought two fingers to my tongue, licking over the pads and bringing them down to work slowly over her clit, drawing out the pleasure as she shuddered beneath me.

She shook her head, bringing her forehead up to mine. "If you take your cock out of me before I come, I'll cut it off. Do you get me?" she demanded. We fit so perfectly, and nothing about this felt normal.

I grinned, grabbing the hem of her neckline and wrenching it down, exposing her breasts to me fully. She opened her mouth to protest, but I slammed into her, knocking the breath from her lungs. If she wouldn't take the dress off, I'd fuck it into scraps.

I leaned all my weight onto my forearm propped next to her and gripped the bottom hem of her dress, ripping it up. I grabbed both ends of the fabric like reins and pounded into her tight cunt, occasionally leaning down to take a hardened nipple into my mouth. I watched her as she took me beautifully, body arched, tits and hips jiggling under the force of each thrust, her walls too tight and warm as she lifted her hips to take me impossibly deeper.

I needed to slow down, to watch the speed and ferocity I was fucking into her with, but every time I tried to adjust my pace, she swirled her hips, pulled me deeper with her claws, and heels dug into the small of my back.

"Don't stop!" she moaned, eyes glassy as she held my stare and Fates help me, I couldn't if I tried. It was as though she commanded me, my body, my cock. Whatever she wanted, I'd give to her. I had no idea how long we fucked, time stopped existing while I was inside of her warmth. I bit and grabbed at her pale flesh, relishing the marks I knew she'd have for keepsakes long after I was gone. Each roll of my hips in sure strokes had the sweetest sounds filling my ears, sharing my breaths, and I worked her clit with each thrust, reading her body. Needing this to be good for her, for the trust in her eyes as I filled her too deep.

The chain that held my silver band dangled between us, and I lifted it over my shoulder, tossing with it the anticipation of the gnawing guilt I felt anytime I fucked someone else. I focused back on Red, taking me deep, giving her all the attention she demanded.

"See, look at you, so full. Like you were made to take my cock, Red, *Hells*," I panted, dropping her dress and settling my forearm up her sternum, the better to grip her throat. Her cunt kept me locked in a vice, and with every drag against her walls, every whimper from her plush lips, I flew closer to damnation.

"Please, right there, *please*," she begged, and my cock swelled, fucking into her in earnest. I squeezed the sides of her throat, and she locked up, so tight she nearly pushed me out. She winced when I plunged back in, meeting me thrust for thrust, and it became clear by the way she tightened around me that she enjoyed a little pain with her pleasure. My cock was so fucking hard it could have busted concrete, mind running away with what I could do with her, what pleasure I could show her, if given more time. My thoughts were stilled as my gaze fell to her glassy blue eyes, shining with pleasure and unshed tears, so full of awe at how I took her, face to face.

I hadn't been in this position in a long time. I preferred to fuck hard and fast from behind, but I wanted to watch her eyes, needed to see her gasp as she fell apart on my cock. I deepened my strokes, but my mind took me back to another time, another life.

The feeling of home and love and comfort. A pair of dark brown eyes, not blue, that hung and reset the moon of my world . . . Dark brown hair, sweet lips . . .

A pair of hands came up to meet my face, pulling my attention to the present, slowing my thrusts.

"Hey, where did you go? Come back to me, come *with* me," she whispered, searching my face as my hips faltered. Red pressed our foreheads together and I stared deep into her intelligent eyes, the blood thundering in my ears and my heart kicking in my chest in warning. This was too intimate, too close. But here I was, staring into the deep pools of her shade, enraptured by the vortex of blue hues that swam within them. A feeling of possessiveness welled up inside of me from nowhere, pushing me closer to the brink.

I felt the moment she reached her release, and I pushed through, riding out her climax. Her body arched up as she cried out, squeezing me impossibly tight, and it was fucking incredible, watching her in ecstasy. I exploded, filling the condom while she pulsed around me, utterly spent, exquisite in her rapture.

We stayed locked together, both breathing hard, engulfed in the comedown of our release. I was still hard inside of her as she pulsed around my shaft, massaging and milking me for every fucking drop. That sensation of owning welled up inside again, deep, forbidden, and suddenly I needed to get this condom off. Needed to fill her up and watch my cum leak out of her. I was desperate to paint her stomach and tits with it, watch it drip from her long, pale eyelashes, see her blue eyes fall shut while she sucked my cock to soothe herself. I wanted to take her apart then spend hours putting her back together.

A shiver rocked down my spine and another wave hit me, causing my cock to spasm as my cum pushed the already tight condom to its brink. Gently, I pulled out and slipped the rubber off, careful to keep her hips pinned underneath me. I twisted the condom up and tossed it into the trash near her bed before settling back between her legs. She was a wet, sticky mess as she gasped for air, and I intended to clean it all up, not ready to be done, not nearly having had my fill. I kissed down her torso and she moaned, her voice a raspy cry against my ears. I licked the sweat and her arousal from her thigh, trailed my tongue back to her cunt and swirled it over her swollen clit. When I pushed a finger inside, she jerked off the bed, calling for god just as a door slammed in the distance.

Red stiffened, her grip ironlike on my head as a few strands broke loose from my scalp.

Muffled sounds filtered their way down the hallway to us. "Z! Yo, Z! What I tell you about leaving your shoes and shit in the foyer? I'm always trippin' over this shit," a deep male voice boomed through the house, laced with exasperation.

I sat up, alarmed. *"Are you fucking married?"* I hissed, voice low.

Red shoved me off her, scrambling to right her dress, looking thoroughly fucked. "No, of course not!" she fired back, "That's my brother. He's also my roommate and is very, *very* good with knives. You need to *go*." She emphasized the word, tossing my T-shirt to me.

"Z, I brought you food. You up?" His voice echoed down the hall, and she launched toward the door, legs nearly giving out as she tested her weight like a damn baby deer. I could hear the thunder of her heartbeat as she slipped the lock.

"Yeah, just got back from the club. Lemme change and I'll be out, bubba," she shouted just as footfalls halted outside of her door. She shot her hand out to me and mouthed, "Don't move."

"Aight then. I'll get it ready. You and Tati didn't drink too much, did you?"

She shimmied out of the ruined fabric of her dress, the silk stained with her own slick and flecks of my cum. "Nah, but Tati found some entertainment for the night so I peaced out. I'll be out in a second, my makeup's a mess and I want to put my hair up," she said, and we heard feet shuffling way.

Big feet. Lots of shuffling. He must have been huge. I pulled up my boxers and zipped my jeans as quietly as I could. I had no idea where my shoes were in this mess of a room. It wasn't dirty, but there were piles of clothes obscuring everything in the darkness.

Red—no, what had he called her? Z?—furiously combed through her hair and wrapped the red locks up in a messy bun. Her makeup was indeed smeared, lipstick smudged down her jaw and over her lips, mascara running from where her eyes had watered. She looked fucking delicious, and my cock ached to be back inside her, my body thrumming with a foreign need.

Z yanked the silk dress off, leaving her almost completely exposed, save for her panties, which I'd all but ruined. Her hour-glass body stopped me in my tracks, mid-pants pull. I did the mental mathematics on how much an ass whooping would be worth to get caught bending her over right here. I was an immortal after all, a mortal man wouldn't do much damage. I crossed the room to her and spun her around to face me, sliding a finger under her lace panties. I pulled them down her legs, ignoring her protests.

"What are you doing?" she whispered.

I looked up at her, pocketing them. "You're about to make me go out a window, aren't you?"

She pulled on a pair of sexy little sleep shorts that strained against the swell of her ass. "Yes, if you'd like to live," she mumbled, and so freshly fucked, she looked delectable.

I grabbed her around the neck and pulled her into me, kissing her reverently. She melted into my touch before coming to her senses and pushing me back.

"Well then, I'm taking a souvenir, Red." I grinned, letting her go. She laughed and tossed my shoe at me, motioning for me to take the window out. I tiptoed across the hardwood and swung open the bay window.

"Hey, Mystery Man," she whispered, and I turned, halfway out the window. She looked beautiful in the pale moonlight, smiling. "Thanks for the orgasms."

I grinned like a fool, licking my lips as I shot her a wink. With one last look, I hopped out the window and dropped the few feet into the grass, the sound of her bedroom door opening and closing shut sending me on my way.

My mind buzzed as I jumped the gate, careful to mind the creak I'd remembered it made when we'd stumbled up the garden path to her porch earlier. My body, my entire being, felt lighter from my release, and I could smell her on me, taste her in my mouth and on my lips. That faint scent of meadowsweet clung to my skin.

My watch alarm sent off several sharp chirps a moment later, and reality hit me, *hard*. The fog in my head cleared more and more from the drink, and as the old familiar pangs took up residence in my body—the same song and dance I'd endured for an eternity—I chastised myself for how reckless I'd been. I stumbled down the empty street, grateful for the darkness shielding me from prying eyes. A small courtyard, open on only one side, rose into view and I all but crawled inside and waited for the final blow to fall.

Zarena

CHAPTER 14

ight flooded the hallway, and the delicious smell of whatever special Andros had made that evening at work filtered through my nose causing my stomach to rumble. My muscles were sore, and I was starving, absolutely *ravenous* after what we'd done. Mystery Man had more than delivered, and a pang of regret welled up inside of me that I didn't have a name to pair with those deep green eyes.

Clearing the hallway, I swallowed down my regrets, determined not to let any societal notions of propriety push me into a guilty headspace. We were two consenting adults, and we'd both agreed to do what we did and leave it at that. I'd only ever had a few one-night stands in my life, and I generally wasn't a huge fan of a fuck and run. I needed a genuine connection to put my mind and body into that intimate space normally. Tonight, I'd just been chasing a high, willing to settle to break my dry spell with Tim or Tom or whatever the hell his name had been. But Mystery Man? With hands dwarfing my own and a wicked tongue? That had been the best ending sex of my fucking *life*. More than once, I'd lost my mind completely and nearly begged him to lose the condom and take me raw, further proof that I was way too horny to be trusted.

Andros lifted an eyebrow at me as I shuffled past him to grab the pitcher of sweet tea out of the fridge. He stood at the center island, doling out portions of steak topped with what I recognized as his famous Orleans sauce, crabcakes stacked precariously on top of each other in the box, and a separate box for gorgonzola-topped asparagus. My stomach practically jumped out of my body.

"Y'all have a good night of service?" I grabbed two mason jars from the cupboards and poured glasses of tea for us. Andros nodded, plating up the last of the leftovers and swiping a tea towel over some of the dripped sauce on the plate. I smiled; even at home he never shook that precise professionalism. It made him an excellent chef.

"You and Tati had a good time? I didn't expect you home so early, honestly. I know how y'all get when go out."

"Yeah, it was good. We had a decent time, a few drinks, some dancing," I said, doing my best to sound aloof. I turned sideways and slid behind him, a difficult task with his immense bulk and my wide hips in our small kitchen.

Andros stiffened as I passed and I swear I saw him *sniff* the air. He turned slowly and lifted the plates from the counter, setting them in front of my seat and his respectively. "Where did y'all end up?"

There was a subtle change in his tone. My brother was often serious but always open and kind to us. I set the tea down next to his plate, then sat with my own, ignoring the twinge of pain from between my thighs, confused at his mood shift. He took his chair and immediately cut into his steak, shoving it into his mouth.

"Oh, we went to this show that Tati wanted to go to, a place called Electric Delphi. It's down off Bourbon, but pretty far down so we avoided all the tourists. The band was great, but it was crowded." I shrugged and dug into my own meal, snapping a piece of asparagus and plopping it into my mouth. The flavor hit me instantly, the rich butter and spices sending sparks of happiness down my spine.

I glanced up and my smile faltered. Andros had gone stone still, his big hands gripping his fork and knife-like weapons. Tension rolled off him in waves. I startled. "Bubba, what's wrong?"

His jaw clenched. "I thought we talked about Electric Delphi. I've heard some real bad shit about that place, Z."

I raised an eyebrow in confusion. "I was with *Tati*, Dro. We were fine the whole time." The panic flickering in my brother's eyes shot unease through me. I leaned in, concerned. "What's wrong?"

Andros's eyes cut to the door, to the windows and curtains, and down the hall, as though he could sense someone had been in his home, in *our* home.

"Those people aren't our people, Z. A lot of shady ass shit goes on there. I want you to promise me you'll stay away. You're not safe there." His eyes fixed on me and for the first time in years, my brother looked scared.

My eyebrows knit together as I studied him. "Andros, what's *wrong*? You're wound the fuck up. Why isn't it safe for us, is there something I don't know that you do?" I asked, setting down my fork to give him my full attention. This reaction was weird and completely out of character for him.

He looked at the door again then looked back at me. "Listen, I don't ask anything of you, Z. I *never* do. But I'm asking now. Don't go there again. Not with Tati, not with *anyone*. Is that a promise you can make me?" he pleaded, his deep voice rising an octave. Whatever it was that had him strung out broke my heart. My brother never acted like this.

"Okay, yeah, I can. Whatever happened though, you can tell me. Of course, I won't go back. It was just a show, Dro. I'm fine," I promised.

He nodded a few times, sucking in a few deep breaths before getting back to cutting into his steak. The rest of the meal passed in silence, even more when he cleaned up the plates and dishes without comment. I headed to bed with a soft good night, but Dro just nodded.

When I woke up hours later to use the bathroom, he was still sitting in the living room, a glass of cognac in his hand, staring at the front door. Waiting.

*

The morning sun woke me in the rudest way possible, bright and shining through the blackout curtains I normally kept shut. They swayed lithely in the meandering morning breeze. Seven A.M. and the air, already hot and thick with the salt of the gulf, was oppressive enough to push me out of bed to the shower.

My feet hit the floor, and I stretched my arms high into the sky, groaning, sore between my legs. I padded to the bathroom, sending a glance toward the living room, half expecting to still see Dro acting sentry.

Whatever that had been about last night was far from over. He'd been so distressed, and tired and frazzled from work, but he would explain *what* made him react that way, and it *would* be soon.

The hardwood gave way to cool tile underfoot as I entered our small bathroom and turned on the shower. Straightening, I headed to the sink to brush my teeth while the water warmed up. I pulled my shirt off and shimmied out of my shorts before grabbing my toothbrush and slinging some toothpaste on it. A quick splash of water later found me scrubbing the remnants of last night's tastes from my mouth, and I felt a twinge of loss knowing I was erasing the taste of *him*.

Mid-brush, my eyes skittered over my reflection and I balked, shocked. I looked different. My normally pale skin had taken on a slightly golden hue, as though I'd spent the day out in the sun. Only, even in the sun, I wouldn't glow like this; *I'd burn.*

Setting my toothbrush down on the edge of the sink, I ran my hands over my naked body. There were purplish bruises every-where, coin-sized ones that would match thick fingers perfectly. I skimmed my hands over the marred flesh of my hips, my waist, my thighs. All the places he'd held on to while he'd worshiped me, holding me as though he was sure I would disappear if he didn't. Tender spots trailed up my chest, around and over the swells of my breasts, and just beneath my collarbone, where he'd bitten and nipped and marked me as his own.

I should have been pissed, but instead, all I could do was remember each touch, each word of praise he'd uttered while he took me. Heat flushed through me and an ache like I'd never felt throbbed between my legs. He'd been thorough in his exploration, in his endeavor to steal my pleasure.

I should have gotten his name.

With a sigh, I wrapped my curls up high on the top of my head and secured them with an elastic before stepping into the shower. The bathroom filled full of steam that billowed around me. The first fat drops of searing water fell against my skin as I stepped under the showerhead, shocking me into the now, stinging my bruised flesh as it landed. I washed carefully, everything but my hair. I only washed it a few times a week, and a small part of me relished the fact that I'd still have him on me somewhere. The rest of what we had done, what we had stolen from each other, slid down with the soapy bubbles off my body and circled the tiled drain.

I showered and dressed quickly, glancing at the clock on the wall. Dro would be gone already, down to the market and the docks to grab the best catch of the day from the shrimp boats for the restaurant. I chose a pencil skirt and a deep green button-down that cinched at my collar and tapered tightly at my waist. The sleeves covered the handprints on my arms and wrists, and I smiled at the reminders of what we'd done last night, little love bites I could carry like secret souvenirs.

The walk to work was warmer than I'd have liked, and I was exceptionally grateful for the sweetest sin of air-conditioning when I walked into the atrium of the Sillah, ten minutes past my clock-in time. My heels clinked across the marble floor, echoing in my wake. I shot a pained smile at Greta, one of the summer's circ clerks.

"Head isn't in yet. Just clock in and say you forgot, I'll back up that you were here on time," she assured me, smiling.

I nodded gratefully. "Thanks, girl. I owe you."

Eventually, I made my way into the Jewel and crashed down at my desk, relieved to be away from the prying eyes of library patrons and more relieved I didn't have to face my bosses right now. They tended not to venture into my domain and that was more than okay with me. I rested my head on the top of my desk, letting my mind quiet in the space, pushing all thoughts of earth-shattering sex and green-eyed sex-gods from my head.

Prometheus

CHAPTER 15

I startled awake, jolting off the dirty ground of the shelter I'd managed to sneak into before being dragged under. Grunting, I hauled myself up and looked around. I didn't recognize this neighborhood in the daylight and had no idea how far I'd wandered before I'd lost consciousness. I stumbled from the alleyway, stiff and sore from the angle my body was bent into for hours. I reeked of sex and oily pavement. In desperate need of a shower, I meandered for a few blocks before hailing a cab, thankfully on shift in the early hours of the breaking dawn. Crawling into the back seat, I barked out Hermes's address and leaned my head against the cool glass.

The drive was longer than I expected but mercifully quiet. Responsibility reared its ugly, logical head now that I was conscious, but I pushed it back down, not ready to face the weight of my actions. I'd been reckless, but what was done was done, and I was on the hunt again.

No distractions.

Despite best intentions, my thoughts drifted back to her cool blue eyes, shining like sapphires in the moonlight, but the jerking halt of the cab brought me down from the cosmos. I grabbed a twenty from my wallet and passed it to the driver, though it was double the fare. With the sun barely rising in an unfamiliar city, I had no idea how to get back on my own, and the cabbie had been a Fate's send.

Taking the stairs two at a time, I pushed through the door at the top of the porch, painted haint blue. Hecate lounged on the floor, propped up on a palette of pillows between Hermes's legs. Behind her, his hands moved deftly through her hair, braiding the long strands with careful precision. She looked blissful and content as he worked, the two of them wrapped in the intimate moment I felt like an asshole for intruding on. It belonged to them, this domestic intimacy. I closed the door as carefully as I could, but there was no way to avoid detection in a house full of gods. They didn't miss my entrance, and one look at my disheveled state had Hermes looking me over with alarm.

"Hells, Theo, are you okay?! What happened?" he demanded. His fingers ramped up speed, finishing Hecate's braids in seconds. The goddess rose gracefully to her feet, crossing the space between us, concern in her eyes I didn't deserve.

"I'm fine. I had a great night, just got caught out during the Reaping."

Hermes's jaw tightened. "You know better."

I nodded reluctantly, turning toward the guest bedroom. "I know," He followed after me.

"We thought you stayed with Dio and Thanatos, or we would have come to find you. Where did you end up staying?" Hecate looked so worried another pang of guilt shot through me.

"I was fine. I've been caught in much worse places during the Reaping, Cate," I assured, hoping they'd just drop it. I was almost in the hallway that led to the spare bedrooms when a gust of air placed Hermes right in front of me, arms folded, blocking my way.

"I'm sure that's true, but then we weren't in the middle of trying to assassinate Zeus and you weren't carrying the only hope we had to find the weapon to do it," he barked, disappointment lacing his tone.

I wanted to glare back but I knew he was right. What I did was irresponsible and put us all at risk. I reached for my breast pocket out of habit to grab the delicate little compass that made a home there. Instead of flannel, the cotton fabric slid soft beneath my fingertips.

Fuck.

Panic shot through me as I dropped my hands to each pocket, dread building somewhere deep inside as realization dawned. My fingers clasped around something thin and lacy. I looked up at Hermes, mortified. Images of my flannel splayed across Red's floor flashed through my mind's eye. A flannel I hadn't had time to grab.

Careless, reckless fool.

"Theo . . ." Hermes began, already putting the pieces together at the look of abject horror on my face. "Theo, *where* is the compass?" His words calm and deadly even. I fisted my hands into my hair, tugging on the strands with considerable force. "Were you robbed? During the Reaping?"

I turned to him. "No, my wallet was there. They wouldn't have left the cash if I got rolled. I . . . I met someone last night. We ended up leaving together, and I think I left it on her floor—when I jumped out of her window."

Hermes's pale eyebrows shot up so high they disappeared into his hairline. Hecate let out a startled, "Oh!"

Hermes's demeanor immediately changed from scolding to one of hope. My stomach churned.

"Theo, that's—that's actually really great that you're getting back out there. Do you know where she lives?" he asked urgently but not unkindly.

"I get out there enough. Don't do that, don't let me off the hook." I frowned, thinking. "Rue something, fuck. It's a blur, that drink I had of Dio's really whammied me. I don't remember."

Hermes slid a mask of calm back over his face and crossed his arms. "You don't. You might still fuck occasionally, but you haven't gone home with anyone since—" he started, but Cate stepped in to cut him off.

Tension rolled off me, coursing through my muscles, in my back and neck and chest. *Fight*, my subconsciousness demanded.

He'd almost crossed a line.

"I'll try to scry for the compass. We'll find it." Hecate offered, stepping between us, everything in my body language a deadly warning.

I could see the carefully veiled concern, the pity. I hated it, wanted to rage and spit and scream for her to yell at me. To be angry. I was getting a pass because I'd gotten my dick wet. Bile rose around the twisted knots of my throat.

"We can fix this," Hermes assured, tone still clipped. Hot shame washed over me. Holding out an arm expectantly, he ushered me toward the bathroom. "Go shower. You smell like someone threw up *in* my nose."

They should beat my ass to a pulp for my recklessness, but it was clear they had no intention of punishing me, so I pushed through and rambled toward the shower, hating myself with every step.

Few things in this world could narrow perspective. One, a hot shower. The other was post-nut clarity. Both crashed over me, tidal wave after tidal wave of self-deprecating chastising that seeped into my skin with every pass of the washcloth in my hands.

Every stroke stripped her from my skin, the ghosts of soft hands roaming over my body, the way she'd responded with pretty little moans each time I'd kissed her. My cock lengthened for only a moment, lost in the memory until another, darker memory washed over me.

Dark eyes. Blood all over the ground, my hands. Blood that ran red, red, red.

Cold water sluiced down my spine, crashing me back to this realm. I turned off the cold spray and ripped the shower curtain back, focused on the task at hand.

Find the compass. Find the blood of Clio. Secure the box. Break the Bond. Kill Zeus.

Kill Zeus.

I toweled off hastily then wrapped it around my waist, securing it with a fold in the front, hardening my resolve with every second. I surveyed myself in the mirror. Three days of stubble threatened to turn into a short beard, and I could use a haircut, my wet hair falling in dark sheets into my eyes. Dark marks colored the column of my throat, small teeth marks that felt right, marring my flesh. A gift Red rewarded me with as I'd made her come, *hard*. A small smile played on my lips, and I found myself grateful for the tangible reminder she'd been real. A wildfire straight out of my fantasy.

I wondered how colorful the canvas of her skin was this morning. She hadn't wanted it gentle, deliberately pushed me to ride out her pleasure. I hoped when she walked, she would be reminded of how badly I'd wanted her, how thoroughly I would have wrung her out if we'd had the time.

Stepping away from the sink, I made my way out the door and down the hall to the open expanse that was Hermes's home. Stark and pristine with no hint of dirt or disorder, no clutter. Just neat. Ordered. A dichotomy of his chaos. I glanced at the row of clocks ticking away at different times on his wall.

Nine A.M.

Hopefully, Red had work today so I could slip in and grab the compass.

I found Hermes and Hecate in the living room, Cate in a salt circle surrounded by black pillar candles, a map of New Orleans spread out in front of her. Their heads bent low as they whispered, bickering at one another like an old married couple. Hermes trailed his fingers lovingly up the exposed ebony skin of her shoulder, the mention of my name stopping me short. I waited in the shadows, listening.

". . . I'm glad he did it. He's been so focused, it's alarming, Cate. He plunged his hand into his father's chest after finding out he's hated him for millennia for no real reason, and he's acted like it hasn't fazed him. That's not normal. And after what he's been through? He deserves to work out some of that stress. I'm not going to pretend to be angry at him when he needed that," Hermes whispered, laying a kiss on her temple.

Hecate leaned into him but shook her head. "I'm not saying to actually be mad at him. But he needs you to hold him accountable. He won't want the pity, and that's what he'll see it as. Theo was on the run for centuries, and every time Zeus caught up to him, he took something valuable, sometimes irreplaceable. Out of his flesh, his heart . . . I'm just saying, give him normalcy. Pretend he's Ares before those three figured their shit out. He doesn't need coddling. I don't think he knows how to receive that kindness right now."

I stepped into the room, willing the embarrassment to ebb out of my expression, clearing my throat.

Hecate gave me a wide smile, and Hermes, to his credit, leveled me with an annoyed glance. "She can't get a handle on the compass. I don't suppose you have something of this woman's, do you?" He schooled his features to feign indifference, and against my will, my affection for Hermes grew. He was trying, heeding Hecate's words.

"Actually, I do have something." I turned on my heel and walked back to the bathroom, retrieving my jeans from the hamper. When

I returned, black lace between my fingers, cheeks burning, Hecate lifted an eyebrow at my closed fist. "There's no way for this to be less embarrassing, but here," I said, opening my palm.

Hermes stifled a laugh, his mask of indifference shattering completely. "You filthy little titan!" he hollered, sauntering over to clap me on the back. I leveled an annoyed look straight at him while he howled with unrestrained laughter.

Looking over his shoulder at Cate, I asked, "Is this what it's like to have friends?" She smiled, nodding. "Great, I hate it," I groaned. "Where do you want these?"

She pointed to a space inside the circle, near the map. I stepped over the salt line, careful not to disturb the candles or salt crystals in my wake and I dropped the lace where she instructed before retreating.

Hecate began chanting in a language even I couldn't understand and the flames of the candles rose higher with each octave her voice climbed. Hermes stood near me, watching her work, mesmerized. The map of the city rose up, up, higher, spinning. The pressure in the room built as she incanted, the tension so taut I could feel the ribbon of magic in the air. Hermes leaned in, the reverence in his gaze replaced with something else, something more akin to concern as he watched her cast. I glanced back at Cate, who looked to indeed be struggling, as though she were on the opposite end of a tug-of-war match and was finding it difficult to gain footing.

"Something isn't right," he murmured. He tensed, then in a flash, was gone, a mighty gust of wind displacing the air in his wake. He broke the salt circle and scooped Hecate up milliseconds before the candle flames exploded, the map and lace bursting into flames of their own volition. I stared, bewildered with my mouth agape as a few feet away, Hermes checked over Cate, running his hands over her arms, her face. Her eyes cut between me and the charred remains of the map of New Orleans.

"What the *fuck*?" I asked, stepping through the circle to scoop up the smoldering paper.

Hecate shook her head. "I'm fine, Hermes." Waving him away slightly before turning toward me. "She's untraceable; a powerful incantation."

Confusion clouded my thoughts.

"I don't understand," Hermes said, still touching Hecate. "I thought she was mortal."

I shook my head. "*She was.* I would have seen it, sensed her if she were like us. She was mortal," I insisted, thinking back. Surely, she couldn't have hidden her divinity from me, not when I had the compass on me. I could see through Helios's and Nick's glamor and see everyone else.

"She could be mortal, but someone, somewhere has put protections on her. Which means she belongs to someone, Theo."

She belongs to someone.

Hecate's words sat like a stone in my gut.

Prometheus

CHAPTER 16

"I need to go for a walk." I turned on my heel, heading for one of the spare bedrooms Hermes insisted I hole up in. The Messenger God opened his mouth calling after me, but Cate put her hand on his arm and shook her head. "Let him go."

The faint shuffling of moving candles and sweeping up salt hit my ears as I closed the door. Uneasiness built in my chest as I dressed in jeans and a plain gray T-shirt and grabbed some socks to slip on. I needed out. I needed to think. My feet moved automatically as I headed to the front door, with no destination in mind. My skin felt itchy and panicked, rippling with anxiety, thousands of frayed threads of synapses firing at the same time. I needed air. I needed to think. I let my feet take me where they willed, turning and moving down streets and through intersections lost in thought under the brutal rays of the southern sun.

How could I find the compass if she was untraceable? Not just to anyone, but to *Hecate*. The damn Goddess of Witchcraft.

Red had been at Electric Delphi, but I detected no aura around her, and while Electric Delphi *was* a spot that catered to Otherworlders, it wasn't *exclusive* to us. It wasn't even exclusive to Greeks. Last night, there had been Norse, a few Croatians, even an Egyptian or two. She hadn't felt like any of them.

I found myself being pulled around the city, much like I had been when I first held the compass, and I didn't even question it when I ended up in front of a bar, some little hole in the wall. I did need a drink, even if it was just to let myself feel less like a moron for a moment.

Pushing open the heavy door, I stepped out of the intense sunlight into the dark belly of the place. Empty bar stools lined the seedy bar, the only true illumination coming from the small red candleholders peppered around on each table. It looked like it was around three A.M. in this place, mercifully deserted. Exactly what I needed.

Quiet seclusion to order my thoughts and come up with a viable plan to unfuck this mess.

I bellied up to the bar, ignoring the sticky pull of grime doing its level best to keep the soles of my boots from separating from the floor. The bar stool creaked as I pulled it back and settled in. The elderly bartender turned his crooked smile to me.

"What'll it be?" he asked, voice ravaged by years of smoking, teeth stained from the nicotine.

"Whiskey. Irish, if you have it. Neat, please."

He obliged, reaching for a tumbler, then a bottle of Jameson. Gnarled fingers sat the short glass in front of me and poured a double. I raised an eyebrow at him in question.

"You've got the look about ya."

I nodded once. "Fair point. Cheers." I raised my glass to him and took a long pull, relishing in the slow burn of the alcohol as it slid down my throat. Setting the glass back down—now about two fingers lighter than it began—I traced the pads of my fingers over and around the purpling bruise on my neck. Desire rocked through me, tinged just slightly with soreness, but I couldn't pull my hand away. It felt like I was close, so close to being where I wanted to be. I drained my glass and signaled for another.

"So, what is it? Heartache or work troubles? Few things can cause the look you're wearing, son." His scratchy voice raked over me, his deep drawl punctuated with that unique New Orleanian accent.

I lifted my head to study him as he pushed the now-refilled glass to me. "Little bit of both," I admitted. "But work, I think, is the most pressing." I took another swig, rolling my lips over my teeth at the burn.

The barkeep grinned. "You want comfort or advice?"

I cocked an eyebrow. He looked battle-hardened, and I supposed this was part of his job. Mortals often spilled their guts to those brave shades tending bars. Glancing around at the empty room, I focused on the candlelight dancing in red glass prisons. "Sure, advice will work. Shoot," I replied, lifting my drink to my lips.

The bartender squared up in front of me, wiping away a few drops of spilled liquid. "When you get to be as old as I am," he began and I tipped my glass higher to hide my grin. If only he knew I was older than mountains, older than parts of this world considered ancient. He drawled on, "You realize that work, it comes and goes. But the love of a good woman? Or man—hey, I don't judge—but a good partner? That'll weather you through most storms."

I glanced down at the tanned skin stretched over calloused fingers, to the weathered, golden band there on his left hand. Thin and well-worn but polished to shine. A love he cherished, a love he was proud of.

"Well, I can understand that. But this ain't love, Mister . . . ?" I gestured at him.

"Adam. You can call me Adam, but don't call me Mister. I work for a livin', son." He barked a laugh, mirth and mischief dancing in his eyes.

I cocked my head toward his wedding band. He reached a leathered hand over the bar and I took it. "Theo. How long have you been married, Adam?"

He lit all the way up like a meteor shower raining over the night sky. "Forty-six years, next May." He preened. Reaching into his back pocket, he pulled out his wallet, and inside, a small plastic bundle of pictures sat together. He opened it up and showed me a black-and-white wallet-sized photo of what could only be him and his young bride. They were holding hands, standing in Jackson Square, looking at each other like they each hung the stars in the heavens. The knot in my chest twisted; I'd looked like that—*once*.

"Her name is Miriam, and she's just, you know, son, she's just my best friend. When we got married, they said I was crazy. But the war had just started, and I knew I needed to do what I could to make her mine. Grab and wring all the joy out of life we could get." He flipped to the next photo, one of Miriam on a beach in what looked like the seventies, hair tied up, in a modest one-piece. A toddler balanced on her knee, both smiling and laughing in the summer sun. "That's our boy, Austin. Married with a few kids of his own now." He went on and on, flipping between each of his photos, telling me the story of his life.

He spoke of good times, then of the harder ones. Such passion and conviction in his voice, that spark of humanity that made them so fucking special, a roaring flame inside this man. It reminded me of what I fought for, what I'd sacrificed to keep alive, what I'd killed and died for. A few hours and many drinks later, I looked up at him, really looked at him. He had to be in his seventies.

"Adam, what are you doing here working? Shouldn't you and Miriam be on an island by now?" I asked, and for the first time, his smile faltered. Dread pushed up in my gut that had little to do with the whiskey floating on an empty stomach. Adam cleared a few of the glasses, avoiding my gaze. He rubbed his jaw and shot me a sideways glance.

"Well, truth be told, Theo, I am retired. After the war, I worked at the power plant out on Market. They closed it, so I hopped over to the Michoud plant, up the way. Worked hard, got my pension.

Miriam and I always planned to travel the world, but we had Austin, and later, his baby sister. She, uh, she didn't make it to cry her first cry. It was a tough time for us all. And after, Miriam wouldn't leave Austin for more than a few days at a time. Certainly not long enough to take a belated honeymoon. The money was never good enough for that either. I worked hard, pulling overtime, but we never had travel-the-world type of money."

I sipped from my glass, taking in his words.

"Few years ago, we were gonna just do it. Sell the house, take the money, and run. But then, Miriam got a cough that wouldn't go away, and the next thing we know, she's got something called COPD. Her lungs don't work right, and the cost of the medication to keep her going and keep her comfortable is a crime. My pension barely covers enough to live, and I had to get this job to help pay for her pills. The owner is a friend of mine, lets me work under the table." He suddenly looked worried, like I might snitch him out.

"I won't tell anyone," I assured him and watched him worry over it just a moment more. "What's the prognosis?" I asked, dreading the answer.

Adam ran his hand over his bald head, a practiced habit to calm himself down, I was sure. "Doc says three to five years. My daughter-in-law stays with her during the day so I can work here. They advised us to put her in a home, but that ain't happening to my *bebe*. Not while I got breath. We all pitch in, we take turns." He scoffed at the mere idea. I hated that he was here, hated he had to work, that they never got to travel.

"What does your son do?"

Adam lit up again. "He's a teacher like his momma. His wife was, too, but she's taking time off to help with Miriam. Plus, they've got babies and daycare is expensive. He's a great teacher. Really cares about those kids."

I took another drink and let my power out, just a peek. I wanted to take the measure of the man, the measure of his words.

It snaked out, silent and invisible to the naked eye, radiating around him, lapping at his aura. There was no lie in Adam's words. Only love and fierce pride for what he and Miriam built, the boy he'd raised.

"You got a bathroom in this place, Adam?" He flung out his arm, gesturing to a door near the back. I stood, downing the last of my drink before making my way into the dinky bathroom, pulling a few quarters from my pocket as I went. Sure enough, a phone booth sat nestled between the men's and women's rooms, as I'd hoped it'd be. I lifted the receiver and dropped in my coins, dialing the only number I knew by heart.

Hermes answered on the first ring. "Hello?"

I shifted, checking over my shoulder to make sure Adam was still at the bar. "Hey, it's Theo. I need a favor."

I heard Hermes stiffen down the line, dropping whatever he was doing. "What do you need?"

"Five hundred thousand dollars," I replied.

Hermes let out a low whistle. "You thinking of skipping town?"

I let out an impatient noise. "No, but I met someone who deserves it. Can you get it over to me? Hades can get you into my vault in the Underworld. Grab two obolos too. You're faster than me."

"Obviously," Hermes replied. I rolled my eyes.

The creak of the chair let me know he'd leaned forward, probably resting his elbows on his desk. "Theo, you know you can't save them all. I know the compass has you twisted up, but you don't have anything to make up for." His voice was gentle.

I clicked my teeth then grounded out: "I know that." I settled my breathing. "Can you do it? Or not?"

He let out a sigh. "Yeah, of course. Where do you want me to drop it?"

I looked around at the sign hanging over the bar. "I'm at a place called Gil's. Honestly not sure where it is in the city. I just started walking and ended up here."

"Give me half an hour, I'll be there," he promised, and with a click, he was gone.

Satisfied, I headed into the bathroom to splash some water on my face. I may have been an epic failure in some regards, but I could help Adam and Miriam. I could give their family a trip to remember, make her final days happy and free. I could help them be together, a life well-earned.

I walked back out and retook my seat, ready to have a theology conversation with Adam. He glanced over when I walked out, surveying my balance. Making sure he hadn't overserved me. *Good mortal man.*

"How 'bout a water?" I asked, and he chuckled and nodded, filling a tall glass for me with ice and water. I drank it gratefully. "Hey, Adam? Can I ask you a personal question? Are you a religious man?"

Adam's hand that had been wiping down his sink stilled, the tension rolling through him. He turned to me. "Truth be told? I'm not. Used to be, but that was Sunday school learnin'. Some of the things I have seen in war just makes you think. All that killin' and bloodshed. If there was a god, he sure turned his eye from that place. Just seen too much, I reckon. Miriam used to, 'til Talia. After, I guess she couldn't reconcile how a god she prayed to could abandon her to that fate. You?"

Religion was a touchy subject for most mortals. Wars had been waged over differences in interpretations, in theology. It was a brutal, bloody business. At his words, some of the knots in my belly eased.

I opened my mouth to speak as the dark room flooded with sunlight. Hermes stepped through the open door, illuminated and shining in the threshold. He sauntered in, his movements carefully slowed after centuries of living amongst mortals. Hermes looked around curiously before approaching us at the bar. Adam turned, giving us a semblance of privacy.

He sat an envelope next to my hand and two obolos on top of it. "You good?" he asked, and I dipped my head reassuringly. "Okay. I'll see you at home." With that, he was gone.

"Adam, could you come here?" I asked, and the old man obliged, though he looked wary now. I slid the envelope toward him, and he surveyed it like it might be a bomb. I gestured for him to take it.

Slowly, carefully, his weathered hand slid over the oak bar, closing around the envelope and coins. "What is this?" he asked, voice uncertain. I'm sure what he'd just seen looked to be shifty business. Business, I was sure, he'd gotten good at staying out of.

"I want you to close this bar up after I leave and never come back. I want you to take what's in that envelope, and I want you to take Miriam and your boy and his family, and I want you to travel the world."

Confusion skittered over his face. He slid the two coins into his palm before flipping the envelope over and opening the unsealed tab. With shaking hands, he pulled a crisp check free, along with a thick sheet of folded paper. The noise that escaped his throat was one of disbelief and shock. "What is this? Is this real?!" he asked, hands shaking.

I nodded. "It's very real, and it's yours."

He turned the check so I could see it, dated and signed by Hermes, with G I F T scrawled in huge letters along the memo line. Six hundred thousand dollars, it read. I scoffed. He just had to one-up me. *Prick.* Adam sat the check on the dry counter, as though afraid it may disappear if it went too far from his sight and unfurled the tri-folded thick paper. I watched him read it over.

"This is a letter to the IRS claiming that the tax is covered on your end and that this is a certified gift." His voice shook and I reached to steady his hand. Liver spots covered the paper-thin skin there, hands that worked for a lifetime to take care of his family. Even now, when he'd earned rest.

"Are you in the mob? Dixie Mafia?" he blurted, eyes on me.

I chuckled. "I am not. This money is perfectly legal. It is clean and real," I promised.

He shook his head several times, rereading the lines. His tongue darted out, wetting his lip as he scanned. "What do you want for it? I'd be dead before I could pay it back." His voice was so torn. Like he couldn't believe it was real.

I gave his hand another squeeze. "I don't need you to pay it back. I've only got one condition." I gestured to his palm that held the golden coins, holding my hand out. "You said the only thing you saw in the war was death, right?" He nodded, confused by my line of questioning.

"Once upon a time, humanity prayed to the practical things. One of those things was the God of the Dead. Long before the age of Christianity, before greedy kings decided they would build a church for themselves, an altar for those to worship . . . Adam, the life you and Miriam have lived is the kind that humanity was promised, the world the creators wanted. Love and laughter, solidarity. The only requirement I have for you is that you get these fashioned into necklaces or pendants or rings. And that you and Miriam wear them until each of you takes your last breath. Never lose them. Never sell them. And you won't be separated, even in death."

I pressed my palms together, peeling back the layer of obfuscation that kept mortals blind to our blatant power just a bit. Blue glowing light pooled from my fingers, marking the coins as blessed by me. Hades would respect the mark. He would make sure they made it together in the Asphodels.

Adam's gaze blew wide, stunned by the smallest glimpse of divinity. Tears leaked from the creases at the edges of his eyes. "Are you him? Are you Death?" he whispered.

I chuckled, ceasing the glow. I reached my hand over and dropped the coins in front of him. He scrambled to pick them up off the bar top like a starving man grabbing food from a feast table.

"No, but he is a friend of mine. He will honor the tokens and ensure you stay together," I promised.

Adam's eyes filled with tears. "What is his name? So, I can thank him when I meet him."

"The one that comes to get you, Death, is named Thanatos. But the God of the Dead is Hades. You pray to Hades. But if you want to get in good with him, pray to Persephone, his wife. He likes her best." I winked.

Zarena

CHAPTER 17

"It was *how* big?!" Tati screeched through the phone, and I lifted the receiver away from my ear before she busted an eardrum.

I spent the first four hours of work trying (and failing) to get anything done. Everything in my body felt . . . *off*. Unsettled. I'd finally broken down and called Tati back. She'd called all morning, leaving messages with the circ desk.

"*Massive*. Like, I for real don't understand how I'm even walking right now," I murmured, careful to keep my voice down.

"Girl, and you didn't even get his name? The fuck is wrong with you?"

I grimaced. "He was just passing through, T. He doesn't live around here, so it doesn't matter." I gnawed on my lower lip, pushing down the uneasy feeling that just wouldn't fucking go away.

What about you?" I teased, turning the tables. "Two of them? You seemed to be having a good time when I left." Tati sucked in a steadying breath and for once there was no witty comeback, no joke. I tensed, Dro's words flowed through my head: *It's not safe for you.* "T?" I pressed, voice hard. If something happened to her after I'd *left* her there . . .

"I'm here. I'm good. It was . . . I can't even really begin to describe it. They were both so different, an ebb and flow of the other—Z, I don't think I've ever been so thoroughly satisfied. There was nothing left of me when they were finished . . ." Her voice trailed off softly. Alarm gripped me. Tati was always in control of her conquests, *always*. But the way she spoke of them? The demure tone of her voice? It seemed heavier, more important.

"What are the names of these sex gods?" I asked, subtly poking for information.

"Dio. And Thanatos."

"Like the Greek god? Is he Greek?"

She let out a small laugh. "Yeah, actually. Greek but spent a lot of time in London, so he's got the accent. You know I'm a sucker for a good accent. Hey though, my boss is walking in. Call you later?"

"Yeah, of course. Go daydream about your tag team while you intake patients." I snorted as she laughed and hung up. Wistfully, I glanced up at the clock—three hours to go, but it was clear I wasn't going to get fuck all done today. I also had a ton of PTO I never took, and I forced myself not to feel even a little guilty as I popped my head into Nessa's office and found her bent low, filing some sort of administrative paperwork. I rapped my knuckles against the oak door, startling her.

I smiled apologetically. "Hey, Nessa, I'm not in a great headspace today. I'd like to pull some PTO hours and head out. Start fresh tomorrow with clear eyes. I wanted to check in and make sure you didn't need me for anything else, first."

She pushed her glasses down her nose and looked me over, concerned. I never wanted time off. "Yeah, of course. You okay?"

I nodded, shooting her a smile. "Had a long night last night and didn't sleep well. I just need the afternoon," I replied honestly. No reason to lie, it was my paid time off and I could use it whenever I wanted, and we both knew it.

"Okay, take the day. I'll file the paperwork for you, just get some rest."

I shot her a grateful smile and retreated from the doorway before scooping up my bag and heading out. I locked down the Jewel every time I left the room, so it was secure. I just needed *out* today.

Stepping into the sunshine, I sneezed immediately, shaking my entire core with force. I hurried down the steps, the sound of my heels clicking slightly on the stone below, but instead of turning left out of the iron gates, I shifted right, following the cracked sidewalk away from home.

Gil's came into view and I smiled. Mr. Adam was a kind man who loved his wife, Miriam, and opened up early so we'd have a place to grab some bar food if we needed out of the Sillah. He was always dropping little nuggets of wisdom, always with a kind word about life or living or loving.

I hurried in, already tasting the fried pickles on my tongue. The tiny bar flooded with light and Mr. Adam looked over the shoulder of a hulking figure, beaming at me. A figure I'd spent considerable time cataloging last night.

"Zarena! Beautiful Zarena! Come in, come in! I want you to meet a friend of mine. Theo, this is Zarena." Mr. Adam was alight with an excited energy I'd never seen on him before.

The figure at the bar turned, the muscles in his shoulders rippling with the effort. Green eyes blew wide with surprise as he took me in. He stood abruptly, nearly knocking over his stool as an adorably boyish grin pulled up his lips.

"She's quite striking, ain't she, son?"

The figure moved toward me cautiously. Like I wasn't real, like he couldn't believe his eyes. His teeth sank into his bottom lip, a wolfishly hungry gleam in his gaze as he took me in.

"She certainly is."

Mystery Man.

Prometheus
CHAPTER 18

*R*ed.

She stood in front of me, a fiery halo of unruly curls, illuminated in the sun like firelight. Her blue eyes swept over me uncertainly, her expression as stunned as I felt, and it took everything in me not to cross this bar and—*no.*

No.

I kept my eyes trained on her face, and it was all I could to not let my gaze wander. Just her face. If I glanced back down at that body, the soft curves that begged my hands to grab, the heavy swells of her breasts that screamed for my lips, my mouth, *Hells—no.*

What the fuck was wrong with me?

"Zarena." Her name tasted sweet on my tongue, and I rolled it around the syllables, savoring the vowels like I'd savored her, wishing I'd known it last night, could have moaned it out against her skin. The knot in my chest tightened, the cord pushing toward her with all its might.

The compass.

Reality slammed back into me, but she still hadn't spoken, hadn't so much as moved a muscle. The door swung shut behind her, bathing us all in shadows once more. I stopped advancing and leaned back against the bar, my head still reeling. *What were the fucking odds?*

"What are you doing here?" she blurted, hands traveling across her chest to grip the strap of her black bag.

I frowned at the same time Adam asked, "You know each other?" Cheery, his voice was practically elated. I'd just made the rest of his life. And afterlife, too, if he played his cards correctly.

Glancing back toward him, I nodded. "We met at a party." I turned back to Red, to *Zarena*. "Actually, this is great luck. I believe I left an overshirt with you?" I said the words gently, praying that Adam would catch the hint and not ask further questions. Zarena's cheeks pinked, such a beautiful shade of crimson. My cock jolted to life, growing just from her proximity. "It normally wouldn't be a big deal, but I had something important in the pocket." I slid my hand up behind my neck uncertainly, pushing my other hand deeper into my pocket. Anything to draw attention away from the massive erection threatening to creep down my leg.

"Oh, umm, yeah, I didn't notice. But, sure, if you need it." She was cute like this, rambling. A fox caught in a snare. She looked over my shoulder at Adam. "I just came in for the usual, if that's okay?"

Adam's smile faltered just a bit. "I'm actually . . . closing up, love. Today is my last day." He looked slightly guilty.

She frowned. "Is everything okay? Is Mrs. Miriam taking a turn?" Concern laced every word.

Adam just smiled. "Oh no, *love*, she's the same. We've just come into some inheritance. I'm gonna get to take her to see the world, just like we always wanted!" There was so much joy in his words, so many dreams he'd thought would never come true. I smiled back at him and shot him a discreet wink.

Zarena shuffled her bag around. "That's incredible, Mr. Adam, that's really amazing." She sounded relieved but glanced between us. "This is a crazy coincidence," she mumbled.

I gave her a small smile. "If you'd rather I wait here, I can. Surely, I can talk Adam into whipping up your regular order if you don't mind grabbing my shirt?" I hated the words as I said them, but she seemed uneasy, unsettled. I didn't want to come on too strong. I had to get that compass back at all costs. My power snaked out for the second time today, creeping over her, searching for the spark of divinity that would expose her as one of us.

Nothing. Just blank silence.

I relaxed a bit, but she looked between Adam and me, warring with some internal argument. After a brief pause, one side seemed to win.

"No, no. That's not necessary. I was planning on heading home anyway. Why don't you just come along? I don't live far." She gestured behind her. "Mr. Adam, I'll come by the house tomorrow and drop off Miriam's requests and pick up her books that are due, okay?"

He beamed. "That sounds great, Zarena. We appreciate you, darlin'."

She turned, gesturing for us to head out, and at once, I was moving, called by her slightest whim. The knot in my chest tightened, pulling me toward the compass.

Once outside, Zarena's full form took me out at the kneecaps. She may not have been divinity, but this woman was a *goddess*. She came up to just under my chin, which was a feat considering my height. Six-five made doorways obstacles most days. She had to be something like five-eleven or six feet, and she was in heels. Long, spiky heels lengthening her already considerable legs. That skirt was holding on for dear life and I wanted, *needed* to peel it down her hips, over her thighs.

Or push it up over her ass, I wasn't picky.

"I'm so sorry about last night." She pulled my attention back.

"No, it's okay." I stepped up my stride just a bit so I could walk next to her instead of being slightly behind. "So, Zarena, huh? That's a beautiful name." *I needed to focus.*

"Yeah, I'm a big fan." She laughed, the sound melodic, like the tinkling of windchimes, the rustle of book pages turning. I found myself leaning into her, shoulders barely brushing. She didn't flinch away. "Are you staying around here?"

I nodded, shoving my thumb behind us. "About six blocks that way, but yeah. Crazy that we're this close." I raked my eyes over her body, taking in her clothes. "I assume you were at work? Am I allowed to know what you do?"

She gave me a coy smile, looking me up and down. "I assume you weren't, or else I need a job that lets me wear jeans and get day drunk at eleven A.M."

A laugh bubbled up out of my chest, startling me. She was funny. I nodded my agreement that I was indeed not working.

"I'm a librarian. An archivist, actually. At the Sillah LaFleur." She gestured to the large public library to our right.

A librarian. An archivist.

My knees buckled. My mouth watered. As if she couldn't get any fucking hotter. I let out a low whistle. "Man, I wish librarians looked like you when I was younger."

She arched a copper-colored eyebrow, pursing her lips. "And what did librarians look like when you were growing up?" she asked. A test.

I shrugged. "Like men." She let out a loud, belly-shaking laugh. The knot in my chest pulled tighter, cinching. "An archivist, huh? Any special projects you're working on?"

She regarded me, impressed. "You know what an archivist is?"

I let out a bark of a laugh at her shock. I invented the specialty I wanted to say, but instead, I simply said, "I spend a lot of time reading and researching. I'm a professor." It was true. I held specialties from every prestigious school in the world, under one name or another. This alias, Theo Forethought, happened to be a professor of literature at Cambridge. I told her so, and her eyes shifted. Zarena swallowed, the tension between us astronomically heavy. I badly wanted to know what she was thinking.

"What brings you to the N.O.?" she asked.

I shoved my hands in my pockets as we walked, not trusting them to behave with her in such close proximity. "Research. I'm shifting my specialty to focus on Ancient Greek prose and mythology. Conferring with a colleague here about some ancient texts." Zarena lit up, and I recognized the zealous hunger for knowledge in those deep ocean eyes. It wasn't possible that my cock got harder, but here we were.

"My emphasis in anthropology was Ancient Greek linguistics and artifacts. I'd love to see what you're working on. If that's okay, I mean, I wouldn't want to pry," she rambled, stumbling over her words, and it was the cutest thing I'd ever seen. I nodded, smiling like a fool.

When was the last time I'd smiled at anyone this much?

"Yeah, I'd love that," I said, wishing it was possible. Still, the way she beamed made me want to give her whatever would keep that smile on her face. "You seem young for an anthropologist. Shouldn't you be out in the field still?" I asked, and some of that shine darkened.

"Well, I have only been back for the last year. I *was* out in the field . . . Egypt, on site for an excavation." Her hesitation caught my attention, a deeper story there. I waited in silence to see if she'd continue, and after a beat was rewarded with a long sigh and more nuggets of insight into who she was.

"I was massively overqualified when I took the position as archivist for the Sillah LeFleur. I have a double masters from Berkeley in Archival Sciences and the other in Anthropology with an emphasis on Ancient Greek civilizations, focusing on linguistics." She hesitated. "Egypt was great. Our team was closing in on what we'd hoped was a preserved village, swallowed in a sand-storm." She slowed her pace to a crawl, and I adjusted with her.

"And was it everything you hoped for, in a first dig?"

She grimaced. "Yes and no. Full disclosure, I was assigned to a team headed by my former antiquity professor. Things got . . . heated, lines were blurred. And before you judge me, just under-stand I know how reckless it was. I just got . . . swept up in it." Zarena looked away, focusing on the sidewalk in front of us.

I clenched my fists, already sensing where this was going. "I'm not judging you, Red. You don't have to tell me if you don't want to. But if you do, I promise I won't judge you. If you can't talk to your one-night stand about your—what I'm assuming is about to be a dickbag—ex, then who can you talk to about it?" I joked, bumping her shoulder lightly with my bicep. I hardly recognized myself. Maybe it was the hours I'd spent with Adam; maybe there was something in the water of this city, but everyone here had a story I wanted to hear. And I really wanted to know more about Zarena. In a different world, she might have been my walking wet dream of a woman.

She let out a small laugh. "Wow, it's that obvious, huh? Yeah, we'd been working nonstop, and he wanted to dig on a left grid where a few artifacts had been initially found, but I had a hunch. Turns out, I'm really, *really* good at guessing where to dig in the sand." The bitterness in her tone soured her shade, and I swal-lowed, waiting patiently for her to continue.

"It was the discovery of a lifetime. It wasn't just a small village, it was a tomb. A female pharaoh, one of the few we've ever dis-covered proof of. As you've surmised, things changed. Suddenly, we weren't a team; he was the leader and I was nothing more than a junior excavator. He took all the fucking credit, even though I'd given him the idea about which grid I thought might give us some answers. He'd refused to share the claim and called me a *'petulant child who hadn't paid my dues.'*" Zarena's hands shot up, mimicking air quotes at the end. My blood boiled but I kept my face smooth.

"He'd not so subtly suggested that should I go public and try to fight his claim, his tenure as a professor and reputation would far outweigh my own, and basically, who were they going to believe? He expected gratitude for throwing me the table scraps of the meal I'd spent two years preparing and then had the poor grace to be indignant at my insubordination," she finished, looking over at me.

"How did you handle that?" I asked, suppressing the urge to ask if she was okay. Of course, she wouldn't be.

"I broke his nose, dumped him, and tucked tail back to the States." She shrugged.

I let out a heavy laugh. "Good girl," I praised, and Zarena's cheeks flamed, the flush spreading down her neck, the sight instantly sobering me.

She gave me a sheepish smile. "I'd been living in my old room with my parents, mortified. I had money, but I came home with no plan, and I didn't even know if I wanted to stay. After a month of partying and wandering and fielding questions about when I was going to 'get back on that horse,' I saw a position open for an archivist. I applied. I got an offer, and I accepted. Then, I moved in with my brother, because a roommate felt better than living at home at twenty-eight. So, that's my sob story," she said, just as we arrived at the creaky front gate of her home.

"And is your brother home right now?" I asked as we walked the path to her steps and climbed up.

She shook her head, digging in her bag for her keys. The lock gave way with a swift turn and we were inside, the air twenty degrees cooler indoors as I trailed behind her, the scent of meadowsweet overtaking my senses.

"He's at work. It's the middle of the day, so he's doing prep. Hold on, I'll grab your stuff," she said, and hurriedly moved down the hallway, heels clicking on the hardwood. Those same sounds announced her return; my blue flannel clasped in her hand.

Relief flooded through me as I reached to take it, but Zarena yanked it back, holding her other hand up. "Ah, ah, not so fast," she practically purred, and every hair on my body stood at attention. "What will you give me for it, *Professor*?" The words hung between us. The implications too.

A soft growl bubbled up from somewhere deep inside my chest, a primal need to make her *want* to bend beneath me. This was a bad idea, a terrible one truly, but the primal, instinct part of my brain silenced the intellectual side I'd been so famous for. I closed the distance between us, backing her up until she was pressed against the counter, scenting her like a fucking caveman. Against my will, my hands acted, wrapping around her body, cradling her neck in a firm grip. Her pulse raced beneath my fingertips, heart beating loud enough for me to hear, and that just did something to me.

Some siren song I couldn't seem to fucking ignore.

"*Professor Theo*," she moaned, the sound pornographic coming from those perfect, red lips.

I ground my hips into her, savoring the sounds she whimpered. My lips fell to her neck, tongue tracing the column of her throat, pushing back her collar to reveal a tapestry of marred flesh that had me leaking in my fucking jeans. I slipped a hand from her waist up to the hem of her shirt and tugged once, popping the buttons, exposing her chest and the strappy black bra beneath the green blouse. The sight of more beautiful love bites I'd left coloring her skin shot through me, and I traced them carefully, lovingly. I wanted to memorize the way she wore them, a secret for just the two of us. Her hand came up to my neck, sliding my collar down to expose the one she'd left on me.

I rolled my hips against her core once, pressing my cock right up against her cunt. More little sounds of pleasure. I brought my lips back to her throat, sliding down over each bruise, kissing away the sting, whispering into her flesh, "Such pretty little sounds, such sweet moans, Red." I slipped lower, kissing down her chest, her sternum, until I rested on my knees in front of her. My hands followed me down and I wrapped my hand over her hip, bunching the fabric of her pencil skirt to expose those milky thighs. Lifting her leg gently, I hiked it over my shoulder, settling between the apex of those thighs. Matching black panties waited for me, soaked through, and I blew a hot breath over her core just as her hands came down to rest in my hair. My shirt slipped to the floor beside us.

"*Please*," she begged, eyes hooded with desire.

I pressed my nose against the lace, slipping up against her clit, and she bowed. "Look at you, Red. So responsive, *so needy*. I'm gonna make a mess out of you, then I'm going to fuck it back into you," I promised, as her hands yanked me flush to her. "Are you rea—" I began, but at that moment, a mighty crash sounded from behind us.

I glanced behind me in time to see two monstrous figures burst through the front door and windows. In a flash, I dropped Zarena and stood, sinking into a fighting stance, protecting her. Two massive LOA warriors stood before us, spears and blades raised. I could feel the fury rolling off them, the raw power. Zarena screamed, but there was no time to explain, to wonder why two of the LOA were attacking us in her kitchen. I had to protect her. Sizing them up, my mind assessed battle strategies automatically, calculating exactly how they'd strike.

And when they did, I was ready.

In that tiny cottage, all Hells broke loose.

Zarena

CHAPTER 19

*C*haos.

The front door was in splinters. Chips of wood and debris scattered unceremoniously amongst shards of glass on the floor as my papa and brother crashed through the front of our house. I shrieked in shock from the violence of their entrance, eyes wide at the spears in their hands. Theo stood in front of me, shielding much of my view, as I hastily tried to right my clothing, mortified, reaching for Theo's shirt to cover my ripped blouse.

"Get away from her," Dro spat, snarling in a way that stopped me in my tracks. His voice had taken on a deeper timbre, deadly and laced with a double octave that didn't sound right to my ears.

Theo straightened up, rolling his shoulders, tensing for a fight. My skin prickled, and I tasted something ancient and spiced in the air. For a moment, none of them moved, save for the thrums of power rippling through the space, an energy my mind struggled to process. I peered around Theo's elbow and locked eyes with my father. He said something to Theo in a language I didn't quite understand, but the cadence lent toward island, the patois of the Caribbean. The words venomous, biting—*a warning*.

Theo answered him in the same language, his accent as smooth and practiced as a native speaker. He cracked his neck once and I saw the subtle shift in posture as he lined up defensively, the same stance my papa spent years drilling into my head. Whatever Theo said enraged him. Lightning flashed over the room, impossible within the noonday shine, but under my papa's skin, a thin membrane shifted like a mask slipping. I felt it, then *saw* it. *Something lived within my papa*, something ancient and powerful and deadly.

A white skull face and eyes that glowed red. Bones around his neck, traditional garb on his body. A supernatural force peered through the cracks of their skin; ancient, coiled in the hollows of mortal bones. Papa's hands glowed faintly with embers, the ashes of a thousand offerings. A warrior.

"So be it," he answered in a language I understood, twirling his deadly-looking spear.

Theo moved first, impossibly quick and graceful for a man of his stature. They moved, meeting blow for blow as the air whipped around us, shattering windows, curtains snapping from the rods. My chest pinched for air as I tried to make sense of what I was seeing, of the smell of ozone and rum, the tang of the ocean and fire that burned my lungs.

A ripple of power blasted me back and I landed against the hard wood of the cabinet with a crack that radiated pain from the back of my skull. My vision blurred, eyes watering with tears, dizzying me enough to force my body to slide down the wall. Theo jumped, scaling up and over the kitchen island with ease. It was a melee of skilled blows, calculated moves, and each moment, I could see the ghosts of something blinking in and out of sight within my brother, within my papa. Dro's eyes flickered milky white, the bulk of him swelling to impossibly fill the room near to the ceiling. Their bodies blurred, fighting in a style I'd never seen them use. Twenty years of training with my papa and I'd never seen him so calculated, so *deadly*. A ruthlessness peeled from his aura, slipping into the fray and I blinked as my head throbbed from where I'd smacked it. Nothing made sense.

Andros flickered back and forth between his normal clothes and the thin veil of power; the glimpse into his soul that showed a traditional warrior, a mighty bone through his nose, colored clay down his dark chest. They lunged their spears at Theo, punching and kicking and maneuvering, but he did not relent, did not falter for one second. He met them blow for blow, not allowing them an inch of movement toward where I was, but they were too fierce. Terror gripped me as I tried to call out, to get them to stop this. If he hurt either of them, I would kill him myself.

"Papa," I managed on a broken gasp, my head splitting in agony in a way that didn't make sense. Was I bleeding? I couldn't tell, but my father's eyes cut to my voice, and he doubled his efforts, slashing and hacking at Theo with renewed vigor.

Dro lunged toward Theo with such grace, such deadly precision, that I screamed as he barreled forward. If they killed him, it would be the end of everything—the end of the world for our family, my *maman*, my sisters. They would never forgive me. I could see the headlines now, the demonization of my papa and Dro. I couldn't let that happen, because of me.

A gust of wind ramped up through our house and a man appeared in the doorway in a vibrating blue. Theo's eyes shot to him, currently blocking and parrying a hammer fist from my papa as my temple throbbed and my vision tripled. Something caustic burned across my skin, a recognition forcing itself into my mind.

"The girl!" Theo managed to grunt. With a terse nod of his chin, the golden-haired man flashed around the room, displacing air until he got to my side. He was fast, impossibly fast, there and here in less than a blink. When he stopped in front of me, I yelped.

His eyes were soft and kind as he offered his hand out gently.

"Hey, can you come with me? It'll be easier on your stomach if you're prepared."

The gentle care in his gaze made me *want* to trust him, a familiarity that didn't make sense. I glanced past him to my papa, to my brother and their flashing forms. To the stranger defending me, who spared a glance back to make sure I was okay even though it got him rocked. My stomach roiled as overwhelming pressure pushed through my veins, stretching my skin too tight.

My heart lurched, my head along with it, and I swayed unsteadily. "I can't. That's my papa, my brother," I choked out. My world spun, heavy and heady, and suddenly this stranger's hands were on me.

And I was burning.

By the sound of his agonized scream, he was too. My blood boiling beneath my skin, burned. I couldn't breathe, couldn't think. When he'd touched me, a sharp agony tore through my bones with a jolt. A barrier broken.

It scorched, his flesh on my flesh.

The scream tore from my throat, guttural and unnatural, blackening the edges of my vision from the intensity of it. Theo faltered at the sound and the loss of focus again cost him. Dro sent a powerful blow to his chest, sent him crashing back into the island. My head reeled as I swayed. Again, the man who cradled a burned hand reached to catch me before I could collapse to the floor. Everything was too loud, too heavy and his touch *burned, burned, burned.*

Someone was screaming in the distance as those burning hands and arms lifted me, cursing and grunting with the effort to get me off my feet. My vision faded to nothingness as I was overwhelmed by the blinding pain where the stranger's skin touched mine. I couldn't think, couldn't breathe as flames tore me apart.

"Get her to safety!" Theo roared from far, far away.

I felt my body shift, the rush of air against my hot, hot skin, and then, at once, a blast of power sent us flying backward, the detonation of a bomb in my living room, threatening to take the whole fucking Ward out with it. The stranger absorbed the impact while I fell, and the burning subsided as something like electricity pulsed over my skin. I rolled forward onto the hardwood of the home I shared with Dro, my brother, *my protector*. Rolling off the strange man, our bodies disentangled, his beautiful face bleeding at his temple from the impact of the fall.

My vision tunneled in and out as hands—*strong hands, safe hands*—were on me. Hands that had roamed over my body just moments before all hell had broken loose pushed stray hairs out of my face, checking me over. A soothing voice whispered that I was okay. Somewhere in the far recesses of my mind, I pieced together that Theo had come for me when we'd been blasted backward. He was fighting but now he was here, heaving his body in front of mine protectively.

"*Papa*," I cried, worry and fear calling out for my own, needing to know they were okay. The world spun and spun and spun, and I was untethered, drifting, unbound.

I heard it, a soft voice, the one that gave me comfort and brought me joy. The voice of the one who loved me unconditionally when I hadn't been her responsibility to love.

"*What in the hell is the meaning of this?*" she hissed, voice clear and calm. I struggled to focus my sight, to see past the bleeding cut on Theo's cheek, to *her*.

"*Maman.*"

Prometheus

CHAPTER 20

Panic slid through me the moment I'd felt the earth crack. The LOA in front of me—*the god* in front of me—had taken one look at Hermes, had caught his scent, and the moment Hermes touched Zarena, he'd struck that mighty spear on the ground. The sheer power that rippled through this tiny house should have been enough to level it, but he'd hesitated. He'd only meant to harm us, *not* Zarena.

No, Red meant something to these deities, the LOA.

He'd meant to stop Hermes from taking her, but in the heat of battle, power and pent-up energy could be fickle to wield. Zarena's blood curdling scream agonizingly tore through the air the moment Hermes touched her. I glanced around through my daze and saw them against the far wall, blasted mid-zoom. Hermes, bleeding from his temple, groaned. Great welts of red covered his forearms and hands. Zarena rolled off him, panting, and crying. I needed to get to her, needed to protect her from harm.

Why were they here? Why her house? Had the compass brought them?

Had Zeus discovered my tryst and sent them to punish me?

My eyes faltered between the others for only a second, barely registering that the demi-god was regaining his bearings, having been caught in the aftershock and slammed into the cabinets himself. One glance at Red's crumpled form had me throwing away centuries of survival instincts, of battle tactics. I turned, exposing my back to them, and dragged myself to her, ignoring the twinge in my leg, one that alerted me the bone was snapped in two.

I *had* to get to her; it was a compulsion.

My hands cradled her body against mine, whispering to her, begging for forgiveness for bringing an innocent into this, for seeing her hurt. I felt the spark of life before I saw her eyes, felt the quiet power radiating from her body before she spoke. Power awakened inside of Zarena, a veil burned away under Hermes's touch.

"*What in the hell is the meaning of this?*" that tone was deadly, primal. A mother's rage and fury.

Zarena wriggled in my arms, and I tightened my grip as she reached for the voice, needing it. "*Maman?*" she croaked, throat raw from screaming.

The small woman stood in the doorway, a look of rage etched into her beautiful face, her brown skin shining with a sheen of golden power. There was no mistaking the divinity there, no hiding the raw energy permeating the room in her rage. She gave each of us a stern look before rushing over to a sweating, delirious Zarena. Red whimpered as the LOA wrapped thin fingers under her armpits, hoisting her from my grip with the barest effort. I rose with her.

"What's happening to her?" I asked, voice uneven.

She stroked her daughter's face, whispering words I couldn't hear. But I felt it, felt the panic recede from Zarena's body, counted the frantic beats of her heart as they returned to normal. Her blue eyes, sapphires of kaleidoscope blues, slowly opened and her mother cracked a beautiful smile at her.

"*Maman*," Zarena choked a sob before sitting up on her elbows gingerly. Her eyes went wide as she took in my bleeding face and torn clothes, the two men behind her, and a groaning Hermes, also bleeding from a head wound. Those blue eyes studied us all and I felt such a sense of relief that she wasn't *dead*, that whoever these people were to her, they weren't trying to kill her because of me. Her eyes settled on the LOA who had cast the shockwave, and I let my aura out, felt my power wrap around his own, tasting the magic on his skin.

Ogou Feray.

The Protector.

LOA God of the Sword and War.

"Papa?" Zarena asked, disbelief in her voice.

He shifted nervously, reeling in his power. He took a step closer to her, but she flinched, and a flash of despair flitted over his face. He opened his mouth to speak, to explain. "*Baby girl*," his voice was a normal tenor now, nothing like the double cadence he'd used earlier, his *true* voice, where he'd warned me to leave or die. "Please, let me explain," he pleaded.

She eyed the spear and sword in his hands, and with a twirl they were gone, completely dematerialized. Zarena leaned into her mother heavily, but her hand still stayed wrapped around mine.

"We need to have a family meeting," her mother said, eyeing us all. "No weapons." Ogou opened his mouth to say something, but she snapped her eyes to his with a stare that could have leveled nations. "It's time, Ogou. We should have done it long ago."

Zarena looked at her with a sinking realization: her family had kept something massive from her.

Hermes slowly sat up behind us.

"One of you better fucking start talking right now," Zarena demanded, the tears welling up in her eyes making my chest tight. I rubbed small circles against her palm. She turned to her mother, who still stroked her hair. "Why did you call him *Ogou?*"

"There is much to tell you, but we have to leave now. The wards here are broken and what we have to tell you cannot be witnessed by others, do you understand?" She focused on Zarena, a serious look on her face. "I know you need answers, and I promise to give them to you. We all will," she pointedly looked around the room at each of us.

Her keen stare settled on Hermes, and she appraised him for just a moment, assessing his aura. "Lord Hermes," she bowed slightly. "You are the consort of Lady Hecate, are you not?" she asked, and his look was guarded. Hermes would give up nothing until he knew her motives for asking. The small goddess smiled, reading his thoughts. "Summon her to us. She is welcome amongst our people. She will bear witness. Tell her Erzulie Dantor has evoked her boon."

A boon was a powerful piece of currency, and once called in, it *must* be honored.

Which is how we all came to be sitting in the living room of a modest but beautiful home in the Ninth Ward of New Orleans.

Hermes sat on a small love seat with Hecate. Hephaestus, who'd been with her when she'd received the message from Hermes, stood behind them. I sat on the couch opposite them, on the side nearest to Zarena, wrapped in a quilted blanket in a reclining chair. Her feet were tucked beneath her, and she'd changed into some sweatpants. She still wore my flannel, and some small part of me tugged at that. The compass was still in the pocket, I could see the outline just underneath the fabric that swallowed her body. Her brother, the one she'd told me about, had been the demi-god taking shots at me earlier, and he sat on the opposite end of the big couch. Her father paced near the door.

No one spoke but everyone sized up the other deities in the room, except for me and Andros. My gaze and his flickered between mundane things in the room and Zarena.

Red hadn't said a word to anyone to my knowledge, and I couldn't imagine what was going on in her head. Why did the LOA adopt her? Why could I feel her power now, and not earlier when I'd searched at the bar? She seemed mortal then, but now? Now I could feel it, that thin membrane sitting just below her skin.

Hermes touched it, and it almost flayed him alive. His hands and arms still bore the scorch marks, but they were slowly healing. That power lived under her skin, a protection I'd never heard of. And why the LOA; what was their stake in this? *What was she?*

Zarena's mother moved gracefully through the kitchen doorway, balancing a tray in her hands laden high with cups, a kettle, and fresh-cut fruit. Zarena picked at a spot in the blanket, refusing to meet any of our eyes. Her mother sat the platter on the coffee table and began to pour a dark liquid into each cup, the heavy aroma of coffee billowing from the tray. I took the cup she offered me. It was warm, but I didn't drink, no matter how much I wanted to.

Hermes shot me a warning look as he accepted his own cup—*not until Cate says it's safe.* An imperceptible nod from me and Hephaestus told him we understood. Hecate swirled the liquid around, then raised it to her lips gingerly. Her nostrils flared, the tension in her muscles relaxing as she took a long sip. The three of us followed suit. I was grateful for the bitter burn.

The lady of the house shuffled to the kitchen and back once more, this time carrying a small piping mug billowing with steam between her fingers. She handed the mug to Zarena, who finally looked at her. Such love in those blue eyes, and in the brown ones that bore into hers. The lady sat in the recliner next to Zarena's, and Ogou crossed the room to stand behind his wife.

Zarena took a small sip of her drink. "Thanks for the tea, *Maman*," her voice subdued, barely a whisper.

"You're welcome, *bebe*," she replied, then looked around at the rest of us. Murmurs of thanks rang out around the room.

She turned to Zarena. "I'm going to have to tell you some hard things today. But before I do, I need you to know, there has never been a moment in which you were not *our* child. Never a moment that you were not so loved, so cherished that the nature of your lineage ever mattered to any of us. We are your family, and what you're about to hear doesn't change that." She cleared her throat and pressed on. "You're going to have questions, and you're going to be hurt and angry. I want you to know we understand, and it's okay for you to feel that way. But I have to ask that you promise to stay until the end, that you hear all we've got to tell before you decide our fate." There was no uncertainty in her words. She accepted that this tale may rip her family apart, but she was resigned to doing it for Zarena.

Red sat the cup on her knee between both hands and nodded at her mother. "I understand, *Maman*. I'll hear you out," she promised. The goddess let out a long breath. "There are things in this world—old things, old beings. They live amongst mortals. You know the story of the LOA, the spirit liaisons between the Vodou practitioners and Bondye. Long ago, when the slaves were stolen from their lands and sold like chattel, they cried out for the gods of their motherland, but those gods were tied still to Africa and could not follow to aid them, to give them comfort. Some felt such sorrow at the ravaging of their people that they allowed slivers of their essence, their power, to travel on the waves and winds, guided by silent prayers and the wails of the weeping. Those slivers took form and gained their own legends. And thus, the LOA were created, birthed into existence by the willpower and belief of the oppressed." The goddess gave Zarena a rueful smile. "That is how we came to this land. That is how we came to be divine."

Zarena looked around, at her father, at her brother. Those blue eyes even flicked to me briefly, waiting for someone to refute what she'd seen with her own eyes. We remained silent, but I didn't miss the way her hand trembled on her mug.

"*You're all gods?*" she asked softly.

Her mother's lips set in a thin line, but she nodded. "We are revered as such, yes. The other pantheons recognize our status as gods."

Tears welled up in Zarena's eyes. She looked at her brother as he shifted forward in his seat, vibrating with nervous energy, leaning toward her. His need to comfort his sister but to wait until his mother finished with what she had to say warred within him.

"You lied to me. You lied. We don't lie to each other—it's our promise." Her voice was soft, but he flinched as though she'd slapped him. The look of betrayal on her face clawed at me. Suddenly, I wanted to do nothing more than put space between us. It was only a matter of time before she looked at us, at me, with the same disdain.

"I wanted to tell you, many times, but it wasn't safe. It wasn't—" but Andros was cut off at the quick by a sharp look from his mother. He went immediately quiet, a silent anger and guilt flaring under his aura. He hated this.

The goddess turned back to Zarena. "Before we go any further, do you have any questions you'd like to ask about the LOA?" Her words were gentle, kind.

Zarena scoffed. "Of course, I do. Who are you?"

The goddess's mouth split into a wide grin. She held her hands aloft and closed her eyes, peeling back the layers of glamor, of her shielded divinity. Her aura washed over me, over us all, the sound of island music, the smell of the sea and salty breeze filled the small room. Sunshine radiated from her darkly burnished skin, and I saw the moment it registered over Zarena, saw the devastation at the truth as her mother glowed and glowed.

Erzulie Mapiangue.

LOA of Beauty, of Childbirth, and Protector of Babes.

The words coiled around me like a serpent, in warning. That same tendril wrapped around Zarena, but instead of biting, it was calm and assured.

"There are many Erzulie, each of us a different sliver of her power, her essence. Each standing sentry for those who need us for particular ailments."

Zarena lifted her chin to her father. "And you, papa?" she demanded.

Ogou Feray slid down his shield, announcing his name, his affinities. She shuddered at his power. He held back, we could feel it; a war deity who couldn't bear to unleash his fury too heavily in front of his child.

She turned to Andros, who shifted uncomfortably.

"I'm no one of importance." He shrugged, but she pinned him with her stare until he raised his hands and slowly, evenly peeled down his defensive barriers. "I'm just Andros, God of Nourishment." It was clear he loved his sister above all and wasn't used to being on the receiving end of her hurt. The instinct to protect her ran deeply through him and being the root of her pain waged war within him. I knew that look of guilt well; had seen it on my own face more times than I could count over the years.

"And the girls? Are they—have they been keeping—?" Zarena's voice cracked before she swallowed the question. *Had they been lying to me too?* she'd meant.

Erzulie shook her head. "Our offspring are born with fractured divinity, having not been made from essence and worship. Not all children develop powers, though all demi-god blood is sacred. They know no more than you did."

It was such a small movement. Still, Zarena's shoulders sagged just a fraction with the knowledge she wasn't the only one out of the loop.

Zarena

CHAPTER 21

The level of delusional denial running laps in my mind threatened to overwhelm me. I was calm, too calm, considering *Maman* sat inches away, in a room mixed with family and strangers, telling me with a straight face she, Papa, and Andros were actually ancient beings.

I glanced over to Theo, to the deep green eyes belonging to the boy tracking my every breath. He and Andros sat as far from each other as possible, but their studious gazes stayed trained on me. Why hadn't he or his friends said anything to refute this? Even as my logical brain raged and rallied against the sheer improbability of it, the utter insanity, hadn't I spent most of my life reading novels and getting lost in the astounding fantasy of books? Did we not have myths and legends for a reason? I'd built a career and life around discovering ancient civilizations who believed in these very beings. Built shrines and temples for them.

Why couldn't it all be true?

Four strangers sat in our house and didn't so much as flinch at *Maman*'s words, and what I'd seen of Papa and Andros. I'd *felt* a strange thrum of energy from *Maman* when she told me her name, saw the lightning pulse off Papa.

Maman fell silent, waiting for me to say something. Waiting for me to process.

I cleared my throat. "Are you LOA, too?" I asked our visitors, doing all I could to keep my voice steady. I didn't want to crack up, so I leaned into the scientific part of my mind, cataloging each of them like a specimen to study and dissect later. The standing one I recognized him from Electric Delphi the other night as the drummer from the band Tatiana wanted to see. And the stunning woman sitting next to the man who'd burned me with his touch. *Hermes*, *Maman* called him. His slender fingers, the same ones that seared my flesh, now circled the wrist of the dark-skinned woman next to him. She was *breathtaking*, a queen, her coppery eyes searching my face. I flinched.

She smiled, gently. "We are not of the LOA, but we are similar in origins. I'm Hecate." Her voice was soothing, washed over me like a caressing warm summer night breeze. Shadows coiled around her easily.

I cocked my head, thinking. *Hermes. Hecate.*

"You're Greek gods?" I asked. My breath caught when the stranger, Hermes, smiled.

"She's quick, that's for sure. Hermes, Messenger of the Gods, at your service." He dipped his head in a quick bow. "Hephaestus, God of the Forge." He gestured behind him at the sandy-haired drummer of the GorgonKnots. Then he slid his gaze to Theo, whom he didn't introduce. He simply said, "You chose well."

Theo stiffened.

You chose well.

Chose.

Theo, who looked like a stone statue.

Theo, who I'd let taste and touch and fuck me.

Theo, who'd *chosen* me.

Bile rose from my stomach to my throat, but I swallowed it down and turned back to the face of the woman who'd raised me. Who'd loved me. Who'd lied to me my entire fucking life.

"What was it all for?" I asked. Her eyes shone, brimming with her will for me to let her explain it all away. I'd promised I'd stay to hear it all out, and surely there was more to it than just this, but my emotions threatened to overwhelm me. Why tell me now? Why all the fighting? I swallowed sharply and steeled my nerves before I could have a complete fucking meltdown.

Maman began speaking again. "I worked in women's shelters for a long time. One night, a woman came in—pregnant, scared, and on the run. But she wasn't just a woman, and she wasn't just fleeing a bad situation. Something was different about her, and the minute her eyes tore through my wards, stripping me bare and revealing my power to her, I *knew*. I just knew that she was of the Otherworld, and she was in trouble.

"She was exhausted but used all the power she had left to make sure I could be trusted. When she passed out from it, my own power welled up, demanding I put her under my protection. That's my job, *bebe*—to protect women and children. I cloaked her divinity as best I could then called your papa to come get us, and we brought her here. When she woke up, she was grateful but guarded, unwilling to tell me who she was or who she was running from. I gave her some clothes and food, and it was a little while before she opened up enough to tell us who she was. Who *you* would become."

Her eyes, warm and soft, pinned me in place. I hung on every word, demanding the heat pricking behind my eyes not to make me cry. If I started, I might not be able to stop.

"She was about seven months along. We debated whether to go to the Council about her, but she begged us not to. Said it would put them in danger, put *us* in danger. Dro was just a baby, not even two yet. The person she was running from was powerful, very influential, and she'd warned us that harboring her would only put us in danger. She tried to run, but there was no way we could let her."

Hermes slid forward, elbows resting on his knees. He hung onto my *maman*'s every word as aptly as I did, but her eyes were only on me. This story was mine. It *belonged* to me.

"After a while, she and I became friends. She cooked, despite our insistence that she rest, helped keep the house, kept it warded underneath our own. She watched Andros while we worked. Eventually, she trusted us enough to give us the full story, or as much as she deemed safe for us to know. She'd been taken by Zeus, a powerful Greek god. He'd kept her bound to private chambers on a remote estate under constant guard. The things she endured at his hands were horrific."

I stopped breathing, stopped thinking. Only one question pushed through my mental stasis, one question I'd asked her a thousand times in my life.

"What was her name?" The house was so quiet I could hear the subtle ticks of the clock in the hallway, moving along.

Maman smiled. "Clio. Your *maman*'s name was Clio. She was fierce and kind, with red hair, just like you, *bebe*."

Clio.

"Impossible." The word short, a curt bark from Theo. His hands balled into fists on top of his thighs, his posture still stiff with subtle panic in his dark green eyes.

Maman bowed her head slightly in confirmation. "I'm afraid, Lord Prometheus, it was. She opened up after a few weeks here and told us, not only her name but a harrowing tale of the nightmare that had become her life."

I loosed a sharp breath, and Theo's eyes snapped to mine. Begging. Pleading.

Prometheus.

Prometheus, the God of Knowledge. *No.*

Prometheus, the *Titan* of Knowledge.

Prometheus

CHAPTER 22

"She was taken prisoner by your God of Gods, Zeus." The words rang through the room like the aftershock of an earthquake. A thrum of anger blasted from my chest, cold fury and rage. I wasn't the only one. Hermes, Hecate, and Hephaestus all stiffened. We knew from Iapetus he'd taken her, but this LOA filled in the gaps with intimate knowledge that turned my stomach.

"Why did he lock her up?" Zarena demanded.

Erzulie sighed. "She had something precious inside of her. A map, of some sort, tied to her essence. When Zeus realized she escaped, he hunted her mercilessly. For five years they ran, going deep into hiding. But as her due date approached, she needed one of her own kind to help with the delivery."

"They?" Zarena pressed.

Erzulie gave her a sad smile. "Yes, *bebe*, Clio, and Zaren—your father. He was a guard, but they fell in love. Then you were on the way, and they knew they'd have to make a break for it sooner rather than later. Clio spoke of him with such love, Zarena. He protected her while she was in that place as best he could. He'd sneak her books and—it feels important to tell you—he planned her escape for years and years. They took a chance coming into the city, hoping to meet with Lord Hades, but when they got here, he was gone. Zeus must have known they would try to get to him, because the moment they stepped foot here, they were hunted. *Brutally.*

"Zaren fell during one of those attacks, protecting your *maman*, protecting you." She leaned over and squeezed Zarena's hand. "He loved you both so much. His sacrifice protected you both, put a sort of lock on her. She was shielded from the Greeks, and after a few bad experiences, she found that none of her own people could touch her. Her skin burned them, causing great painful welts. It was embedded into her very blood. That protection passed to you when you were born. But it meant that she was exposed, without it."

"That's why you couldn't touch me." Zarena's eyes cut to Hermes.

"She'd felt me, that day she stumbled into the shelter. Said the strings of the Fates pulled her feet to us. She saw the Medusa sigil on the unmarked door and knew it was a safe haven for women in need. She maybe was hoping to find a fellow Grecian, but instead, she found me." Erzulie's ghost of a smile dropped sadly.

"I delivered you, you know. Even then you were stubborn, waiting for your own time. She was a week overdue, but you made her wait until you were ready. Born in the middle of a hurricane; can you believe that? It raged outside, and whether you'd called it to you or you were called to it, I knew the moment that blast of power entered this world with your first cry that you would be a force."

"She abandoned me."

Zarena's mother shook her head, and when she spoke, the unwavering conviction in her voice was unmistakable. "Not in the way you think. She held you, even though the protection in your veins burned her to do it. She passed every bit of love, every semblance of strength into you. But Clio knew he would come. They could track her again. So, she held you, arms blistering with fire, and kissed your forehead that burned her lips as she made me swear that we would shield you and protect you. That he could never know you existed. She named you Zarena, then handed you to me. She said, 'Raise our girl to be a wildfire,' and while I wrapped you tight, she slipped out the back of the house. We didn't even realize she'd gone for several minutes." Tears shone in Erzulie's eyes, full of pain, fresh and raw as it must have been twenty-eight years ago.

"What happened when she left? Did she . . . Why did she . . . ?" Zarena began but her father, Ogou, buckled at the hurt we all heard in her voice.

He rushed to kneel in front of her, taking her free hand between his own. "I ran after her. I tracked her, intent on telling her we'd find another way. But when I caught up to Clio, she was surrounded. She saw me, moving in the shadows, preparing to attack. I can show you, if you want to see. It will be difficult, and maybe too much, but it is yours to decide.

"We've kept so much from you because we *had* to. It was her final request on this earth. But I won't ever keep anything from you again, baby girl. If you want to see, I'll show you. And after, if you hate me, I'll bear that too. I should have done more to protect you both; for that failure, I will wear your pain."

Zarena regarded him with such love, such sorrow. Her dad was her entire world, and his betrayal cut her to the bone. But my girl, so thirsty for knowledge, raised her chin to meet his gaze stoically.

"Show me."

He lifted a hand to stroke her cheek. "Okay, Z. I'll show you." He stood, pulling a small knife from his back pocket. Hermes and Hephaestus tensed but Ogou raised the glinting steel to his fingertip, pressing until blood welled at the tip, then let the bead drip into the tea mug perched on her leg.

He then turned and moved to me, offering his finger. "As one of yours, you have the right to know as well—to bear witness to what *he* did to her." The venom in his words at the mention of Zeus straightened my shoulders, made me respect Zarena's father even more. Gratefully, I raised my cup to him and in went his lifeblood. He repeated it with Hermes, Hecate, and Hephaestus, then with his son, Andros. Erzulie, I was sure, had seen it many times before.

"Drink."

We did.

I drained the rest of my chicory coffee and placed my mug on the side table atop a wooden coaster. The edges of my vision blurred as Ogou raised his hands, his power pooling out around us. Zarena sucked in a sharp breath, and it took everything in me not to stumble forward and take her hand to reassure her.

Darkness ripped around me, street after street. The wind howled and rain pelted in thick sheets. The hurricane. She'd gone in the middle of the storm. Panic rose in my chest—in Ogou's chest—at her scent, how faint it had grown in just a few minutes. A soft silver glow, the only indication of divinity had come this way, quickly dispersed in the rainwater.

I pushed on, and her scent grew stronger, just a little farther and I could bring her back to Erzulie. We would convince her that we were family, that she could be safe. But then, I heard them, their jeers and sharp tones. The thick scent of "other," of metallic lightning, tasted on the air.

There she was, backed into an alley. A sword, heavy and scream-ing for blood, materialized in my right hand, my short spear in my left. I would make quick work of the five who cornered her, spill their blood in the name of Erzulie, in the name of war.

As if her thoughts were a shout, Clio's eyes pierced through me just as I was to lunge, pinning me to the shadows. A voice, melodic and calm, drifted into my ears, a sound as beautiful as music, as reverent, wrapped me up and held me close.

"Don't. Don't come for me. Think of Erzulie, of Andros. Of Zarena. You can't risk your own for me, but I can protect you all

like this. You're her family now; her father. Protect her, Ogou, as you would them. If you show yourself, they will know a LOA is involved. They will look."

Her words wrapped around me, soothing the base instinct to kill, to spill blood, to protect what was my own.

A crack of lightning split the darkness for only a moment, and in its wake, stepped Zeus. Hatred roiled beneath my bones for this predator, as the rain halted in a small circle around the block. We were in the eye of the storm, one he'd made. I felt it in my bones.

"Clio, Clio, what have you done, pet?" His voice too smooth, dripping with false comfort. He was a tall god, large in stature, his golden hair shorn close to his neck. Crackles of lightning flitted up and along his arms, over his shoulders as he approached her.

Clio put her hands protectively over her stomach, still swollen.

Zeus stepped closer an inch, tsking and shaking his head. "Did you think you could keep my child from me? That there was any-where in the cosmos you could go that I wouldn't find you? Come now, stop this madness. You need to come home and deliver our son in peace." He held a hand to her, gently, reasonably.

Clio lifted her chin in defiance. "I don't belong to you, and you will never have him, Zeus," she spat, and pride flared in my chest at her strength.

The thunder rolling around us shook the earth, and a sliver of careful composure slipped from Zeus's face. His lips tightened into a thin line. "Oh, but you do belong to me, pet. You are mine to keep, hold, fuck, use, breed . . . And as for my son, I will have him. He will be raised to be strong, and he will be taught the old ways."

Clio didn't so much as flinch at his casual admittance of his repeated violations. I raged against the power she'd used to cloy my senses, to hold me here in the shadows.

"I'd rather die a thousand deaths than let you touch me again, you fucking monster." Clio spat on the ground, and Zeus took two more steps closer.

Fifty feet separated them now, but I knew he could close that distance with little effort. Clio lifted a knife, one dripping with black ichor, and I blanched. I knew what that was, knew the True Death it meant for Greek deities if they were infected with it. Poisoned Ambrosia.

Zeus stopped dead. "You don't have the nerve," he whispered. The sounds of the storm raging around us went deathly still.

Clio shot him a look of pure hatred. "To make sure you never get a chance to hurt him, I would. I've seen your fate, Lightning Bearer. You spend eternity cold and alone, shackled in Tartarus forever." She raised the knife, but before she could thrust it into her belly, a bolt of electricity materialized in Zeus's hand. He hurled it at her, impaling her in the chest. Rage and horror washed through me at the sound of her bones impacting the brick wall, the smell of singed flesh.

Clio choked and sputtered, but before Zeus could move to her, she rallied. "Fuck you," she gurgled, and plunged the knife into her stomach, over and over and over.

A scream of rage, of white-hot fury, bellowed from Zeus and he zipped to her, fast as lightning, but the Poisoned Ambrosia was in too many places, too deep inside her womb.

The acrid sludge began to rot her flesh, melting it like battery acid, and before he reached her fully, her entire abdomen was gone. The bolt of glass that impaled her kept the top of her body intact, but Clio's head lolled lifelessly, her wild red curls singed around her.

The binding holding me loosened.

I felt the very moment her soul left this realm.

Tears, hot and thick, rolled down my cheeks. "Goodbye, my friend," I whispered into the darkness, hoping she would hear it, that she would know how loved and protected Zarena would be.

Zeus plunged his hand into her chest, looking for something, but when he wrenched his hand free, he let out another howl of rage. Whatever he was looking for, her last true act of defiance was to deny it to him.

I slipped through the shadows, back through the walls of the hurricane. I would come back and bury the body of my friend once they were gone.

I would protect Zarena from all threats. This I vowed to Clio.

The blinding light of reality blinked back into my sight. I glanced around. Hecate had tears in her eyes and Heph looked like he may be sick. Hermes was a ball of rage, white hot, and ready to kill. He and Clio had been close, had even shared a tryst or two in their day. He loved her dearly as a friend, and what was done to her was a crime of the highest order.

I looked at Zarena, to the tears that filled her brilliant blue eyes. She sat and listened to so much tonight, but this. This was too much. I could feel it on her, the despair.

She looked at Erzulie. "Am I his child?" was all she asked.

Erzulie grabbed her face between her hands and shook her head vigorously. "No, *bebe, no*. Your father *was* Zaren. When Zeus assaulted her, she was very careful to make sure a child never resulted. Muses are different from the rest of the Otherworlders. They are told by the Fates how many children they are to have and with whom. To defy it would cause the greatest of consequences.

"When she found out about you, she called in a boon to one of the Fates. It's how they escaped. The Fate spun a tale about how the baby belonged to Zeus, how it was to be a child of great strength. A boy since she knew you'd be a girl. Sowing seeds of misinformation to throw him off your trail, to not kill you if he ever found out. But Clio loved you, *bebe*. She trusted us with you."

Hermes cleared his throat and rose, disentangling himself from Cate. He approached Ogou slowly, extending his hand. "I knew Clio since the dawn of her existence. She was one of the finest beings to ever grace the cosmos. Thank you for being there with her, at the end. Thank you for telling us, *showing us*, her story.

We will avenge her." His words were sharp as steel, a boon of the highest order. Zeus had earned himself a blood debt from the God of Messengers, Lord of Thieves, and Hermes *always* paid his debts. Ogou slipped his hand into Hermes's and shook once. "We are in your debt, for keeping her daughter well-loved and well-guarded. Please accept a boon, from me to you."

Hecate stood and Erzulie rose to meet her. They spoke, voices low, but I couldn't look away from Zarena. From the tremble in her lip, the defiant way she bit her cheek to stop the tears, but it was too much, too quickly. When the first sob cracked her chest, a tether snapped in my own, and I was up, off the couch and across the small room, pulling her into my arms. She sobbed, breaking apart against my chest, burying her face in my neck, soaking my skin with the salt of her tears.

Zarena

CHAPTER 23

I let Theo—*Prometheus*—carry me out of the living room, and to my surprise, no one made a move to stop him. I was a mess, snot and tears and sobs spilling from my lips, threatening to bury me alive. I felt weak, so foolish.

But I was grateful to have seen her. Clio. My *mother*.

She was so beautiful, earth-shakingly so. And even at her end, she'd fought. She fought him *for me*. She'd sacrificed so much, gave everything she had, so that *I* would have the life I did, with the family *she'd* chosen for me. A family I loved more than anything. Guilt crashed through me, crushing me under the weight of a thousand bricks, drowning me like a flood from the Mississippi. I wished a tidal wave would come and bury me down in the mud and the silt and leave me there. How many times over the years had I *hated* her, *cursed* her for leaving me?

Theo walked me into my room—how he knew which was mine I had no idea, but I found myself back in my high school bedroom. Books were scattered over my desk and my floral lilac comforter, but I didn't care.

He sat us down carefully, with my body still pressed against his, while wave after wave of grief consumed me. His hands were warm, a soothing fire over my shivering skin, comforting even as they left goose bumps in their wake, the air too cold compared to them. I was surrounded by his arms, his steady breathing. This man, this *god*, didn't care that I was ugly crying all over his chest. He let me. He held me, and I had a lot of complicated feelings and questions about that, but they could wait, they had to. I didn't have the capacity for much else.

The door creaked as my brother poked his head in. I could hear murmuring voices from down the hall, but I couldn't bring myself to care.

"Z?" Dro whispered.

Theo stiffened, his arms banding just a little tighter around me. I turned to Dro and the sorrow on his face, the guilt; it broke me too. Another tiny shard of my family base chipped away, but I reached a shaking hand to him and he sagged with relief, approaching gently.

"They need to speak with you," he said over my head to Theo.

"It can wait," Theo grunted, the low rumble in his chest a soothing white noise. I clung to him a little tighter.

"I'm sorry, but it can't. I'll stay while you go. I need a minute with my sister too." Dro replied, but his words were soft, almost reproachful.

Theo studied him for a moment, then flicked his gaze to my face. I sniffled then nodded a few times, knowing that no matter what, Dro had me. He was my rock. Reluctantly, Theo shifted, settling my body onto the bed before leaving the room.

Dro slid onto the covers, pulling me into a fierce hug. We were quiet for a long while. Long enough for my sobs to turn to hiccups, for the tear tracks to dry on their own, leaving my skin irritated and raw.

My brother was my mountain. He was the steady rock that held our family tethered together. We had always been the closest among our siblings. We protected each other.

I should be angry about the lie. I should rage and claw and kick and scream at the betrayal. But Papa had *shown* me. I'd seen with my own two eyes what she'd asked of them. She'd begged them to protect me, and I knew myself well enough to know that if I'd have been told who I was—*what* I was—then I would have sworn vengeance. I'd have sought out the people of my own kind, devoured the knowledge I could get, and then I would have gone after that motherfucker with everything I had.

"I'm sorry," Dro whispered.

I hugged him tighter. "I know," I answered, and his breathing faltered. "When did you find out?"

"When I turned sixteen. I'd shown some power. Remember when I punched Eric Delgado so hard it cracked his ribs?" he asked, and I nodded. He'd beaten the shit out of him for looking up my skirt. That kid *was* a real dickbag.

"Papa smelled the residual power coming off me when I got home. I was so scared; I thought he was gonna put a belt to my ass. But he brought me to the temple and explained our family legacy instead."

"How, how old are *Maman* and Papa?" I asked, slightly afraid to know the answer.

"Old, but if you tell *Maman* I said that I'll lie, then whoop you myself," Dro chuckled.

"Have they . . . Are we the first kids?" I should have asked them, but he was here and this was normal and familiar. Dro had always been the one I had the hard talks with, and my chest was too tight to try and speak with them right now.

He sighed. "As far as I know. The chance of their offspring not being demi-gods who could protect themselves was a risk they weren't willing to take, considering the climate during when they'd been worshipped into being. They didn't want to bring a Black baby into slavery, and then into segregation. I think I was the experiment, to see if I could survive."

My face blanched with horror. "Are the other gods like that?"

He shook his head. "No, most of the other pantheons were created in their divinity from the power of the universe. We were created from slivers of essence, then worshiped and revered into divinity. In many ways, it makes us much stronger. We were brought into being by the will of the people. That's why there are many versions of Papa as Ogou. *Maman* too," he finished thoughtfully.

"And you? Are you a sliver of power too?"

He chuckled. "Girl, hell naw. I'm one hundred percent *original*." He pursed his lips and hit me with his classic side eye.

"Are there many other LOA around here?" I wasn't sure if it was polite to ask but I wanted to know. I *needed* to know if I was going to survive this world.

"A few." Dro shrugged, taking me up and down with him. "A lot of the Old Guard keep to the temples. Not many live freely out in the real world. For them, it takes practice to blend in. I know a good bit of demis, though." He fell silent while I processed his words.

"Dro?" My voice was low, tone serious. "Don't ever fucking lie to me again. I mean it."

He nodded. "Promise. Pinky promise, Z." He held out his pinky to me, and I took it into my own. That was our bond since childhood. He was as solemn in his vow as my papa had been in the one he made to Clio. He wouldn't betray it.

"*Sooo—*" Dro let out a long sigh. I already knew what was coming. "Prometheus, huh?" He laughed, low and steady, but his tone was lighter, almost teasing.

"Oh, my damn, I had no idea. I don't think he knew who I was either, Dro. Also, why does *Maman* call some of them Lord and Lady, and then others are just their names?"

"Lord and Lady are titles of respect. Lady Hecate is legendary, even among our people. Lord Hephaestus and Lord Hermes, too. They're a continuous source of good, and they've fought many battles in their time. They come when one of us calls for aid. But Zeus is a piece of *shit*," he spat, relaxing back into the headboard.

"She called Theo Lord," I recalled.

"She did. Though, I doubt she'd have honored him with the title if she walked in on what I did. You're lucky I was through the door first and Papa rolled in after. He may have killed him on the spot if he'd seen him about to go down on you. And in the kitchen? I *cook* there, Z. Gross. We *eat* there," Dro chastised.

I shrugged. "He was trying to eat too." That earned me a look of faint disgust. "Was this why you didn't want me around Electric Delphi? The Greek gods?"

"Yeah. Papa told me to keep you away from there, and another club, Styx. To keep you out of the Shadow Marché, anywhere other deities banged around, but especially the Greeks. Add that to the list of shit I didn't do well," he grumbled.

A soft knock at the door had me sitting up. We fell silent as *Maman* peeked in.

"I need you to come out here, *bebes*. I know you've heard a lot, but there are some other things and they're pressing." She sighed, looking so tired.

Dro slipped out of my bed and ruffled my hair. "Come on now. Let's go figure out how you're gonna bring down this bitch."

Prometheus

CHAPTER 24

So many questions. I had so many questions and barely any answers. The first one hit me like a ton of bricks as soon as I walked out of that bedroom. Hermes was on me in a flash.

"How the fuck can you stand to touch her?" He turned my hands, my arms, over between his fingers. Fingers, I noticed, still marked with freshly healed skin. I'd smelled his flesh burning; it had been extensive.

"I don't know," I managed to choke out. And I didn't. I had no clue what was up with me. No idea why when she cried, I *had* to go to her. A compulsion. It was mandatory to make her stop hurting. I felt it in my chest.

"And you two just met randomly at Electric Delphi? And then you just happened to run into her at that bar getting day drunk? Something you *never* do?" I could see the gears turning behind his eyes. "Where's the compass?"

"In the pocket of the shirt she's wearing," I ground out. I itched to get back in there, hating the door keeping her from my sight. I needed to make sure she was safe and protected. Just being in our presence put a target on her back.

"What if . . . what if you pulled the compass from Iapetus and that power, that *pull*, transferred to you? Neither of you had the compass when you ran into each other earlier. What if . . . *you're* the compass now and *she's* the map?" Hermes's eyes were alight, excited.

I shot him a weary look. "That's not what my father said. He was clear about the compass." I didn't want Zarena involved in any of this business, especially knowing who she was.

"It wouldn't be the first time a prophecy was misinterpreted." Hermes shrugged and I wanted to punch him in his throat. "Plus, she's the blood—*Clio's* blood. She's the map." His words trailed off as Hecate approached.

"Can I talk to you for a second?" I asked.

She nodded, concerned. I stepped back and she followed me, dismissing Hermes with a quick kiss. He, mercifully, took the hint and zoomed over to where Heph and Ogou were deep in conversation.

"What's going on?" Catc asked, and my chest heaved.

"Something is wrong with me. There's something. Like a tether. She's down the hall and it's too far. That's not normal." My eyes darted around, whispering low as I dug my fingers into the tight knot that had taken residence in my chest.

Hecate studied me. "Maybe it's the beginning of a ma—" she began but I silenced her with a look.

"It's not. This is . . . It's . . . I think it's the compass. The tether between the compass and the map. Hermes thinks that's what the pull in my chest has been—to her. But if she's spelled against us, then how did I find her in that club? And if I could track her, could *he*?" She knew exactly who I was talking about.

Hecate frowned. "Did you drink anything that night? Like out of the ordinary?"

I thought back to that night. "Just the one drink from the cock-tail tray. It was a red liquor and looked the safest. No smoking."

Cate's eyes widened with understanding. "That was for *clarity*, Theo. There was already a pull to her, but it was dampened by the glamor that made you not focus. I would bet, if you compared them, all the places you were being dragged through were places *she* visited."

"We slept together, Cate. I *can't* be connected to her. It would be terrible," I ground out.

A sharp huff of breath right behind me slapped me upside the head. I knew before I turned whose face I'd see waiting for me. Knew by the tone, the subtle shift in the very air in the room. Knew by the way Cate's eyes widened just slightly in regret.

I closed my eyes and steadied my breathing, then turned to see Zarena, inches from me, her hand still outstretched like she was going to touch me.

Hurt.

My chest ached and I didn't know if it was her feelings leaking into me or my own regret. *Fucking idiot.* I should have noticed her entering the room.

I opened my mouth to speak, to say *anything*. "Zarena, I—" But before I could muster up a weak apology, fire burned behind her eyes and she pushed past me without a word, careful not to touch me at all. I brought my thumb and forefinger to the bridge of my nose and bowed my head, closing my eyes.

"Real fuckin' smooth," Hermes grumbled, suddenly at my side.

I shot him a look that promised death by a thousand cuts, but he just ignored me and wrapped his arms around Cate as Hephaestus walked over.

"Erzulie is ready to give us the floor. We've got one chance to pitch this to her, so everyone just be easy," he said, not missing the pointed glare coming from Hermes and Cate. He looked between us. "What did I miss?"

I turned and walked back to the couch to sit, ignoring Heph's exasperated groan as Hermes filled him in. Andros sat on the other side of the couch from me again, but this time he was more relaxed. Whatever he and Zarena talked about centered him, and I envied that easy posture.

One by one, they trickled in and retook their seats. Only this time, Zarena looked everywhere, *anywhere* but at me.

"So, how does this all fit together? Why did you guys show up here?" she asked Hermes, who looked smug as shit that she'd chosen to speak with him.

"We have a plan to take Zeus down. It's not going to be easy. In fact, it's a fucking long shot at best. But there's a chance." He looked at her then, his pale blue eyes cutting a laser into the dark pools of hers.

"Tell me," she demanded, sitting forward in her seat. I locked my jaw; I *knew* that look, the determined posture. Zarena was like me in many ways, and the promise of vengeance welled up inside of her like a lifeline, some semblance of control after learning her life was not her own.

And so, Hermes told her. He recalled every word my father spoke about the map and the library and Pandora's Box. Everything about Hera. And she listened—*really* listened. When he was finished, she sat in silence for a long while, contemplating. He had spoken for an hour, Hecate and Hephaestus filling in bits of information to supplement, but she never even once looked my way.

That cold shoulder was arctic.

There was a determined look on her face when she turned to Erzulie and nodded. Dread, twisted and heavy, sank in my gut as she turned to Hecate and said the words I would have given up half of my organs to never hear her say.

"When do we leave?"

Zarena

CHAPTER 25

*I*t *would be terrible.*

I'd come to thank him for his kindness, for the way he seemed to understand that I was at my limit, and the full force of his words hit me like a slap to the face. That, coupled with the look of pity on Hecate's face had me wishing I could melt into the fucking floor.

What we'd done had been just sex between strangers, and now that was over.

Done.

It was certainly not fucking happening again.

Hermes gave me the perfect solution to push all thoughts of Theo from my mind—*vengeance.* I wanted to take Zeus down, to destroy him. He'd kidnapped my mother and raped her who knows how many times. Killed my father, then hunted and forced her to take her life. I would make him pay, and make sure he knew whose child swung the sword.

I needed to learn how to wield a sword.

Maman looked fearful, but to my parents' credit, neither tried to stop me when I agreed to go with them. Dro, however, stood ten toes down that he wasn't letting me go off on my own.

"I'm coming with you," he'd announced, and his tone was so final, so absolute that save for a few terse glances, no one rendered any objections.

An hour later, I'd packed a small bag and met them all in the living room. Hecate gave me a sweet smile, and I drifted over to where she was talking with *Maman.*

"Promise you'll be careful and that you'll stick with Dro?" Papa said, wrapping me in his arms and squeezing tight. I nodded, holding on to him with everything within me. I was still angry, but I was also about to embark on some dangerous shit. Now wasn't the time to be a petty brat.

Maman had small tears in her eyes, but they shone with something else, something tender. "You're my *bebe,* you know that, right? As close as blood, Zarena. I've loved you since before you were born, childe." She placed a kiss on my cheek, and I bit back the well of emotion pooling inside my chest.

"I love you both, so much. Thank you for loving me," was all I could say.

Papa gently peeled *Maman* away, hugging her tightly. Dro crowded into our space as they kissed and hugged him as well.

"Kill anything that gets near her," Papa growled.

"I will."

The others formed a loose circle, holding hands. Hephaestus had a free hand, as did Theo. I grimaced. If I let Andros hold my hand and then grabbed Hephaestus, it would scorch the Greek. Theo gave me an apologetic look as he realized my hesitation, the implication clear—we had no choice. I rolled my eyes and stepped beside him, adjusting my ruck on my back, only touching him at the very last moment. Dro stepped between me and Hephaestus and grabbed our hands.

My skin against Theo's felt itchy—too warm, too electric—in his palm. I wanted to rewind it all back, to erase all the kisses and touches he'd stolen, but Theo tightened his grip like he could tell I wanted to pull away. His thumb traced a slow circle on the top of my hand, and I bit back a frustrated groan, hating the way my tension eased slightly.

This turned into the never ending one-night stand from hell.

Not the sex, but the finding-out-I'm-a-half-immortal-being-and-oh-yeah-I-had-a-titan's-dick-inside-of-me.

Heat flamed through me at the memory of what we'd done, what we had been about to do when my brother and father busted in. Theo's head snapped to me like he could feel my arousal, scent it in the air. His eyes were wild, hungry, as Hecate lifted her arms and slammed them down. Shadows enveloped us on all sides, and I was falling, screaming, through a dark abyss.

*

As quickly as the darkness was summoned, it abated, and my feet slammed into damp earth, hard. I stumbled with the buckling of my knees, but sure hands were on me, catching my fall just before I hit the ground. A hand wrapped around my torso, cradling my ribs as he helped me stand, and I ignored the white-hot bolt of electricity that shot straight to my nipples when that hand grazed the underside of my breasts.

Mercifully, Dro stepped over to help, pulling me gently from Theo's grip. The titan straightened just a fraction and turned to speak with Hermes without a word, leaving Dro and me to look around at the dark realm we'd landed in.

Inky blacks of storm clouds painted the midnight sky above us; a large river, glowing blue seemed to sing the saddest song I'd ever heard, flowed just a few feet from us. The water was bioluminescent, and I stepped closer, transfixed. So lovely. So refreshing. It sang to me, both in my *maman*'s voice and another's—a voice that pulled something taut in the deepest buried parts of me. A memory, long forgotten. If I could just touch the water, just dive right in, I could hear that sweet voice again, I could—I reached out, fingers inches from the water.

A sharp tug ripped me from the river's edge just millimeters from the surface, and I slammed back into a mountain, or a boulder, something heavy and living and true. The air expelled from my lungs as I reached toward the water, wanting, *needing* to hear that voice again. Shackles held my arms down, wrestling me into a prone position. A voice, a *panicked* voice, ripped me back to reality, back from the edge of mania.

"Zarena, *look at me*," Theo ordered.

That voice, that deep timbre giving the command shot a different memory through my mind, one that had my cheeks flushing. Lips grazed my ear and my heart sped up. Theo breathed heavily against my neck, and when he spoke, I felt it in my chest, the rumble from his pressing between us.

"First rule of the Underworld, Red. Don't touch the Styx. *Ever.*"

The Underworld.

"Like Hell?" I asked as my pulse rocketed with panic. Theo's arms stayed coiled around me, but I quickly moved out of his grasp, in desperate need of air that didn't smell like him.

No strings, no emotion. I could respect that.

Knocking the coarse sand off my jeans, I turned and offered him my hand. He looked at it in surprise then took it, and I did what I could to hoist up his massive frame. He rose gracefully, unfolding his legs with ease.

"Why are we out here in the open?" Theo asked, cocking his attention to Hecate. She turned to take in the terrain around her, but before she could answer, a deep voice spoke from a mass of roiling shadows.

"My orders."

I squinted into the empty blackness that leached all light from the air around it and was startled when a man, tall and broad, stepped out of it. He was pale, built more like Hermes than Theo, but every stride he took forward screamed predator, screamed of destruction and retribution. I took an involuntary step back and bumped into Theo's chest. His arm came up, his hand settling on my hip. I ignored it and kept my eyes trained on the new threat in front of me. Andros stepped in closer to my body, shifting protectively. His hand twitched, likely debating whether or not to summon his spear.

Hermes, however, scoffed. "Hades, what the fuck? You can't just stop us mid-portal! You know how dangerous that is?" He sounded annoyed and not the least bit fazed, but I'd heard the name he'd called this man, this god.

Hades.

The God of the Dead.

Hades simply strode forward, eyes on me. I did my best not to shrink away from him, to hold my chin high. He was beautiful, a deadly sort of handsome that could rip apart the universe; drown empires—such was its devastation. He regarded me with a cold, unflinching stare and I gazed right back. Theo's fingers gripped tighter at my hip, steadying me, lending me his power.

"You are the daughter of Clio?" Hades asked sharply.

"I am," I answered coolly. "You are Hades?"

"Indeed. Is it true that you cannot be touched by Greek hands?" He regarded me with a steely gaze.

"That seems to be the case."

His eyes flicked to my brother, inching ever closer, then to the hold Theo kept on me. "Yet Prometheus is touching you now and he isn't on fire." It wasn't a question, more of a simple observation.

I lifted my chin. "Perhaps he's made of tougher stuff than most Greek gods?"

Hades arched his eyebrow in surprise. A little smile ghosted his lips, some small amusement. "That he is," Hades replied. "Welcome to the Asphodels. I was greatly saddened to hear the news of your mother; I knew her well." His tone was steel-like but sincere. "I stopped you here because we have company in the palace. I wanted to warn you." He gestured to Theo, who shifted, suddenly alert.

"Who is it?"

"Epimetheus. He was visited by emissaries of Zeus." Hades's tone dropped like an avalanche as he said Zeus's name.

I racked my brain, trying to remember the name but it meant nothing to me. A minor deity, perhaps? Theo stood ramrod straight, head on a swivel. He moved me then, slightly behind him—wedging my body between his mass and Dro and the craggy rocks jutting behind us. I made a noise of protest.

"I'll see him, but Andros and Zarena need to hide. I don't trust him, Hades. I need to figure out what he knows." Theo scanned the landscape once more as if he could see any potential eavesdroppers.

Hades nodded. "He is with Seph and Ares." His words were half-amused.

Hephaestus perked up. "Ares? Is Ditey here, too?" His tone was guarded, but those brown eyes lit up with a fire so rich and full it was nearly indecent.

Hephaestus, God of the Forge. Married to Aphrodite. Cheated on by her and Ares, right? Something about a net? I took a deep breath and prayed to whatever beings we were supposed to pray to that I wasn't about to witness some sort of lover's spat.

"Got here just before you did. I think she's in your chambers." Hades turned to Andros and me. "We'll portal you into the throne room. Theo, we'll meet Epimetheus in my chambers. If you are satisfied after your talk, come find us. If not, we can send him packing with him none the wiser."

Theo gave a quick jerk of his chin in understanding, and Hades turned, arcing his arm lazily through the night. His shadows responded immediately, opening up a crack of light that danced merrily on the other side of the threshold. Hades gestured for us to step through.

Theo turned to face Andros and me, and the subtle tension in his jaw let me know he wasn't happy about separating. "Don't eat or drink anything unless Hades says it's okay. If he serves it, it's fine. If you see anything growing, do not pick it, and most certainly do not eat it. When in doubt, ask a shade or someone else. You get me?"

He crowded my space, bending slightly to stare directly into my eyes. His body thrummed with nervous energy and his gaze flicked briefly, so quickly it could have been a hallucination, to my lips.

"We get you," I whispered. "Be careful, okay?" I hated the trembling in my voice. I didn't want him to go, to leave us in the fucking Underworld alone. Dro and I needed him to help us navigate.

Theo smirked. "You worried about me, Red?" His breath fanned over my face, and I had to arch my neck to look at him even with my height.

I rolled my eyes. "Only that you may get murdered before you can give me all the insider info on the others," I grumbled, and Theo laughed—a real, rich, and full laugh.

His hand trailed up my arm, then down to the pocket on his shirt that held the infamous compass. He dug two fingers inside and lifted the golden trinket, adjusting it into his palm while I tried desperately to ignore the heat that seeped from his fingers through the fabric to my chest.

"I need this back, but you should keep the shirt. Looks good on you. Now, go on. I'll see you soon." His fingers grazed the side of my jaw as he retreated. Only he and Hades remained. I flushed slightly, then rushed to the portal, ignoring the curious look on the God of the Underworld's face.

The last thing I heard before the portal closed was a bark of laughter and Theo's grumpy, "*Oh, don't you fucking start.*"

Prometheus
CHAPTER 26

By the Hells, I had to find a way to stop touching her.

Epimetheus stood casual and relaxed as ever inside Hades's chambers. A current of electricity thrummed over my skin, and I steeled my thoughts against focusing on those who were no doubt just on the other side of that left wall. Epimetheus's mouth split into a wide, easy grin as we approached. Hades settled behind his massive desk; the wood was so deep and rich in color that it would have been at home in Tartarus.

"You came." His words were guarded, but his posture and tone betrayed how shocked he was to see me. I couldn't blame him. I had deliberated for a moment earlier about blowing him off completely, but I decided against it—I needed to get Epi's account of Zeus's visit firsthand. To get a feel for what *actually* went down straight from his mouth.

"Of course." I gestured to the two chairs opposite Hades, and Epimetheus sat down, looking tired and bloodied. His cheek was bruised, his lip busted.

He turned to me. "What did you do to piss Zeus off this time?"

"The usual: defying his word, taking issue with the rape and murder and torture he likes to inflict, breathe. I could go on, but we don't have that much time. I assume that's his handiwork?" I grumbled.

Epi's grin faltered. "I mean it, Theo. He's on the warpath. And yeah, he decided to remind me what happens to those who aid and abet fugitives. He was cagey with his questions, so I have to assume that whatever shitstorm you've caused is important." He leaned forward onto his elbows to hold my stare. "I want in. Whatever it is. If that fucker suffers, I want in."

I had never seen this side of Epi, and it made me cautious, to hear him declare against the God of Gods. It was never a secret the disdain he held for me, or the litany of sins he blamed me for. Hades studied us both; fingers steepled together in front of him.

"I don't have a grand plan. Just pressing a few buttons to try and get him to back off." I threw as much casual aloofness into my tone as possible and sat back, linking my hands over my abdomen.

My elder brother would have none of it. He straightened, sucking his teeth as he too, leaned back.

"I know you killed him. I know he's dead, and I know it was you." He regarded me with cold calculation, and it pierced me, the charge of murder. This sin was mine. If he knew, then so did Zeus.

I shifted slightly. His eyes clocked the movement. The guilt. *Fuck.*

"Old scores. You know how I hate to leave revenge unfulfilled." I gestured my hand like I was referring to the weather and not the enormous weight of patricide that threatened to eat me alive anytime I closed my eyes.

Epimetheus let out a frustrated sigh, running his fingers through his golden hair. "Prometheus, cut the shit. I know you killed him, and I know you trapped his shade down there. You don't just casually make a day trip to Tartarus for something as simple as revenge. And seeing as how Ares is the only one that can get into that part of the prison, this was coordinated. Zeus didn't outright say it, but he dropped enough subtle clues. He's readying for war, Prometheus." His words sliced through me, cutting to the quick. Epi's eyes blazed with a cold fury I'd never seen before.

"Why now?" I asked, curiously.

"I have my reasons. They're no concern of yours, but my face, for starters. You're not the only one he treated like a second-class citizen, Prometheus. I suffered too. The brother of Atlas and Prometheus. The son of Iapetus."

I looked over at Hades, who still hadn't spoken. He inclined his head to me, a subtle deference. *It's your call.*

I loosed a breath and turned back to Epimetheus, throwing out a soft prayer to the Fates that I wasn't dragging him into a conflict that would end with him being run through by a thunderbolt. "We may have found a way to cripple him. There's . . . a relic that could sever his power long enough to deal a kill shot. Be sure before you hitch your wagon to this cause, Epi. It could get you killed." My words were meant as a warning, but I saw him disregard it with less than a thought.

"How do we find it?"

I took a deep breath and prepared myself for the chaos that would mean introducing Zarena and Epimetheus.

"Not it—*who.*"

Zarena

CHAPTER 27

The Underworld looked nothing like I thought it would. I wasn't sure if the lack of hellfire and brimstone threw me off, or if it was just the lack of . . . general misery? Every person here, the servants—or shades, as Hecate had whispered to me when one asked to take my bags to my room—looked content and happy to be here. If the woman hadn't had an eerie, greenish glow to her and grayish skin pulled taut over her jutting bones, she could have been a concierge anywhere.

The palace towered, massive and imposing from the banks of the Styx, but inside, it was welcoming. Cozy, even. The walls were stone, the floor too, but one side was a completely open terrace, and the view was incredible. It looked like the night sky and the pictures I'd seen of the Northern Lights. We didn't have anything like that in Louisiana. There were fields and mountains and glowing bodies of water, exotic and colorful dark flowers and trees. I didn't know Hell was supposed to be *beautiful*.

Dro found me staring out at the vast expanse and nudged my shoulder. "Shit's wild, right?"

I nodded, glancing over at him. "Is this what the LOA have, too?" He shook his head. His locs were tied up in a high knot on his head, and he looked every bit the demi-god I now knew him to be. How had I never noticed the power thrumming off him before?

He caught my stare and shot me a grin. "It's different for us. It's less of a place and more of a slip between the veil of reality. You feel it now, don't you? You can taste the power in the room?"

I crossed my arms and turned away from the view. "It's wild. Like how did I not get it before? I can taste the air, the way every-one has their own—I don't know—scent? I just know that this power *belongs* to you. It's as simple as how I know the sky is blue."

"You're *aware*. I can feel it coming off you too. You've always had a spark, but here with these people, it feels like an exposed livewire. How are you taking all of this? You're . . . eerily calm, Z." His concern laced through the words, that protective instinct too ingrained into the fabric of his person to let it go, so I opted for honesty.

"I don't think I've really grasped what it all means. I think, right now, I'm just taking in information and storing it in little boxes to unpack later. I don't want to show any weakness around them. The break is coming, I know it. But for the moment, I think if I'm being honest, curiosity is pulling me through. And rage—at what happened to her, what he *did* to her. I want to take him out, and I want him to know her kid did it." I'd never meant words as truly as I did at that moment.

"Any way I can help, I'm here." He threw his massive arm over my shoulders and squeezed.

We looked out over the rest of the room, at the others who sat at the large stone table. A round, massive hunk of natural stone rose up from the ground, laden with papers and plates of food. Hecate sat on Hermes's lap while running her long fingers through his hair. The air around them shifted, ebbed and flowed, with the movement. Their love was strong, a living thing.

Hephaestus sat across from them, casually laughing, but the room still as the double doors burst open, followed by a joyous squeal of excitement. The God of the Forge whipped around, was out of his chair in an instant, a massive smile on his face as the most beautiful woman I'd ever seen leaped into his arms. She wrapped her legs around his waist, her long blonde hair curling around them both. Hephaestus dug his fingers into the flesh of her ass, and I shot Dro a pointed look as they proceeded to devour each other. Loudly. She was gorgeous, a powerful aura permeating the air around her with the smell of salt water and jasmine.

Aphrodite, Goddess of Love and Beauty.

"His wife, according to lore," I whispered to Dro, and he arched his eyebrows as if to say, *no shit*. Thundering boots rounded the corner of the doorway, causing both of us to tense.

"*APHRODITE!*" a deep voice boomed, and the largest man I'd ever seen blasted through the door, a lethal predator nearly the size of Theo. His muscles rippled from the exertion it must have taken him to run here; his dark hair was plastered to his face, breath causing his chest to rise and fall rapidly. He halted immediately, dumbstruck by the sight of Aphrodite and Hephaestus entwined together.

I stopped breathing as the mountain of a god's aura washed over me. *Ares, God of War.* His feet ate up the stone floor between them, an intense look on his serious face. The myths said Ares and Aphrodite cheated on Hephaestus, and when the War god reached them, they broke their kiss. Ares pointed at Aphrodite, a curved bangle hanging from his wrist. "You. Big trouble," he barked, then slid his gaze to Hephaestus. "You. Come here."

Hephaestus cocked an eyebrow at him but moved closer anyway. He adjusted Aphrodite up on his hip so he could hold her with one hand and angled his body toward Ares. Then, the God of the Forge shot a muscled arm out and wrapped his fingers around the God of War's neck, pulling him close with a mighty jerk. A band of three rings I hadn't noticed before gleamed on his ring finger as he squeezed, bringing Ares's face down to meet his.

"Hey baby, did you miss me?" His tone took on a low vibrato, hungry and seductive. Aphrodite swung her gaze between the two of them, glassy-eyed and breathless, as they eye fucked one another right in the middle of the room. I couldn't blame her one bit. The hand collaring Ares drifted up the thick column of his tanned throat, a slow caress that had me weak in the knees. Hephaestus's thumb slid over Ares's lower lip, and I swear to all that was divine and holy, Ares let out a low whine that had me flooding.

"You know I did," Ares pouted, sliding his hands up, one on Aphrodite's hip, the other on Hephaestus's wrist.

The God of the Forge cocked his head to the side with a devilish smirk. "Oh, my poor baby. Did you two stay out of trouble?"

Ares shot a side eye to Aphrodite, who squirmed. "For the most part." He shrugged noncommittally. Ares's body leaned into Hephaestus's touch, docile under command of the blond god. Hephaestus was clearly in control here.

It was hot as fuck.

Hephaestus pulled Ares in, kissing him with power and pure dominant force, melting the God of War. Aphrodite pulled their attention with a small whimper and then both had their hands on her, lips kissing her neck and fingers tangling in her hair. I pressed my thighs together at the sheer sexuality pouring off them. Andros took a step away from me, clearly uncomfortable with the waves of passion himself.

"It's been two days, you three. Cool it a second, won't you?" Hades's exasperated tone cut through the haze of lust filling the room. Theo and the unexpected visitor trailed behind him.

Ares shot him the finger. "Keep talking; we'll tag team her right here," he growled, but Hephaestus shot him a warning look. Ares rolled his eyes. "Sorry, Hades. You know how it is."

Instantly visions of being fucked like that flashed through my mind and heat flushed my neck and chest. I took a step closer to the open terrace, desperate for a breeze, or maybe a balcony to jump off because I was far too worked up over just witnessing that shit.

Theo took a step toward our direction but stopped himself. The hesitation was subtle, but I saw it, if only because he drew my eye as soon as he walked into the room. The visitor walked near him, and I couldn't quite place it, but they were different yet somehow similar. The visitor was tall, built much like Theo, but with a smattering of blond hair that looked kissed by the sun. While Theo had a short, trimmed beard, the visitor was clean-shaven. Muscles rippled under his plain black T-shirt, and he walked with such confidence it was impossible not to stare.

His head whipped toward me; brown eyes pinning me to the spot as a set of perfect teeth flashed a wicked smile, sharpening his face with a jaw that could cut glass. The stranger instantly pivoted, making a beeline straight for me and in seconds, he was right in front of me, towering in my space. Dro stepped over, blocking access as he stared down the new god among us.

The god held out his hand, large and strong with tattoos that rolled down his forearm and dipped around his wrist. "Epimetheus, but you can call me Epi. I don't think we've met." His eyes smoldered into mine, shameless in his flirtation. Behind him, Theo stiffened, green eyes locked on the interaction.

I let my mind open to the power radiating from the god in front of me. It wasn't as potent as the others. *Epimetheus, Titan of Afterthought and Excuses.*

I suppressed my urge to laugh. As far as monikers went, that was certainly a choice.

"Zarena," I replied, extending my hand. He took it, bowing low and sweeping his lips over the back of my hand. Instantly, he let out a yell and surged back, shaking his hand and staring at the red welts bursting to the surface of his skin.

I snatched my hand back, mortified. "Oh shit, I'm so sorry!" I said, clasping my hands together. Epi regarded me with an intrigued look, shaking his fingers. I had forgotten I couldn't be touched by Greeks.

"Nice party trick." He grinned.

"It's a new development," I mumbled, wincing.

"You're . . ." He stared at me intensely, and I fought the urge to squirm. His eyes raked up and over my body, almost hungrily. "Muse," he finished, continuing his perusal, unaffected in the least bit by the daggers Dro was shooting at him, until my brother cleared his throat.

Epi studied him for a moment. "LOA." He turned back to Theo, lifting his chin. "Interesting company you keep now, brother."

Prometheus

CHAPTER 28

*B*rother.

I suppressed the urge to kick his ass on the spot. Epimetheus acted without thoughts of consequence, and that quality was adorable in its childlike innocence for some, but as a millennia-old titan, it was reckless bullshit. And he *touched* her. My fists clenched so tightly in my pockets the fabric groaned in protest.

Mercifully, Hades cleared his throat, pulling everyone's attention back to him. "I think it's been a long day and—at the risk of sounding impolite—I'd like a few hours with my wife and child before all of this fuckery truly begins." Hades turned to face Andros and Zarena. "The shades will show you to your quarters, and food will be prepared and sent up from the Upper Realm for you. I assure you that it is safe to drink and eat what is delivered."

"Thank you, Lord Hades. Your hospitality is appreciated," Andros answered formally. The authority that flowed from him—one that spoke to the strength of the LOA—was befitting of his people. Hades inclined his head. Andros smiled and returned the formal gesture before stepping closer to Zarena.

"We can pick this up tomorrow," Hades continued. "Epimetheus, you're going to be in the guest quarters in the East wing. We're completely full on this side, but I'm happy to portal you there should you need it."

"And you three." He rounded on Hephaestus, Ares, and Aphrodite, who were standing together, Aphrodite tucked between the two of them. "Stay in your wing. *I mean it*. We all need sleep, and we can't do that if you're sluttin' up the corridors."

"Yes, dad," Ares rolled his eyes, earning a death glare from the God of the Dead. "Great, so we're done here for tonight?" He asked, clapping his hands together. Hephaestus shot Hades an apologetic look, but Ares just turned and hoisted Aphrodite up, throwing her over his shoulder. She screamed with amusement as his big hand came down, slapping her on the ass as he strode out of the throne room with Hephaestus close behind. Hades shook his head slowly, staring after them with a mix of amusement and annoyance on his face.

Zarena

CHAPTER 29

"I'll take that portal, Hades, thanks." Epi shot me a heated look. "I'll just have to figure out another way to casually bump into you, beautiful." The boyish grin was endearing, but hearing that nickname come from him sat an uncomfortable weight in my stomach.

"*Zarena*, please. And I'm sure you'll figure something out," I replied, a quiet but playful rejection. Epimetheus slipped me a wink as he stepped through the waiting shadow portal Hades conjured for him.

"Come on, I'll take you to our quarters," Theo offered, and the air stalled in my lungs.

Our quarters?

If I had to share a room with him, I wouldn't survive it. We'd been interrupted earlier—when he was inches away from eating me out. I had savored the way his hands had roamed over me possessively. The way he'd felt inside of me the night before.

A cold, sliver of regret washed over me, sobering my thoughts.

That would be terrible, he'd said to Hecate.

It was just sex before, and it seemed he wasn't interested in repeating the situation now that we couldn't be strangers. I followed him in silence, Dro hot on my heels. Theo didn't speak, didn't offer to show us around, just straight to our quarters, which turned out to be an entire house clustered into rooms, like those at Versailles. Our bags were there when we arrived.

He turned at the door. "This is for both of you. The suites are split by a sitting room. I'm just right there." He threw a thumb carelessly over his shoulder, pointing to the other door. "If you need anything . . ." Theo hesitated.

Dro pushed through our door, letting it fall closed naturally with a small click, no doubt attempting to give us a moment of privacy.

Theo and I stood there, letting the air charge around us with a heavy, awkward silence. I shuffled my feet, as he ran a hand over the back of his neck, just as he'd done earlier at Gil's.

"Try to get some rest. I'll see you in the morning." His tone was oddly formal for someone who'd had my nipple in his mouth less than twenty-four hours ago. I had half a mind to tell him as much, but then he was gone, disappearing into the sanctuary of his room without another word.

*

I couldn't help but fall in love with the way my room was decorated. There was a huge, four-poster bed decked out in midnight blues and blacks, and the ceiling moved, tracking the constellations in real time. And in the en suite bathroom, the tub was made from a giant cut of what looked like sapphire. I spent an hour just soaking in it.

As promised, dinner appeared an hour later, and it was incredible. Even Dro lost himself in it, and he was the pickiest person I'd ever seen with other people's cooking.

We didn't talk much. A thousand things raced through my mind, each tendril of thread leading down a deeper, darker rabbit hole, but Dro seemed content that I was eating and didn't push me for conversation. He looked a little alarmed when I announced I was heading to bed right after dinner but still made no protest.

I changed into a comfortable pair of pajama shorts and a sleep cami before sliding between the luxuriously cool sheets. They felt like clouds, were the perfect temperature, and the bed was the exact firmness I needed. Hotel Hell wasn't so bad. Soft starlight above my head caught my attention, the constellations ever changing as they sailed across the sky. For hours, I traced their ebbs and flows as my mind raced. There was too much information to process, too many questions.

I couldn't settle.

With a groan, I threw back the covers and slipped out of bed, padding over to the door. I peeked out and found the sitting room empty and let out a sigh of relief. I loved my brother, I did, but I needed to take a walk and clear my head, not have him hovering to make sure I wasn't about to fall apart. I mean, I might be, but I didn't need company for it. Sitting idle never worked to cure my restlessness, and ever since I was a child, I'd sometimes sneak out and walk under the moon to think.

I moved quietly across the sitting room and opened the door to our chambers, checking over my left shoulder to make sure the coast was clear. I snicked the door shut behind me and turned to check the other side of the corridor, only to smack squarely into a large chest, one I'd be up close and personal with not once, but twice in the last twenty-four hours.

Thick arms banded around me, arresting my fall, and when I looked up, I knew it'd be him.

Theo smiled softly down at me. "What are you doing out here, Red?" His eyes raked over my body, catching briefly on the tops of my breasts, and a bigger part of me than I cared to admit took pleasure in his perusal.

"Couldn't sleep." I whispered, keenly aware that I was still pressed up against him and begging whatever gods we were supposed to beg that he couldn't feel the way my nipples hardened at his proximity.

Over my head, he looked down the hallway, into the darkness.

"Come on, I wanna show you something." His breath fanned over my face, the faint scent of whiskey greeting me. Prometheus righted my body but slid his palm down my arm and took my hand in his, before dragging me along the hallway.

"Where are we going?" I whispered, lengthening my stride to keep up with his longer legs.

He turned back and grinned. "To my favorite place."

Prometheus

CHAPTER 30

"This is fucking insane, Theo." Zarena's breath caught as she took in the room around us. She stood in the middle of the Asphodel Library, the heart of our wing. Her eyes shone, bright blue, alight with wonder and joy and *hunger* as she took in the massive shelves that towered thirty feet above our heads, set into the stone. She stepped closer, hands tracing the delicate spines of the ancient tomes no mortal had ever touched.

"Do you like it?" I asked. I'd been uneasy all evening, the knot in my chest pulling tight, the compass's need to be near the map, but I could have done without the other implications that seemed to go along with it. I craved being near her and it was dangerous, for both of us. I let my gaze fall onto Zarena's strong build, soft curves, and perfectly fuckable swells of breasts and hips.

I wanted her, *badly.*

I'd already jerked my cock in the shower to memories of last night, palmed my length until I conjured the vision of her full lips opened for me while she came, and it meant nothing in this moment, watching her arch up on her tiptoes in those teeny tiny shorts.

"It's amazing. I want to live here, with all these books. I bet I could read for the rest of my life and never finish them all." The happiness that radiated off her was a beacon and the knot in my chest pulled toward her, desperate for her warmth. I wrapped my fingers around the research table—piled high with whatever Hades had been working on—to keep myself grounded. "I doubt that. You'll live for a very long time."

She turned to look at me, confusion etched onto her face. "What do you mean?" she asked, biting her bottom lip. I suppressed a groan at the way her teeth sank into the delicate flesh.

"You're a Muse," I ground out.

"Half-Muse," she corrected.

I shrugged. "Doesn't matter. Muses are divine by right. You're as powerful as most minor gods, even demi. You'll live forever, if you aren't taken out by supernatural means. In other words, dying of old age isn't in the cards for you, Red."

Zarena tilted her head thoughtfully, crossing her arms. The movement pressed her considerable breasts up, and my eyes zeroed in on the yellowing bruises. Bruises I knew would line up perfectly with my fingerprints, my teeth marks. I suppressed a groan working up my throat just as a wave of arousal dosed us both. Zarena sucked in a breath. Desire, hot and intoxicating, drifted up through the stone floor, a radiating need that set my blood on fire and flushed her pale skin. I watched as her blue eyes peeled down my torso, over my arms, then farther down to where I knew my cock would be tenting my pants. Another wave, a jolt this time, sent her reeling.

I quirked my ear and the sounds of moans and panting filtered up to me. "We should go. I didn't realize we were over their chambers."

Another bolt of desire sent Zarena careening backward into a shelf. She grabbed it like a lifeline, chest heaving, but all that did was bounce the perfectly natural weight of her breasts beneath that barely there camisole. The desire was so heavy, so thick, it eroded my self-control.

"Is it Aphrodite? And Hephaestus and Ares?" she panted, rubbing her thighs together.

"Yes, fuck, we should go, Red." I ground out as another wave hit us, but she moaned, eyes rolling back as wave after wave of sexual energy pulsed through her. Zarena's hand slipped from the shelf, roamed down her stomach, searching lower, the pads of her fingers teasing delicately over her body. She stared at me, eyes locked and daring me to object, as if I could. I hardly had the self-control stone cold sober, but wanting her, the weight of the compass and key, it was an insatiable urge to fucking possess. I was transfixed on the movement of her fingers, more animal than man as I devoured her body with my gaze. My control ebbed from my grasp, and I gave her a subtle nod, one that had her biting that fucking lip in the way I wanted to.

Her hand slipped under the waistband of her shorts and the moment she made contact with her clit, the whimper that ripped from her lips undid me.

"Fuck it," I growled, launching forward, crowding her space, as I crashed my mouth against hers. The kiss was rough, filled with need and want and repressed desire. I trailed my way down the column of her throat, hellsbent on finishing what we'd started this morning, kissing and nipping until I knelt in front of Zarena. Her fingernails dug crescents in the flesh of my shoulders, possessive and primal as I ripped those little shorts from her body, exposing her hot center to the cool air of the library. I silenced every instinct for self-preservation, every scream and protest that this was a bad idea until need saw that every doubt in my mind was destroyed.

Repeating the motion from this morning, I hiked her leg over my shoulder and slid my tongue up her thigh, tracing around her clit, and if one person tried to interrupt us, I'd rip them the fuck apart. Zarena writhed on top of me, grinding her core against my mouth, seeking and so fucking eager, the most delicious meal I'd ever tasted as I slid a finger up her slit.

"You turn me into an animal, Red, fuck," I groaned, as Zarena rolled her hips, impatient and so fucking desperate for me. I sucked her clit between my teeth, applied pressure until she quelled, until her back arched. Not relenting an inch, I worked a thick finger inside of her silken cunt—so soft, so fucking perfect.

"Is this what you needed, Red?" I asked, lapping through her lips, applying just a slight pressure to her clit while curling my finger inside of her. Her little moans shot through my body, and I wanted to taste her in every way, all day every day until we died. Her chin fell to her chest as she watched me, open mouthed and dazed, high on pleasure.

"Y-yes," she moaned, "please don't stop, d-don't ever stop."

I pressed a second finger inside her, her hips seeking relief bucked in response. I left no part of her untouched, paying careful attention to the way her body jerked and responded to my movements, the ragged heaves of her breaths as they left her lungs in staccato bursts. I slowed my fingers and looked up at her falling apart, caught in the rapture of her pleasure, achingly fucking decadent under my control. The bookshelves rattled, shaking not only from the ferocity in which I devoured her, but the speed at which I took her. My fingers twisted and crooked, dragging rough strokes along the softest parts of her flesh, massaging from the inside until Zarena's legs started to shake.

"So *responsive*." I praised. "That's my good girl."

Zarena whimpered as I explored lazily with my tongue, all the while keeping that rhythm inside of her that had her eyes rolling. She was close to exploding; I could feel it in the way she pulsed, the way her muscles tightened in her legs and abdomen and her release became a singular focus as fire licked through my veins.

"Take your time, Red. There's no rush. I could taste you on my tongue for days. Twice we were interrupted, so I want two orgasms from you with my mouth, then I'll fuck the other one out of you." I meant every word. There was no rush, if it took her hours to get there, I'd give her every fucking stroke, just to feel her fall apart, but she was so good for me, didn't keep me waiting. Zarena locked up around my fingers, shooting her body back into the bookshelves so hard I knew the stone would leave marks. I kept stroking, relentless in the pursuit of her pleasure, greedy for it as she trembled and cried out my name as she came.

"That's one, Red, but I think we can get you higher. Do you want that? Relax for me, give me what I came for."

And she did.

The second orgasm tore through her with no warning, rolling in from somewhere deep inside. She squeezed my fingers in a vice lock, but I pushed through, sucking on her clit, laving the flat of my tongue over it in pulses. Her toes curled, muscles bunched and tense as she gripped me close, holding on for dear life as books fell around us, crashed to the ground, spines askew. A deluge of fluid drenched my fingers and wrist, and I lapped that up too—the sweetest nectar, the essence of life. Zarena, shaking and boneless, slumped against the bookshelves with those sultry, hooded eyes was the most salacious sight.

I needed it tattooed on my fucking body.

I stood, kissing her hard, just as Zarena wrapped her hands around my neck, our bodies responding so well to one another. Sexual chemistry like this was rare, the way we anticipated what the other needed, freely gave it. I lifted her, carrying her body to the research table, pushing books to the floor as I crawled up her sinful body. Her pale thighs flushed with heat, the red such a perfect bloom of color, and I nearly lost myself as I imagined what she'd look like with *my* marks on her there. Red welts of handprints, of fingers dug into soft flesh while I fucked her with every ounce of power I possessed.

"Not the books!" she shrieked, still panting and shaking and breathless as more pages fell to the floor.

I grinned as she opened her knees, allowing me to settle against her with ease. Fingers fumbled at my belt, her trembling hands desperate to have me as she unbuckled my pants and slid them down just a fraction, freeing my leaking cock. Zarena put a hand on my chest and stroked my length from root to tip. Her bare skin felt so fucking good against me.

"I don't have a condom," I remembered, pulling back.

The hand on my chest grabbed at my shirt, hoisting it higher so my bare skin was flush on hers. "It's okay. Just . . . are you sure you want to do this?" Her breathing sharpened, a moment of uncertain vulnerability flashing in her eyes.

I nipped at her chin, and she lifted it to me, still so fucking responsive. "Of course I do," I assured her, grabbing her face in a gentle grip. "There is no place I'd rather be than inside of you, feeling you come on my cock. You are perfection, Zarena. I haven't been able to get the taste of you out of my mouth." I answered honestly.

Zarena smiled and pulled me to her. The kiss was slow, exploratory even, no rush or hurry as she stroked me slowly in her sure grip. When she wrapped her legs around me and crossed her ankles, she lifted her hips, sliding herself along the hard ridge of my cock, her soaked core molten and inviting as I throbbed in her palm.

"*Look at me*," I commanded, and she brought those beautiful blue eyes—eyes more precious than the oceans—to stare into mine. I canted my hips, reaching between us to slip through the mess I'd made of her. Our fingers brushed as I angled my crown lower, and that first slow thrust past her entrance shook me to my fucking core. Zarena kept her eyes on mine, never faltering as I slid into her, filling her with careful strokes, inch by fucking inch. There was no discomfort on her face as her mouth dropped open on a gasp, but I needed to feed her more. I hooked my hand under her thigh and pushed it up, nearly coming on the spot at the sight of it alone as I sank deeper into her tight cunt.

"More," she demanded, eyes rolling.

I kissed her, speeding up my thrusts, pushing harder. Each press rocked her body beneath mine, but she kept fucking strangling my shaft as she flexed and tightened. I gripped her in a tight embrace and flipped us over, settling her body over mine. Zarena yelped at the sudden movement, bracing her hands on my chest as gravity helped pull her farther onto my cock.

"Take your pleasure, Red. Come on my cock like my good fucking girl. Let me see my cum drip out of you," I growled, taking her hips in my hands and rolling her body back and forth. She mewled beneath my touch, the sounds sending bolts of pleasure through my muscles as I slid my grip to the inside of her powerful thighs and glided my thumb over her clit while she rode. This view was fucking magnificent, and I couldn't settle my eyes on just one part of her. I wanted it all, needed to take my time memorizing it all.

Zarena's hands roamed her body, gripping the fabric covering her tits and I decided then that I hated that fucking shirt. I let her continue to ride and reached the hand not on her clit up her torso, palming her breasts. Twisting the fabric in my grip, I wrenched the top hem of her sleep shirt down. "That's better, baby. Take it, wring me fucking dry." Zarena started to shake again, constricting around my cock, and I felt the pull beneath my spine, curling up from my balls, a reckoning like nothing I'd ever felt.

"So close . . . uh, I'm . . . Fuck—" she choked, and I slowed the circles on her clit, my own fingers shaking as I tried to hold on to my control.

"There's no rush, baby," I panted, knowing good and damn well that was a lie as she milked me for everything I was worth. She threw her head back, right on the edge, as she used me to work herself up. Zarena's muscles tightened, shivering, but right as she crested, she lost it with a frustrated little growl that had my lips tipping up. I knew what she needed, could feel it pulse through me like a second lifeline, and I wanted to give it to her. She chased that high, working so fucking hard for it, but she needed *more*. A heavier hand. *Less control.* I sat up, holding her body close to mine as we flipped, and I rested her ass on the edge of the table.

My hand gripped her neck so tightly her eyes flooded with unshed tears, her sweet cunt strangling me with every squeeze against her pulse point. Zarena whimpered with a sigh, and I knew that this was the right move as she turned languid in my arms. Surrendering so sweetly.

"Ah, this is what you want. You want me to take this cunt? To hold you down and empty inside of you? Use this tight little hole as my own personal fuck toy?"

Zarena nodded frantically as I licked a trail of sweat up the side of her face, savoring the taste of her, the tension. Her body pushed flat to the table as I hoisted her legs up, blue eyes watching with fascination as I sank inside with considerable force. She cried out, fingernails digging into the flesh of my thighs as I held her in place and unleashed. The faint sound of beeping punctuated each slap of wet flesh on flesh, but I was lost in an inferno, two bodies merging in a firestorm of need, of push and pull. I buried my cock to the hilt, stilling as incoherent words fell from her lips. I pinched her clit and she cried out, back bowing off the table, liquid gushing around my cock as it leaked from her like a waterfall.

The force of her orgasm hooked me deep and I came on a cry, every nerve in my body flayed raw as she took and took and took. I kept thrusting, kept my gaze locked on her, watching where we were joined with eyes half-hooded. In the reflection, I watched my cum drip out her body around my cock, pearly trails of release that painted us both so vividly in the low light. Seeing it coat and slide over my shaft had her tightening once more, and she came again before I could finish unleashing, a thousand tiny deaths.

I rubbed slowing circles over her swollen nerves, smearing our cum over her flesh, awestruck at the sight of her slick lips swollen and still split wide around my length. "You look so good stuffed full of me, Red."

The beeping of my watch grew louder, louder, and then I felt *it*. I finally felt the pain the orgasm masked, that being inside of Zarena had held at bay. My hand came up to my side, clutching at the unbearable agony speared through me. I couldn't speak—couldn't warn her—as the Reaping overtook my body. With a heave, air arrested in my lungs, my cock instantly chilled as I fell from the cradle of her warmth and slammed to the ground.

Zarena

CHAPTER 31

The blissful euphoria in the wake of the earth-shattering, rolling orgasms Theo gave me evaporated the instant I watched his body fall to the stone floor with a sickening thud. Panic slid through my chest as I scrambled off the table, the first test weight of my body almost too much for my numb legs. He laid face down on the ground, arms and legs bent at odd angles, and all I could think of was getting to him.

"Theo!" Scrambling toward him, I grabbed his massive shoulder and pulled, attempting to turn him onto his back. Adrenaline slammed through my veins, but he was heavy, and my worn-out muscles strained with effort. I tried twice more with no luck, but on the third, I managed to use my knees for leverage, and he flopped onto his back, smacking hard into the stone with an audible crack.

I crowded his torso, reaching for his face only to look into his open, wide eyes. The once sparkling green gems dulled as I saw *nothing*. No movement, no shine. Just a lifeless gaze staring straight ahead into the abyss. I reached a trembling hand to the pulse point in his neck, willing myself to detect any sign of life.

Nothing.

My heart stopped in my chest. Blood rushed through my ears, a freight train of howling sound.

Dead. Dead. Dead.

I screamed, the sound ripping from me could have shattered glass, as I scrambled back from his lifeless body. Prometheus was dead *and I had killed him.* His skin was still warm, blanketed by a thin sheen of sweat from the exertion of sex, his still-hard cock twitching against his abdomen. My back hit a bookcase, and I curled in on myself, bringing my knees up and wrapping my arms over them. Hot tears splashed down my face as I tried to process what I was seeing, reason reaching down to break past the numbness sliding up through my chest.

Voices, loud and frantic, sounded from somewhere in the hall but I couldn't bring myself to call for help again, couldn't try to save him.

Theo was dead.

Dead. Dead. Dead.

Hephaestus and Ares barreled through the door, both shirtless with unbuttoned jeans hanging low on their hips. Ares had a sword in hand—an *actual* fucking sword. Hephaestus carried a hammer as they scanned the room, assessing for potential threats. I wanted to open my mouth to speak, to beg them to *help* him, but I just couldn't break the surface. Cold like I'd never felt before settled over me, seeping deep into my skin and wrapping around my bones.

Dead. Dead. Dead.

The word replayed in my head, an earworm consuming my consciousness. My thighs were a mess as my release and his cum leaked onto the floor beneath me, but I couldn't rip my gaze away from his face. That beautiful, devastatingly handsome face with kind eyes that cut straight through me. The mouth that kissed me and devoured me and whispered such terribly delicious things against my flesh while he filled me. All the parts of the man that had shattered the veil between my normal, boring life and this land of gods and monsters.

Dead. Dead. Dead.

"For fuck's sake, Theo," Ares said, exasperated, lowering his sword. He and Hephaestus shared a look before glancing over at me, but all I could focus on were *his* still open eyes.

"What's going on?" A soft, melodic voice trilled.

Muffled whispers, and then, suddenly, Aphrodite knelt in front of me. "Zarena? Zarena, right? I'm Ditey. You're okay; everything's okay," she whispered, and I wanted so badly to believe her. I shuddered with the numbing cold, and she looked over her shoulder. "Get me his shirt," she commanded, and then there were soft, dainty hands on me, covering my body in the T-shirt that still smelled like him, that was still warm. Several sharp, painful breaths escaped her lips as her skin touched mine.

A sob wracked through my chest. Aphrodite pulled me to her, cradling my head as fat tears splashed over us both. I heard her partners protest as the contact of her skin on mine singed, but it wasn't until we could *smell* the burning that she pulled back and gave me some distance. Hephaestus pulled her hand to his, soothing over the scorch.

"Zarena, it's okay—he's okay." She comforted me, ignoring the disapproving set of the God of the Forges' jaw.

I shook my head. "He's . . . he's . . . *dead*." I managed to eke out after several pauses to catch my breath through the tears. I stared at his perfect body, as still as marble on the ground. Ares had found a throw blanket from somewhere and draped it over his torso.

Aphrodite held my attention, the blisters on her hands already healing. "He's not dead. He's okay, Zarena. He's going to be *okay*." Her words were so confident, and I wondered if perhaps she was crazy. Gods *could* die. My mother had; I'd seen it in the memory Papa showed me.

I pulled back, needing her to listen. "He's dead, Aphrodite, and I killed him. I did. He's dead." I sobbed.

She smoothed her fingers through her hair. "Tell me what happened. Go slow," she coaxed, and I nodded, sniffling.

"We were just looking at . . . at the library when we felt—" *Hiccup.* "We felt something well up from somewhere below the floor, and it just got the best of us and we, you . . . you know." I gestured to the table, to the discarded papers and books that were upturned, to Theo's naked form.

"And that happened, and then he, you know, he finished and—" My voice broke. "And then he was on the ground, dead. He just fell," I finished, my voice barely a whisper.

Ares let out a howl of laughter overhead. "Oh, fucking *amazing*. I promise that's the way he'd have wanted to go," he chuckled, and Hephaestus shot him a reproachful look.

"Ignore him," Aphrodite said and reached her hands down to grab mine. She hissed at the contact that I vaguely recognized was burning her, but she didn't stop. "Zarena, I need you to listen to me. Prometheus is *not* dead. Not really." Her words seemed sincere, but the cold truth of his situation still stared at me from ten feet away. "It's complicated, and he *definitely* should have explained it to you, especially with it being so late, but he will return. Soon."

I glanced at Hephaestus, searching for confirmation of this insanity, and he nodded gently. For the first time in ten minutes, my heart beat again. "I don't understand," I breathed, and they all gave me sympathetic looks, even Ares.

"Sometimes Theo dies. It's *not* permanent and you did *not* cause it," Aphrodite said, emphasizing her words.

I stared at her blankly. "What do you mean he *sometimes* dies? Who just randomly fucking dies and it's no big deal?" My voice cracked, raspy and raw from strain.

"It's better if he tells you when he wakes. Just think of it like a long nap. It's normally no more than a few hours. Should be less since we're already in the Underworld," Hephaestus offered kindly. "We should get you to bed; you've had a big shock. I promise we'll send him to you when he wakes. Little Love, your hands; let her go."

"If you want to see him, we mean. Come, let's get you into a bath," Aphrodite added, ignoring her husband's command. I looked back at her beautiful face. She held so much light and love in her gaze and, in that moment, I would have done anything she asked me to.

Slowly, she escorted me to my room and ran me a bath, silent but not uncomfortably so. I was grateful for her presence; grateful she let me sit in solitude with my own thoughts while I processed what little information I could.

Then, she tucked me into bed—careful not to touch my body again—and sang me to sleep.

Prometheus

CHAPTER 32

y shade landed swiftly on the banks of the Styx, cursing Zeus the entire time. My mind raced to Zarena, to what she must be going through. Guilt wracked through me. I came inside of her.

Then I fucking died.

Mortification cut through me at the realization someone would come to her aid when she screamed or ran for help, and I'd be face down, naked, with her slick still coating my cock. I'd never recover from this, on any front. I grumbled to myself and peered out over the river, pressing the tattoo that adorned my ribs.

I saw him, that ghostly specter that ferried the shades across the river to the Asphodels. Charon and his barge floated silently up to the small dock. I gave him a wave and stepped over the bow of the boat.

Evening, Prometheus. You are late. I feared you would not come. His words echoed in my head, his voice gravelly and calming.

I gave him a sheepish smile. "I was detained, but I made it." I knew he worried about me, about all of us.

Dangerous game, boy. You know that it is harder to rouse from your waking death the longer you push the Reaping. I was afraid he had finally caught you.

I stepped forward, resting a hand over his skeletal gnarled one. "Oh, come on now, ye of little faith. I'm a lot harder to kill than you're giving me credit for," I joked.

A warm rumble passed through my mind—the sound of Charon's laugh. *And yet, here you are, day after day on my boat. It would be more accurate to say you're easy to kill but hard to keep dead. The distinction is important.*

"And what would you like for next month's tribute?" I asked.

Charon's robed shadow cocked its head thoughtfully, considering. *I should like to smell the sea. It has been many, many years since I've indulged.*

Sadness gripped me. Charon had once roamed free of this land, the child of Nyx and Erebus. An altercation with Poseidon over a mortal woman resulted in his disfigurement. Zeus had allowed the insult to go unchecked, siding with his brother over Charon. He'd been humiliated, mutilated, and forced to stay in the darkness. It rotted him, from deep within his bones. Thanatos found him wasting away and brought him to Hades, who helped him and gave him purpose. A way to be worshiped in his own right, with the placement of the coins as his tribute.

I nodded at my old friend. Charon was often the only deity I let have contact with me over the years. The covenant of the Underworld passed after Persephone's taking dictated that Zeus could not come here, or he would risk war with Hades. It was often the only time I found sanctuary when I was on the run.

The side of the boat bumped into the far bank and I smiled at him. "I'll see you soon, Charon." And with that, I was up and over the bow, careful not to touch the water, boots sloshing on the muddy bank.

I started the long trek through the Asphodels, my mind heavy with the issues pressing on me. I needed to find Hecate, figure out what about this compass and map business pulled Zarena and me together constantly. I needed to visit Hermes and get a game plan for finding the Library. I needed to find Zarena and apologize for . . . *everything*. Part of me hoped she'd refuse to see me, while the other part, the one buried in my chest, raged against the very thought. I felt it then, the pull in my chest. This fucking compass pointed straight to her, to the map she held within her blood. I ground my teeth, annoyed by the forced connection. It wasn't her, and I knew I had to apologize for that comment she'd overheard, to explain to her that she was amazing, but how would I do that? Where would I even begin?

Sorry, I love fucking you but the attraction between us could completely be fabricated by this thing that lives within both of us; it'll probably fuck right off once we get to the Library?

The alternative was even worse.

Actually, having *true* feelings for her would be a death sentence. It was already risky enough with her being in my orbit.

No, I couldn't afford the weakness, couldn't expose myself like that to Zeus again. Couldn't put her through the trauma, the danger that comes with being loved by me.

The poison in my touch.

I balled my hands into fists, willing them to forget the way her body bent to mine, how much her need to be dominated and used oozed out of her. How she'd felt beneath my fingers, all soft and pliant.

No. I would put those thoughts away and be responsible.

Keep her safe from the destruction that lingered in my touch.

"You are in *big* shit, my guy," Hermes announced the moment my feet crossed the threshold of the throne room. I grimaced. He, Cate, Heph, and Ares were seated in their usual places around the table.

"Really, man? What were you *thinking*?" Hephaestus's usual calm tone all but disappeared under the weight of his disappointment. "She thought she'd killed you."

Guilt rolled through me, a fresh new wave to compound with the tide that tried to drown me during my entire journey back to my body. The moment I woke up, I'd dressed and fought every urge to go to *her*, to let that tether in my chest bring me to Zarena on my knees and beg for her forgiveness. Instead, I forced myself to find Hermes and Hecate first. I needed real answers for her before I made this right.

"I *wasn't* thinking. I can't think around her because of this shit," I admitted on a frustrated grunt, slapping my hand over my chest once. Cate lifted an eyebrow in question.

"There's a pull. I've been talking about it since I touched the compass, but ever since that night at Electric Delphi, it's constant, *demanding*. It's fucking with my head, and it's causing me to act impulsively, which is dangerous, and worse, it's cruel to Zarena." I sat, shoulders slumped in defeat.

Ares scoffed. "Are you trying to tell us that the sexual tension we could cut with a knife when you're in a room together is the compass? That you wouldn't be fucking her if not for it? That sounds like absolute bullshit, Theo." Ares crossed his arms, staring straight at me.

I rubbed my palms over my thighs and bit back the shitty retort I could feel on my tongue. *They are friends. They're trying to help.*

"Of course, I would *want* to, but when have you seen me act like this? Even with . . . Even before." I swallowed back the words that threatened to choke me. "Zarena's beautiful and funny and smart as fuck, and we would have enjoyed a good time, and then gone our own ways. But you don't understand; this is like a compulsion. I have very little control over my faculties around her, and when she's not in my sight, I feel antsy, ready to crawl out of my skin. Right now, I'm fighting every part of my body that's screaming to go to her."

Ares's eyes softened just a bit. "You think I don't understand that, Theo? I experience that every day of my life." He glanced at Heph, who gave him a look so full of love and adoration I had to avert my eyes. "That's what the Bond is like."

I flinched. "This isn't that," I gritted out, as Cate reached a hand to touch my wrist. I recoiled slightly at her touch, but she just squeezed for a moment before breaking contact. I looked at her, pleadingly. "Is it possible it's the magic? In your opinion?"

Her dark eyes cut into my own and I felt her then, rooting around inside of me. I did my best to unlock the doors, to make her access swift. Hecate's magic coiled around my chest, the tendrils of darkness caressing the cord there. She retreated and shook her head.

"It *might* be the magic's way of ensuring the compass and map found each other once the compass was freed. Also, she's a muse, Theo. Sexuality is how they . . . *inspire*. Not always, but you know as well as I do that it's how their divinity presents. We should also consider that it may be more, may be the beginnings of a Bon—"

"*No*. It's not." I cut her off swiftly and, thankfully, she made no more protests.

"So, what are you going to do? Because there's a traumatized girl upstairs—only just having found out her mother was brutalized and then sacrificed her life to keep her safe, and that she, herself, is a muse. Not to mention that her entire family are LOA and have lied to her for her entire life. Then, you died while fucking her, Theo. You should pay her therapy bills for her entire immortal life," Hermes said, reclining back in his seat and propping his feet up on the table.

"I didn't die *while* fucking her." I defended.

Ares barked a laugh. "The naked body I covered up said otherwise. Nice cock, by the way," he chuckled. Hephaestus elbowed him.

I gave him the finger. "We'd just finished, asshole. And I'm going to tell her the truth, I guess. She deserves to know. Enough shit has been kept from her. I just needed to know that I wasn't crazy, and this shit between us is some Fates-damned horseshit. Not to mention that having any sort of feelings for me, any attachments at all, is deadly. She may as well wear a beacon for Zeus at that point." I threw my hands up in the air in frustration.

"She's already got a target on her back, Theo," came Cate's reply.

I nodded. "I know. I can't add to that." My voice did not falter.

"Well, you're in for it after you talk to Zarena. Aphrodite is *pissed*, Theo. We can probably temper her anger tonight, but with the state we found that girl in. She's gonna take her pound of flesh. You don't fuck with the Goddess of Love like that." Ares let out a low whistle to emphasize his words.

"Whatever she needs to do, I'll understand." I turned to Hephaestus. "How bad was it?" I asked, dreading his answer. The look on his face said it all, the quiet understanding and undercurrent of anger. *How could you be so fucking reckless?*

"Bad." I nodded once and stood, scraping back my chair.

"I'll make it right. I'm going to tell her the truth, and I just, I need us all to be on the same page. No more snide remarks; no more trying to push us together. When it's over, it's going to be shitty enough. Can you all promise to respect that?" I asked, giving each of them a look.

They swore they would, in their own ways.

"And enough with the not-so-subtle suggestions that it's more than it is, okay?" I added.

Hermes cocked an eyebrow. "That depends. You going to tell her about Bonds?"

I wanted to smack him upside his smug face. "*Fuck you*, Hermes." And with those parting words, I left them to, no doubt, dissect the shitshow that had become my life. The journey through the palace felt loaded, each step I took eased the tug in my chest but added weight to my conscience.

Bad.

Hephaestus would not have lied. The bitter taste of regret coated my tongue, mixed with the sweet taste of Zarena still on my lips.

I crept through the doors of Andros and Zarena's chambers and moved immediately to the door on my right, allowing the tie between us to take my feet to her. I cracked the door silently, and the sounds of quiet, steady breathing filled my ears.

Asleep, she was asleep. Good sign.

I stepped into the room, closing the door halfway. I felt the daggers being shot into my back twist as I turned to find Ditey curled up next to Zarena—close but not touching—giving me a look of pure fury. I raised my hands in mock surrender and paused.

She slowly and carefully unfurled herself and slipped out of bed, stopping right in front of me. "Tomorrow, you and I are going to have *words*, Prometheus," she hissed. "I'm so fucking disappointed in you. She deserved better."

I nodded, letting the guilt and shame show on my face. The anger in her eyes faltered momentarily at whatever she found there, and then, without any goodbye, she was gone, slipping out the door and sliding it closed.

I stared down at Zarena, breathing softly and dreaming, her red curls fanned over the dark pillows. For the first time in a long time, there were no racing thoughts as I climbed into bed behind her. Just the lull of steady breathing like a metronome, calling me home.

Zarena

CHAPTER 33

Warmth surrounded me, covering my arms, chest, back, and thighs with comfort so deep it seeped through my skin and muscles and into my very bones. The earthy smell of Theo settled around me; the large arms and hard chest pressed against me belonging to him. His breathing settled to match mine, and I felt the moment he let his body relax against me.

My heart constricted.

This was an impossible game we were playing; his hot and cold antics were giving me whiplash. I toyed with the idea of yelling and screaming and calling him every name I had ever learned, and a few Tati had taught me, but I was too content. Tomorrow I would rage; tomorrow I would demand answers.

His head rested in the crook of my neck, and when he pressed his lips lightly to my shoulder, the overwhelming rush of emotion that welled within me shuddered through my body. Theo's grip became iron, binding me to him in safety, letting me know I could fall apart as I needed. Salty tears leaked down my cheeks, wetting the pillow below me as relief shot through my chest.

I hadn't truly allowed myself to believe he would return. Despite their insistence, and against all I'd learned about the fantastical realities of this world, those hours he'd spent away from his body—away from this realm—I'd *felt* them.

"I'm sorry. I'm so sorry," he repeated, holding on to me so tightly I knew I would bruise. As I curled in on myself a little more, he followed, shielding my body with his massive frame. The weight felt good, felt like it kept me tethered to the world. Like without it, I might float off into the abyss, past the constellations that swirled on the stone ceiling. I let him hold me until I cried myself out and drifted back to sleep.

*

My body woke lazily, still pressed against the warmth that was Prometheus, only differently. We'd shifted through the night, and instead of him spooning me, I was splayed across his chest, his giant hand nestled on my lower back and the other cupping my face and neck, my leg thrown over his thick thigh. For a moment, I just lay there, not ready to face the implications of what waking up meant. The sky outside was still in its perpetual state of darkness, and the watch on Theo's wrist was somewhere around the middle of my back.

It took me a moment to realize my bladder was screaming in protest. I suppressed a groan at the mere thought of moving. Theo's thumb traced lightly over my jaw, letting me know he, too, was waking. The steel bar of his cock pressed into my inner thigh, and I was conscious not to move my leg at all.

"Hey there." Theo's sleepy voice rumbled through him, his words vibrating my chest. It was low and delicious, and my body grew warmer. We were so close, entangled together, and I flushed as I looked up into green eyes, half-hooded, flicking from my lips to my own eyes. I wanted him to kiss me.

I might fall apart if he did.

Theo ran his thumb over my lower lip a few times then, with what looked like great effort, tilted his head back to stare at the ceiling. "As much as I want to flip us over and bury myself inside of you, we have to talk."

His words cut through me like ice, cooling the fire building. I went to pull away but his arms constricted around me, his hand pressing down on my bladder, and I was reminded it was angry at me.

"I need to use the bathroom. Half-human, remember?" I joked, and he let me go slowly, eyeing me like he didn't believe that was the reason I needed to move. I slid my leg over his cock to get off the bed and briefly relished the slight hiss that escaped his lips as I practically ran to the bathroom, grateful for indoor plumbing in the Underworld.

When I'd finished, I washed my hands and pushed back my unruly curls. I studied myself in the vanity mirror over the sink, fighting the urge to cringe. I looked horrendous, eyes rimmed red from crying all night, my cheeks puffy, hair wild. I sighed.

This talk wasn't going to end well, I felt it in the way he'd held me. It was goodbye. I steeled my nerves and swished some water around in my mouth. I'd brush my teeth later, but for now, I needed to make sure he was still there.

Theo was still lying down on the bed when I returned, and I shuffled my feet, unsure if I should just get back in or if he was going to get up. He answered my unasked question with a flick of his wrist, directing me back to the covers. I stumbled forward, scrambling onto the bed, annoyed at my own obedience. He sat up, propped himself against the headboard, and pulled me into his lap. Instinctually, I rested my head on his chest as he stroked my hair.

"I'm so sorry about last night, Zarena. I shouldn't have been that reckless. I'd like to tell you that was the last bit of wild I have in me, but considering our situation, I don't know if I can do that." The sensations pulsing from the circles he made on my skin shook through me.

"What did happen?" I asked. "You were just gone."

He looked down at me. "You've heard the story of Prometheus? About the eagle and my liver?" he asked.

"You stole fire for the humans to thrive, and Zeus punished you by chaining you to a mountain. The eagle pecked out your liver and each night it regrew," I answered, drawing on my brief stint of mythological obsession that everyone I knew had in the eighth grade.

Theo nodded. "When we began to lose our powers, Zeus had to consolidate where he exerted his magic, and I was freed from the mountain, but the curse remained. Every night, the Reaping happens, and my liver fails. I die and make the trek through the Underworld to find my body again. I've got the timing down to a science at this point, but I was . . . distracted." His eyes raked down my body. I suppressed a shiver.

"There's no way to break the curse?"

He shook his head. "It's old magic, rooted in deep hatred. We've all tried, for years and years. It was easier to adapt than to hope for a cure," he answered simply.

"That's horrible."

He squeezed me in his arms. "It will happen again and again. I don't want you to be scared when it does. I'll come back. Haven't not yet," he chuckled. "Now, onto the next bit. You heard me talking to Hecate, and I want to be clear about something."

My mind floated back to the words that had haunted my thoughts for the last day.

"I did *not* mean that you were terrible. I meant that the connection between us is dangerous, and being shackled together won't end well."

I stiffened, casting my eyes down.

Theo let out a sigh. "Do you remember Hermes telling you about the compass and map? How your blood was the map, and the compass would lead us to you? Hecate and I think that the magic is forcing us to be pulled together. That this connection we're feeling is supernatural in origin, and that when we find the Library, it will most likely dissipate."

The words slapped me across the face, and I pushed back from him, sitting up to look into his eyes. "You think it's not real? And that's why it would be terrible," I repeated, searching his eyes.

"I think that the map and compass were spelled to always find each other. Magic demands payment in many ways. I think you're stunning, and I love being inside of you, but I don't want you to wake up after this is over and feel violated, like your choices weren't your own because of a spell. Neither of us consented to this."

My mind whirled, wrapping around his words. "To be clear, forced connection or not, you would have still approached me the other night?" I asked, bracing myself for his rejection.

He grabbed my chin and lifted my face to meet his gaze. "Without a shadow of a fucking doubt."

Close, his lips were so close. I felt the building urge well up inside of me and knew, tether or not, I would have let him fuck me in that club. Against a dirty wall. In the back of that cab.

"Do you regret it?" I asked.

He thinned his lips into a tight line. "Yes and no. Yes, because I'm afraid of what this will become when the fallout hits. No, because you taste like fucking magic, and watching my cock sink inside of you will be tattooed on my memory forever. But when it's over, the feelings will go with it. I don't want you to have regrets, and I don't want to hurt you."

I listened carefully to his words; his last sentence sobered me.

"You're sure that we won't feel this for each other once we get to the Library?" I asked, gesturing between the two of us.

"I have no doubt. This is the result of magic; both the compass and map, and also *yours*, muse." Theo touched the pad of his finger playfully to the tip of my nose.

I considered for a moment, moving to straddle his lap. He cocked an eyebrow but brought his hands up to rest on my hips anyway.

"*My* magic?" I asked, curious, slowly grinding over him. Theo's eyes darkened as he watched me move, all predator.

"Yes. Muses are incredibly sexual beings. Sure, being in their presence is enough to spark *some* inspiration, but fucking one?" Theo blew out his breath, then gripped my hips hard, controlling my movements. "That's the truest form of inspiration. It's probably why your shitty ex was able to discover that excavation site. But when the pull is gone, we won't feel whatever this is, and I don't want you to be hurt. Separating magic from reality is hard. *Incredibly*." He pushed and pulled me against him.

The desire coursing through me amped up.

"Even for you?" I asked, and he nodded, breathing deeply. I considered it. "We're adults, Theo. If we're going to find the Library, we can't do that if we're denying these . . . urges. I don't know about you, but I don't want to pretend I don't want you when there's a massive cock eager to please me. And if we get inspiration out of it, then so be it. If it's truly going to go away, I don't see the point in punishing ourselves for something that isn't our fault." I meant the words as I said them, looking back. I needed some base connection normally, *intellectual stimulation was best*, but I didn't need forever. A sexual relationship, one that curled my toes and made me squirt, seemed like the least the universe could do for me, being as it wanted to upend my life lately.

Theo's hands stilled, his green eyes searching mine. "It wouldn't be safe, being near me. Zeus won't care that it's magic pulling us," he cautioned, but I saw it in his eyes, the gleam of something dark and possessive, even as he warned me away.

"I'm already going to be a target. I refuse to let him take anything else from me. So all that's left is for you to decide: Do you want to enjoy the time we have and then part as friends? Or deny us both and watch me take my pleasure elsewhere. Because I will, and not because I'm being spiteful. I just can't function being this wound up all the time," I admitted, and the hand circling me tightened possessively. My core throbbed.

He lifted me gently, setting me next to him on the bed. Rejection and a hot wave of humiliation settled over me. Theo climbed out of bed and left my room, and I sat there, dumbstruck. He hadn't even had the courtesy to answer with words. Anger welled up inside of me, and I hopped off the bed, intent on finding him and—

The door opened before I got three steps toward it and Theo slipped in, sliding it shut behind him quietly. I cocked my head to the side, confused. Every muscle in his body was tight, coiled to spring, as I waited for him to speak.

"I locked the door and spelled it to be soundproof, for Andros. Take off my shirt, Zarena."

Oh, fuck yes.

I obeyed, slowly lifting the hem and stretching it over my head until I was fully exposed to him.

"Good. Now be my good girl and get on your knees."

My world crumbled apart around me, as I sank down, knees nestled against the soft rug.

Theo stalked to me slowly, deliberately. His eyes devoured my body like he was deciding which part of me he'd destroy first. I shivered as he walked around me, snatched up his shirt before wrapping it tightly around my wrists. He was rough in a way that had every cell in my body aching for him. Desire pooled between my legs, dripping down my thighs. When my wrists were bound behind my back, Theo circled back to stand in front of me. Slowly, he unbuttoned his jeans and slipped his hand inside to unleash his massive cock.

And it *was* massive.

Up this close, I got to see it, appreciate it. Thick and hard, Theo's length stood straight up, veins pulsing under his grip as he stroked in rough, hard tugs. I settled up off my calves, chest heaving, my body shivering in a way that had nothing to do with the cold. I needed to feel him in my mouth, had to taste him slide down the back of my throat.

Theo's eyes burned into mine as he took in the bruises blooming over my chest before stroking my cheek in time with his cock.

"Choose a safe word, Red. Make it good," he instructed. A bolt of desire rocked through me at the order.

"Flame," I breathed. He nodded, pleased.

The hand stroking my cheek ghosted around my collarbone, tracing the purples and yellows there, just as he had last night. He gripped my neck and brought me up to him. I arched, opening my mouth expectantly, head angled up to look at him. My lips kissed the soft skin of his sack and Theo let out a hitched breath.

"I should be more careful with you, Red. Marking up your beautiful skin like that," his voice low and full of quiet wonder. It was almost as though he was reminding himself to take it easy on me. Every ounce of my body rebelled against the notion. I flattened my tongue over the seam of his balls and slid my lips forward, leaving wet trails against his shaft as his green eyes burned into mine, tasting myself on his skin.

Oh yeah, we were so fucking doing this.

Prometheus

CHAPTER 34

I stared down at Zarena with her mouth open, tongue licking up my sack, her fiery red hair and watercolor bruises kissing her skin and for once, my life was good. I stroked her cheek, fisting my cock in my other hand. Her eyes shone, blue orbs bright and heavy with lust. So damn eager.

"Don't be. I'll heal," she soothed, and it took everything in me not to blow all over her face. She was perfect—her eyes, her mouth, that warm cunt.

I gripped her chin harder, stretching her neck to me. "You're going to be a dangerous fucking addiction, aren't you?" I whispered, and she smiled wide, eyes full of heat. She laved her tongue along the underside of my cock, the sensation electric against my skin as I stroked steadily, loving the way she struggled against the bindings on her wrists. She arched, presenting those pretty tits to me, pushing to take more than what I was giving.

"I'm going to show you exactly how I want to be sucked, and then I'm going to come on this pretty face. When we're done here, you're going to go see Hecate and get a tonic for birth control. Once you're on it, I'm going to pump you so full of my fucking cum it'll be spilling out of you, until I can see it sliding down these beautifully thick thighs. Do you understand, Zarena?" She shuddered at my use of her name, and I made a note to use it for these moments when she was slipping into a subspace. She was so subservient, under the right guidance, her eyes glossy, cheeks and chest flushed.

She nodded slowly, but I gripped her chin with force, locking her hungry gaze. "We've been over this. I need your words."

"I understand," she panted, breathless. I relished the rapid rise and fall of her chest, tight with anticipation, the need radiating off her. I'd fucked her only hours ago until she was shaking, but she was panting for it now, begging for it and Hells, I'd give it to her. My need was feral for her, but there were some things we needed to discuss first, before I let the baser part of both of us loose.

"Do you have any words you don't like?" I asked, forcing us back on task. She considered for a moment.

"Pussy. I don't like it. And I don't want to be called a whore or slut, unless it's *yours*. I'll be *your* slut, but not in a general sense. Does that make sense?" She batted those long eyelashes up at me, and I bit back a moan, stroking the side of her cheek.

"It does. You want to be used for my pleasure, because that's how you get your own. I'll call you my little cum-slut for as long as it feels good to you. The second it stops feeling like praise, you *will* tell me, and it ends. Do you have any hard limits?" I asked, still stroking my shaft. Her gaze was locked on the movement, and I slapped the underside against her lips to draw her attention back to me, smearing wetness across her lip. "Focus, Zarena. Do you have any hard limits?" I repeated.

"None that I can think of. The safe word is good, touch check-ins too," she replied. I rewarded her with a kiss, pressed against her brow. "What should I call you?" she asked. I paused.

"What feels right to you?" I countered.

A slow smile crossed her face. "Sir."

I grinned. "Are you ready for me to brutalize your throat, beautiful girl?"

Zarena licked her lips. "Yes, Sir. Please, let me taste."

I leaned down once more, unable to resist the urge to kiss her soft lips slowly, stealing the breath from her lungs. "Get over here and slip those perfect lips over me," I demanded, slapping one of her perked nipples hard with the flat of my hand.

She moaned, rocking up on her knees, opening her mouth for me. I angled my cock down and pushed past her lips, my pace agonizingly slow. Her lips stretched tightly over my length, teeth tucked, like the queen she was. Halfway in, I tested her with a shallow thrust. My toes curled with every kiss, every lick of her wicked tongue over my sensitive skin. Zarena hollowed out her cheeks, molding to my cock in an airtight vice while I pushed to the very back of her throat. I let out a low groan from the pleasure rippling through me.

"That's it, relax your throat for me." I felt the muscles in her throat go languid as I pushed my tip past the tight ring of resistance, filling all the space in her mouth. One hand fisted in her hair, the other caressed the delicate skin of her lips stretched around me. "Fuck yes, Zarena. I'm so pleased, feel what you do to me when you're my good little whore and swallow me down."

The scent of her arousal permeated the room, addictive, and I lost control for just a moment, slamming into her throat with wild abandon. Tears streamed down her cheeks, and a delicious flush stained her chest and the top of her breasts, but I counted her breaths, knowing she didn't need to breathe, but not knowing if she knew that yet.

"So fucking beautiful when you cry," I grunted, pulling back from her slightly so she could suck in a lungful of air.

Zarena choked and sputtered, spittle and precum pooling around her lips. I leaned down, licking a tear from her cheek, trailing kisses across her brow. My hands wrapped her red hair around a tight fist, and we both groaned as I sank back inside of the wet, hot cavern of her mouth. She bobbed and swallowed, ripping my shade from my body with every swipe of her tongue.

I wrenched my cock from her lips after the first shocks rolled through me, and fire ignited in her eyes when a spurt of cum landed on her tongue. I held her hair in a tight fist and stroked in front of her, loving the way she arched her back to me, pressed her heavy tits high into the sky for me to see. She was a magnificent tapestry of desire, wanton and sexy as fuck on her knees, hands bound by my shirt.

"Look at me, Zarena. Open your mouth and take this load and I'll reward you. I'll make it so good." Promises and praise fell from my lips as she opened her lips wide and stared into my eyes as I stroked. The sight of her submission, the supplication, it undid me. My toes curled, hot cum erupting from my tip in wave after wave of bliss that painted across her chest and neck and lashes in communion. I stared down, chest heaving, blood roaring my ears as she wore me with pride, utterly pleased with herself as her skin shone with my desire. I pulled her up to stand and turned her around, untying her wrists before spinning her back to face me. I gripped her chin, soaked with my release, and walked her back to the four-poster bed.

"Back to the bedpost," I growled, and she obeyed. "Wrap your hands around the pole." I tied her wrists once more, so she was bound to the bed, and checked her eyes once to make sure she was still with me. I should end this here. I'd told her I would. She wasn't on birth control, and I'd already fucked her hard and fast in a moment of weakness earlier, but she looked too delectable, too hungry and I had no self-control left in this body when it came to this woman. Her chest heaved as her pink tongue darted out, swiping the cum off her lips with a flourish.

"I can't wait for Hecate. Do I have your permission?" I worked to keep my voice even, but I was seconds away from dropping to my knees and begging her for another taste.

"Yes, Sir," she smirked, lips glistening.

Smiling my approval, I praised, "Good fucking girl. I wanna hear you scream for me, Red."

Zarena locked her ankles together around my lower back as I hoisted her up and slid a finger into her, pleased to feel how wet she was. Her head fell forward as she watched me slide my cock through her lips and press in.

"You like to watch, Red? Look how pretty this cunt looks stuffed." I gripped her neck, forced her chin to her chest, giving her a first-row seat to the depravity of her taking me to the hilt. The first push was impossibly tight. Zarena's cunt gripped me harder than any mouth ever could and my legs shook slightly, my cockhead still sensitive from when she'd sucked me off.

"Yes, Sir. I love watching that cock disappear inside of me, filling me up," she panted as I slid my hand down to play with her clit in soft, teasing strokes, Zarena's eyes flew to mine. "Don't, please, Sir. Don't tease. Finish me. Please, I need it." A noise of approval ripped from my chest at her words.

"So pretty when you fucking beg for me, sweet girl. You're my dirty fucking whore when you need to come, aren't you? Look at you, covered in my cum." I punched up my hips, burying myself as deep as she could take me. Zarena moaned after each thrust, and it was the sweetest music I'd ever heard, nearly unraveling me. I bent low, sucking her nipple into my mouth while I circled her clit in quick strokes tasting myself, her sweat, this moment. "Come for me, Zarena. My good little slut loves to come on this fat cock, doesn't she? So do it. *Now*," I demanded.

Her blue eyes locked on mine, completely lost to the command as her body spasmed, squeezing and convulsing. She was shaking, dripping as she squirted around me. I fucked her through it to the very last moment, fighting back the second orgasm that tore through me, but then I was emptying inside of her, watching the cum slide in and out of her, and with a final thrust, I was done, utterly fucking spent.

Zarena trembled from the aftershocks rocking through her as I grabbed her legs with ease, unhooking them and lifting them as I knelt, placing them on my shoulders. Obediently, the muscles in Zarena's core flexed, and I watched my cum drip out of her abused cunt, swollen and beautiful. I gathered a rogue stream and stuffed it back inside of her before bringing my mouth to her clit. I caressed my tongue over it greedily.

Zarena's eyes blew wide, staring down at me with a half-drunk expression. "*I can't, I can't again,*" she whined, still shaking.

I grinned up at her and sucked harder, unrelenting. "Use your safe word, Red. Otherwise, I want one more. So you'll find a way to manage." I wanted for words that would never come, and she cried out as I devoured her, occasionally stopping to slip any of my cum she let escape back inside of her, growling against her flesh.

"I love watching my cum leak out of you, Red. A dangerous fucking addiction, indeed."

Zarena

CHAPTER 35

Theo lifted my sore body, cradling me to his chest as he walked us into the spacious bathroom. Boneless. He'd fucked the soul from my body, and I was nothing more than a mess in his arms. As Theo laid me gently into the sapphire stone basin, water rushed from the taps behind us. I braced for cold but only found pleasant warmth from both the tub and the water gently filling it. Theo stepped out of his clothing then bent my torso forward so he could maneuver his massive bulk behind mine. Once situated, he pulled my back against his chest, and I settled comfortably against him.

His hands were on me then, thick fingers kneading gently into my shoulders as the tub filled to cover us, the warm water lapping at my collarbone. Theo pulled a stone from the ledge and lathered it with sweet-smelling liquid before sliding it across my skin. I blew out a pleasantly surprised breath at the warmth the stone contained. My muscles relaxed under his touch and I hummed, content. At my approval he chuckled, a deep rumbling sound that sent vibrations through my torso.

"You did so well for me, Red." The stone roamed over my torso, my breasts, and then down, down to my core. He veered at the last minute, massaging my sore thighs and hips before bringing it back to my neck. "Did it feel good?"

I smiled, eyes closed. "It felt so good. This magic pull is something else. It's like I'm starving for you always. I wanted to be good for you," I confessed, as he ran a trail up the column of my neck; the pads of his fingers digging gently into the muscles sore from his thrusts.

"You were. It pleased me very much, watching you lose yourself. The way you take my cock is a work of art."

His touch was soothing, so fucking comforting. I snuggled back into him, loving the way his voice sounded echoing off the walls in this tiny slice of heaven. His fingers grazed a particularly sore part of my jaw, and I let out a soft hiss. His hands stilled for just a moment. "I was too rough. I'm sorry, Red." Regret tinged his voice.

I tilted my head back, searching for his eyes. "You weren't. You were attentive and I loved it. I've never been able to squirt before, and you've made it happen each time we've fucked. That alone should tell you how good it was for me." I lifted my chin a little higher to kiss the underside of his stubbled jaw.

His arms wrapped around me, pulling me tighter to him. "Do you always want it like that? Rough? Is it the only way you can let go?"

I paused for a moment, considering. "No, not every time. I can get off just fine without the Domination, but I love it when I can get it. It's just—I'm so often in control of everything in my life. Men love when a woman is certain and can demand what she wants, but when you need them to choke you to the point of unconsciousness just to get a moment of peace, where thoughts are silent, most men tend to balk. On the other hand, some take the liberty to go too far, and it borders on dangerous without the fun. You read me and my body like a book with pages waiting to be spread. So, no, I don't need you to bruise me or fuck me into oblivion every time. Sometimes I'll want to please you, to be in control. Sometimes I'll want something softer."

His fingers traced soothing circles into my spent flesh as he pressed his lips to the delicate skin just under my ear in a soft kiss. "Whatever you need, however you need it. Use me to take the pleasure you've been denied."

I flooded, heat rolling off me in waves. All soreness ignored, I ground my ass into his crotch and felt intense satisfaction as his cock grew instantly hard.

"*Zarena*," he rasped, tone sharp. "You need to rest. You're still half-mortal; surely, you're sore?" His fingers traveled south, sliding around, teasing my core.

I sucked my bottom lip between my teeth, biting back the twinge of pain I felt through the pleasure. I *was* sore.

"I want more. Just a little taste, Theo. I feel so empty right now." I whined. It was ridiculous, but I couldn't stop. It was like my body knew there was an expiration date on this and was determined not to waste a single damn moment with him.

Theo looked torn, clearly wanting to be back inside of me, but the protective, domineering part of him knew I needed rest.

He pursed his lips. "A compromise?" he offered.

I tilted my head. "I'm listening."

"We have a big day ahead of us, and everyone will start moving around in a few hours. You need to relax and get some sleep, but I know you won't do that if you feel like you've been denied, and since you were such a good fucking girl for me, you can straddle my lap and I'll slip my cock inside of you, but you must lie down and try to rest. No moving, no rolling those beautiful hips. Rest. And first thing when we wake up, we find Hecate and get you safe. Fair?"

"Deal."

A grin cracked his face as he leaned down to kiss me softly. "Insatiable. Come on then, up you get."

I twisted my body until I was facing him, my knees falling on either side of his hips. I snaked a hand between us and wrapped my fingers around him, stroking once. Theo groaned and tilted his head, eyes hooded as he watched me work beneath the water. I lifted onto my knees and lined his crown up, teasing the tip over my clit.

"Settle down, pretty girl," he warned.

I held his gaze while I sank on top of him. Mother of hell, I was fucking tender; but he was hard and warm, and the heat felt so good. He collared my throat gently, bringing my body down to rest flush against his chest. Theo tilted my chin up and the kiss he gave me was soft, and caring. I bit and nipped at his lips, savoring my taste on his tongue.

I was so full, stretched wide around him, every breath pushing my body down harder on his shaft. Every single ridge and vein of his cock rubbed against me with delicious pressure, and I bit into his pec to stop from crying out. Theo reached over to the shelf near the tub and grabbed the only book he could reach, shushing me with gentle caresses as he opened the tome, spreading his wide fingers to hold the pages open.

I tested my hips once, but the hand he held under the water pinched my clit, stilling me.

"Behave," he ordered.

I relaxed into him when his fingers rolled my clit between them. Careful to keep my hips as still as possible, I clenched and unclenched around his cock, milking it for my own satisfaction. With his fingers playing with me, he began to read from the book he held, his voice a lullaby reverberating through my chest as I sank into the gentle warmth of him.

"In the beginning, there was a spark of life that erupted out of what was known as Chaos, and from it, titans were born . . ."

Tiny trembling orgasms rolled through me in gentle waves, my eyes drifting closed with his cock still buried inside of me, listening to the history of his people.

Our people.

Zarena

CHAPTER 36

Soft rustling roused me from a deep slumber. I reluctantly opened my eyes to find myself in warm blankets and Theo very carefully getting dressed. He sat on the edge of the bed with his back to me, silhouette illuminated in the soft starlight. My breath caught, seeing him in the earliest breaks of morning. He slipped his shirt over his shoulders and smoothed it down, much to my dismay. I reached a hand to touch him, and every muscle in my body screamed in violent protest.

I whimpered and he turned, concern etched into the lines of his face.

Devastatingly beautiful.

"Regretting that last round, Red?" he teased, whispering low. A cocky grin split his handsome face as he leaned over to press a kiss to my lips. His hand came up to brush back a rogue curl as I nodded, pouting. "I told you we should have gone easy. You haven't learned how to heal yourself yet."

"Heal myself?" I asked, bewildered. My entire life I'd never been a particularly fast healer. "Is that something I can do now?"

Theo peppered my face with sweet kisses, muttering against my skin. "You were born divine, Zarena. You were always able to, but the skill must be exercised, just like any other muscle. The more you learn, the more powerful it'll grow. I can teach you," he offered.

The thought of him tutoring me sparked a forbidden fantasy deep inside of me. Last night when he'd read to me, coaxing orgasm after gentle orgasm from my bones while he simply warmed his cock inside of me had been the single hottest encounter I'd ever experienced.

Theo pulled back, eyes wide. "You cannot be *serious* right now! You're barely able to move and you're aroused?" His face shone with amusement and I reddened, knowing I'd been busted. I buried my face in the covers, but the movement wasn't appreciated by the rest of my body.

"I mean, it's kind of your fault if I'm being honest. You can't go all dominant-forbidden-professor on me and not expect me to want your cock immediately. It's inhumane. And if you teach me how to heal myself, I'll warm that pretty cock every fucking night."

Theo let out a bark of laughter. "Just this *once*, I'm going to soothe the ache. Next time, you're going to learn how to do this yourself, alright? You've gotta learn. But right now, we need you at full capacity. It's time to find that Library."

A spike of adrenaline surged through me at the prospect and I nodded eagerly. Theo clapped his hands together once, then rubbed them furiously. I could feel the power between them, sense the charge in the air that moved around us. He roamed his hands over my arms and chest and hips, fingertips flitting down my thighs. Every movement pulled the ache from deep within me. When his hands came together at my core, he cupped me gently. I gasped at the relief. Too soon he pulled his hand back, but the pain was dulled considerably. I shot him a look.

He grinned. "Gotta leave you with a reminder, Red." Theo winked, and then with all the speed and grace I could never possess, he was on his feet. "I have to go talk to Hermes; I had an idea last night while we were . . . soaking. You could even call it inspiration."

I sat up, pooling the sheets up to cover my chest, now unmarked and perfectly smooth alabaster. His eyes roamed over my form, lingering on the skin just south of my collarbone. I saw the gears turning behind his eyes and realized the moment before he sprung what he was about to do.

Theo jumped back onto the bed, pushing me flush against the mattress with his bulk as I squealed. His lips traced down my neck and over the tops of my breasts playfully. "So fucking beautiful like this, Red. What are you doing to me?" he whispered into my skin between kisses. The stubble of his short beard tickled, as I squirmed, giggling under his touch.

Theo selected a spot just above my right breast and sank his teeth down. He sucked at the skin, bringing the blood to pool under my soft flesh, and a small purple bruise appeared.

Just one. Just for him.

"Happy now?" I teased as he peeled himself off me and stood once more, moving for the door.

"It'll do for now. Find Hecate." And then he was gone.

I gave myself twenty minutes of self-pity for my soreness and anger at horny-last-night Zarena; she'd gotten us into this mess. I found myself lying in bed, missing the warmth stolen when he walked out of my room. I couldn't wrap my head around how this kind of connection could be fabricated, a product of magical artifacts working together to unite two beings, only to take it away. But Theo had been sure—and Hecate too—that it would simply cease once the job was done. It might have been smarter to cut it off at the root, but what was done was done. I'd ride this train until reality righted itself.

I grabbed some leggings and a workout sports bra that braced me tightly, the one I used to wear while running. A thick pair of socks gave extra cushion in my well-worn hiking boots. I dressed quickly. I had only packed practical clothing since Theo warned that we'd be venturing onto darker paths with uneven terrain. I wanted to be ready.

I let my feet carry me down the same hallway we'd taken the day before to get to our chambers and found the room at the end bustling with activity.

Ares and Hephaestus stood in front of the circular table inspecting an impressive array of weaponry. Ares gripped a pistol expertly in his hands, assembling it with quick strokes while Hephaestus finished sharpening a dagger he then slid into his boot.

As I slowly approached, Ares dipped his chin toward me. "You alright?"

"I am." I nodded. "Much better than last night. Thank you both," I managed to stammer, "for showing up."

Hephaestus's answering look held nothing but radiating kindness amplified by my clear view of him. Blond hair pulled into a knot on his head with wispy tendrils escaping to frame the canvas of his handsome face. Stunned at how *beautiful* everyone was I blew out a breath. How did anyone manage to get anything done around here?

"Not a problem at all. I'm just glad things are better," Hephaestus replied.

I excused myself to seek Hecate and found her sipping something hot from a mug, staring out through the open terrace that overlooked the Underworld.

"Hecate?" I called. Her long hair was wrapped around her head and piled high with silver hoops adorning some of the strands. She was such a fierce beauty, and though I knew she was one of the older ancients, she looked as young as my sisters.

She smiled and turned to give me her full attention. "Zarena, hey! Good morning. Did you sleep okay?" she asked. "Theo told us about what happened. I'm sorry you had to go through that."

She stepped toward me and the quiet thrum of power that slinked around me comforted my thoughts. I wondered if I'd ever evoke such power.

"Actually, I need to ask you a favor. I don't know how long this is going to take, having never been on a quest before, but I'm still half-mortal and for the past, I don't know, fourteen of those mortal years I've gotten my period, as mortals do. Is there any way to, I don't know, stop it? I can't imagine doing all this shit while also bleeding out over everything in the wilderness. I don't know if that's something you can do, but I figured it couldn't hurt to ask?"

Understanding flashed in her eyes. "Yes, of course. I can take care of that for you, and if you want to learn how to control and command your body, we can teach you that too. Is there anything else?" she asked, and I had a feeling she knew the other reason I'd sought her out, the verbal agreement I'd given Theo.

My neck flushed. I pressed my hands together awkwardly. "Actually, there's another thing." I paused but Hecate didn't interrupt, just waited. I took a breath—it was just sex, and we were both adults with nothing to be ashamed of. I glanced around anyway to make sure we were alone.

Hecate caught my gaze. "Anything you tell me stays here. Even from Hermes," she promised.

I sighed with relief. "Theo made me promise I'd come see you about getting on birth control, but I'm already on the pill. He was adamant that I came to you though. Is this inappropriate? It feels inappropriate," I choked out.

Hecate let out a small laugh; deep and warm. "It's fine." She shook her head, still laughing. "I'm glad you came to me. I can help with that too. Theo's right. Mortal birth control is fairly ineffective against gods—especially one like Prometheus."

I gave her a confused look. "What do you mean?"

It was Hecate's turn to look uncomfortable. "He's the spark of humanity. Life incarnate. That makes him particularly *virile.*"

I twisted my hands nervously. "Does he have children?" I blurted, unable to keep my mouth shut.

Hecate gave me a look of sorrow, and I read it there in her eyes: *He used to*.

"No," she replied as my heart ached for him. "I assume you didn't have protection in the library?" she asked, switching gears.

"Correct. Or . . . early this morning," I said, doing all I could to ignore the embarrassment rising in my chest.

Hecate drained the last bit of whatever was in her cup and swallowed thickly. "I'll get both of the things you asked for."

I sagged in relief. "Thank you. Truly."

Hecate gave me a small smile. "You're going to be good for him, I can tell."

Prometheus

CHAPTER 37

"He knows Iapetus is dead. He knows you have the compass. No chance in Hells he doesn't have the roads to the Mountain blocked." Hermes grimaced. I felt inclined to agree with him.

"Right, but what is the alternative?" Ares asked. "It's the only way to find the path."

I considered the possibilities.

"Umm, what's the Mountain?" Zarena's sultry voice cut through the air and I straightened just a fraction at her presence. She walked up to the table, and I had to grab onto the cool stone to keep my hands to myself.

Hells, she was going to kill me.

I spent the evening buried inside of her, and yet a fire burned within me at the mere sight of her here. The tightest leggings I'd ever seen hugged her close, accentuating her perfect hourglass figure and round ass. Her sports bra had clasps up the front that lifted her tits, and it fit her more like a little vest than anything. A small sliver of her waist showed through her two-piece, and my mark peeked just a little above the neckline of her top.

Epi let out a low whistle, and I had to swallow down a growl. My fingertips bit into the marble of the table, pieces grinding into fine powder under my touch. Hades cleared his throat next to me, shooting a pointed glance between my face and the falling slivers of stone on his floor. I gave him an apologetic look and took a deep breath.

Epi scooted over, making an opening for Zarena to slip into that gave her better access to the battle map. My already thin self-control pulled taut.

At least he couldn't touch her.

Small victories.

"The Mountain is the convergence of the Fates. For our people, all quests begin there. There are many pathways, but they all lead to the door there called the Mouth, located near the base of the Mountain. They are designed to test your mettle, make sure you're worthy. Many have perished far before they even began their journey," Hades answered as Zarena sank her top teeth into her bottom lip, studying the map.

Hells.

"We have the numbers. He can't possibly take us all together. Zeus won't risk upsetting the balance that way," Epimetheus argued.

Ares shook his head. "He would if he was worried we were getting too close. He loves nothing except his power and the control it brings him. Besides, we *don't* have the numbers it would take to defend against him."

"There are plenty of us right here, and we have Hades. He's one of the Big Three, not to mention Hecate and us titans. Hells, even Helios could probably be persuaded," Epi scoffed nonchalantly.

"I'm not going; neither is Persephone." Hades glanced at me with a subtle apology in his gaze, but I shifted to bump his shoulder. I knew why he couldn't come and I understood.

"Wait, are you kidding? Why would we leave the ringer at home?" Epi asked incredulously.

I bit back the words I wanted to spit at him: *Impatient. Reckless. Selfish.*

"Hades and Persephone have to protect the Underworld. Three of the four paths to the Mountain are here, and if they aren't in residence, Zeus could use it to his advantage. And they have a child who needs them both intact. Same for Helios. He and Nick have a child to consider and, though he would come if called on, I ain't asking unless we have to. Hermes and Hecate are being called away to work another angle, another piece of this. So, as far as the numbers go . . . it's us," I said, glancing around.

Epi folded his arms across his chest. "Medusa? Artemis?"

"They'll be guarding the other path." I leaned over the map and pointed to the landmark I'd circled. "Last night, I had some time to think, and I believe I've found a way to get us there in one piece. To the Mountain, at least. Hephaestus, can you replicate the compass?" I asked, pulling the trinket from my pocket and tossing it to him.

He looked it over, roaming his hands across the nooks and crannies, studying it carefully. "Yeah, I could. What are you thinking?" he asked, intrigued.

"I want you to make me two more." I pointed to the stairs just off the banks of the Styx. "We start together here. Then, we split here, at the Ravine of Regrets." I slid my finger up and over. "At that point, we each get a compass. None of us will know which is the true one and which is the decoy. Three teams. Three paths. Meet up here, at the Mouth. We wait for twenty-four hours. It's a long shot, but it would at least thin their efforts. This is our domain, we know the roads. Three chances to make it." Silence settled over the table.

"Aphrodite, Heph, and I will take the Warden Path. I know it well," Ares offered, and I thanked him silently with a dip of my head.

"Epi, you and Andros can take the Cliffs. Zarena and I will take the Crucible." I pointed to each point on the map.

Andros let out a snort, folding his arms over his chest and rising to his full height. "Absolutely not. Where she goes, I go."

I'd braced myself for this, knew it was coming. I turned to him but before I could answer, Hephaestus beat me to it.

"You can't go there. It is only for those with Greek blood." His tone was reasonable, but Andros was having none of it.

"Then she and I will swap paths with your brother. We won't be separated," he insisted.

"It's the safest path for her, the one with the most direct route. Theo is intimately familiar with the terrain and can cover it in twelve hours if he's running. It's only part of the journey. We'll reunite," Aphrodite explained.

Zarena exchanged an uneasy glance with an immovable Andros. "No. If she's doing this, we're *together*. Leaving her with one person against the odds we are facing isn't a chance I'm willing to take."

Ares lifted his eyebrows. "Are you suggesting that Prometheus can't protect her? Easy, warrior; you're still young. He's been slaughtering enemies on the battlefield since the dawn of time. I assure you, I've seen him take life as swiftly as he gave it. You will respect him. He has shown you the same courtesy."

I gave him an appreciative smile and held up a hand. "I'll protect her with my life, Andros. I swear it."

Zarena reached a hand up to comfort Andros, who'd gone silent. I could see the struggle within warring behind the demi-god's eyes.

"I'll be safe. We need you on the other path, Dro," she whispered.

In the end, it was her gentle touch that swayed him.

Zarena

CHAPTER 38

Three hours later, we all gathered in the atrium of the palace, laden down with survival packs, rations, and weaponry. A low buzz of nervous energy permeated the space around us, and I glanced over at Andros, who stood sentry by my side, wound tight.

I nudged his shoulder. "Truth or dare?"

He glanced down, lips thinned. "Truth."

Of course, it was. It had been truth since I'd dared him to streak through Mrs. Brown's vegetable garden in the eighth grade.

I grinned. "How badly are you hoping to get down to the kitchens and meet whoever has been making our food?"

A small smile cracked the corner of his lips. "Fucking bad, bruh. Did you try those grits this morning? After this is over, I'm breaking in. I need answers."

I bit back a laugh behind my hand. We'd sat for a quick breakfast while Hephaestus worked his forge to replicate the compass. The food served was insanely good, and Andros even helped himself to seconds. The table had been piled high with bacon, ham, eggs, grits, potatoes, and pancakes. Aphrodite made a plate to deliver to Hephaestus, but Ares stayed behind. He and Dro had, between mouthfuls, discussed some of the firearms Ares made ready when we arrived. I smiled with how easy they seemed to be, their banter sharp and biting.

Soldiers were always the most comfortable around their own kind, and I knew enough about the God of War to know he'd served his fair share in battle. Dro had, too, during the four years he'd spent in the Marine Corps. After the Gulf War, he'd come home and thrown his mind and body into serving people through cooking, often volunteering at soup kitchens. He kept a small table in the back for any veteran down on their luck that just needed a hot meal. Feeding people had always been a love language of his, but now that I knew what LOA powers lurked beneath his skin, I realized it was an outlet for his divinity.

"Your turn—truth or truth?" he asked.

I arched my eyebrows at him. "If there's something you want to know, Bubba, just ask."

His gaze flicked to Theo, deep in conversation with Epimetheus and Hades. "Are you being . . . careful?" he asked, and I could see the effort it cost him to be calm.

I snorted once. "Oh, yeah. I have the pocketknife you gave me on my person at all times." I tapped my left boot. He rolled his eyes.

"Z," he chastised, "I'm being for real. This shit between y'all seems intense. I don't want you to get hurt." Concern shone from his brown eyes, and I was reminded that I had the best big brother in the entire world.

I snaked my arm around his waist and leaned into his ridiculously large bicep. "I'm being careful. We're figuring things out."

Part of that was true; I was being careful. I'd downed some sort of supernatural anti-pregnancy concoction that Hecate slipped to me during breakfast while Theo's eyes zeroed in on me as I discreetly poured the vial into my orange juice. His heated gaze tracked the liquid as it slid past my lips like it was giving him permission to fuck and fill me to our hearts' content.

Perhaps it had been.

"I ain't fuckin' with the brother," Dro mumbled.

I looked up at him, confused. "What? Why? He's a bit of a flirt, but I think he's harmless."

Dro went rigid under my arm, turning me to face him full-on. "None of these people are *harmless*, Zarena. They're gods, Greek ones at that. Their world is full of backstabbing and killing and selfishness. Do not for one second forget that. You're half their people, I get it, but the things they've done to each other, to gods they've known their entire lives . . . You need to be cautious. Don't let your guard down for even a moment. I know I won't."

"I got it. I'll be careful, Dro. Are you going to be okay with Epimetheus?"

He scoffed, rolling his eyes. "I'll be fine. He's not trying to get in *my* pants." He shot me a pointed look and I made a face. It wasn't that Epi wasn't good-looking—he was just as hot as the others—but for some reason, his gaze made me uncomfortable in a way Theo's didn't.

"Head on a swivel, just in case," I teased.

A portal surged to life across the room, and we looked to see Hades, arms wide, concentrating on the whirlpool of darkness rippling there. Theo was by my side in a blink, hoisting my pack from my back and adding it to his own, ignoring my protests.

"After you." He placed his hand on the small of my back and ushered me forward. I tried and failed to ignore the sparks dancing up my spine at his touch.

My boots squelched on soft ground as I stepped through the rippling shadows. The landscape around was magnificent and menacing, all at once. We landed on the banks of a river; the same river I'd almost dove headfirst into. The others filed through, and then the roaring of the portal was silenced with a snap as the smoky tendrils dissipated.

Ares approached me, armed to the teeth with two swords crossed elegantly over his back. "I assume Ogou trained you with your brother?" he asked, and I nodded. He reached his hand toward me, palm up. Balanced on his hand was a dagger, sleek and beautiful.

"Take this, please, just in case. If you press here, it will extend into a spear. Do you know how to use one?" There was no condemnation in Ares's tone.

Dro stepped up. "She can more than hold her own," he replied, and my heart swelled with the surety in his words.

Ares nodded approvingly. "Good. Press here and it'll retract again. And if this one gives you any shit, make sure he meets the business end." Ares gestured to Theo, who tried to hold back a smile.

"Fuck you, too, Ares."

"Not with that anaconda, Prometheus."

Theo flushed bright red.

"This way!" Hephaestus called. We filed out, careful not to get too close to the water's edge. This side of the banks bordered a shale hunk of rock, rising alongside us like a wall that stretched into oblivion. In many places, we had to walk single file to squeeze between it and the Styx. Hephaestus led the charge, followed by Aphrodite, Ares, me, Theo, Epi, and Dro.

We walked in silence for a while, with Ares scanning the area every few minutes, assessing for threats. Hades explained this journey had to be taken on foot, void of magical aid. In this way, our powers would be greatly reduced, almost like mortals, which for me, meant nothing really changed. The pace was fine, and at least there weren't any bugs. The mere suggestion of traipsing through the bayou like this had me cringing at the thought of the mosquitos.

A few miles in, the path widened enough for a few of us to walk shoulder to shoulder, and I watched in fascination at the interactions between Ares, Hephaestus, and Aphrodite. Their banter was lovely, often with Aphrodite or Ares saying some wild shit and Hephaestus looking at them both with a mixture of love and wariness. Clearly, he was the Dominant of the three, and they wanted to please him. I thought of the way I'd seen Hephaestus kiss Ares, how Ares spoke of double-teaming Aphrodite right in front of us . . .

Theo's pinky brushed slightly against my own as I accidentally leaned toward him, sending sparks rippling up my body, exploding at my nipples.

"What's going on in that head of yours?" he asked, but I clammed up, unwilling to meet his gaze. The last thing I needed was everyone around us to hear I'd been fantasizing about him taking me that way with someone else. Who, I didn't know, but I liked the thought of being shared, just to try it out once. Theo eyed me like he'd been able to read me with no effort. My chest felt hot.

A hard body smacked into my front, drawing my attention back to the Underworld, Ares's swords centimeters from my face. Theo's arms wrapped around me to steady my frame. I'd been so engulfed in my thoughts I hadn't realized we'd come to a halt.

Ares turned to me, concerned. "You good?"

I nodded, embarrassed. "Lost my footing. Sorry."

Theo's hands held me just under my rib cage. I'd thrown his flannel around my waist just in case it got cold on the hike, and he toyed with it before reluctantly breaking his hold. His thumb caressed over my hard nipple as he drew back, and I knew he had not only read me, but he was teasing me over it.

I turned around and glared at his sly grin. "Asshole," I whispered, but he just brought his hand up, brushing his knuckles over my cheek. I turned my attention to the others, and the massive set of stairs settled into the side of a mountain. They were uneven and jagged, some steep and some too narrow. I couldn't see the top; it became obscured with dark clouds some distance up.

"How many are there?" I asked.

Aphrodite shrugged. "I don't know that anyone's ever counted. I think it changes anyway, depending on the quest. There are chutes that act as escape slides for those who want to give up, but I'm afraid that won't be an option for us."

With no preamble, Ares began the steep climb. Hephaestus followed, and soon, we were again single file, climbing and climbing until my legs were jelly and I hated the world.

Prometheus

CHAPTER 39

arena's ass peeked out at me occasionally from under my flannel as we climbed, and I decided this was a special kind of torture, one that kept my dick hard as a rock with no chance for relief. We'd been at it for a while now—over three thousand stairs if my count was correct. Zarena's breath came out in ragged spurts at times, but for the most part, she kept her breathing even and deep. Her powerful thighs rippled with exertion, and I wanted to sink my teeth into them. She was about eight steps ahead of me and the view was exquisite.

A low whistle rang out from behind me and I turned to see Epimetheus, hot on my heels, staring fire at her while she climbed. I reached down and smacked him upside the head. He was so enamored that he hadn't seen it coming.

"Stop ogling," I snarled, and he shot his eyebrows up, rubbing his skull gingerly.

"Why? It's not like you're going to do anything about her. Chaste Prometheus, Patron Saint of Self-Denial." He snorted and I grimaced. With anyone else, he'd have been right. But with Red . . .

"Knock it off, Epi, I mean it." The possessive grip of the compass burned through me, enough to steer the venom in my tone toward my brother. He didn't take the warning.

"I bet she's wild in bed, redheads always are. I wonder what she'd sound like coming on my cock? I can't touch her without burning the shit out of myself now, but she smells so good, I may risk it. I've never fucked a muse before . . ."

I turned around quickly, halting our assent, but before I could wrap my hands around his neck, Dro's fist connected with the side of Epi's jaw.

"Watch your fucking mouth, or I'll toss you down these fucking stairs." Andros's god-power pushed to the surface and his appearance rippled, putting his LOA on full display. He pushed past Epimetheus and me, blocking our view of Zarena from below.

I turned back to Epimetheus, who was glaring at Andros. "That's his sister, prick. What the fuck were you thinking?"

He tore his gaze back to mine. "I was just trying to fuck with you, Theo. I know you've had her; you smell like each other."

"She's wearing my shirt. That's why the scent is there," I countered.

He raised an eyebrow like he couldn't believe the denial. "Whatever you say, man."

We finished the rest of the climb in silence as I considered my brother and what drove his interactions. He was impulsive, with no self-control. In many ways, it was what had made him an easy target for Zeus, who'd offered him the gift of a bride then saddled her with an undeniable temptation. He knew Epi would buck against my warnings about accepting anything from him, and he made her beautiful and cunning and smart. Epi never stood a chance, poor bastard.

Exhaustion burned in my muscles and lungs by the time I hauled myself over the last step and collapsed on the ground, breathing hard. The others were in similar states after climbing roughly eight thousand steps.

"Make camp; we need to rest," Ares barked, hauling himself up. He and Hephaestus made quick work of securing a perimeter as I stumbled up to set a fire. The darkness up here was oppressive, and we needed the warmth. The wind whipped around us in sporadic gusts while I searched for kindling. Andros and Zarena unpacked the bedrolls, laying them out. I was pleased that she'd put mine next to hers, and noticed Andros set himself up on the other side of the fire from us; Epi's was next to his.

Once the fire was blazing, I pulled some of the rations from the pack and heated them over the flames, enough for each of us to have a decent-sized bowl. The soup was hot and warmed my bones from the inside out. Exhausted, we ate quietly together around the fire. When the dishes cleared away, Aphrodite rose, stretching her arms high into the midnight blue sky. "There's a creek just through those trees. I'm going to get a quick bath in before this starts," she announced and was gone.

Ares jumped up immediately, Hephaestus rising behind him. "Don't wait up for us." Ares winked and then they, too, were gone through the dark trees.

"We should get some sleep," I suggested in the awkward silence they left in their wake. "Today was the easy part."

Without protest, everyone settled into their bedrolls.

The fire crackled and danced merrily while I listened for the lulled breathing that announced when both Andros and Epimetheus fell asleep. I glanced at Zarena to find her blue eyes staring into the starless sky. Slowly, I slipped my fingers over hers, pleased when her pinky wrapped around mine, radiating sunshine.

"You did well today," I whispered just barely loud enough for her to hear. Zarena scooted closer, until just an inch or so was left between us.

"I felt like my body was on fire the entire climb. What if I'm not strong enough to make the trip?"

Turning my head to fully look at her, I clocked the way she worried the inside of her cheek and squeezed her hand reassuringly. "It was a hard climb. You did better than some gods I know who've attempted it."

Her head snapped to me, eyes alight. "Really? Like who?"

I ran my thumb across the back of her hand absentmindedly. "Apollo tried once. He made it halfway up before he cried sanctuary. A couple of demi-gods over the years, most of them the offspring of Zeus looking for payback. It's a hard test, that's why it's there. To deter. Then there's Ares, who's made the climb more times than I can count."

"Are all the myths true? Like, are they accurate? Because in the lore, Hephaestus and Aphrodite were unhappily married, and she and Ares . . ." Her voice trailed off.

"Most of the myths have truth to them in some way but think of them as gossip rags. There's a kernel of truth surrounded by propaganda. *That* particular myth does hold some weight. Hephaestus and Aphrodite were forced to wed, but they weren't unhappy. She simply loved Ares too. But Heph did catch them together, and their Bonds were shredded to ribbons for the next few thousand years. It took them a long time to find their way to each other, and a lot of pain. But they did, and recently too. They've been married less than a year."

"Wait, what's a Bond? Like a marriage?"

My throat constricted. This was dangerous territory for me. I forced myself to swallow, to control my grip on her hand so I wouldn't break it.

"Kind of. You can be married and not Bonded. Among our people, marriages can fade and be broken. Bonds are forever. Many marry intending to never Bond because in the event you want out, it's not possible.

"There have been a few examples through our history where Bonds were forced by Zeus or Hera, against the will of the recipients. Heph and Aphrodite were one such union. They'd known Ares and Ditey were in love with each other and that Zeus had forbidden it. They forced the Bond, but I don't think anyone expected Heph and Ditey to fall in love too.

"Before they were Bonded, Hecate tried to help Ares and Aphrodite by performing a Bonding. But she isn't the Goddess of Bonds—that lies solely with Hera—so their union was corrupted. It ate them all alive, trapping them in this weird love triangle."

Zarena's eyes were wide as she listened. "What made them get together after all these years?"

"Aphrodite almost died. I don't know the specifics, but they worked out their shit. Went through death trials to get their Bonds reforged. It's the first multiple Bonding in our history. Now, they're happy as fuck and it's all of our problem." I chuckled. She squeezed my hand.

"And Hecate and Hermes? They're Bonded?"

I shook my head. "No, not yet. They're together, but they're not Bonded. Bonds make you vulnerable; it's literally your heart existing outside of your own body. It's power too. But a weakness that can be exploited. Losing a Bondmate . . . It's the most vicious pain our kind can experience. A thousand deaths would be more merciful. Hades experienced losing Persephone, for two thousand years. She wasn't even dead, and he was destroyed." A shiver rocked through me as I fought to keep the old wounds from my voice.

Zarena faced the sky once more, awed by inky splotches that painted the navy canvas.

"Isn't Hades like . . . Persephone's uncle?" she asked, voice so low I had to strain to hear it.

I snorted. "You have to let go of mortal expectations and associations. They share no blood relation in any way, not in the way DNA works. We're made up of . . . essence. Yes, that often comes from sex but not always. Aphrodite was born of the ocean. Athena burst out of Zeus's temple. Familial relations are what we make them, but there is no human DNA to confuse it. Persephone was born of a union between Demeter and Zeus, but as I said, there are some preconceived notions you must leave at the door when you're talking about our world."

"Are they safe out there, in these woods?" she asked, her mind wandering back to Ditey and the boys.

I grinned. "Ares is a killing machine, and I would wish a lesser fate on almost any enemy than someone who interrupts his pleasure with his mates." Zarena's breath hitched as a shiver ran through her at my words.

"You're thinking about them sharing, aren't you?" I guessed, grinning at the beautiful stain of red that crept up her neck and cheeks.

"Yes," she admitted, reluctantly.

"You were imagining what it would be like earlier on the stairs, weren't you? To have them fuck you at the same time?"

"No. Well, yes. Not them, *exactly*. Just to be shared. I've never done that before."

I lifted my fingers to caress her arm and released a relieved breath. "Who do you see when you think about two cocks being inside of you?" I whispered.

Zarena tilted her head back to the sky as my fingers danced down the side of her breast and along her torso, searching.

"I . . . I . . . You," she answered honestly.

"And?" I prompted, flattening my palm down, toying with the waistband of her leggings. "What do you picture when you think about it?"

Zarena's eyes slipped closed the farther my hand went, teasing the soft tufts of hair just over her core.

"I'm on my back, legs bent. You're standing above me, gripping my face."

I circled her clit once. She gasped.

"*Shhhh*, quiet, Red. Wouldn't want to wake everyone," I cautioned, and she clamped her hand over her mouth for a moment as I slid through her wetness. "Then what?"

The hand closest to me drifted over my torso, those perfect fingers moving slowly across my skin. She slipped her hand beneath my jeans, caressing my already hard cock. I sucked in a sharp breath when she began to stroke slowly, in tandem with the movement of my fingers.

"You have my throat in your hands, and your cock is in my mouth. My head is pushed back so far that you're choking me with every thrust. I don't know who's fucking me, but they're going hard."

Zarena's perfect mouth opened in a gasp as I pushed two fingers deep inside of her tight cunt, grinding her clit under my palm. Not to be outdone, she squeezed her fingers around my shaft and ramped up her strokes, slipping her thumb to work under the ridge of my crown. I shimmied my jeans down with my free hand, giving her space to work.

"This is a terrible idea," I choked out when she slipped her palm over my tip, smearing my arousal all over my shaft, all protestations ceased. Her hands, like her mouth and cunt, were pure magic, pure divinity.

"Don't you dare stop," she growled, and the need to please her ramped up in my blood. I curled my fingers inside of her, pressing against the soft flesh, coaxing her pleasure.

"You'd talk to me, ease me through it while I'm being dominated, stretched full. His hands would be rough, grabbing my tits in a hard grip and using them to ride me. You'd pull out your cock, slap it over my mouth a few times. I'd be a mess while you coached me through it, telling me what a slut I am for you both, how well I take your cocks."

Her words had me so close, so on edge that when her hand slipped higher in a steady rhythm, I had to pin my hips to the ground to resist fucking up into her tight fist.

"You're taking these cocks so well. Look at me, Zarena." I watched her head fall to the side as she warred with the instinct to give in—to let me pleasure her, dominate her—and the need to finish me off.

We stared into each other's eyes under the ink-stained sky, the fire so low it was barely embers in front of us while we got each other off. My orgasm crested at the same time Zarena's thighs clamped together around my wrist and I knew she was ready to come with me. I exploded over her hand, twisting and sliding up and down my shaft. My cum was everywhere, streams painting her delicate wrist and my torso as I felt her fall apart around my fingers, quivering with those piercing eyes still locked on mine. I took my time pulling out of her, stroking her softly through her comedown.

While my breath came heavily as I struggled to control my heart rate, Zarena's fingers scooped up the spend on my torso and what was still on my cock. Bringing her fingers to her mouth, she licked them and the back of her hand clean. I almost came a second time when that tongue darted out, tasting me.

"Right where you would be," she moaned, and I was a second away from flipping her over and burying my still-hard cock inside of her, consequences be damned. "Good night, Sir," she whispered sweetly, turning over with her back to me.

I tucked my cock into my jeans and pulled my shirt over my head to clean up what was left of the blowback, before I licked Zarena's arousal from my fingers, relishing her taste.

My eyes drifted closed in a heavy sleep, the second in two days. When the Reaping came for me, I was already out.

Zarena

CHAPTER 40

Dawn never really came, no sunrise to let us know it was time to move, but I'd barely slept, my mind racing. Theo's arms were around me, his torso pressed right up against my back. His steady breathing felt so natural, so right that I almost woke him up and ended whatever this was right here.

He was so earnest and sure that this pull between us was just the magic, but every moment we spent together burrowed him deeper into my skin, infused him into my marrow. When this was over and he left, he would take that part of me with him and I wasn't sure that was something I was ready for. The fair thing to do would be to tell him how deeply it affected me, but this was crazy, right? It'd only been a few days, but the connection between us from the very first moment we laid eyes on one another felt different. Intense.

You're going to be a dangerous addiction, he'd whispered, but I was the one on the precipice of falling over the ledge. He was the kind of man that stayed with you long after he was gone, and I could logic it all away, but the fact remained that a part of him called for a part of me, and when it was over, it was going to gut me.

He'd whimpered only once as he'd died last night, and though I knew he'd find his way back, I'd bristled, so close our shoulders touched, feeling the warmth drain from his body. It took two hours for him to breathe again, for that first gasp of air to break the dark silence around us. Warmth flooded through him as I shook with relief. Not long after, he'd curled into me and I'd let him, grateful just to know he was alive.

I should be fair to both of us and be honest about the complicated feelings twisting me up, but that meant losing his touch, losing the way he mapped my body with care, losing sight of him sinking into me. I weighed the cost as the sky bloomed from midnights to bruising purples; knowing even as I played devil's advocate, I wouldn't end this. I'd never been a quitter before, and with my world turned upside down, Theo was a lifeline. A port in the storm raging around me.

I slipped from his hold gingerly, doing my best not to wake him, but he cracked an eye as soon as I stood.

"Where are you running off to, Red?" His sleepy drawl was sexy as hell, his voice a rasp against my skin. I had to focus to keep my knees from buckling.

"Bathroom. And I need to brush my teeth." His taste lingered in my mouth. I needed it out so I could think clearly.

He nodded, sitting up. "Straight through those trees is the creek. This area is protected thanks to Ares and Hephaestus, so you're safe. But be careful, those three could be anywhere," he teased, and I rolled my eyes before grabbing my small hygiene bag from my pack.

He stretched, exposing his bare torso, folding those large hands behind his head as he laid back giving me a perfect view of the eagle tattooed across his side. It was so realistic, so lifelike. His eyes raked up and down my body, drinking me in.

I tore across the clearing and set off for the trees before my better sense was overridden by the feral little horny gremlin, those green eyes activated with less than a look. The clearing of trees thinned in the middle, the shade lightening. I stepped over several gnarled branches as I made my way through; the blanket of protection in the air coated my skin in an electric thrum. I wasn't sure if the magic was just stronger here or if I was homing on it in a way I'd never known to do before. There was still so much I needed to learn, so much to explore.

Voices caught my attention, carried on a gust of wind tearing through the clearing. No, not voices. *Grunts.*

Deep, guttural moans ricocheted off the trees, amplified by whatever sphere of protection settled over this place. The wet smacks of flesh on flesh startled me, and then, at once, my hearing zeroed in, amplified as though I were mere feet away from the source. My head whirled.

"*So fucking tight . . . squeezing my cock so well.*" Hephaestus's voice slammed into me, his tone low, authoritative. Heavy panting followed his praise along with a sharp crack like a slap.

"*Who said you could touch your cock, Ares, hmm? That's mine. If you want to touch it, you ask nicely.*" Another slap, another moan.

"*Beg me for it, Ares. Beg me to touch it and I'll make you sing, baby.*" A breathy moan resounded, shooting straight to my core.

"*Please, please,*" Ares begged. The unmistakable sounds of a cock being jerked reached my ears, and I stumbled before steadying myself against a tree as a wave of lust washed over me, much like it had in the library of the Underworld.

"*There you go, my good boy. Aphrodite isn't here to swallow this cock, so shoot it in my mouth while I fuck this hole . . .*" A strangled cry fell from Ares's mouth.

"*Fucking delicious.*" Hephaestus praised between thrusts, and images of him licking the cum from his lips and mouth flashed through my mind. "*Again,*" he demanded, more sounds of him fisting Ares's cock ramped up. I almost choked on air, rife with sex and desire.

"Zarena!" Several snaps in front of my face brought me crashing back into my body, breath heaving. I looked around bewildered.

Aphrodite crowded my space, immaculately put together with her long hair in a high pony, an amused smirk on her face. "It's about to get really good; I hated to interrupt but you looked a little panicked."

Shame washed over me, burning up my cheeks being caught with my proverbial hands down my pants. The sounds grew louder. More frenzied. *Fuck.* I focused on literally anything else, willing their intimate moment to remain between them. "I'm so sorry, Aphrodite. I wasn't trying to listen, it was—" I began, mortified, but she waved away my apology.

"Oh, call me Ditey. And no worries, they aren't shy. They're intentionally being loud to punish me." She rolled her eyes. At my confusion, her lips quirked in a mischievous grin. "I like to watch, but I was 'bad' last night so I don't get to this morning." I stifled a laugh, knowing that whatever punishment she got she probably enjoyed. Game recognized game, and the Goddess of Love was as much a brat as I.

Relatable.

Ditey's eyes fell onto the small bag clutched in my arms. "Are you heading to the creek? I was too. Want to go down together?" she offered. I nodded, eager to get out of this clearing. The dense greenery gave way to a small river flowing with soft luminance. It didn't feel sinister like the Styx when it reached out for me. Ditey bent near the edge and washed her hands in the water. "If you go around that rock you'll have some privacy."

I returned a few minutes later, a little more grounded. Following the Goddess of Love's example, I dipped my hand in the flowing river, finding it cool to the touch, but not frigid. Squatting down, I uncapped my toothpaste and coated my toothbrush, doing my damnedest not to laugh at the act of such a mundane task when I was in the literal Underworld. Aphrodite remained quiet as I brushed, eyes trained out over the water, small tensions radiated from her, as though she were working herself up to something.

"I knew your mother," she finally said. The silence sat heavier between us as my hand slowed to a stop. Heart beating too fast in my chest, I spat out the rest of the foam in my mouth, rinsing with the cold water. The agony in the way she spoke unsettled me. The regret sharpened her words to points that stung to hear.

"People keep telling me that they knew her, but they aren't really telling me things about her." I sat next to the Goddess of Love and Beauty and waited.

Aphrodite sucked in a deep breath, nails digging into the tops of her thighs. "We were friends, for a time. You—" she faltered, side-eyeing me wearily—"look so much like her, Zarena. It's a little unnerving." A weak laugh left her full lips, it too, bitter. I leaned in just a bit closer.

"I don't know what you know about our history, but things were not always as they are now between the boys and me. Many times over the years we were estranged, and we took lovers. Well, Ares and I took lovers. Heph preferred the company of friends rather than taking others to bed." She glanced again at me nervously, picking at her nails.

"Your mother was enigmatic, and, much like you, when she entered the room, people noticed. She was also incredibly just, and fairness mattered to her. I used to joke she should have been the muse of justice, or that she was possibly the child of Themis, Theo's mom." A dark look passed over her face. "Not that it would have been possible, of course. She was long dead before Clio came into existence." A sharp jolt sliced through me. Theo's mom. Long dead.

Like mine.

"I thought there were rules for killing gods, that it was forbidden?" I asked. "Theo and Hermes explained why it was a big thing that Iapetus was gone."

Aphrodite's eyes softened. "There are but Zeus bends and breaks the rules he wants. Themis died during the Titanomachy—the great war between titans and gods. More of our people than I care to admit were lost. And Persephone killed Minthe a little over a year ago. It's rare and ill-advised, but it *does* happen. There's a reason the justice systems throughout human history have been corrupt. Theo has tried his best to make sure Themis wasn't forgotten, and we've done what we can to immortalize her, but the absence of her power is noticeably felt every time an injustice goes unpunished."

"That's so terrible."

Aphrodite swallowed, her throat working around words that obviously cost her something to share.

"Yeah. It is. Clio was the only muse not sired by Zeus, and it was horrible the way he lusted after her. He couldn't touch her, yet. She was protected as long as she stayed at the Temple of Apollo, as long as she held on to her maidenhood. If she gave herself to another and a marriage wasn't arranged, in his mind, she would be fair game. He couldn't take her by force the first time; muses have their own rules, deep law laid down by the Fates. Completely barbaric, but rules are rules." Disgust laced her tone as my stomach tightened with unease.

"But your mother was willful. She met Adonis and fell for him, and he loved her. When Zeus found out about their affair, he watched her like a hawk, waiting for her to give herself to Adonis. He planned to claim her for his own, as though she were a prize for him to take. I spent a lot of time in Zeus's camp and figured out what he was up to, and though I begged her to end it, begged her to either push for marriage or to stay at the temple. She refused to be tied down. I—" Her voice cracked.

"I am ashamed of how badly I hurt her and will never forget the look of betrayal on her face when she walked in on us together, but it kept her safe. For a while. She hated me from then on, and I deserved it, but I would do it again, if it meant giving her a little more time."

Tears flowed unchecked down the sides of her cheeks. My hands shook. "Zeus got to her anyway in the end, but I heard she made him suffer for it though," she said miserably. "I wish I had done more. Gotten her out of there for good. She died, thinking I betrayed her, and I did. But I loved her anyway."

For years and years, she'd sat with this. A small part of me envied her and the others. Envied their grief. It was tied to tangible relationships, to real memories and moments. Something I'd never get to have. I started to reach for Aphrodite but then remembered my touch would scorch her and drew back.

She looked at me ruefully, sniffling. "I'd deserve it if you did."

I shook my head. "I can't speak for her, but in my book, I've got no beef. I don't agree with the way it happened, but I know things like this aren't always black and white. I have a best friend who I love more than my own life, and if I knew a man planned to kidnap and violate her because she refused to heed my warnings, I'd rather she hate me than go through that pain. You tried to save her." Anger welled up in my chest, bitter and hot at the mere thought of Tatiana in danger. "The only one who needs to suffer is Zeus." I stood, brushing the dirt from my bottom.

"And he fucking will," I vowed.

Aphrodite rose, giving me a grateful smile as we set off back toward camp. She felt lighter, but I felt hardened. Ravaged. Each new piece of my mother's life stoked a pyre of rage inside me, consuming in a way I'd never known. I sucked in a deep breath, settling my mind. There would be time for retribution. I needed to pack this feeling away and save it for when I could use it to my advantage.

I turned to Aphrodite, searching for a change of subject, and with my newfound divinity, there was no shortage of questions. Instead of something profound, or intellectual, I blurted, "So, Hephaestus and Ares are fully together, then each of them with you? Is that normal in our world?" In the end, curiosity won out against my good manners.

She smiled. "It was unheard of to Bond to more than one person—our case was an exception. But many of our kind don't believe in the conventional roles that apply to relationships."

I cocked my head and gave her an appreciative look. "Good for you, girl. I mean that."

She laughed. "They're a handful, for sure. If you have any other questions, I'm an open book."

I considered for a moment how much of that she meant.

"I never thought Ares would be a bottom? But I guess there's something to be said about stereotypes," I commented, the filter between my brain and mouth all but broken. She let out a wail of laughter, raising her eyebrows.

"Babes, Ares hasn't ever bottomed for anyone other than Heph in his entire existence. That man is pure dominance; it *leaks* from him. But . . . Hephaestus can bend steel to his will, and Ares is nothing if not a weapon of war, forged from iron. He is very much in charge when it's just the two of us. Sometimes Heph lets the control go; with each other, they switch. They swapped three or four times last night."

"Oh, my damn, did y'all get any sleep?"

She shrugged. "We're possibly heading into battle. Bloodlust gives us strength far better than a good night's sleep ever could."

"Noted."

Prometheus

CHAPTER 41

Zarena and Aphrodite returned to camp a little after Heph and Ares made their way in, and I was grateful for the restraint I'd shown in not immediately going to get her when she'd been gone longer than expected. With camp packed and ready to move, I dug around in my bag for the three identical compasses forged by Hephaestus. I felt a small twinge of guilt at the subterfuge; none of them knew that I no longer needed the compass to find the Library. No, I needed *Zarena*.

Hermes came to the same conclusion I had: Keep the loop as small as possible; and that loop consisted of Zarena, myself, Hecate, Hermes, and Hades. Too many in Hermes's mind, and he'd said as much when we informed Hades. I hated that I was inclined to agree with him, but in the event of an attack, it was better for them to try to take an object rather than a person. I tossed a compass at random to Andros and another to Ares.

Epimetheus rolled his eyes. "What, I don't get to carry the compass? Don't trust me, brother?"

"What happens if you're attacked and need to take your beast form? Does your lion or bear have pockets now, or have you taken to changing into a kangaroo in the heat of battle?" I asked. He threw up his middle finger, narrowing his eyes. "Nice, real mature."

The rest of our company milled around, readying for their goodbyes. A small lilac growing near the tree line caught my eye, and I bent down, scooping it up. Aphrodite moved to speak with Hephaestus, leaving Zarena alone to check her pack, her pale eyelashes dusting over her cheeks as she focused on her task. I sidled up to her quietly, tapping her shoulder.

"Hey there," she said, eyes catching on my hand as she did a double take.

I flipped my hand over to reveal the tiny purple flower.

The gentle smile she gave me was radiant, the brightest light on this mountain shelf. Zarena's curls, pulled back into a ponytail, bounced around in the Asphodel breeze. Tiny wisps escaped the tie, framing her face like a portrait, like a dream. Her fingers brushed mine as she lifted the flower carefully between her fingers, twirling the tiny stalk to examine it. I looked at her, staring at the bloom, wishing I could freeze time and capture the moment. Here on a mountain surrounded by darkness, she was as resilient as these flowers, the freckles dusting the bridge of her nose a spray of fire against soft skin, the startling blue of her eyes bright. I couldn't look away.

Then she began to shake. Her smile faltered, eyes glossing over, her body still as death. I stared horrified as her eyes rolled, milky whites eating up the crystalline blues, her grip on the lilac a stranglehold.

"Red!" I shouted, taking her shoulders in my hands and giving her a shake. The others rushed over, all but Andros keeping a respectful distance, but she was seeing without seeing, somewhere neither of us could reach.

"Z, can you hear me?" he asked, pushing me out of the way. I surrendered one shoulder, the loss of touch an agony, but at his voice, a small bubble of laughter broke past her lips. Melodic, nearly childlike in wonder. The cloud in her eyes cleared, the smile on her parted lips returning, then falling as she took in our panicked faces with confusion.

"What's wrong?"

"What's wrong?" Andros asked, eyebrows knitting together as he towered over his sister in concern. "You went full *Exorcist* on us for a second, Z. What the fuck was that?"

Her face lit up in alarm. "I did? I didn't know. I just touched that flower, and I don't know what happened, but I saw its life. Saw the seed germinate and split and breathe through the soil; watched it reach toward the sky and bloom in the darkness. It was beautiful, Dro. I felt the magic it took to build, felt the rush in the soil." She gripped his shoulders back, speaking animatedly, eyes bright.

Aphrodite cleared her throat. "She's a Witness."

Reverent words, spoken in a manner that lent to the greatest of powers. The Goddess of Love pushed forward a few paces and lifted the bangle she kept loose on her wrist so Zarena could touch it without touching her skin. Wordlessly, Zarena reached out for it, the corners of her eyes squinting down as though she could see something the rest of us couldn't. My grip on her shoulder tightened as again, her eyes went white the moment she touched the metal.

Her eyes blew wide as a thousand emotions passed across her features. Sorrow, joy, happiness—silent tears fell down her face as her eyes returned to their usual blue. Her body trembled beneath my touch, cheeks shining from the tear tracks.

She turned to Hephaestus. Broke from my touch and walked right up to him. "You sacrificed yourself for them," she said, her voice shaking. Heph regarded her carefully but dipped his chin in confirmation. "And you'd do it again."

It was a statement rather than a question, but Heph answered anyway.

"Without hesitation."

They stared at each other for a long moment before Zarena wiped her nose and tears with her arm. "I saw it. So much of it, all these moments. How is that possible?"

Ditey shifted. "A Witness is a type of oracle. Oracles of divine birth are extremely rare. Witnesses even more so. Hecate is one. Melia as well. It works differently for each of you, but it seems like yours is triggered by objects imbued with emotional significance."

"Are you sure? That's never, I mean, if I was born with it, why is this the first time that's ever happened?" She asked, retreating closer to me, seeking comfort. I relished it, opened my arms to tuck her against my side, not caring how reckless the motion was.

"You're in the Underworld. Think of it like being submerged in a pool of divinity. It's in the water, the earth beneath us, even the air. You're breathing it in, and your powers are waking up," I answered, brushing a tendril of her hair back as she stared up at me, face open and earnest, seeking knowledge. I wanted to feed it to her, dripped from my lips to hers, the rest of our company forgotten.

"While Persephone was imprisoned, nothing grew in the Underworld. I think what you witnessed was the burst of magic that flew through the land at her homecoming. I think it caused that flower to grow, making it significant. You witnessed it Become. This bangle was forged with love and heartbreak and choosing. It being remade after Hephaestus died was a crucial part of my Becoming," Aphrodite offered, breaking the spell between us. Zarena took a step backward, slipping out of my hold, heat blooming over her cheeks.

"Is it dangerous?" Andros asked, eyeing us warily.

"She'll learn to control it," Aphrodite assured him, before turning to lock eyes with Zarena. "But be careful. Not all parts of Becoming are pleasant; you'll feel those just as deeply."

*

Zarena stayed close to Andros while we made the trek to the Ravine, their heads bent low. Aphrodite's revelation bounced around in my mind alongside everything else, and I wondered what Zarena might see when she touched me. Fates knew I was held together like a mad scientist's doomed fair project, Hells, I had the emotional and physical scars to prove it. A shudder rippled through me at the mere thought she could be subjected to the darkness that dwelled just below my skin. The last thing that woman needed was me bleeding all over her.

Questions without answers plagued me all the way to the grove where the Ravine diverged. Each path offered its own resistance, its own obstacles, but they all led to the same point. An opening on the path revealed four distinct roads as we huddled together. Andros hugged Zarena tight against him, crushing her in massive biceps as she buried her head in his chest. When they finally broke apart, his jaw set, the LOA looked ready to burn down the world. "Keep your stance steady. Don't drop your fist on the follow through," he reminded her and she dipped her chin. Next to her big brother, she looked young.

So fucking young.

"I'll see you soon. Promise." She extended her pinky to him with a watery smile that he returned with a strained one, hooking his own around hers.

"Promise." He stepped back and hoisted his pack.

I turned to my own brother, hovering awkwardly just out of the way. "Be safe, Epi. If you get into trouble, get to the Cave of—"

"Cave of Mentax—yeah, I know. I've made this trek before, remember?" He shifted uncomfortably. He *had* made this journey once, to save his wife, Pandora. An unsuccessful journey, but he'd gone all the way. Seeing Andros and Zarena together twisted a tiny knife between my ribs at the contrast with my own brothers. We never had a chance to become close, the wars and politics of Olympus stripped those opportunities away.

The death of Pandora destroyed the rest.

I clapped him once on the shoulder. Across the crossroads, Ares shook Andros's hand firmly. "Give 'em hell," the God of War barked. The LOA shot him an understanding grin. Ares turned to Zarena, careful not to touch her. "Remember, the business end is for anyone who gives you shit."

"Will do. You be a *good boy* and stay out of trouble." She smirked as Ditey snorted with laughter.

Ares shot her an amused wink as he hoisted up his ruck and started down the path. "I like her," he quipped as he passed before stopping to add, "don't die, fucker" to me over his shoulder. The rest of us moved to the beginning of our respective paths, nervous energy thrumming through the gathered.

Zarena stared at the solitary empty one with confusion. "What's down the fourth path?"

A unanimous "Labyrinth," resounded from the Greeks, unease clear in our tones. She pursed her lips, the implication clear. "Yikes."

"Twenty-four hours," I reminded everyone, bringing my watch up to synchronize. The others did the same. "We'll see you at the Mouth."

Step by step, we set off down our respective paths, delving deeper into the Hells until the surrounding trees thickened to the point of obstruction. I listened out for lurking threats, senses on high alert, but the Asphodels fell silent around us. The only sounds filling my ears were from our own breaths and the crunch of the path underfoot.

Zarena

CHAPTER 42

The trees thinned the farther along the path we walked. Fresh earth gave way to sediment, hard and compact, devoid of color or life. Theo stayed quiet, but I didn't mind the silence. Every day I'd taken in more unbelievable information, and I feared I was getting close to my limit. Those neat little boxes I compartmentalized it all in started to rattle on the shelves of my mind, some close to overflowing. How much shit could one person be expected to find out about themselves, their family, the universe before they were allowed to crack? I shivered from the barren cold settling in my bones from the frigid air.

We hiked higher along the barren landscape, the air razor thin as it sliced against my lungs, the open space oppressive as I tried to unpack a little of the clutter in my mind. I was a Witness, which meant I'd started to manifest some god-like powers. The academic in me took the reins, studying the events on a replay in my mind's eye as we moved. I'd watched the flower bloom, felt its magic blossom in a state of awed nirvana, but touching Aphrodite's bangle felt much different. Watching Hephaestus use his hammer to break apart the earth, sacrificing himself and the most horrific monster of nightmares in a pit of lava evoked the opposite reaction.

Extreme emotions wrapped up each of those objects, one joy, one pain, leaving me to conclude that it was those extremes calling me that produced visions. Otherwise, I'd be having a moment touching everything. Each item in this world had a story, a thousand hands that touched it. What made me *see*, I hypothesized, was some sort of extreme psychic imprinting on the physical object.

Too much. It was too much.

The emotion of those moments, the pain and loss of the circumstances of my birth, it all welled up in a wave, battening back the barriers of logic and reason even as I clung to them, digging my fingers in until my hands went numb from the effort. As if my thoughts were screaming for him, Theo grabbed my hand in his, brought my trembling fingers to his lips. "You wanna talk about it?"

I sniffled, looking away. "Would it be okay if I couldn't right now?"

He nodded, stroking the back of my hand with his thumb. "Of course. We can talk when you're ready, but I'm here. I can't even imagine what you're going through." Sincere words from kind lips. I melted into his touch a little more, needing what I knew I couldn't ask for, but Theo didn't make me voice it. He stopped, pulling me up short, his hands roaming over my exposed shoulders, pushing warmth from his palms over the goose bumps covering my arms.

He cursed under his breath. "Red, you're freezing. Why didn't you say anything?" I didn't protest as he pulled me close to him, slipping his hands down to the knot holding his shirt around my waist. I just stood there, cold and numb as I watched him quietly undo the tie and make quick work of sliding my arms through his flannel. I barely registered him pulling me against his broad chest. Warmth slammed into me, like a cozy fire emanating from his body, and I arched into it, seeking it out as I snuggled closer. Theo's arms wrapped around me, and it felt so fucking good my knees almost gave out.

"We've been walking for hours. Shit, Red, you're a popsicle."

I didn't bother to tell him the numb was probably from delayed shock, not the weather, because I simply didn't have the energy. But something he'd said gnawed at me, causing me to pull back, bewildered. "Hours? What, no? It's been like maybe half an hour," I protested, but Theo lifted his watch to my face, showing me the twenty-four-hour countdown.

Twenty-one hours left.

"You've barely spoken the last few hours, I figured you were in deep thought, but I'm worried you're disassociating. I was going to suggest we stop in another hour or so to rest, but now I think we should sit for a second." Concern dripped from Theo's words as he walked us over to a felled tree and set the packs on the ground. He'd refused to let me carry mine, but the burden didn't seem to be getting to him as much as I was sure it would have weighed on me. He sat flush to the ground, his back against the spruce, and signaled for me to climb into the gap between his legs. I scrambled to sit, groaning as he wrapped me up tightly in his arms. I laid my cheek in the crook of his neck as the tension drained from my muscles.

"Tell me what's going on in that head of yours," he whispered, cupping the back of my neck to keep me close, but I slid down, until my ear pressed against his chest, the strong, thumping of his heart a soothing metronome. Wrapped up in the heat of him, it was hard to focus on his question.

He repeated it.

"Do you think Epi and Andros are okay?" I asked instead.

He grunted. "If Andros hasn't pushed him off the Ravine by tomorrow, he'll deserve a medal. My brother has a particularly special ability to get on everyone's nerves," the half-hearted joke landed with a bitter backbite.

I sucked in a deep breath, inhaling that rich smoky scent radiating from him. "What's the deal with you two? Siblings fight, sure, but there is something deeper that doesn't sit right."

Theo gently massaged my calves resting over his lap, letting out a sigh. "We're almost twins, but not in the mortal definition. Different mothers, same father, born around the same time. Our father left his to Bond with my mother, and his never recovered. When Epimetheus was born, he inherited an extreme version of my father's shortcomings. I inherited his need to assess every angle of a situation. Epi was brazen and reckless where I was forethought. It often put us at odds." The rumble of his voice felt good, the vibrations a soothing balm.

"Our father did not abandon his other children; we have an older brother, Atlas—the one who held up the world. He made sure to love us, to try and teach us the things that were important to him, but he loved my mother beyond all. Her name was Themis, the Titaness of Justice." I squirmed uncomfortably, hearing the quiet ache in his words, knowing from Aphrodite the source of that pain. "I think, in a lot of ways, Epi resented our family, and though my father tried, I don't think the love my brother got was what he wanted. Or perhaps it was just his nature to be a shit." He shrugged. "Either way, after the war, our father and older brother were imprisoned. 'For their crimes' according to Zeus. Hermes told you about that. Epimetheus fought with my mother and I." His voice faltered. "She didn't make it."

I tightened my grip on him as I turned my head to press my lips over the fabric covering his peck. Theo swallowed back the painful memory, throat bobbing above me.

"During the war, our world was destroyed and we had to rebuild. Only I was able to give life. Hephaestus could shape mortals, but he couldn't breathe into them the spark. Epi had an affinity for creating animals, and so together we were tasked by Zeus to begin rebuilding. We did a decent job, but Zeus was cruel to the humans, hating how they cared for me. He was content to let them dwell in despair, but I wasn't. By then, the cracks with the God of Gods were starting to show, and I was, you could say, disenfranchised with his brand of ruling."

Beneath me, Theo stretched, readjusting us lower, allowing me to lay my head back on his chest. "Some years after we reforged the world, he gifted Pandora to Epimetheus. Zeus had Hephaestus shape her from clay and the rest of the Olympians bestowed her with gifts, but he needed me to give her life. When he asked me to do so, he didn't tell me what he planned to do with her. He said he needed a guardian for an artifact, and it was easier to imbue a golem than to trust the corruption of others. He also said he'd allow the humans to use fire so they could build civilization, something they desperately needed. I relented and gave her the spark of life." Theo's face turned away, his features rife with guilt and regret, tone haunted.

"When Zeus gifted Pandora to Epimetheus as a wife, I was immediately suspicious. I warned him not to accept gifts from Zeus, but Epi was so shortsighted, completely enamored with her. I mean, how couldn't he have been? She was designed *for* him, bestowed the most precious gifts from each of us. But she had that fucking box—well, jar. He brushed off my concerns, called me jealous of Zeus's favor, called me bitter. They lived together happily for a time, but I never trusted her, something always felt *wrong* about the situation. One day while Epimetheus was at sea, Pandora gave into temptation. She opened the box and all Hells broke loose." He absently stroked my hair.

"What happened to her after that?" I asked, dreading the answer. The fates of women in our history always ended horrifically; his pause confirmed as much.

"She became despondent when it happened—according to her attendants. Stopped eating. While he was held up at sea, she wasted away, whether from her own guilt or something she'd unleashed from that jar pushed her over the edge. My brother came home and found her in her wedding dress, laid out in their bed with a vial of the Styx in her hand. Wasn't able to down the entire thing, but it was enough to take her life. She didn't leave a note."

"Poor Epimetheus," I said, horrified.

"He wouldn't let me bury her, wouldn't let any of us lay coins on her eyes for Charon. Instead my brother grabbed his sword and began the trek to the Underworld, banging on the gates until Hades let him in. He demanded to see her, but Hades couldn't find her shade. I think he expected her to be waiting on the banks for Charon until he got there and that's why he wouldn't let me pay her toll, but Pandora was never human, and she wasn't a god or an Otherworlder either. With no answers from Hades, he marched right up the path, determined to get to the Fates. Word is, he made it to the Mouth, and Clotho took pity on him. She said that because Pandora was *made*, not born of mortal or divine essence, she had no shade to speak of. 'Borrowed divinity' they called her. He hasn't been the same since, and he blamed me for it. Said Zeus punished her by giving her the box because he was trying to get to me."

I opened my mouth to protest the claims but couldn't. His knowing look told me it was true.

Anger rocketed through my bones, bolstering me from the numbing disassociation. I pushed up, careening my neck to look right into his eyes. "Every time anyone opens their mouth in association with Zeus, it's either murder, rape, sorrow, or fear. Why the fuck hasn't he been dealt with?" I demanded, fire burning me up. Theo released his hold when I moved to stand, watching me pace, boots wearing a path in the dirt. "All of you are so damn powerful, but you couldn't band together to take the fucker out?"

Theo rose with a resigned sigh. "It's not that simple, Zarena. As we explained, he's tethered with an unending well of power.

The last time I defied him, I wound up chained to a mountain with my liver being ripped out each day. He's not mortal, but he's incredibly resourceful and cruel beyond anything you can imagine. It's not lack of action; it's lack of result." His words stopped me in my tracks.

"You stole the fire. But he said they could have it if you gave Pandora life?"

He crossed his arms. "*He lied*, and they were starving so I fucking took it. Not just me, but Hestia too. She gave it to me. When I got caught, I kept her out of it. She's a saint and didn't deserve punishment for doing the right thing." Not an ounce of regret radiated off him. I knew if he had the chance to do it all again, he'd steal that fire a hundred times over.

I squared my shoulders, emboldened by his unflinching conviction. "Let's get this shit done."

Prometheus

CHAPTER 43

I glanced nervously at my watch for the four hundredth time in an hour. The thirty-minute rest cost us precious time, but I couldn't tell Zarena that. She'd needed it after practically falling apart on the hike up, retreating further into her own mind. The taste of her overwhelming anxiety stifled the air around us, making the grounding moment necessary for her. For both of us, really. Zarena rallied, spurred on by righteous indignation, and if we pushed hard enough, we might make it to the halfway point in time.

The climb up and over the steep crag of jagged rock jutting up from the base of Mount Caucasus was a brutal one. I hoisted myself up, using a foothold to propel my body over with forward momentum before sliding to the ground on the slanted, shale slope. The moment my boots hit the cursed ground my body tensed.

It recognized these mountains, the smell of iron in the air.

Zarena slid down behind me and I turned automatically, arresting her momentum before her boots slammed into the ground. I told myself it was instinct, but the truth was, I felt unmoored on this desolate rock. I just needed a moment to feel her touch, to know she was real, and I wasn't stuck here alone. *Again.*

Memory after memory battered against my mind, the smell of the air choking me, the grains of sand crunching beneath my boots, and blood, so much fucking blood . . .

Zarena's body responded to mine, and then her crystalline eyes filled my vision, concern etched in the lines of her face. Flecks of dark gray in her irises growing larger as she sensed my panic. Warm hands cupped both sides of my face, used firm pressure to bring our foreheads together. "Theo, where'd you go? Talk to me," she begged as I breathed her in, filling my lungs with the scent of her sweat and perfume, sucking in greedy gulps around the knot in my throat.

I hadn't been here in five centuries, but five hundred years of freedom was a drop in the bucket compared to the sentence I'd served.

"Prometheus, where are we?" she asked sharply. When I couldn't steady my thoughts, she leaned up, pressing her mouth gently to mine. I leaned into the warmth of her lips, the steady pressure of her body pressed to mine.

"Mount Caucasus," I croaked. She shook her head, searching my face, not understanding the weight of this place, the terror of it. "Th—this is where I was imprisoned," I panted, willing my lungs to calm.

Zarena placed a hand over my chest and brought mine up to rest on top before covering them both with her other hand. "Focus on my breathing. You are okay. We aren't stuck here. We can leave right now if we need to. You are not chained to a rock. I'm here with you. I'm here with you," she repeated. I latched on to her voice, to the feel of her, to the warmth between us, until the buzzing in my head quieted to a murmur. We stayed like that, inhaling in tandem, Zarena regulating my breathing.

Too long.

We began the ascent, working together to scale the cliff faces and crags of broken rock. Zarena kept my hand clasped in hers while we toppled the first hurdles. The climb took hours. Hours we didn't have, but we were closer, nearly there, when the real panic settled in. The air was thinned—too thin for even us—slowing our progress as strength waned from us.

We'd lost so much time.

"The halfway point is there," I panted, pointing to the ridge still too far away. "We've got to get to shelter before the Reaping takes me. I won't be able to protect you when I'm out."

Zarena didn't waste her breath on the questions burning behind her eyes, choosing instead to throw everything she had into getting up the rest of this mountain. She held her own, but she, like me, was fading fast. Sweat and grime streaked down her arms, the side of her face, the only sounds between us grunts of exertion and the grind of rock under boots as we shuffled up the side. We rose steadily, but the darkness grew thicker with every passing minute, spiking my panic.

This was a place of limbo, hidden behind the thinnest veil. These same mountains existed in the mortal realm, but like the Sea of Monsters, what dwelled below was far more sinister. The looming proximity of my rock, the prison fashioned for my captivity, tightened my already overworked chest. I panted, arms and legs burning in protest, aching bone deep.

"How long?" Zarena choked. I knew what she was asking.

"Thirty thousand years."

She balked. "Theo—" she began but I waved her off and hoisted myself up the waiting ledge.

"Later. Now, climb." She acquiesced with a grimace as I boosted her up to the next rung, fingers screaming from the effort of dragging my ass up these cliff faces.

The darkness fell in sheets of black shadows, and with it came the first pains. I pushed through them, wheezing against the onslaught, summoning every ounce of willpower I possessed to get up to the cave, to get Zarena to safety. We hit a stride, eating up the mountainside, and she matched me step for step; determination etched in the grit of her teeth, the furrow of her brows.

Nearly there. Just a little farther.

Pain ate up my torso in earnest, just one level away from that prison I swore I'd never return to. I couldn't bear to be stuck here again, dead on the same ground that claimed me sunset after sunset for endless lifetimes, but the strings of Fate are cruel and didn't seem to give a damn about what I wanted. The last vestiges of purple twilight gave way to waves of black, the shadow creeping over the mountainside menacingly. My left leg went numb, the Reaping accelerated to match the timeline of being back on this fucking mountain.

Every day at sunset . . .

Mortification washed over me, ripping open my wound metaphorically and physically. This Reaping was painful, more painful than I'd experienced in so long. The magic was still potent here, still thick with the hatred of the curse.

The iron whispered to me, caressing against my shade.

Welcome home, it cooed, demanding its pound of flesh. *How we've missed your screams, Prometheus.*

And I *did* scream, then. My hands slipped, sweat slickened as I clawed against the smooth mountainside. I fell, blood pouring out the jagged wound on my lower abdomen, hot and thick as my heart galloped to its end.

Fates, just let it fucking be over.

Small hands wrapped around my wrist, arresting my fall. A sickening crunch, followed by radiating pain had my eyes cracking open. Zarena sat on her ass, feet braced on either side of the rocks above me, straining to pull me up and over the ledge to her. Her beautiful face contorted in pain, sweat beading down her temples, her teeth gritted.

"Theo, help me. Don't let it take you, *fight!*" she demanded. Through the haze of torment, her voice was a thunderbolt, shocking my chest, I bled out against the rocks.

"Deadweight," I choked, coughing up a deluge of blood, coating my lips and chin. Bloody flecks sprayed over her pale wrists, already marred with dirt and grime from the Crucible.

"Fight for me, damn it. Prometheus, don't leave me up here. Fight for me!" she sobbed, her fingers slipping from the sweat and blood and tears, but her pleas rooted me in reality, her voice a war drum rallying me to serve.

Fight for me.

An extinction burst of adrenaline surged through my body, one final, desperate act of self-preservation and with a grunt, my numb leg found purchase on the ledge, allowing Zarena the leverage she needed to drag my body over the bedrock.

A groan clawed its way out of my chest as she rolled me over, dragging my torso to her lap. My lungs strained, fighting around the blood clotting in my throat. Dark blotches peppered my vision as I tried to find her face around them, every atom in my body knowing this Reaping was unlike any I'd ever experienced.

"I've got you, *shhh*, it's okay, I've got you," she sobbed, cradling my face. Tears dripped from the tip of Zarena's nose, dirt smeared across her cheeks, and in the reflection of her glassy, tear-filled eyes, I watched the light leave my own.

Zarena

CHAPTER 44

Prometheus was dead in my arms.

Again.

Covered in muck, he bled out from his abdomen on the mountain he'd been imprisoned on for thirty thousand years. Everything about this Reaping felt different, somehow personal. Like the mountain itself reached up from the depths of its core and gripped him tight, unwilling to let loose the prisoner who'd escaped again.

When the last vestiges of warmth drained from his body, I pushed to my feet and took in the terrain around us. We were exposed on this ledge, to the elements and whatever creatures lurked on this mountain, easy prey a man down. With considerable effort, I hooked my forearms under his armpits and heaved, using what little strength I had left to haul him away from the cliff's edge. "Stupid fucking hulking mass of a titan," I grumbled, inching him backward little by little. My muscles screamed, fingers rubbing raw against the material of his shirt as it slipped and slid around my grip. "Did you bench press the whole mountain while you were up here? The fuck, Theo." I spoke my frustrations into the waning twilight, grunting into the silence settling over this place like a tomb.

I laid him down as gently as I was able before collapsing beside him, panting from the exertion of dragging him just a few feet back. I gave myself a few minutes to catch my breath, all too aware the air in my lungs grew sharper, colder as the night rose around us.

Assess your surroundings, my papa's voice ghosted through my mind, and with it the litany of survival skills he'd spent years ingraining into us.

With a groan, I pushed up onto my elbow and rolled to my feet, allowing some grace for the stiffness in my muscles. Cold sliced bone deep and it wasn't like I could huddle against Theo for warmth in his state. I avoided looking at him, terrified that he wouldn't wake up like he had before. I made myself move, dragging myself around the small expanse of the shelf we found ourselves on. At the very back, a chunk of flat rock rose up to hip level. Morbid curiosity drew me closer.

The rock Theo lived and died on for millennia was permanently stained with blood. Even in the low light, I could pick out the differences in color, golds tarnished to copper, deep reds stained to rust. I reached into my pack, ignoring the ache in my blood-stained hands to grab the thermal blanket and a military-grade glow stick, courtesy of Ares. The sound of the tube cracking between my fingers reverberated through the alcove, bouncing off the walls with a menacing pop. Liquid sloshed loudly as I shook the thick cylinder in my hands. Bright neon light cast an eerie glow over the stone, drawing my eye to primitive markings hidden in the shadows.

I stashed the glow stick between my teeth and hoisted myself up on the side of the rock to examine the space closer. Something powerful called me here, a shimmer reminiscent of the one I'd seen on the lilac stem, Aphrodite's bangle. I glanced back at Theo, but he remained unmoving. Swallowing, I lifted the light higher, battling against the shadows surrounding the walls. Cautiously, I inched closer, feet scraping over the killing stone.

My heart shattered.

Thousands and thousands of tiny hieroglyphics were written in neat rows, scratched into the mountainside. Intricate sigils, foreign to my eyes, but the anthropologist in me was already cataloging patterns, understanding these markings for what they were—the words of a man desperate to not be forgotten.

Thirty thousand years and none of the people he fought next to now came to get him? Thirty thousand years to rot? Against the unease swirling in my gut, I brushed my hand over the smoothed stone, dug my fingertips into the slim markings. My mind quieted as I traced the crude sigils. The etches reached for my power, presenting a thread to me. My head snapped back as the glow stick fell from my fingers.

Flashes of a clean-shaven Theo, naked save for a piece of cloth slung over his hips. Frantic scribbling, the words on the wall sparse. He had only just arrived. Fresh blood lay splattered on the mostly clean stone.

Another memory, in this one he had a beard. It was short, much like the one he had now. More blood on the stone, more words on the walls.

Another flash and another, each showing the progression of his captivity, until the last frame found Theo on the floor of a blood-caked stone bed, heavily bearded. An eagle tore at his flesh with fervor. There were no empty spaces left on the walls, now. His green eyes stared into the abyss above and I knew that this was a vital part of his Becoming—the moment he'd given up. Broken.

My head snapped back as the memory relinquished its hold, the whole of it startling me. To witness that kind of pain, the desolation of it. I swiped up the glow stick from where it'd rolled across the rock, found it nestled between the set of shackles I'd seen on Theo's wrists in the visions. Their power did not call to me, did not show me sadness. Instead, they hissed and lashed out, bucking against my audacity to Witness. My hands shook as I reached for them, knowing this would tear me apart but needing to see it anyway. My fingers wrapped around the nearest shackle and the agony was instant, ripping a scream from my throat, buckling my knees as the memory dragged me under.

"Take the fire back, Prometheus. There's no need for you to be here on this mountain. We will find another way," Hades pleaded, *but Prometheus just laid on the rock, staring ahead. His beard shorn short, his stone not so bloody.*

"No." His reply firm. *"The fire stays with them."*

The vision shook apart and rematerialized, this time a little later. The wear and tear on his body and psyche was evident. The eagle landed near him, devoid of its ferocity. No, the eagle scooted up to him, nudging its head against him softly as though offering comfort. Theo lifted an uncertain hand and stroked along the feathers on its back.

"Will you hurt me today?" he asked. *The bird let out a quiet coo, looking almost sorrowful as it inclined its head in response.*

The bird began to devour his liver, pecking through barely healed flesh with hesitation. Something in that resistance made Prometheus want to fight. He'd been chained to this rock for a hundred years, and this bird couldn't even be bothered to do its job quickly. Every peck was agonizing. Prometheus looked at that eagle with every bit of hatred he harbored for Zeus, targeted it as the weapon of the God of Gods, and unable to quell the rage, he snapped.

Dirtied, blood-caked hands struck quickly, taking the eagle by surprise. In moments, there was a crack, so small, but echoing in the silence. Before his eyes, the eagle began to transform, and Prometheus found his hands no longer wrapped around the neck of a felled bird but instead circled a woman. She was beautiful with wide, surprised lifeless eyes, her neck bent at an unnatural angle.

His grief shook the very mountain holding him. Prometheus scooped her body to his chest, holding her close as tears streaked down his dirty face.

The wail he let out broke my heart into a thousand shattered pieces.

"Hesione . . . Hesione . . ." He called her name. Over and over again, on broken sobs, as though some enchantment could undo the damage done. Her long dark hair fell in waves around them as he rocked her body, buried in sorrow.

A mocking laugh filled the air and then he appeared, a cruel smile on his face. Malice shone in Zeus's eyes, those dark chips of blue-black obsidian completely devoid of humanity.

"Look at what you've done, Prometheus. Your own wife! Does your selfishness know no bounds?"

Horror sliced through my gut as realization washed over me.

"Why?" Theo sobbed, a devastated mess on the ground, cradling his dead wife. A wife murdered with his own hands.

Bile rose in my throat.

"Why not?" Zeus shrugged.

I hated him, wanted to run him through where he stood for his unchecked cruelty.

Zeus bent down low to push a lock of Hesione's hair from her forehead. Theo struck his hand away, but Zeus only chuckled.

"Every person you love, or who is foolish enough to love you, will meet a similar fate. You are a rot, Prometheus."

My vision cleared the cold wind stinging my face. I reeled, adrenaline and anxiety and rage twisted together like snakes in my gut. With a heave, I fell forward, bracing my hands on my knees as I hurled my guts up over this wretched fucking stone. I wanted to reduce this mountain to rubble, to erase it from history.

Grabbing the glow stick off the ground, I stalked back over to Theo's lifeless body, needing to have my hands on him, feel the moment he returned. If he returned.

He better fucking come back.

Rage bolstered my strength as I hauled him up to rest, his back on my chest, covering his body as best I could with the thermal blanket. The cold settled over us, deeper, as I pulled my dagger from my boot and laid it across his torso, knuckles nearly white from my grip.

"This mountain will never take another fucking thing from you ever again," I promised. The words flew from my mouth like a curse, spoken loudly enough for Zeus, the Fates, the very mountain itself to hear me, daring them to challenge my resolve.

I kept watch for the rest of the night.

Prometheus

CHAPTER 45

It took me three hours to find my way back from the Underworld, but it only took one look at Zarena's blood-stained face and furious expression to know she *knew*. Her dagger was clutched tightly in her hand, keen eyes searching the darkness for any threat. I took a deep breath, the movement calling her eyes to mine. In them flashed emotions so powerful they threatened to rip down every stone in the wall I'd built around me.

Pity.

Sorrow.

Anger.

Rage.

And something softer, more tender. Something I couldn't let myself dwell on. She'd stood sentry over my body, in this place of my nightmares. I tried to sit up but her arms tightened. "No—not yet. I just need to feel your heartbeat for a minute."

She sounded so shaken. I settled back, obliging.

Heavy silence wrapped around us like a cocoon of angst. My pulse quickened, waiting for the moment she'd speak and break what was left of my defenses, but she waited, avoiding my gaze. My eyes touched past the chains tethered to the rock, to the walls of the prison I spent lifetimes writing on. The stench of vomit wafted over on the wind, a condemnation in its confirmation. What she'd seen had been so traumatic she'd thrown up.

She knew.

I opened my mouth to speak. Closed it. Acid crawled its way up my throat, nausea rolling as I braced myself, ready to hear her cut me down. To hear those lips condemn me for the selfish monster I knew I was.

Zarena just held me close, rocking us gently, quietly counting our breaths. I was too much of a coward to make her stop, but that too, felt wrong. Receiving comfort, after what I'd done. Guilt ridden, I gently untangled our limbs and stood, glancing again at my watch. "We should get moving."

My voice came out harsh, more bark than anything, but Zarena made no comment as she rose and dusted the dirt from her backside and legs. I hoisted our packs as she sheathed her dagger back into her boot and followed me to the next ledge. We worked our way up the Mountain in crushing silence, but I found the ache in my chest eased the farther from that stone we moved. When it was a tiny prick in the landscape and our breaths hitched from the climb, I called for a pause.

Zarena slumped to the ground, back against the ledge, legs splayed wide in front of her. I winced at her disheveled state—bloodied clothes, red smudges and grime on her cheeks and hands. Her wild red hair was sweat soaked, dampened with the exertion. Dark rings circled her eyes, but when she looked up at me, I couldn't hold her gaze from the embarrassment, the guilt.

"We should talk about it," she took a swig from her canteen.

"Did you sleep at all?" I asked, deflecting. Zarena was having none of it.

"No. Prometheus, we *have* to talk about it."

I kicked at the ground with my boot, sending debris sliding off the side of the ledge. Hands on my hips, I turned to face her general direction but couldn't bring myself to meet her eyes. "You're not going to let this go, are you, Red?"

She rose to her feet, stepping into my space. I fixated on the spot of mountain just past her head, taking two deep breaths through lungs flayed raw.

"Prometheus. Look at me."

I couldn't. My name coming out of her lips felt like a slap. No nicknames, no brevity. Just the cold hard truth, coiling between us. She waited. I dragged my gaze to hers, terrified and anxious about what I'd seen in those eyes.

"What happened was not your fault—" she began but I held up my hand.

"Don't. Don't make excuses." My words were sharp claws that drew a clear line in the sand. I prayed to the Fates that she'd heed the warning, but the look on her face promised she wouldn't.

She came closer, so much closer to me than she'd been, and that proximity was dangerous because I was unwell. The last vestige of my control was a fraying rope, one she threatened to unravel just by being in the place with me. Her words grated at the walls of my mind and the rage-beast I kept locked inside rattled its cage in warning. She was getting too close to digging out the scar tissue in my side, and it wouldn't end well for her. For either of us.

"It's *Zeus's* fault. He is responsible for so much horrible shit, Prometheus. Thousands and thousands of years of misery and torture and unabashed cruelty. How could you possibly blame yourself after everything?"

Flayed to the bone, my control snapped.

"Because it *is* my fault!" I hissed, pressing into her space until our chests nearly touched. "My hubris brought this about. You think I don't hold Zeus responsible too? Of course, I do. But it doesn't change what *I* did. You think that was the last time he took everything from me? Think the worst of what I endured was on this fucking mountain? You don't know me, Zarena. You don't know shit about what I've survived. It's fucking exhausting, and the only thing that's kept me going all these years is the thought of tearing him apart from the inside out."

Her eyes were stone, her resolve a bastion that refused to give me an inch. She put her finger on my chest and pushed back. "I don't know you, Prometheus? You're going to stand here and act like the last four days haven't felt like a lifetime? I've seen first-hand what happened down there." She flung her hand out in the direction of the pit. "I've held your lifeless body in my arms every single fucking night since the day I met you. I didn't ask for this, and I sure as shit would have preferred the quiet, *normal* life I'd been living, but guess fucking what? That wasn't my real life—this is." She grabbed my hand. Pressed it against her chest. "There's a reason we found each other," she whispered, near a plea as sparks danced from her fingers, electrifying my skin.

I stared past her face again, pushing down the overwhelming feelings threatening to drag me in the undertow. "Yes," I said flatly. "The compass and the map are literally destined to find each other, Zarena. It's not real."

Zarena stiffened, but she didn't recoil. "That's bullshit. You're afraid and you're pushing me away. It's obvious that's what you do. To *everyone*. You think that if you pretend you don't actually give a fuck about them that Zeus won't know that you do? That's insanity. You may as well let the people around you love you. They already do, whether you accept it or not, so get the fuck over yourself and grow up. All these years on this Earth and you're just as emotionally stunted as modern men."

Her words sliced through my chest, surgical in their precision. Dissecting. It was me rearing back, desperate for some distance between us as the single thread holding my beast inside snapped.

She didn't deserve it, but I unleashed.

"You don't think I *want* to? You think I enjoyed spending my life on the run? You know, I thought like you once! Once, some years ago, there was a long while where I thought maybe he'd given up. Eighty years went by without so much as a peep from Zeus or his lackeys. I met someone. Let myself fall in love, against my better judgment. I was terrified—for months, years even. But time went on and we were safe. It lulled me. We had a son and a life. A decade in, I came home late and they were *butchered.* I let my guard down for one fucking moment, just enough to learn to breathe again, and he *brutalized* them. My son was driven into the wall with a spike; his body ripped to shreds. And my wife? Helen was—" My eyes glazed over, my mind wrapping in on itself against the onslaught of images.

"So don't act like I'm being self-sacrificing like some sanctimonious prick. How many people would you have die before you fucking listen to me? And all this because I taunted him, I just knew I was smarter than he was. I made an enemy of Zeus and everyone I've ever cared about has suffered for it. So, excuse me if I don't take notes from you on how to keep the people I care about safe!" I roared, properly losing my shit, chest heaving, heat creeping up my neck. Zarena stood, unflinching while I raged, listening as I got it all out, until the only sound on the mountain was my ragged breathing. Even the wind quieted around us.

Zarena sniffed once, lips tightening. She lifted her chin high, defiant, and squared right up to me. I towered over her, but she remained unbowed.

"The pain you've endured is immense; I'm not denying that. If you want space and distance, I'll oblige you. I don't care what the consequences are; I want Zeus dead. Not just for you or my parents, but for all the damage he's done. As far as this goes"— she gestured between the two of us, her voice hard as steel—"we can call it right now. No need to wait until the tether snaps. This isn't healthy. You have a long road ahead of you, and I can be there as your friend, but I won't be your punching bag. I'm a *person*, Prometheus, not just a map, not just a convenient fuck. I'm a *person* and I deserve more respect than what you gave me today. You've been through a lot, being here is traumatic and I recognize that." Her tone flattened as she crossed her arms protectively over her chest, exuding confidence and power. "But I'm telling you now, if you ever speak to me like that again, I don't care how fucking big you are, I'll fold your clothes with you in them. Got it?"

I couldn't recall how we'd gotten here. Couldn't defend my actions. Zarena was strong and intelligent, and she was right. This wasn't healthy, and no good could come from taking this any farther than we had already.

"I got it."

Zarena

CHAPTER 46

Theo and I climbed the rest of the jagged mountainside in complete silence. His demeanor remained subdued, and all my anger dissipated over the last hour or so. I understood *why* he'd lashed out—wounded animals backed into corners often did—but I'd meant what I'd said. I deserved more respect than to be screamed at, and I didn't take abuse from anyone in my life, tethered together supernaturally or not.

I flung myself over the last ridge, but my grip slipped and I nearly tumbled back over the edge. Theo was there in a flash, strong arms hoisting me over like a child being pulled from a swimming pool. His touch flamed along my skin, and I ignored the way it made me feel. Prometheus backed away just as quickly, either out of anger or needing physical distance to fight the tether.

I took a drink from my canteen.

He pointed to a path that wound down into a copse of trees. "Through there," Theo grunted, turning on his heels to make the descent. I followed.

The sound of our boots crunching against the gravel grated on my already frayed nerves. I sped up, lengthening my strides, unable to stand the sight of his tensed back for another damn minute. My anger had always been quick to flash, but also, quick to fade. The energy it took to keep up this silent treatment was exhausting.

"I resented my siblings for a really long time," I admitted, breaking the silence by voicing a secret I'd never told anyone. A peace offering. Maybe Theo was ready to take it or maybe he was as sick of the silence as I was, because for whatever the reason, he asked, "Why?"

I sighed deeply. "Now that I know I'm a muse, a lot of things make more sense. Remember the library I work for? A few years back, when I first started, my coworker and I discovered a room hidden with a secret passageway. It was a treasure trove of artifacts that went back centuries, rich with the histories of the Afro-Caribbean people who were enslaved and brought to New Orleans. It was incredible, and the wealth of knowledge inside was so vast that we started calling it the Jewel. I'm now the archivist for that collection, but I remember when she found it, this glazed look came over her face. It was crazy, this woman walked right up to the shelf and pulled the right book like she'd known it was there all along. And though I was so blessed to be present for that moment, I resented it. All my life, those around me had surpassed me and achieved greatness, and it was like I was always just a minute too late.

"Dro became the incredibly skilled chef de cuisine at one of the best and oldest restaurants in the city. My sister, Cece, is a musical savant. She's maintained the first chair in cello our entire lives. When she first showed interest in music, Papa worked three weeks straight overtime to get her a cello—she was six. She attended Julliard on a full-ride scholarship. Now, she plays in the New York Orchestra and lives in Brooklyn. My other sister, Drea, is an incredible artist. She never went to college, she *could* have. Parsons School of Design offered her a decent ride, but she turned it down on a whim and bought a one-way ticket to Milan.

She designs couture for celebrities to walk the runway." I took a breath as Theo soaked in my words.

"I felt so happy to see them all thriving, but something always nagged at me that I couldn't quite get there too. Almost. I could *see* it. *Taste* it. But I just couldn't get there myself." I shrugged. "Selfish, I know. I wanted something of my own, and now, knowing why I never got it doesn't make it feel any less shitty. Being a muse sucks dick."

Theo burst out laughing at my candor. A reluctant smile tugged at the corner of my lips as he ran his hand over the back of his neck, looking down at me with a bemused expression.

"You'd be surprised to find *all* your aunts felt the same way. They felt that inspiring was important work, but not having their own agency to create and discover felt like a cruel cosmic joke."

We came to a stop in a valley between two mountains; a wall with a massive cavern opening set into the recess of the rock, filled with the inkiest black shadows I'd ever seen. Weighted air fell heavier here, steeped in old magic.

"Is this it?" I asked, moving closer to what I assumed was the Mouth. He nodded, stepping beside me. The area was huge, dwarfed in the shadows of the mountains, with a river that cut along the left side of it. To the far right were two more paths that led deep into the nothingness.

"Which way will they come from?"

Prometheus turned to study the pathways. "Ares and Co. will arrive from there." He gestured to the farthest from the right. "Epi and Andros from there." He pointed to the opposite side of the riverbank. "Now, we wait. They've still got a few hours."

He sat down with our packs. I dug through mine, grabbing a spare cloth and heading for the river. "Is it safe to touch the water?"

Theo glanced up from his notebook. "Yeah, it's the river that feeds the spring for the Fountain of Youth. I've never tasted from it before, but it should be fine. Refill your canteen if you want."

I wasted no time plunging my grime-caked hands into the cool water. The area around my hands colored light pink as I scrubbed hard, determined to rid myself of Theo's blood, of the reminder of the mountain's cruelty. The water kissed over my skin in a gentle caress, peeling back the layers of hurt and pain and dirt, lapping at my wrists and forearms playfully. This water was ancient and knowing; a deep well of magic that felt almost alive. I scrubbed until my hands were raw, so deep in my task that I almost missed the sound of voices coming from behind me. I whipped around and found Ares, Aphrodite, and Heph jogging up from the bowels of their pathway. They, too, were disheveled and battered, but intact.

I abandoned my washing to hurry to them.

"What happened?" Theo asked, voice sharp.

Ares shrugged him off. "Manticore," he grunted. A large gash over his eye bled freely down the side of his face, making his grin at my arrival downright feral.

"Any sign of Dro?"

They all turned to face the banks at once. Nothing sparked on the horizon, no movement save for the plants shifting in the wind over the water.

"They still have a little time." Hephaestus offered, kindly, glancing at his watch. I checked my own, which served to do nothing but amp up my anxiety. Minutes. They had minutes, according to these clocks. Theo watched me, carefully schooling his features to appear calm, but I saw the tic in his jaw, the pulse jumping in his neck. No matter how strained his relationship with his brother, the Titan of Knowledge was worried.

Swallowing hard, I picked up my pack and walked toward the water's edge, leaving the three of them to recount their story to Prometheus. I uncapped my canteen, drank down the remnants inside until I was sated before refilling it to the brim in the crystal-clear water. I screwed the cap back on and stowed the canteen in my pack, rechecking rations we hadn't used, organizing just to keep my hands busy.

Waiting.

Seconds crawled into minutes, ticking like sap trickling from a tree. My eyes constantly scanned their horizon, every moment that path stayed empty twisted my stomach up tighter. Andros—if something happened to him, it would be my fault. What would I tell our parents? Our sisters?

That he'd survived war only to die on some busted ass path in the Underworld? An Underworld he didn't belong to, at that. Every horrific thought I had no business thinking rolled through my mind, all worst-case scenarios that ran up my blood pressure just imagining the hypotheticals. Another peek at my watch.

Two minutes.

One.

I turned, ready to argue with Theo, ready to tell them I wasn't fucking leaving without my brother when I saw it, in the low light. I squinted as the glint of a neon beam peaked through the trees, fast approaching. I stood, searching.

Without warning, Epimetheus and Andros barreled through the tree line, bodies bent in a full sprint over the river.

"RUN!" Dro screamed, waving his hand wide for us to move. They splashed through the shallow wade of the river, arms and legs working overtime. Andros smashed into me like a freight train, pulling me behind him through the calf-deep water. On the riverbank, Ares stood on high alert, eyes trained on the path they'd come down, dual swords unsheathed. A mighty roar broke through the clearing, shaking the trees and earth below us, nearly knocking me off my feet. I drew the knife spear Ares gifted me from my boot, gripping the handle tight as we formed a line on the banks, weapons drawn.

Two trees, taller than four men, snapped apart as the biggest creature I'd ever seen broke through, heading for us.

A monster of a man with a thick torso and the head of a bull.

"The fucking *Minotaur*?" Heph whispered, shocked. He shifted in front of Aphrodite and Ares protectively. The God of War rolled his eyes with a wounded noise and pushed his husband back behind him.

Prometheus grabbed my arm tightly, shouting, "We need to get out of here. *Now!*" It wasn't a command he had to give twice. As a unit, we turned to run into the darkness of the Mouth, so close to completing this questing road bullshit. We made it two steps.

Two steps, and the world shook apart, blasting us wide from beneath the soles of our feet.

Prometheus

CHAPTER 47

haos.

The maelstrom of battle whirled around me, a clash of swords and spears and teeth and horns. Zeus hadn't just sent his undead Minotaur but soldiers as well. Demi-gods, by the smell and dulled power rolling off them. So many, *too many*, especially with the beast to contend with.

Ares and Andros tag-teamed the shade of the Minotaur, slashing and stabbing and corralling it as best they could. Hephaestus drove his hammer into the skull of a demi-god, spraying brain matter everywhere. Pieces of gray spattered over me as I tangled with two assailants. They smelled like ocean brine, an instant giveaway that these weren't Zeus's progeny—they were Poseidon's.

A silver moonlit arrow flew past my ear, lodging in the eye socket of the demi-god oozing in front of me. He swayed, buckling as his sword clattered to the ground. I turned to see Artemis and Medusa barreling up from the path of the Mortal Realm, two more divine beings gave us better odds. Relief rocketed through me as the Goddess of the Hunt sliced through the melee, zeroing in on the massive beast snarling between our friends.

Aphrodite and Zarena fought back-to-back, barely any space between them but enough that Ditey wouldn't burn. I snapped the neck of a Son of Poseidon who'd lunged in, presenting it to me like an amateur. I should have been paying more attention to the beasts around me, but I couldn't look away from Zarena. She moved with concentrated precision, strong form—relaxed and lithe. She moved with purpose, extending her follow-through punches. Every blow she landed to bare skin was made more painful by the burning damage erupting from her knuckles. Such grace, such raw power pulsed from her that every move of her assault was a dance. I was mesmerized.

I paid for that lapse of concentration when a fist connected with my face in a crushing blow that blackened my vision momentarily. I shook out my head, then I was back at it, grappling with cursed offspring. Poseidon mated with sea beasts and creatures often; as a result, not all his children looked normal. Illustrated clearly by the fishlike features and seaweed hair of this creature who screamed in rage before spitting a green mass of gunk into my eyes. It burned, searing against my skin. I raged, clawing to get the venom cleared as it ate away at my flesh. I buckled, hitting the ground hard, pain pulsing in and out as the creature advanced over the top of me in a blurred silhouette.

A part of me felt relief that this may be the end, that the fight could be over. He raised a curved blade, a maniac gleam in his bulging eyes.

Blue-black gore rained over me, drenching my torso and face with blood as the creature's head was severed swiftly from its neck. Epimetheus stood behind it, a blade in each hand, covered in shallow cuts and marred skin. My brother kicked his boot out against the creature's stilled frame to knock it onto the ground. His swords glistened with ichor as he shifted both blades to one hand, extending his free hand down to me. I took it, letting him yank me to my feet as he returned my nod of thanks. With more work to be done, we threw ourselves back into the fray.

Bodies dropped around us as my eyes searched for Zarena, desperate to catch a glimpse of her. A flash of flame-red hair whirled, and I homed in on her just as she headbutted a massive half-man who'd wrapped her up. Her fighting skill was something few mortals could achieve. Her father trained her well. Andros had his spear out, chipping away at the Minotaur with each thrust. He was strong in his LOA form, pulling from the power of his people.

A sharp cry rang out, sending panic flooding my system. I turned to see Aphrodite being dragged across the ground by her hair. She kicked and fought, but before I could move, Ares and Hephaestus advanced, a lethal, imposing unit as they broke into a run. The God of War pulled his fist back just as they reached the demi-god with his hands on their wife. The force of Ares's blow exploded the rib cage out her assailant's back, blood and viscera spraying out with the spikes of his bones. Hephaestus scooped up a bleeding Aphrodite.

Only the Minotaur remained. They descended on him, the Goddess of the Hunt latched to the beast's back as Medusa slashed at the creature with her blades. A mighty groan signaled Artemis's weapon finding its mark as she shoved the steel deep into the junction of its neck. It crashed to the ground with a sickening crunch.

The whistle of metal drew my attention just as a trident sliced through the air with the grace and speed of a javelin. I twisted unnaturally, narrowly avoiding the impact as it sailed past me, impaling Ares in the chest. Hephaestus roared as his husband fell, blood gushing from the punctures in the God of War's chest, spewing from his lips. Aphrodite's fury-filled cry pierced the air.

In the river, Poseidon rose from the depths, leaking rivulets into the wake washing over the bank, carrying more of his kin with him. Medusa slid through with two long batons, her tiny frame and wild snakes striking out as she weaved through the battlefield like a ball of furious rage. She'd clocked these fuckers as Poseidon's immediately, and I felt great satisfaction at the vengeance she wreaked. She deserved this, and so much more.

Medusa kept her pace, eyes locked on the God of the Sea. Her snakes coiled around her, hissing and tasting the shift in the air. She wore her rage like a shield—a living, tangible thing. Poseidon sneered as she squared up to him, fierce and unafraid. Twin batons slid down to rest in her palms as she rocked back in a fighting stance. Andros locked eyes with me and we advanced together, flanking her. I gestured my fingers over my eyes to say, *Stay clear of the snakes.* He inclined his head.

"Medusa, you're looking . . . tight." Poseidon drawled, eyes raking down her body like the sleaze he was. Andros and I both closed in, ready to rip him apart, but batons came up to halt our movements.

"Poseidon. You aged like milk," she spat, looking serene and unaffected by his proximity even as she read him for filth. "I assume you're coming for blood?"

He conjured another trident in his grip.

Medusa smiled through bloodied teeth. "That makes two of us."

Then she lunged.

Zarena

CHAPTER 48

The God of War groaned and hissed through clenched teeth, hands shaking as they hovered over the trident buried in his chest. Hephaestus and Aphrodite crowded him, his head cradled in his wife's lap, eyes bulging as they searched for her face. The wound gushed, a thick deluge of blood flowing from torn flesh over the unsteady rise and fall of his chest. The gore of it rooted me to the spot. It looked—*unsurvivable*. He sputtered, choking on the blood bubbling up from his throat, as Hephaestus crowded over him, gently assessing the wound, soothing his partner in hushed, even tones as his hands stained red.

Turning to me, he barked, "We need to get this out of his chest. He can't heal with it inside."

The urgency in his tone snapped me to attention, the rushing sound of swords clanging and creatures dying flooding back to my ears in a deafening crescendo.

"What do you need me to do?"

"Grip it tight and when I say, pull with everything you've got." He gestured to the handle. Ares's eyes rolled back in his head, exposing the whites of them to us. Hephaestus brushed sweaty strands of dark hair back from the God of War's face. "Ares, look at me. *Look at me*, baby," he demanded, tone raw and cracking around the words.

Ares's eyes refocused. "We need to get this out. It's going to hurt, I'm so sorry. Stay with me, okay? Stay with us," he ordered.

The corner of Ares's lips tipped up in a lax, bloody smile. "I love it when you're bossy."

The God of the Forge wasted no more time. Turning to me, he dipped his chin in hurried measure. I lined up over Ares, planting my feet with purpose just under his rib cage. Power thrummed off the trident, warning me it had something to show me, but I couldn't worry about what horrors I might see. Ares needed this thing out of him.

"Now!"

The command bolted through me as I gripped the metal between my fingers, wrenching with all my strength. A mighty squelch and the sounds of scraping bones met my ears, mingling with a strangled cry from the God of War. The metallic taste of blood lingered in the air as I held the trident aloft, but I had no idea if Ares was okay. My eyes remained transfixed on the trident, unseeing the world around me. The flashes came, quick and fleeting, but informative.

Poseidon being dragged out of a bar by Zeus . . .

Zeus demanding repayment for something . . .

Zeus telling Poseidon to stall until he could get there . . .

"Don't touch her. She's mine."

The snap back to reality was visceral, the trident still in my hands humming menacingly. Beneath me, Aphrodite and Hephaestus worked over their Bonded, hands on his chest, pushing their power into him, while blood gushed around the gaping holes in his abdomen. I stumbled back, dropping the trident as they healed him, holding breath trapped in my lungs for a beat, then another. I gasped in relief when the light returned to the

God of War's eyes. He pushed up, attempting to get to his feet, ignoring the protestations of his partners. I dropped to my knees beside them. "Poseidon is stalling, waiting on Zeus to get here."

Hephaestus's head snapped to me, alarm on his face. "It's still the Underworld until we're in the Mouth, to risk outright war with Hades." His eyes darkened as Epimetheus jogged up, breathing hard. "Hades and Persephone will have felt the moment Poseidon's trespassed; we'll wait here for them. You go. Get Prometheus."

The titan didn't hesitate, sprinting back toward the melee where Artemis, Medusa, Theo, and Dro met Poseidon and his lackeys toe to toe. I didn't want to leave my brother, but there was no way he'd abandon the fight.

"I'll go," Hephaestus assured, sensing my reticence. Seemingly satisfied his Bonded would recover, he pressed a kiss to Ares's forehead. "Stay here," he commanded. The God of War frowned in his wife's arms, looking more than pissed at being sidelined with three puncture wounds still leaking.

Ares raised his blade with a still shaking hand, offering it to me. "You know the rules, Z. Business end."

I took it gratefully. "Anyone who gives me shit—even Theo," I replied.

Ares barked a laugh and then winced in pain. "Especially him."

Then hands were on me, urging me to stand, the sounds of metal meeting metal filling the air. Theo raced with me to the Mouth, Epimetheus hot on our heels. My legs burned, exhausted from days of rough terrain and emotional battery but I kept pushing. The titan gripping my hand didn't falter or give me the chance to, either. We barreled right into the dark abyss of the Mouth, no time for questions or concerns about what might be waiting on the other side of the veil.

Sound ceased to exist as we broke through the barrier. I floated, untethered as I soared through a shadowed oblivion of the murkiest night sky. The depths were endless. I was abandoned by a merciless pull of gravity, an abrupt jerk somewhere around my wrist shifting my direction.

I fell.

Wind rushed around me soundlessly as I swiftly, hurtled through the depths of the very fabric of the universe, a place existing outside of space and time into something cold and wet and bone-splitting. Glacial water invaded my nostrils, stung my eyes as I struggled to adjust to the intrusion. My lungs screamed out for oxygen as I plunged beneath the surface, limbs thrashing wildly, but every drag of my hands and feet through the water met the resistance of a strong current. Bubbles of expelled air pushed past my lips, my vision tunneling around the edges, the agony of my lungs arresting in my chest unbearable.

All this, just to fucking drown.

My mind quieted, the cold numbing my fingers and toes, as I slowly blinked in the dim light. A sense of peace washed over me, an acceptance working overtime to keep me docile as my body shut down. Strong arms seared an inferno against my chest, wrapping tight. My hands floated lazily in front of me as I was pulled through the darkness. I choked, water expelling past my lips as my head broke the surface. Dizzy, I sucked in shallow breaths, greedy for the oxygen as air stung like needles against my face.

"I gotcha, Red, I gotcha. Breathe deep for me," Theo commanded, hoisting my body up and cradling me to his chest, exiting the water with ease. I shivered, teeth chattering from the cold, tiny crystals sticking to my lashes as the Titan of Knowledge cleared the dark pool of blue-black water and laid me down on hard ground. "That's good, good girl, you're okay," he soothed as I curled in on myself, knees bending, arms tucked tight as I instinctually tried to consolidate warmth. His fingers moved, radiating an impossible heat, branding my skin wherever he touched. The cold receded enough for me to get my bearings.

We emerged in a large cavern, the light too dim to see more than a few inches in front of my face, but I could hear the echo of our shuffling bouncing off the walls, the frantic beating of my heart beating a tattoo against my rib cage.

"Come on, we have to move," he urged, lifting me until I was on my own feet. I leaned against him, seeking the warmth of his skin. I had no clue how Theo could see enough to know where we were going, but his sure steps never faltered. Slowly, the air grew thicker, warmer the farther we went, until I could no longer see my breath in white puffs with every heave. Theo clutched me tighter as my teeth chattered and I stumbled over rocks and uneven ground. With a grunt, the ground swept out beneath me as Theo carried me against him. I had nothing left in me to argue.

"Do you th-think they m-made it?" I stammered, shamelessly planting my face firmly into the crook of his piping-hot neck. He was a small sun, radiating his own energy, commanding it to seep into my frozen skin. He pressed his chin to my head and blew out a breath that warmed my face, the tips of my ears.

"Yes. I could feel Hades; he was close. Poseidon royally fucked up, stepping into the Underworld. He knew better." Theo's voice echoed through the cavern as we walked. My body shook as I attempted to orient myself.

The path rose on an incline and with each ascending step, the darkness ebbed quickly until so much bright light filled my vision I had to squint. I struggled to adjust, shielding my eyes after days and days in the Underworld's dimness. Theo stepped into the sun, the warm glow illuminating his tanned skin as he sat me down gently in my wet clothes. I shivered, from cold or shock I wasn't sure. I didn't protest when those hands roamed over my neck and shoulders, pushing in more warmth with every caress, but as my eyes adjusted, my jaw dropped. Stepping away from his hold, I stared, transfixed by the impossible sight in front of me.

An oasis of sorts occupied the land sprawling before us. Grecian buildings dispersed between waterfall cliffs and jungle vegetation, perfectly preserved, the marble looking as natural there as the nature it nestled in. The bluest sky I'd ever seen swept overhead, dotted with painted clouds too perfect to be real. The city was neatly kept, deserted, as though its inhabitants had simply up and left one day. On top of a hill to the east sat a massive structure, a great Parthenon.

Epimetheus peered out over the horizon. "That's gotta be it, right?" he asked, pointing out. "Did either of you think to grab the compass from Hephaestus? I got ours," he said, pulling the brass object from his pocket. Theo shuffled uncomfortably.

"I didn't, but it's not a problem. We don't actually need them; just needed Zeus to think they were necessary."

"You're telling me I almost got gored by a fucking Minotaur going after this thing when it fell out of Andros's pocket, and we didn't even *need* it?" Epimetheus demanded incredulously. "Un-fucking-believable." He threw his hands up as Theo lent him a terse nod in confirmation.

Shrugging off his bag, the jilted titan sifted through the pockets, frustratingly pulling out dry clothes. He muttered under his breath, seething into the tense silence between us. I shuffled uncomfortably, eyebrows raising in alarm when he unexpectedly yanked off his shirt, revealing the hard muscles of his abs and toned chest. I kept my eyes locked on Theo's, careful not to let my gaze wander for a second at the sound of a zipper yanking down.

I turned away as he shucked his wet jeans down his thighs, quickly busying myself with my own pack, grateful for the waterproof spell Hecate placed over them before we left. Throat tight, I grabbed a set of dry clothes and slipped behind a huge boulder to change, leaving the brothers alone in the clearing. When I returned, I found Theo fully dressed, apologizing to a still-shirtless Epimetheus.

Up close, without the shock of hyperthermia, I got a good look at the titan staring sourly at Prometheus. The skin over his chest was ravaged with what looked like burns, darkened around the edges in a way that reminded me of decaying flesh, but if they were painful, he made no mention. Unease coiled through me; a wrongness I couldn't quite place nagged at my subconsciousness as I traced the unusual wounds, not quite torn enough for blunt weapons, not smooth enough to have been a blade.

He caught my eye as I scanned over his collar bone, sending what I'm sure he thought was a smolder. "See something you like?"

I didn't bother to hide my eye roll. "Yeah, open wounds really do it for me. Put on a damn shirt." Theo's shoulders shook with silent laughter as Epimetheus snatched his shirt up and slipped it over his head. I turned my attention back to the city, shielding a hand over my brow to better see the building on the hill.

It certainly *looked* like a library.

But it didn't feel like one. I couldn't explain it, except to chalk it up to the map inside my blood, urging me on. There was a gentle pull, growing stronger by the second, just around my ribs. I grazed my hand over my torso in wonder. It felt warm, vibrant. *Alive*, as I took two steps in the direction it called for, the tension slackened in that tether as I approached Prometheus. The familiar feeling I got right before I knew something big was coming during a dig vibrated down my body. For years, we'd called it my superpower, that dumb luck urging me to dig in one quadrant over another, but now I knew. *It was me.* My calling as a muse. I leaned into it, trusting myself, trusting my gut.

"I think it's this way."

Epimetheus glanced back to the building on the hill skeptically, but Prometheus? He moved instantly, falling into step beside me. His faith was a comforting validation, but unneeded. I *knew* this was the way. "Weren't we supposed to meet the Fates?" I asked, looking around like they might pop out from behind a corner or something.

"The point of the Questing Road is to get what you want." Epimetheus answered. "You're the key. You wanted to come here, and the Mouth took you to where you needed to go."

"I see the logic in that," Theo offered as I fumbled around the side of my pack for my canteen. My throat felt ravaged from nearly drowning, then freezing.

"Trust me, that's how it works." Epimetheus muttered matter-of-factly. His demeanor shifted, subtly, but I noticed, even if Theo didn't. I slowed my steps, the movement positioning me between the brothers instead of in front of them, but it didn't alleviate the uneasy feeling working through me. I drank down a few gulps of liquid to clear the seawater from my throat, letting the still cool water soothe.

The effect was instant. A surge of energy tore through me, rejuvenating my body from the inside out, leaving me feeling refreshed, as though I'd slept a very long time. I tried not to let the worry over Dro overtake my thoughts as I followed the pull inside, letting it guide us through a labyrinth of abandoned buildings and into the woods, far past the ghost town of what had once been the civilization of Atlantis.

Prometheus

CHAPTER 49

"No offense, brother, but I think your map's broken," Epi whispered. I elbowed him hard in the ribs and he doubled over, letting out a sharp grunt. We stood on the edge of a large lake just outside the city. Zarena, hands on her hips, chewed on her lip in confusion and disappointment. She'd been certain the Library called to her, pulling her blood to lead us to its steps, yet a whole lot of nothing stood in front of us.

Except a beautifully placid lake.

"I don't get it," she sighed, shaking her head. "I can still feel the pull. It's telling me that it's *right here*. What'd I miss?" Zarena asked, turning to me for answers I couldn't give her.

I tried anyway, walking to the edge of the lake, crouching down to see myself reflected on the glassy surface. "The tether to you pulled me around the city for weeks before I finally found you in Electric Delphi. I don't know what the rules are any more than you do, Red," I admitted.

Epi wandered off down the other edge of the lake, giving us some privacy. She started toward me, but as though she was reminding herself of her declaration on the mountain, she pulled back, folding her arms over her chest. I bit back a groan. Not being able to touch her was a special form of torture, but she was well within her rights to demand the distance. To protect herself from me. I swallowed, the taste sour on my tongue. After her admission in the Crucible, I knew how badly she wanted this, a discovery all her own.

"I'm sorry I'm not a Muse and can't inspire you to find it," I offered.

She smiled, but it didn't reach her eyes. I hated that too.

I straightened, giving her a moment to collect her disappointment and was just on the precipice of suggesting we check out the building on the hill, when she turned to me, fingernails digging into my forearm, her eyes lit up with an idea. "Kiss me."

I reared back, uncertain. "*What?* No. What? You said—"

Zarena cut off my unsteady stream of consciousness with an impatient wave of her hand. "I know what I said—and that still stands—but we need inspiration, and didn't you say the most potent way to get that with Muses was sex? Like, sexual connection or whatever?"

Fates, I hated the way my body responded, so fucking eager to touch her when I should be doing all I could to stay away. As it was, I had to will my cock to stay still. My fingers brushed across my lower lip as I pretended for both of our sakes to even need to consider it. "Just one kiss?" She nodded, eyes already on my lips. "You're sure?"

Instead of answering, Zarena fisted my shirt between her fingers and hauled me to her, the force of her power bowing me over. Soft, her lips were so damn soft, tender flesh I sucked between my teeth, nipped at as I lost myself in the taste of her. Zarena moaned, back arching as I fisted the curls at her nape, our tongues hungry as we consumed. The very real probability that this would be the last chance I'd get to taste her sent me into a state of frenzy. Her body molded against mine, so fucking pliant and supple it made me ache. She tilted her head back, offering the column of her throat to me and I sank my teeth into her neck like a sinner of the highest order, leaving my mark on divinity I didn't deserve to touch. Her hands locked around my neck, pulling me against her, as though there was any space left to eradicate. Calloused fingers wrapped around her throat, the most decadent pressure, eliciting beautiful little whimpers as she moaned against my mouth. I swallowed those too.

Her hand slipped lower, sliding over my stomach and under the waistband of my jeans. The heat from her fingers grazed the area just above my cock and I groaned, sending vibrations through us both. I knew that if she touched me, I'd come all over her hand and make her lick it clean while I fucked her against every available surface. *The trees, the ground, the fucking bottom of this lake . . .*

The trees, the ground, the bottom of this lake . . .

I froze, hating myself. "Stop," I managed to choke out. I couldn't do this touching her. *Fates.* I pulled back, breathless, lungs screaming for air that tasted more like her as I sucked in a breath. "The lake. It's in the lake."

Zarena's head snapped to the water, that glassy-eyed lust in her gaze receding with every second we weren't touching. Running her fingers desperately through the destruction I'd wrought on her hair, she turned to the lake, tossing her long curls over her shoulder. Her gaze snagged on my crotch before flicking back to my eyes, pale eyelashes fluttering.

"You've got a little . . ." She waggled her eyebrows suggestively. Glancing down, embarrassment flamed hot up my neck as a decent-sized wet spot stained the light jeans dark.

Fucking Hells.

Zarena

CHAPTER 50

"How far down do you think it is?" I asked as Epimetheus made his way back over to us.

Theo squinted into the blue water, both of us mostly recovered from that kiss. I ran my finger over the tender skin of my bottom lip, studiously ignoring the ache building between my thighs.

Mostly.

"I don't know; I can't see through the enchantments, but Theo can go down first and check if you want?" Epimetheus offered. A reasonable suggestion, but I didn't like it, felt even more resigned not to split up when the titan huffed impatiently as I shook my head. He looked tense, edgy even. Alarm bells blared in my head. The thought of being stuck up here alone with Epimetheus twisted me up and I'd been a woman all my life. I'd known too many women with bad experiences to ignore my gut.

"No, let's just go together. I can hold my breath for a decent amount of time," I said.

Epimetheus snorted. "You can hold your breath for as long as you need to. You'd be shocked what that mouth can do."

Okay, that wasn't something I was imagining. His words oozed past playful flirting into unwelcome, sleazy innuendo, even though I knew he'd seen Theo and I practically face fucking out here minutes ago. Hell, I had a claiming mark in the shape of his brother's teeth blooming over my throat as we spoke. Theo ground his teeth together, muscles tensing. He heard it too.

"Keep on, and you'll discover how many ways it can tell you to go fuck yourself. Besides . . . I've been a Muse for less than a week, I don't know everything," I said defensively, doing what I could to steer the conversation into less dangerous waters. Epimetheus remained unbothered by the shift in our moods.

"Maybe in the Underworld, but we've been gone—oooh, what—three months topside? Working on an accelerated timetable here. That's why your power is growing; it's not being stunted by the mortal realm. If you don't want to breathe, don't. Command your lungs to stop."

"Three months?" I balked, seeking out Theo. He nodded. *Fuck.* My mind raced with implications of my absence. My job. Tatiana. *Oh, shit, Tatiana.* She was going to kill me for abandoning her like this.

If I didn't drown trying to breathe underwater, first.

"We go together then," Theo announced, pulling both of our packs on his shoulders again. I eyed the lake's edge apprehensively.

"I just tell my lungs to stop?" I asked, raising my eyebrow skeptically.

Theo offered his hand, palm open and patient, unlike his brother. The other titan brayed and grumbled like a bull at the wait. Ignoring him, I slipped my fingers over Theo's, letting him guide me into neck-deep water. The slope was steep as I bobbed on my tiptoes, water lapping around my ears. Well, *I* was neck deep, Theo's massive body was only chest deep, his fingers clutched in mine as I worked through the nerves of this lunacy. He crouched slightly in the water, lowering until we were face-to-face. His free hand slid around my torso, warming me with his touch. Gently, he pried his fingers from my grip, completing the circuit around my body until both of his palms rested on my back, each over a lung.

"I'm going to help you, but you have to meet me halfway. When I say take a deep breath in, then once we're submerged, release that breath entirely. In your mind's eye, I want you to imagine deflating a balloon all the way and order your lungs to *obey*. You don't need them to breathe. You're a divine being, Zarena. And I am here with you; I won't let you drown." His soothing voice washed over me, calming my pounding heart.

Epimetheus rolled his eyes. "I know Zeus can't technically get us down here, but I'd like to find the box before the turn of the next century if that's alright with you two."

Theo scowled, shooting daggers from the corner of his eye at his brother. "Fuck off," he spat before turning his attentions back to me. "Ignore him; he's a miserable bitch." I let myself get lost in the deep emeralds of his eyes, of the lichen striations bursting around his pupil in contrast. "Eyes on me. You ready?" he asked. I focused, sucking in a long breath. Theo guided us lower into the water, pulling me against him. The water rose over my chin and mouth, my nose and eyes. Deeper and deeper, until we were enveloped in the cool waves, weightless in the abyss once more.

His eyes pierced through me, an anchor I held on to as I steadied my mind and forced trapped breath from my lungs, picturing a balloon just as Theo instructed. Bubbles erupted from my lips, and my mind screamed, even as I willed myself to not panic. I concentrated on Theo, on the strong hands on my back. Two quick pulses from his palms jolted power through my lungs, expelling the last remnants of air from my body in a flurry.

Panic clawed up my throat, lungs burning, water stinging my nose and windpipe as it filled all the spaces water should never be.

Theo wouldn't let me drown. I could trust him. I did trust him. My shoulders relaxed as tension slowly released and I opened my mouth, stopped fighting the intrusion of the water. Stopped thinking of it as an intrusion at all. My mind stilled as we floated, dark strands of his hair catching golden in the rays of light permeating the surface. He smiled, beaming with pride. For a moment, time stopped around us. I felt safe enough, for the first time since this chaos began, to appreciate the fantastical wonder around me. *A muse.* Magic and power. The same wonder I'd chased on excavation sites, in the thousands of hours spent pouring over texts older than most countries, it was *here*. All around me. *In me.*

And it started when this man, this *titan*, blew through my world. Prometheus held me with no expectations, no new bombshells to drop on my life.

Slowly we sank, lost together in the ambient light.

My eyes adjusted as we drifted, locked in our embrace. My world quieted, my mind settled, but the pull under my ribs yanked me closer, pressing me against his chest. Heart to heart, the rhythms galloped between us, slowing together until they danced as one indistinguishable sound. Theo cupped my face. I held his gaze, a thousand unspoken words passing between us. His thumb traced over my jawline in soft touches, my fingers tangled in the hair over the base of his neck. Bright schools of fish swam around us, their yellows and blues reflecting off the sunlight from the surface. For the rest of my days, I would remember this moment, this feeling of surrendering to a power higher than even the gods.

Fate.

Our feet sank into swaying grass, a looming shadow bathing us in shade. Though I was certain the moment I saw the vast, submerged building we were in the right place, I couldn't feel the pull of it. No, that hummed in the space between Prometheus and me. It grew no less powerful when he released me enough to swim us over to the cold, marbled steps of this Grecian temple.

It rose high, cutting an imposing silhouette against the surface of the lake behind it, at least twice the size of the Sillah. Several other smaller buildings sat in a circle around it, each with columns decorated with carved Greek sigils along the top. My brain struggled to unscramble the letters, blurred in the light, but I knew I could read them, if I focused. They were a part of me. I let my eyes sink shut for a breath, centering myself. When I reopened them, the sigils descrambled, revealing all their secrets to me.

Giant caches, labeled like stacks in an ancient style of the Dewey Decimal System. If I could cry underwater, my tears of joy at the sheer magnitude of this would have drowned us all. Theo squeezed my hand, drawing my attention back to a tipped spear resting above the solid, wooden doors. A lock to key, I slid my fingers across the shaft, knowing instinctually what I needed to do to get us inside. The skin split under the blade of the spear, still pristine and deadly sharp despite its watery home. Crimson blood bloomed over the water in inky tendrils that we watched swirl like a vortex around us before floating over the lock on the door. Clio's blood.

My blood.

The doors lowered like a dam, sucking the surrounding water and our bodies inside, something neither of us were prepared for. We crashed together over hard marble, Theo's body absorbing the brunt of the fall as water poured in a deluge from my nose. I coughed, gagging as I fell to the side and wretched, dry heaving the last dredges from my lungs and esophagus. Above us, the doors righted themselves before the chamber could fill up. The knee-deep water that made it inside retreated along tiny grooves set into the floor, flowing back out through the wall by some perversion of physics. I stood, soaked from head to toe, and looked around.

Theo stared in wonder at the glass-domed ceiling above us, at the fish that were giving us a show as they wove and swam around the Library. Two obelisks stood to either side of a set of steps that led up into a massive cavern of intricately carved and gilded white marble, veins of midnight blues and gold shining against the polished stone. Bookshelves lined row after row behind them, and I stumbled forward, caring little about the mess I was making over the clean stone.

Theo fumbled over a large copper disc suspended in the middle of the floor, a mirror positioned just beneath the glass dome. Moments later, a large flame erupted from it, illuminating the upper levels with reflective mirrors that caught the firelight. I stopped breathing, as the light danced, traveling from row to row, shining on shelves thought to be lost to humanity forever. A sob clawed its way up my throat, tears hot and stinging, watered my eyes as I took it all in.

The Library of Alexandria.

Was screaming appropriate? Should I even fucking care? I spun slowly on my heel, in awe of every inch I could see. This was a place I'd only dreamt about. Once burned to the ground. The greatest lost collection of cultural wealth in the entire world, and here I stood, dripping goddamn lake water over the pristine floors. Theo looked over his shoulder at me with that devastating smile of his and I knew, at that moment, he *saw* me. He understood what this meant—the weight of this discovery. It was the single greatest thing I'd ever been a part of.

Something for myself.

Finally.

Prometheus

CHAPTER 51

Emotion pulsed from Zarena, strong and vibrant as the fucking cord in my own chest, and I could no longer deny that this thing between us wasn't just an aftereffect of a talisman, or some series of insane invents to ensure a compass found a map, or magic. Or rather that it *was* but an older magic—one born of stardust and prophecies and the very fabric of the cosmos. I felt her joy like my own fucking beating heart, clear and strong and wild as she beamed at me, devastatingly beautiful in her rapture.

I was completely and irrevocably fucked.

Two great loves in my life came and went, but neither ever produced a Bond. Bondmates weren't always predestined, rather forged over time, feeding off the inner makings of our essences. No one knew how the Fates decided which webs to weave together, and more than a few had wasted a boon asking. Tens of thousands of years on this planet and *nothing*. But four days with this infuriatingly incredible woman?

It was over for me.

I gave myself just a minute, just one minute to look at her. To take in her strength, her beauty. The intelligence that called to me on a primal level—to desire, to hunt, *to claim*. One minute, before I let the reality of our situation set in, let the panic slide through my veins like the icy waters of the Styx.

One minute, cut short thirteen seconds by the impatience of my fucking brother.

"Ogle later, we need to find the box," Epimetheus barked. I was unsure which of us he meant—Zarena looking around the Library, or me looking at *her*.

"Give her a second," I snapped, rounding on him as he crossed his arms impatiently.

I took a moment to look at Epi and what I saw set me on edge. He'd been far more injured in the melee than he'd let on, and up close, I saw the wounds that hadn't managed to heal—even though they should have. His skin was torn and bubbled up in some areas like he'd been burned; his eyes blacked with bruises, his lip, split in two. I reached for him to examine the scope of his injuries, but he waved me off with a bark and backed away.

"How badly are you hurt?"

"I went four rounds with the Minotaur. What did you expect, Prometheus?" He clipped, but that biting undercurrent of anger told me every word cost him effort. Zarena approached, her head still in a daze, but Epimetheus was already gone, taking the steps two at a time.

"What's wrong with him?"

I shook my head. "I think he believes if we get to the box, it'll have a clue about how to get Pandora back." Sadness settled over me for my brother, for the loss he'd endured.

"He really loved her, didn't he?"

I looked at Zarena, knowing if what he felt for Pandora was even a fraction of what I'd felt for Hesione or Helen or Zarena, it would have been enough to break him in two, losing her like that. There was a special kind of heartache from a love that voluntarily left this world. "I think he truly did."

Zarena reached for my hand, and I didn't fight the pull, so grateful for her touch.

"Let's see if we can find her then."

We walked, hand in hand. I let Zarena lead, feeling her power shift and permeate the air unfiltered, guiding her to wherever she needed to go. Past the main stacks of books and artifacts, down a tall hallway with constellations painted on the ceiling, we finally found Epimetheus in a study-like room, eyes glued to a wall full of identical jars, which looked a lot like the one Pandora was charged with protecting.

"Your mother sure did have a sense of humor using decoys to thwart Zeus," he grumbled.

Zarena grimaced, moving to examine the round urns, burnt umber–colored terracotta pots with identical sigils adorning the clay. Her fingers grazed over the jar nearest her, and instantly, her head flew back as a vision overtook her, eyes glazing over.

It lasted less than a moment, before she returned to the now, eyes watering. Breathless.

"What did you see? Pandora?" Epimetheus pressed, fidgeting.

"No. Just my mother walking in a field of flowers." Her voice trembled, the vision a gift of memory. It wasn't hard to surmise what the Muse of History had done, before locking this place away for good.

Clio imbued these jars with her dearest moments, ones that helped shape her, precious snapshots of a life her daughter would never have otherwise seen. Now, Zarena could Witness, whenever she wanted.

She worked methodically, her hand roaming over jar after jar, shelf after shelf. More soft smiles for me, more pitying smiles for Epimetheus, whose scowl grew more pronounced with each perceived failure.

Zarena's hand ghosted over the second to last jar on the third shelf up, and I bristled at the strangled cry ripping past her lips.

Something was different about this vision. She whimpered, body trembling with anger, tears falling with abandon down her cheeks. Epimetheus and I exchanged a tense look, but the need to go to her, to take away anything that could give her pain flooded through me, the strongest surge of adrenaline to *protect, protect, protect*.

Whatever she saw filled her with sadness and rage, more deadly in its fury than any storm.

Zarena

CHAPTER 52

These jars were a keepsake trove my mother left for me. I knew that, like I knew my name, like I knew the sun rose each day. When Zeus made her build this place, she hadn't built it for him or even for herself. She'd built it for *me*, knowing one day I'd walk these shelves. See these memories. Her memories, her blood.

My blood.

Some jars made me cry from joy and laughter; some settled peace over me, observing her in quiet moments. It was surreal, gathering the most important moments of her lifetimes, memory I could hold in my hands and experience like a home movie. She showed me in her own way how to care for the Library. Left instructions on how to read the shelves, understand the artifacts and their importance.

But I knew the minute I hovered over the next jar something sinister awaited me. The story it bore Witness to would not be one of joy or contentment, the taste of sorrow was rife in the air. This was the jar Epimetheus sought. The one Theo did too. My fingers grazed the side, and I resigned myself to the incoming pain as it transported me to a time long ago, to a house by the sea.

The taste of salt from the sea floated in on the breeze, and a woman, so beautiful she could be comfortably compared to Aphrodite, sat at a table in a home that overlooked the open ocean. Pandora was radiant and lithe, delicate as a flower, with her dark hair and pale gray eyes.

Hushed whispers filtered through the room, cloying and sweet and tempting, surrounding the lady. "Come and see, Pandora. Come and see. We only want to gaze upon your beauty, come and see," they whispered, and she swatted them away as a horse would a fly. She leveled a glare at the jar sitting on the mantle above her hearth.

For years and years, those voices whispered to her, tempted her to just take a peek, but she resisted. The distractions of her household kept the wolves at bay, but when she was alone, in times such as these, the curiosity ate at her core, fraying the edges of her sanity. When Epimetheus was home, she was so enamored with her husband, with his laughter and kisses and lovemaking, that the voices quelled their demands.

But Epimetheus had been at sea for Poseidon for a week and the voices grew louder, emboldened and incessant. They clawed at her mind in the waking hours and when she slept, slithered in her dreams, taunting her with their wicked words. Seven days she resisted, seven nights she'd been denied peaceful slumber. She glanced back at the jar, palms itching to just touch it, to run her fingers over the terracotta and feel its ridges. The jar was just so beautifully made, as she had been.

"Just like you!" they whispered to her.

She stood, shuffling on her feet, chewing on the inside of her cheek. Just a touch and her mind would quiet, she just knew it. Her feet ate up the short distance between her table and the hearth, and she froze, waiting.

"Come and see," they cooed, urging her on, pulling to her. Pandora's finger slid over the top of the jar, felt the groove in which it sat, tracing lovingly over the ridges and grooves and intricate designs there.

"Just a peek, then rest."

She was so, so tired and so tortured; she just needed relief, just one moment of peace without their whispered demands.

Once more, her fingernail dug into the ridge, this time in earnest as she applied just the tiniest bit of pressure. The lid moved just a fraction. Pandora stopped breathing. Waiting. The world had not yet ended, and the whispers grew louder, more excited. She slid the lid around, toying with the seal.

"Just a peek and then you can sleep, beautiful Pandora."

It wasn't a conscious decision in her mind, to lift the lid. It happened like love—slowly at first, then all at once. One moment it was nestled safely over the jar, the next, it rested flat against her palm, and she was staring at the opened jar. Silence. Blissful silence blanketed the room, her mind. She sobbed in relief, shoulders relaxing. It was over. It was over and the world hadn't ended.

The room erupted with a howling menace as stream after stream of dark entities entered the world. Some so ancient had been cramped in that jar since before the sun shone, some as new as baby's breath, bred within, the progeny of the dwellers of chaos.

Pandora felt sorrow and despair as it sank through her, burrowing against her skin like a brand. Horror sliced through her as the weight of her actions registered in her sleep-deprived mind, and she tried to recap the lid, tried to right it again, but the force was too great. She was too, too tired.

When the tornado of demons fled the jar, leaving nothing but the stench of rot and decay in their wake, a trembling Pandora peaked inside with a tear-streaked face to see not darkness, but a tiny tendril of light swirling closer and closer to the opening of the jar. It wasn't like the others, the ones that fled with malice. No, this was something pure, loving. Forgiving. She wanted it to be free, found herself rooting for it to break the surface and taste the salt-tainted air as it struggled to flee, a little weaker than the rest.

She had half a mind to reach in and scoop it out, raised her hand to do just that, when a giant hand slammed over the jar, another wrenching the lid free of Pandora's grasp. Zeus stared down at her, grim and serious. She stumbled back, clutching her chest, quaking with fear. He replaced the cap and set the jar back on the mantle before turning to Pandora, the young one breaking apart with the weight of what she had done.

"You have to help me, Zeus!" she cried, wringing her hands and clutching her stomach.

He crossed to where she sat and scooped her up into his arms. "Shhh, shh, Pandora. Do not cry, all is well," he soothed, stroking her hair.

"How?" She sniffled, his touch foreign and uncomfortable but his grip held like iron. "How can all be well? I failed at my charge and now those . . . those things are loosed upon the world."

"You did not fail, Pandora. You did exactly what you were created to do."

Pandora stilled, struggling to reconcile the words of the God of Gods. She pulled from his grasp, breathed a sigh of relief when he let her go freely. "I do not understand." she whispered.

Zeus's beautiful face split into a sinister grin, shedding the kind, jovial persona she'd always known him to have, trading it for something darker. "You were always supposed to let out the woes and despair, as punishment to Prometheus and his arrogance with mortals," he spat the last word, and Pandora flinched.

"Why would this affect Prometheus? He was not charged with keeping the jar shut," she whimpered, tears flowing freely down her cheeks.

Zeus let out a dark laugh and crossed over into her space once more. Pandora shrank back, hitting her hip against the table. Zeus's gaze licked down her body in a way that she knew was dangerous.

"Because Prometheus was too cunning to accept anything from me, but he values family, what little he has of it. This will ruin Epimetheus, and in turn, your shortsighted husband will blame his brother for your loss. Prometheus tried to warn Epimetheus about receiving my gifts, but your husband is a petulant, foolish god, girl. Unworthy of a prize such as you. Tell me," he mocked, crowding too close to be proper, "has he fucked you well?"

Pandora flinched at his words, shrinking in on herself in every way she could.

The God of Gods trailed a finger over her trembling face, and she closed her eyes at the contact, a tear streaming down her cheek. "Aphrodite did her job well in bestowing your beauty. It's wasted on Epimetheus. I think I'd like a taste."

Before Pandora could beg him not to, before she could even cry out, he was on her. Zeus gripped her throat so tightly her eyes bulged, his rough hands ripping at the fabric of her pale blue chiton. The hand strangling her throat thrust her backward on top of the place settings on the table. A plate bit into her back and she cried out, pushing at his chest.

"That's right, fight me for it." His hot breath on her face, her ear, everywhere as he kissed her hard, bruising her lips, forcing her mouth open. Zeus kicked her knees apart while she tried desperately to keep her thighs together. He only laughed, mocking her feeble attempts, lording his power over her.

Relishing in the breaking of her.

Tears flowed unchecked as she begged and pleaded for him to stop. "Zeus, please, I am married. I love my husband, please, please." But he just pressed himself against her, a sadistic smile on his face as she sobbed. His hand scraped against her bare flesh as he lifted her legs, ignoring her attempts to deny him. Bile rose in her throat, choking her words. A large hand, licked from palm to fingertip slathered against her, a precursor for the violation. He took her without mercy, reveling in her pain, tearing her with his force. He never lessened the hold on her throat while he violated her against the table—the table where she shared loving meals with her husband.

He spoke words, insults to her cries, ambivalent to her protestations. "This is . . . Yessss. Such a good whore, exquisite . . . Should have fucked you before I let him touch you, stretched you wide . . . Scream for me, whore . . ."

He carried on for hours, ignoring the tears and the blood and the whimpers she managed to eke out. She sobbed with relief when he finally pulled out of her body. Pandora sank to the floor, ravaged. Above her, The God of Gods stroked himself to completion, one hand holding her face up in a bruising grip that cracked bone. He left himself there, on her face, in her mouth, adding humiliation to what he'd done.

Left no part of her she could retreat in.

Breathing deep, he brushed back his unruly blond locks, tucking himself away as he straightened. "You will speak of this to no one. I created you, woman. I own you now, and I will have you whenever I wish. Be ready for me tomorrow, I have not had my fill yet. I will ensure Epimetheus is held at sea so our fun will go uninterrupted."

He left her there, on the floor, blood staining the chiton Epimetheus had made just for her. She lay on that floor until the sun set outside, and when she forced her abused body to rise, Pandora dragged herself to the bathhouse in their home and fell into the water.

Be ready for me tomorrow.

But she would never let him have her again. She could not hope to endure it.

And so, she didn't.

I turned to Epimetheus, staring at me with a wary gaze and in it, I saw a darkness. The flesh of him grayed, like he was rotting from the inside out. He reached to touch the jar, but on instinct, I blocked his contact. Icy fingers rested over mine in the movement. An electric current seared through me. Epimetheus's eyes locked on mine, and this close, I clearly saw the brown irises bisected with onyx blues. His eyes were split as though *he* were being split in two. I realized, a beat too late, his skin wasn't burning from my touch.

He knew things he shouldn't have, and now he touched me without pain, free and clear.

I raised my leg and kicked him in the chest with every ounce of power I possessed, putting some distance between us. His body flew through the air from a magic I didn't know I possessed, bolstered by my anger. Epimetheus landed gracelessly across the room against an ornate, circular portal that gazed into what looked like a deep, rippling ocean. Theo whipped around in alarm, eyes on his brother as the titan struggled to right himself.

"Did you tell him my mother built this place?" I demanded.

Theo put it together the same moment Epimetheus let out a sadistic laugh.

"Is that what gave it away? Damn, I'm losing my touch." He stood on shaking legs, pieces of skin flaking off in sheets—as though he was shedding.

"*Zeus*," Theo spat.

Epimetheus raised his arms wide and slipped into a mocking, low bow. "Zeus, indeed."

Prometheus

CHAPTER 53

"Where is he?" I demanded, reaching for the knife on my thigh. Panic rose, but I stifled it. There would be room to dissect *how* this happened later.

The monster wearing my brother's face shrugged. "He's around. I don't really know the mechanics behind it, but he's in here." He tapped his forehead twice before taking a step closer to Zarena. "You truly are a thing of beauty. The resemblance to Clio is uncanny." His split irises flicked over her form in a hungry perusal. "I wonder if *everything* feels the same."

Zarena let out a low growl, leveling the dagger Ares gave her at him. "Fucking try it," she snarled.

Zeus cocked his head. "In due time. Now here's how this is going to go: Give me the jar, and I'll give your brother back." He spoke directly to me, but it was Zarena who answered for us both.

"Better idea. I kill you both, right here and now." She countered, inching slowly to her left. Her eyes flew to mine for a split second, but I understood. *Flank him.* Zeus barked a laugh, sending another bit of my brother's flesh to the ground.

"How did you get in there, Zeus? Did he let you in? What did you promise him?" I asked, thoughtfully. The fucker's eyes bounced between Zarena and me, backing just out of reach. We circled each other like sharks waiting on the feeding bell.

"Pandora. I get Zarena, he gets her back."

"I suppose you failed to tell him you couldn't actually bring her back? Everything about her was borrowed, and more than half of those people would rather be eaten by a chimera than do anything for you."

Zeus remained unfazed. "I have my ways, Prometheus. You of all people should understand how creative I can get, once provoked . . ." he trailed off, leaving the threat hanging between us. "I'm bored of this." He brought his hand up, summoning Epimetheus's maul. I called my own sword to me, closing my palm around the hilt of it as he twirled his weapon lazily. We squared off against each other, but his eyes continued to clock Zarena as she moved, and that scared me.

"Heard you'd been sampling my goods, Prometheus." Zeus tsked in disapproval. "Though, I do suppose it's fair considering just how much I enjoyed that mortal woman of yours. What was her name? Hailey? Hannah? Ah, yes . . . *Helen*. Exquisite cunt. Did you know she, quite literally, *choked* to death on my cock? I shoved it right down her throat unt—"

He never finished vocalizing that thought, because, despite my better judgment, even knowing it was a taunt, I charged, summoning every ounce of my busted ass divinity to do it. Rage poured through me with the action, hotter than any forge Hephaestus ever stoked, more savage than any enemy Ares ever faced. It was a living, breathing entity and it demanded retribution, payable only in the spilling of blood.

Zeus's blood. And my brother's, for good measure.

The bastard blocked and parried as I struck, fast and precise, but I never relented, not for a damn moment. He was a formidable fighter, but the weight of his possession seemed too much for Epimetheus's body to handle, and every rush of his divine power burned bits of flesh from the titan, a vessel overwhelmed by the power Zeus wielded inside of him, but I didn't allow to make me complacent. Even in his confined state, Zeus was vicious in his savagery, with an endless well of power thanks to his Bond with Hera.

A bolt of red hair flashed in my peripheral as Zarena struck him hard, slicing cleanly into his thigh with Ares's sword. Zeus let out a hiss as blood flowed freely from the cut, staining his denim-clad thigh with crimson. He maneuvered away from us, regrouping.

"You've got some fight in you, I'll give you that," he remarked to Zarena, spitting blood on the marble floor. "I'll enjoy break-ing you."

She rushed him, all anger and violence, but I flung my arm out protectively, snatching her back, unwilling to let her get close enough for him to put his hands on her. Zarena raged but made no move to disobey even as she vibrated with rage.

He cocked his head to the side, assessing our contact point, the protective stance, sensing the tangible tether between us. "Prometheus." Amusement clouded his tone as he shifted his gaze between us. "You just can't help yourself, can you? Have you learned *nothing*?"

It didn't matter that he saw what she meant to me; he wouldn't live long enough to do anything about it. He would die, maybe not tonight, but we could trap him in Epimetheus's body until it broke down completely. Buy ourselves enough time to get the jar to Hermes and Hera. But I need Zarena out of here. For her to take Pandora's box and go out the way we came, get it to our people at the Mouth.

"How long have you had him, Zeus?" I asked, switching gears, buying enough time for his vessel to weaken. A vicious wound opened along Epimetheus's neck, necrotic and rotten as black, foul-smelling ichor leaked out with my brother's blood. Zeus's power burned through the titan's form, I just needed to draw this out.

Keep him talking, he loves to gloat.

I ignored the nagging sorrow creeping in at the knowledge that my brother becoming a casualty was likely the only chance we had, but he had chosen this. Opened up and let Zeus in, without care or regard for what Zeus would do to me, to Zarena. Our entire life, I'd made excuses for him, but even if I wasn't the one who struck the killing blow, his body would not survive this form of diabolical possession by the God of Gods. There was an order to things. A balance.

This was Epimetheus's bill, come due.

"In here?" He gestured lazily to his body. "Since the Mouth. Snuck in when Poseidon showed up. I knew it would alert Hades that *one* of us was trespassing, but I figure he'd have his hands full with Poseidon. But I've been in your brother's ear for decades."

Zarena's thumb traced across my flesh, an arrow pointing to the jars. I grunted once, barely a sound in confirmation. She had to get to the jar to ensure he couldn't get what he came for. We were in tune now, one unit that understood the other without the need for words. Just a tether. I wanted to tell her I loved her, or that maybe I was falling in love with her. I wanted to pour everything into our Bond, to will her to feel it wrap around her heart and lungs until she *knew*.

The pads of her fingers pressed into my skin once, twice.

Together, we surged, each moving in a different direction. Her boots thundered off the hard marble leading to the shelves and my own war cry filled the room as I blocked Zeus's path to her. I didn't dare look back to see if she made it out of the room. I had to trust that she could.

Zarena

CHAPTER 54

My lungs burned in protest, but I ran. The sounds of the fight were brutal. The clash of steel thundering against the stone echoed through the hallway as I gripped the jar to my chest and tore through the Library. I sent up a silent prayer to whomever may be listening that my usual clumsiness would relent long enough for me to hide this artifact from Zeus, then return to help Theo.

Theo.

Every step carrying me away from him felt like I was running through mud, the atoms in my body screaming their demand to get back to him. Zeus would kill him. He'd use Epimetheus's body as leverage, counting on Theo's inability to do severe harm to his brother, but Prometheus knew what was at stake if Zeus got this jar. What it would mean for everyone, without a path to taking him down.

My heart pounded in my chest as I descended the stairs three at a time, in an unprecedented show of grace and agility, and tore off through the stacks. I swept my eyes around the vast room, searching for someplace to hide, finding nothing usable. Everything here

was for display, not discretion, and it wasn't like the orange clay
didn't act as a neon sign against the gold and teakwood of the
other artifacts.

An agonizing roar ripped through the Library, and the very
foundation shook in response, tilting the world on its axis.

No, not the world, I realized as I fell forward. *Just me.*

I fell, knees buckling under the ripple of pain radiating from
my torso. The marble floor rose to meet me, cold and unforgiving
as I smacked into it, my head cracking against stone. I tightened
my arms around the jar, doing everything in my power to buffer
it from the impact as shockwaves of pain rippled through me,
agonizing and unrelenting. Another sharp stab, this one like being
tased by a thousand volts of 'fuck you' ripped a scream from my
throat, punctuated by rapid footfalls from somewhere behind me.

Large hands gripped me by the hair, searing my scalp, the stench
of rotten flesh making me gag as I was dragged back across the
floor. Zeus bent to wrench the jar from my fingers, tucking it into
the crook of his arm, triumph in the horror of his face. He yanked
at my hair, ripping out strand after strand in his unrelenting grip,
speaking words through broken teeth I couldn't understand. Pain
radiated through my shoulder, my hip as he dragged me back to the
study kicking and screaming and clawing. I gouged valleys in his
wrists, his forearm, the mottled flesh tearing away in strips under
my nails. Every step back up to the dais banged into my legs and
hips and back, and Zeus relished every cry, every jolt of pain.

Still, I fought.

The grip on my scalp tightened, flashing my vision white as he
lifted me to my feet, leashed by my own hair.

"*Look!*" he demanded, words slurring through the meat suit
rapidly decaying around his consciousness.

I screamed.

Theo's body was impaled through the chest, limbs bent at
unnatural angles, held aloft by two spears that went through the

marble ground. Blood ran freely as his head bobbed toward me on broken groans, his green eyes glassy, filled with rage as he struggled to stay conscious. I could taste his fear and panic as though it were mine, and with it, the rage burning through him at seeing Zeus's hands on me. Of hearing me cry out in pain from every twist of the fucker's fist in my hair.

Zeus bent low to whisper in my ear, "I honestly expected more." His hand shifted to the nape of my neck, arching my neck painfully, forcing me prone to look in his eyes. His irises flickered between brown and black slowly as he spoke above me, touting his own accolades. I shut him out and searched those eyes, seeking out some sign Epimetheus was in there. It was something I should have been able to do with my powers, surely, but I was still a fumbling baby deer in all things divine.

Throwing all caution to the wind, I winged it, hoping Epimetheus was somewhere beneath the gore and cruelty, listening in.

"Epi," I pleaded. "Epimetheus, I know you're in there. Please, *fight*. Fight him."

Zeus let out a sharp laugh, a twisted smile overtaking Epimetheus's once handsome face. "Why would he fight it? He *wanted* me in here, begged me to use him as I saw fit."

I ignored Zeus, speaking directly to the titan inside, focusing on the flecks of deep brown. "He hurt her. Pandora didn't kill herself. She loved you. While you were at sea, he tricked her, *raped* her, he—"

A sharp smack rocked through my jaw, rattling my bones. My head snapped back, the blow stunning me as blood rushed down my nose, filling my mouth. Theo roared, thrashing against his crucifixion.

"Lies."

I pressed on, refusing to be silenced. "Epi, he did. I *saw* it. She was wearing a blue dress, the color of her eyes. E-Ep-Epimetheus, *please*."

Another hit, this time a backhand that landed so hard blackness dotted my vision. I didn't know how much a half Muse could take, but I was willing to bet it wasn't much more. The copper tang of blood flooded my mouth, and I spat it up at him, adding to the twisted macabre puppet he wore.

"You're a vile, repugnant psychopath who's raped countless women because you're too pathetic to get one to voluntarily touch your dick. She begged you, told you how much she loved her husband." I swallowed, tongue swelling in my mouth as murder shone in Zeus's eyes.

But so did something *else*.

"I'm not a man, you worthless bitch. I'm *the God of Gods*. I don't answer to you or anyone else." He jerked back, slamming my head to his body, and jerked us back, jar tucked under his arm. My feet fought against the floor in vain, scuffing the marble in a trail of blood and ichor. Zeus pulled me over to the swirling archway as I thrashed, but my strength waned. Pulling a coin from his pocket, he tossed it in. The portal pulsed, flaring to life with the brightest light.

Zeus grinned, looking over to Theo. "You're going to live because I *will* it so. And through this little connection you two have, you're going to feel *every fucking thing* I do to her. *Every. Single. Thing.*" He pulled me up to press my body flush with his and licked up my cheek. My stomach turned.

Theo roared, thrashing so hard one of the spears buckled. The momentum sent him careening to the floor in a tangle of metal and blood. I watched in horror as he tried to crawl to me, dragging his massive body through the remnants of his brother, my blood, desperate to get to us. I struggled as Zeus hoisted me toward the massive structure containing the portal, the golden frame separating this reality from whatever lay beyond. I dug my fingers into the side of it as he tugged, kicking and screaming in any way that I could. I didn't want to die like this. I wouldn't go quietly, if this really was it.

The biting grip on my scalp stilled, loosening. Squinting through my rapidly swelling eyelid, I was met not with a pair of split obsidian irises, but the solid, warm browns of Epimetheus's.

"Show me." He struggled to speak, war for control inside of him one we both knew he couldn't win, but he was trying anyway. I didn't know *how* to show him, I hadn't learned that yet, but instinct took over in this trial by fire. I grabbed his face, thinking of everything I saw, every sordid, soul-crushing detail, and I put it in the mind of the titan who'd betrayed us.

Zeus sneered through black irises, now firmly in place. Panicked, I grabbed for the side of the portal again, fingernails scraping divots into the edge, straining with the effort to stay grounded. Theo roared, halfway across the floor, leaving bloody smears in his wake. He wouldn't get there in time. I had to save myself or die trying.

The body beneath me shifted, releasing my wrist. "Do it," Epimetheus croaked, a haunted, devastated sound as I turned to him. Ares's dagger shook in his unsteady grip as he offered it up to me, the portal roaring behind us, this rotting corpse the only barrier keeping me from being sucked in. I didn't thank him. I didn't hesitate. Epimetheus nodded once as my fingers gripped the hilt, the titan letting go as brown gave way to black one more time. I knew Zeus could see, could hear.

I leveled the dagger at him. "I'm going to kill you," I snarled. "I'm going to rip your heart out of your chest and shred whatever is left. For you, I am Death and I'll be seeing you soon, mother-fucker." I pressed the jewel on the hilt, extending the dagger into a spear as Ares had instructed. It punctured through the soft flesh of the hollow of Epimetheus's throat with a sickening squelch, tearing through the rotten skin and bone and tissue with ease. Blood splattered my hands and face as the force of the blow blasted his body into the swirling abyss.

The portal stilled.

I dropped like a stone to the ground, the taste of blood a constant flavor on my tongue. Theo crawled toward me, and I reached for him, dragging my body across the floor to his. His chest covered mine and we collapsed together in the blood and ichor and gore. He held me close, his breath on my cheek, until Prometheus's heart shuddered to a slow stop. There was silence until darkness took me.

Prometheus

CHAPTER 55

Hades and Thanatos were waiting on me when I landed on the banks of the Styx; concern etched into every line of their faces.

"What happened, mate?" Tos asked.

"Later." I pushed past him, eyes searching for Charon. "I need to get back to Zarena."

"Is she hurt?" Hades put a hand on my shoulder, but I shrugged him off. Primal power shuddered through me; an all-consuming need that thrummed down the Bond to get to her. She'd been a fierce, avenging deity, striking in her brutality, but she was alone while I was incapacitated, and I'd seen her crumble.

"I need to get to her, Hades. *Now*."

He studied me with cold calculation swimming behind the icy blue eyes that bore into mine. The God of the Dead flung out his hand. A portal appeared, ripping through the fabric of his realm and I didn't wait, didn't hesitate. I jumped through and, at once, was transported to the stone archway deep inside the palace, the same one that would transport my shade back to my body. I put my fingers on the cool rock, grounding myself in the familiar sensation of floating as it carried me to *her*.

I slammed back into my body, aching from the beating but the wounds were already knitting themselves back together by the time I opened my eyes. Underneath me, the steady sound of Zarena's breathing filled my ears.

"*Thank Fates*," I cried, relieved even as blood seeped between our bodies. I couldn't tell how much was hers and how much was mine.

I rolled off Zarena with a groan, cradling her face in my hands. The skin over her eye was broken, already purpling from Zeus's blows, her plump lip split from where his knuckles struck. Anger and shame battled inside of me. I should have protected her. I should have fought harder, been smarter. As I stroked the hair out of her face, I vowed that I'd never let anything touch her again.

Her small hand wrapped around my wrist, and the sigh of relief that cracked my chest produced an audible cry.

"Hey, don't. Wherever your head's at, bring it back." Her voice was rough.

I grabbed her hand, bringing it to my lips. Kissed her palm, pressed the warmth of it to my face. "I'm sorry," I whispered, lips moving along the soft flesh of her wrist. My breath hitched, chest tight, and I could barely form words over the overwhelming anxiety that rocked through me. "I'm so sorry. I should have—"

Zarena didn't let me finish my train of thought. She shifted into a sitting position, crying out as she favored her ribs gingerly. "Prometheus, I'm here. I'm alive and so are you, and he's gone. He's gone and he can't get back here."

She rested my palm on her chest with both hands so I could feel her beating heart. So strong, so steady. Something wet splashed over my cheeks, and it took more than a moment to recognize the tears falling were my own.

"He didn't beat us. We survived," she assured, holding on to me. "He didn't win. He didn't." She repeated the words like a mantra, then held me like that, the same way she had on the mountain, with unrelenting strength and conviction.

I loved her. *I loved her.*

"Pandora's Box. He has it. We're never going to be able to break that Bond." It was a quiet misery, seeing him fly through that portal clutching that jar. We'd escaped with our lives, but we'd lost the thing we came for, the only piece of the puzzle that mattered in defeating his reign of terror. The hands rubbing circles on my back stilled, an amused expression on her face.

"Did he now?" I sat up, a flicker of hope sparking in the embers of my resilience at her expression.

"I'm pretty sure I saw him fly into oblivion with it."

Zarena's blue eyes twinkled with mischief. "Ah, I suppose he did. But I wonder what he will do when he realizes that jar contained nothing more than sentimental value to me. He can't see the memory it contains, but he'll learn soon enough it's not what he came for." Hope sparked, impossible yet eternal, in my chest.

"How?"

She gave me a smug look. "When I got to the shelves, I knew he'd come after me for the jar and I knew he'd seen where it was on the shelf. My first instinct was to grab it and hide it, but I also knew he'd be expecting that." She explained, walking me through her process. I brushed my hand over her busted lip, infusing warmth and healing. "I swapped the jar for the one next to it and ran while you had him occupied."

"*What?*"

Zarena untangled herself from my legs and stood as best she could. I rose with her, letting her lean on me as we hobbled over to the wall of clay artifacts. She bent, careful not to jostle her ribs, and hoisted up a jar that sat to the right of the empty space. "*This,* Theo, is Pandora's Box."

I stared at her, mouth agape, all thoughts that should have been scheming in my mind quieted. Quieted around one single thought, a solitary truth that clawed up the insides of me, pried open my mouth, and blurted it into the cosmos. I closed the distance between us, bringing my hands up to cup her face.

"I have to tell you something, and I have to do it right now, before another second passes." The words rushed out in a frenzy, but if I didn't say them, I might die. *Again.* "Every time I've let myself have a little bit of happiness, some small pocket of peace, it's been taken from me one way or another. I have no family left, a liver that kills me every night, and I push people I care about away because letting them close has always been a death sentence. But I can't. Not with you. This thing between us is real. I look for you in a room. I feel your light even when I'm in the Underworld and it guides me back home to you. I hardened my heart a long time ago, and you just up and decided that wasn't the way shit was going to work, and now, you're so far inside of my shade I don't think I can ever carve you out. It's a little broken in here," I admitted, pulling her hand up to press against my chest. "But if you want it, it's yours. Hells, even if you don't, it's yours. I don't have any expectations, but I'm done leaving things unsaid. I was in denial about what you meant to me, what the pull was that stitched us together, because loving someone in that all-consuming way *terrified* me."

Zarena's expression softened as she listened intently to me pour my heart out.

"It's broken, but it's yours. I can be better for you. I *will* be better," I stammered. We stood there for a long time, neither of us capable of doing more than just existing in each other's space.

A single tear slipped from Zarena's face, drawing a clean path through the blood and grime. Then she opened her mouth and shattered my heart.

"I don't want that, Prometheus."

Zarena

CHAPTER 56

It might have been more humane if I had shot him; the look of devastation on his face couldn't have been more earth-shattering. Theo swallowed thickly, jaw snapping shut as he tried to step back, but I moved with him, clinging to his fingers. "Wait. Let me explain. Can you give me that?" The look on his face told me he would have given me anything I wanted.

I sucked in a deep breath and continued, "I know that this was more than just some magical artifacts pulling us together. Even when you were so damn sure, I wasn't, and I knew by the end of this, I'd be the one bleeding out on the floor over you. I hear what you're saying to me, and the hopeless romantic in me wants to let you pull me into your arms and break me apart on this floor. Like, a lot more of myself than I'd like to admit wants that very badly." Theo's confusion ricocheted out of him and into my chest. The cord between us sparked and breathed, and it was *unnerving*, feeling so many emotions that weren't my own, but it felt right, where it sat, moving and flexing beneath my skin.

"I don't want you to be better *for me*. I don't need you to prove anything to me. What I need is a partner who will do the work to get his own shit together. I need you to want to be better for *you*. You've been through so much, Prometheus, lost so much. You've paid penance over and over again, and you have to learn who you are without that.

"Zeus is still out there. My road to vengeance is just starting, but your road to healing must begin somewhere." I grabbed his face between my hands and brought his forehead down to rest on mine. His eyes fluttered shut. I let mine as well, just feeling him through touch and energy.

"*I want us.* But I want you to do the work for *you*, so there can be an *us*. I'm gonna love you, loudly, from right here. When you're ready for me—truly ready—you come let me know. I'm patient, Theo. You're worth waiting for."

Theo's eyes snapped open, green orbs swimming with unshed tears. I lifted my lips to his and he hesitated, unsure if this was okay in light of my declaration. I waited for him there, needing it to be his choice to close the distance.

Softly, slowly, tenderly, he *did*.

THREE WEEKS LATER

We spent weeks cleaning up the mess Zeus made and exploring the Library. Epimetheus's body was discovered somewhere in the Sea of Monsters.

As for the two of us, we were stranded in Atlantis for a few days before we discovered how to properly use the portal. Theo was able to communicate with the others on his nightly jaunts into the Underworld, but it wasn't a long-term solution. But the great thing about libraries is the treasure troves of information buried within, and *this* place held all sorts of secrets. I spent my days in different parts of the stacks, gorging myself with knowledge, familiarizing myself with systems and artifacts. It wasn't long before I had that portal figured out, and we were able to bring a few of our companions through.

Hecate established a connection through an orb, much like a phone line, so we could communicate across the realms in the between moments. Andros, Medusa, Hecate, and Hermes took up residence in some of the guest housing in the city, and putting hands on my brother had me sobbing like a baby. There was a safety in family, after nearly dying at the hands of a psychopath, and I'd never been so grateful that Clio had found her way to my folks. The first two weeks, Atlantis was crawling with our people full-time, but by the third week, no one stayed over, and that was fine with me.

Theo and I had Atlantis to ourselves once more.

Clio built this place to be a haven for history, art, and literature. It was the greatest gift, to be the custodian of such vast history. A task Prometheus and I took very seriously. Each time I picked up an artifact my mother left for me, I gleaned more about her, and it helped me to feel a little closer to the woman who sacrificed so much so I could live. We found several tomes that seemed to be journals, accounts of my mother's history. Small snippets of herself she'd left behind, and, piece by piece, it framed a picture of who she was.

Theo took the words I said to him to heart. He met with Hygieia, the Goddess of Mental Health, twice a week. Now that we'd learned how to raise the Library from the lake, they sat on a bench near the shore and talked. I gave them their privacy, and I never pressed him to speak about his therapy. He never pressed about mine either.

And, fuck, was I in it. My parents and I had a strained relationship for the first time in my life. I understood why they kept everything from me logically, but feelings weren't always logical, and that breach of trust rocked the very foundation of my family.

Dro split his time between here and the N.O., picking up the slack at the restaurant from his absence. Papa explained his disappearance with the excuse that he was taking care of a sick family member, so he still had his spot, and purpose. I was grateful our little adventure into the Underworld hadn't stolen that from him.

As for my career—it was safe to say my reputation was, unfortunately, trashed to hell. Academic abandonment wouldn't go unpunished, and it had taken a visit and sizable donation from Hades to have them halt my program. I was given a sabbatical, but even with the God of the Dead's financial backing, I would be the subject of whispers and rumors, but there was nothing I could do about it now. I had to put that out of my mind to sort out later, because left to my own devices, I'd spiral over all the things that couldn't be changed. The last thing I needed was a pesky little mental breakdown upsetting the careful house of cards I'd built to keep my shit altogether. No, the Sillah would be tomorrow's problems; today had plenty of its own.

Theo and I slept in the same house, a sprawling open concept that I originally mistook for the Library. It sat high up, overlooking a waterfall, and giving us a bird's-eye view of the lost city. We had separate rooms, Theo clearly tried to respect my wishes. Every night, we'd say good night and part ways. But every night, around two A.M., one of us would slink into the other's bed. We wouldn't do anything, just sleep, sharing warmth and physical space. The Bond in our chests only truly at peace when we were together.

I wanted more and stopped beating myself up about that a few days in. Theo was made for me and my body called to him too. Every waking morning showed the proof of that wedged between us, but he kept his word and never made a move, which made me burn for him even more. Self-restraint on a man like that was infuriatingly hot. Made me want to brat him real bad, see how far I could push before he broke.

But that wasn't healthy, and we were learning.

Hades and Hermes told us to take a month for ourselves, that they would work on Zeus from the Underworld. We were safe here, a truly impenetrable fortress city that he couldn't get to, not without me. We rested and we read and we tried to heal. It wasn't over, this war. In fact, it had just begun. But for now, we would take whatever moments of peace we could get.

Medusa fucked Poseidon all the way up. To hear Dro tell it, she'd beaten the breaks off the God of the Sea in a furious storm of blades and venom. I found it fitting that he'd wear those scars he inflicted on her forever on his face, for all to see. It wasn't enough, but it was a start. When he fled, Medusa tried to follow, but Dro held her back, earning him a few bites himself. He didn't seem bothered in the slightest. I had a sneaking suspicion that the reason he split his time between us and the N.O. was because of a certain gorgon that kept a similar schedule.

But that was none of my business.

Prometheus
CHAPTER 57

iving out these last few weeks with Zarena in our little bubble of tranquility was a dream. So peaceful. And hard with the amount of therapy I'd been in. When I called Hygieia, she didn't hesitate, and for that I was grateful. We worked together to heal my mind, and the quiet moments I spent with Zarena healed my shade.

Every day I fell more in love with her. Every day I jerked my cock in the shower to avoid claiming her until I was ready. It was a slow torture, watching her walk around or lounge in the sun in a barely-there swimsuit, and not be able to bury my face between her legs. But she had been clear: She wanted me to work on me, and she'd be there when I was ready.

Judging by the rock-hard cock I had fisted in my hand while hot water sprayed down my back, I was fucking ready.

After my morning ritual, I set out to the Library. As I walked the streets of this hidden paradise, visions of what this place could be one day flashed through my mind. In a world without Zeus and Poseidon, where we could be free to study and teach and spread knowledge. Where I could love freely, without the fear of death hanging over our heads. Streets filled with life and laughter, our friends and families and children.

I walked to the lake's edge, to the above-ground entrance to the library. We kept it exposed now—the process of lowering and raising it was a nightmare, as we'd discovered. But the beauty of this city was that Clio had built it for Zarena to care for, and she took her job as a custodian extremely seriously. If I'd have let her, she would have slept in one of the small alcoves nestled throughout the Library just to be closer.

I took the stairs two at a time, eager to see my girl. The pull in my chest told me she was close, but the buzz of electricity under my skin, that thrummed when she was touching me, complained it wasn't close enough.

The first-floor mezzanine was empty, as were the rooms leading to the Blue Room, a nickname she'd lovingly bestowed upon it because of the portal that lived there as a permanent fixture. Zarena had spent weeks excavating the Library's secrets, and as its custodian, it opened for her and let her climb around in its bones. Every day she discovered something new, some small ability tucked away in an unassuming book.

The portal had been one of those secrets. It was traversable only with an amulet containing Zarena's blood. She'd had me help her make six, gifted to each of our people. Hermes, Hecate, and Hygieia each held one; Hades as well. Her brother, Andros, held another, and Ares, the last. The God of War had taken a special interest in Zarena's swordsmanship training. Every day they met to run drills, and each day she got a little closer to kicking his ass.

The portal lit up and I watched as Hygieia stepped through, her long hair braided back into a neat plait. She wore her scrubs and overcoat; her large round glasses pushed low on the brim of her nose. In her hands, she held notebooks filled with our sessions. I knew she would never betray my confidence, but the thought of my deepest fears and shame being written out for just anyone to take always set my teeth on edge.

"Bench or workshop today?" she asked. I considered.

"Workshop. I have something I'm working on," I replied, and she nodded, gesturing for me to lead the way.

My workshop was in one of the annex buildings just outside of the Library. Some were filled with artifacts or books, but on the fourth day of exploration, I found this one filled with clay and sculpting tools.

Sculpting had been one of my great joys in the days before I knew nothing but sorrow. It was precise and methodical work, unforgiving in its demand, but still artistic. I enjoyed pushing the clay and stone to temper beneath my fingers.

I'd learned that the need to control was wrapped around the lack of control I'd had over my life for thousands of years. Therapy was brutal but sometimes enlightening. I enjoyed the bits where I understood the why. I hated most of the rest.

We entered my studio and Hygieia made her way over to the couch and settled in. I grabbed my apron and began moving around, prepping the marble in front of me for today's work. I grabbed my chisel and small hammer and began the subtle tapping, indenting the marble.

The sound of pages being turned filled my ears as Hygieia began. "How are you feeling today, Theo?" she asked, her voice kind and detached. *Professional.* It didn't matter that I'd known her for eternity. When she was here in that coat with her notes, I was her patient.

I grumbled at the question. It was the same opening line she used each session, but I bit back the sarcastic retort working up to my lips, pushed past that defense mechanism. I struck the marble repeatedly.

"I'm uneasy today," I responded. Hygieia's mouth lifted just slightly. It was the first time I hadn't deflected or made a joke or been outright rude at her opening question.

She shifted, leaning in with fascination. "Do you want to tell me about it?"

I liked that about Hygieia, that she gave me choices. She didn't tell me what I needed, didn't chastise me. If I said I didn't want to talk about it, she would switch tactics and move on to something else, tabling the topic for another day.

I pressed my chisel up and delicately tapped. "When I woke up, Zarena was gone. She's been out in the city all day, but I haven't seen her yet." My chisel flew over the hard stone, and Hygieia made a note on that infernal notepad. A muscle in my jaw ticked, but I stayed it, and instead, focused on the marble slab taking shape in front of me.

"Why do you think that upset you?" A simple question.

I halted my chisel to regard her thoughtfully: "Because her being out of my sight for even five minutes paralyzes me," I admitted on a quiet breath.

"Because Zeus might take her? Hurt her?"

I considered. "Yes and no. I think about all the ways she could be taken away from me, and not just because of Zeus. He's a big factor, sure. But not just him. There's a lot of bad in the world, doc. Any of them could take her."

Hygieia made another scrawl. I ignored the barbed quip rising in my throat.

"That's reasonable considering what you've been through. So, what do you intend to do about it?" My chisel slipped.

"What do you mean? There's nothing I *can* do, right? I can't wrap the woman up in bubble wrap and lock her in this place forever. She's her own person." The words left a slightly bitter taste in my mouth because that's *exactly* what I fucking wanted to do.

Hygieia leaned in. "So, you're going to suffer in silence? Like with the mountain, when Hades begged you to get off the rock?" Her words sliced through that particularly fresh wound, and I flinched.

"That was different," I defended.

Hygieia raised her eyebrows. "Was it? Sure, the magnitude of the consequences was heavier then, but doesn't it go back to the same core? You suffering for the comfort of others?" The words hung heavily between us. I couldn't refute her logic.

Hygieia leaned back, tossing her golden plait over her shoulder as she studied me. "Do you often keep how you feel from Zarena?"

"Zarena knows I love her," I snapped, breaking off a piece of marble accidentally.

"Because you tell her?"

I frowned. "I told her once." She needed me whole, I wasn't there yet.

"Why are we here, Prometheus? Is it just because Zarena *told* you to get your shit together?"

I considered her words. Truthfully, when Zarena first suggested I talk to someone in a professional capacity about everything, I was desperate to do whatever she wanted to prove to her I was serious about us. But after these last few weeks, something changed. I needed this, even when it left me feeling flayed raw after.

"At first. But it's changed from what it was; the meaning behind it is different. I want to be worthy of her, and I don't think there's anything wrong with that. I don't want to say I love her then bleed all over her. That's not fair. And—I think I *want* to get better. I don't want to live in constant vigilance. I want peace like we're building here in Atlantis. But yes, I do want to make her proud."

"Tell me why you love her, Theo."

I let out a low whistle. "I don't know, doc. I think she just . . . She *sees* me. Sometimes right through me, but for the most part, she looks. And she listens. Like last week, with the stones." My voice cracked.

Last week, Zarena and I talked about Helen and my son, how I buried their bones in an unmarked grave so Zeus couldn't find them or hurt them again. The next day, she'd led me out to a small grove of trees with six markers. One for Helen and one for my boy—she'd had Thanatos find them and bring them here to rest. Another was a joint marker for Pandora and Epimetheus; moved with respect, she'd made sure of it. Two were for my father and mother; the last, for Hesione—a small eagle statue. She brought my family to me, a place to properly mourn their deaths. Tears stung the back of my eyes just thinking about it.

"It isn't just the Bond between us that forces a connection. That might have been how it started, but she made me fall in love with her. Not the Fates."

"And when do you think you'll be worthy of her? Where's the goalpost?" Hygieia prodded.

I stared at her, unsure. "Aren't you supposed to tell me? You're the professional," I volleyed back, but Hygieia was ready.

"There's no *I-Graduated-from-My-Trauma* medal, Theo. Only you decide when you're allowed to stop punishing yourself. *You decide*—not me, not Zarena. You get to choose when you get to be happy." She let the silence sit between us as I mulled over her words. "I think that's enough for today. I wanted to ask about the Reaping. Did the water work? Are you experiencing any side effects?" she asked. I shook my head.

Zarena was obsessive about figuring out how her own protective magic was nullified against Zeus and Epimetheus and spent days going over things in her head. But then she remembered the only thing she did differently was drink from her canteen full of water from the spring that fed the Fountain of Youth. Which led to research in the stacks. Then her on the orb to Hecate and Hermes for hours. From there, they decided to test a theory about the restorative powers of that spring. One that seemingly ended my nightly death cycle by stripping the curse from my body. At least it had for the last two weeks.

"Nothing yet, doc. But if that changes, I'll make sure you're the first to know." I dragged my hands over the marble, willing my power to polish it smooth.

Hygieia stood and admired my work with an appreciative gaze. "It's an accurate likeness."

I grinned. "That's the plan."

Zarena

CHAPTER 58

Theo left a note in the Blue Room asking me to meet him in his workshop, and as I walked up the stairs, nerves tingled in my stomach. Nothing but calm was coming from the other end of the Bond, but I hadn't ever been in his workshop. It was his space to create and let out his frustrations.

My hand shook slightly as I pushed through the wooden door. It was immaculately tidy, with a green velvet chaise and a large coffee table; the navy walls lined with tools used to sculpt clay and chisel marble.

In the center of the room stood Theo, bare-chested, his jeans slung low on his hips. My heart stopped as I took him in, but a second heartbeat roared to life deeper inside of me. It had been ages since I'd had him, and my mouth watered thinking about the last time, how he'd taken and taken and made me see the inevitable heat death of the universe.

His green eyes flicked to mine before traveling the length of my body. A slow smile graced his lips, and I was struck by his longer, shaggy hair, how it fell in waves around his eyes. He crossed the room with quiet grace and grabbed my hand, pulling me close.

"Theo? What's going on?" I asked in a low voice, though I had no idea why I was whispering. Something about this room felt sacred, holy. I wanted to respect it.

Theo walked me over to a large statue about his height, covered with a thin white sheet. He turned to face me, head bent low to focus on my eyes. "I love you, Red. I love you, and not because I can't help it. I love you because I deserve it and I deserve you. I'm not better—I don't know that I won't always be broken in some way—but I won't deny you or myself anymore. I tried to respect what you wanted, keeping our distance while I worked out my shit, but I'm not going to do that anymore. I'm not going to deny that I want to be inside of you every moment we're awake. I've got an extra three hours I haven't had in millennia, and I'd rather use the time fucking you with my tongue."

His words ripped a fire to life inside of me and I pressed my knees together, breathless.

"I'm done denying myself. So, if you don't want me to touch you, you better speak now. Because if you don't, I'm going to claim you, Zarena." He pulled my hand up around his neck, crashing our bodies together, emerald eyes ablaze. His free hand traced down the side of my face, reaching around to tug at my ponytail holder, freeing my hair.

"Tell me you love me, Red. Tell me you're mine," he begged.

I leaned into him, pressing so close I could feel the thrum of blood flowing beneath his skin. *This* is what I wanted from him. To see him recognize what he wants and let himself have it. "I've been yours since that night in Electric Delphi. Mark me up, Sir. Claim me."

Theo twisted me around, putting my back to his chest. I glanced curiously up at the sculpture while his hands roamed my body. "Pull the sheet," he instructed.

I tugged on the loose fabric until it slipped over the marble and pooled at our feet on the floor. The sculpture beneath left me dumbstruck. A perfect replica of Prometheus, every line and plane of his muscled body on display. It was so lifelike, so incredibly detailed, and when my eyes traveled farther south, I found the only difference. The cock on the statue wasn't quite as large as his, but it did have long, thick ridges that cascaded down the shaft. There were smooth mounds strategically placed around it, erotic and tempting and I shuddered with anticipation against him.

"Do you like what you see, Red?" he asked, grabbing my chin to arch my head back, greedy for my eyes.

I nodded, still entranced. "It's stunning. I especially love the cock work,"

His body shuffled us closer, until I almost touched the marble. The hand holding my chin traveled down my chest, over my nipples, and down my torso, teasing. His other hand he pressed to the chest of the marble, and the call of his power overwhelmed the space around us, teasing over my skin. Thick fingers danced with crackling white light, light he sent pulsing deep within the statue's torso. The buzz of magic in the air wound me up, already so desperate to feel him. Theo's fingers slid around my clit as he swallowed my whimpers, claimed my mouth, every sound, for his own.

"I remember a good girl who once had a fantasy," he teased, kissing the shell of my ear. I ground my ass into his groin, relishing the stiffness I could feel pushing back. "She wanted me to fuck her throat while she was on her back getting used. But I don't share, do I, Red? So, what was I to do? You know I can't deny you anything. If my girl wants it, she gets it. But only *my* cock, only *my* cum gets to drip down this perfect cunt."

My eyes drifted closed as I drowned in his words, so fucking turned on by the possessiveness in his voice. He slapped my clit and I cried out, eyes flying open. The little air left in my lungs evaporated. Where once stood a marble statue was now a very *alive* and in-the-flesh Prometheus.

Very alive.

I bounced my gaze between them, synapses misfiring. "Is he . . . is he real?" I stammered.

The living statue smiled Theo's smile. "I'm real, Red. Just a bit of my essence split into this vessel. Do you want to touch?" he asked, sandwiching me between them. His flesh was warm against me, hot as the titan at my back. Familiar green eyes stared down at me, and my core fluttered, dripping with arousal.

What a fucking man, my man.

I slid my hand down and wrapped my fingers around the exquisite cock, giving a languid stroke just to see. The ridges massaged against the inside of my hand, and I couldn't wait to experience how they felt inside of other parts of me. They both groaned, panting around me. "So, you can feel everything?"

Theo, behind me, nodded. "It's me, he's not another person. I'm just straddling my consciousness. Now, where were we?" he asked, and then they were both on me, hands roaming and squeezing, pulling my shirt over my head and peeling my shorts from my thighs. They lifted me easily, carrying me to the large mahogany table, one a little rough, one a little gentle as they positioned me on my back. One crawled up my body while the other disappeared for a moment, returning with two sets of leather restraints.

"Let me see if I remember this right," he teased, grabbing my hands one by one and securing the leather straps around my wrists before wrapping each of them around a table leg. "I think, in your fantasy, I was here." He stood over me, eyes on fire.

The other Theo kissed over my chest, yanking down my bra and exposing my nipple to the air. His hot mouth closed over it as he bit down, hard enough to jolt me from the table, before soothing it with his tongue. He trailed down over my abdomen and spread my lips wide, using the end of his tongue to work me up. Hot breaths kissed over my swollen clit, fire licked up my body from his touch, but I felt so empty, I needed *more*.

"And he was there." Theo's mouth locked over my cunt, licking and sucking like it was his last meal. Moaning, I was a shaking, writhing mess under that wicked tongue.

"I *love* those fucking sounds, Red. Keep making them for me, that's a good girl."

Theo undid the belt around his hips and slid it free, all the while tracking the bends and arches of my body. The crest of my first orgasm rose within me, and Theo wrapped his belt around my throat, securing it with a sliding knot. He jerked once, straightening my neck with ease.

"Look at me, I want to see your eyes when you come," he demanded as I shook, waves and waves of pleasure rolling through me. "Do you know how many times I've beat my dick these last few weeks to visions of those perfect tits, that greedy little cunt? I'm going to make this fucking count, Red," he promised, unbuttoning his pants and slipping out his hard cock.

I opened my mouth, waiting patiently, and he smiled, one hand sliding over my cheek, one holding the belt in his hand like reins. The hand on my cheek came down with a sharp crack just as the other Theo pushed a finger inside of me and I saw stars. Theo snapped the reins for me to look at him, and I immediately obeyed his command. He brought his cock up to rest on my face, slipping the head over my lips and cheeks, smearing pearlescent streams across my skin.

"Beautiful," he whispered, eyes softening for just a moment. He bent low and kissed me deeply while my cunt squeezed and writhed around another set of fingers.

Theo straightened, that hard look back in his eyes, and without gentleness, he thrust his cock into my mouth, stretching me wide with no warning until the tip kissed the back of my throat. At this angle, I was wide open for him and I sputtered, fighting the urge to gag as he thrust in, each time a little deeper, using me for his pleasure, feeding into mine. Tears welled up in my eyes at the delicious pressure and then my knees were bending, folding me up, and a very different cock nestled at my entrance. Theo fucked my throat with voracity, and through my tears, I watched him holding the belt slowly tightening around my neck in his hand, riding my throat, green eyes cast down on me.

It was a heady thing, knowing how I commanded all this man's attention, knowing that for as long as I breathed, he would come whenever I called. Another hand reached up, swiping my tears from my cheeks and I looked down to see that Theo wrapped his tear-stained hand around his intricate cock before settling between my thighs.

"I love you," he whispered, and the juxtaposition was over-whelming as he slid into me, carefully, reverently. Like I was the most divine being in the universe, like the secret to life lived at the apex of my thighs, but he needed to ensure I felt it. The cock may not have been as large as the one fucking my throat, but it was still big and full and ribbed completely for my pleasure. My toes curled, legs spasming and Fates, this was the sweetest reward for the shitshow of the last month.

"How does that cock feel, Zarena?" he asked, knowing I couldn't answer around the one pounding in my throat. I tried anyway, sending vibrations up his shaft. "That's right, does my little slut like it when I fuck her from both ends? I bet you'd love it if I had my cock in that ass, too, wouldn't you? You'd be a beautiful mess, stuffed so full, my cum leaking out of every hole."

Theo's thrusts in my mouth were beautifully painful, but it was his words that drove me higher, had my first orgasm barreling toward me. At the same time, the man between my thighs hoisted my legs to him and bent me to drive in deliciously, whispering words of praise. "I've missed this cunt, has it missed me? It's so pretty, so hungry, gripping me so tight. But I can't come yet, not until my good girl does. Come on my cock, Red. Drown me while I fill you up."

He was both devil and angel, playing to my degradation kink and praise kink simultaneously. It set me off like a firecracker and I soaked him, making a mess that he fucked me through, extending my high with every circle over my clit.

The belt holding my neck hostage tightened, clipping my airway. His cock was so far down my throat, his balls slapping me in the forehead with each thrust, and I was powerless to move, pinned to the table and bound. Just the way I wanted it. No fantasy could have ever compared, not to what Theo could give me. My mind stilled. My body hummed. I sank into the feeling, trusting Prometheus to take care of me in every way.

"Do you want my cum, Red?"

I moaned around him, my tongue sloppy over his tip, but the fire blazing in his eyes reflected the most depraved visage of me as he erupted, splashing over my lips. Chest heaving, he continued to stroke until my cheeks and lashes dripped with him too. Warmth pooled inside me, as Theo thrust and held his stroke, pinning my hips down. "Take every drop, that's a good fucking girl." I flexed my inner walls, milking his cock at the praise, relishing how he filled up all the space inside me.

The belt pulled free from my neck, my hands untied as the other Theo fell backward, panting. Then I was up, up, dripping cum onto the table as Theo climbed behind me, positioning me on his lap at the edge of the table. His cock nestled in the cleft of my cheeks, and I stiffened. Knowing what was to come, terrified of the stretch, but desperate to feel him claim the last part of me.

"You can take it, Red. I'll make it feel good. Won't it feel good for me to drip out of you?"

My body melted into his touch. Strong arms lifted me from the front, enough for Theo to drag his cock through my folds and slip inside, coating himself in the mess there. I moaned at the feeling of him filling me, flexing to trap him inside but he was gone again, and I was boneless and relaxed, as another set of arms supported me, massaging my neck. He cradled my forehead to his chest while Theo's fingers worked inside of me. He took his time, stretching and slipping and sliding, adding lube and his spit and more of our cum to the mix. It was a tease, a lesson in restraint as I lay there and took what he gave me, as they peppered me with kisses and sweet words until all that was left was *want*, a desperate need to have him inside of me.

The first push of his head against my ring of muscle had me crying out, but a finger working my clit and several more slowly pushing inside made pain give way to pleasure. Higher, they worked me in tandem until with a strangled moan, Theo was fully seated, splitting me apart.

"Relax, that's precious, just float, Zarena, I love you so much my prefect girl," the voice at my back rumbled sweet nothings that sank me through the fucking floor while the arms at my front pulled me down, whispering, "My good little cock-whore, come here and lick me clean."

I opened for him, sighed with content as he pushed his cock past my lips. There was no rush, no performance, just something for me to savor and him to warm his cock in while he watched a perfect replica of himself fuck my asshole.

In and out, slow and methodical, until Theo cradled my face in his hands, pulling me off his shaft to bring my eyes up to his.

"Fates, you look so perfect like this. Ruined. I need to see those pretty eyes, lay back now, that's right." The body at my back reclined, pulling me with it, my hips gripped between two strong hands, pinning me in place as he stroked lazily in and out. I smiled as the other crawled up my body, feeling warm and buzzing, even more so when a blunt head strummed over my clit.

"One more, Zarena. Give me one more."

I wasn't sure which of them said it, but I was nothing more than a vessel, a livewire of need, shaking and quivering with the intensity of being between them. Pressure pooled at my entrance, a sigh breaking past my lips as he slid home. With both inside, moving in tandem, palming my breasts and slipping fingers around my throat, I saw stars and gave him what he wanted, dragging them both with me.

When he came this time, there was nothing delicate about it. I whimpered as he kissed me, full of him, full of my own release. Connected in a way that defied the laws of the cosmos.

And when Prometheus was done thoroughly ravaging my body, he carried me to the bathing pool, taking care of the most tender parts of me. Ensuring I had water and massages and the sweetest words pressed against my tender flesh as he doted, body and mind. He only protested once when I climbed onto his lap, tired and spent, seeking the feel of him where I missed him most.

And it was here, in the Library of Alexandria, that my Titan of Knowledge slid back inside of me, stroking my hair as he read me to sleep.

Acknowledgments

For this one, I would be remiss if I didn't remind everyone that without Nessa, there not only wouldn't be a *Myths & Muses*, but there also wouldn't be a Dark Fates. Thank you, my girl, for always pushing me. Never stop giving me shit, okay? I know it's your love language.

To Paris—I wrote this novel in a tiny studio walk-up in Paris, in cafés along the Siene, at four A.M. after staying out too late in the 15th knowing I had to be up for class by nine A.M. This novel built my French reader base, thanks to proximity algorithms, and to this day, every time I look at this book, I see Paris in the spring. I see chances taken, and a life well lived.

To my agent, who keeps me going when I'm sick of everything. I appreciate you more than you know.

To Snow, who brought Theo and Z to life half a dozen times over, who worked so hard to get her body right, because representation matters.

To Rachel, for the development notes and care you put in every manuscript you return to me.

To ArtyWings for the beautiful new chapter headers.

And to Britt, Jess, and Dana, for keeping me going when I was in pass page hell and ready to toss my computer in the bayou.

The Dark Fates, and I, are nothing without all of you.

SIX MONTHS AGO

"It's fucking loud in here!" Z shouted over the wild punk music blasting from the stage.

"Yeah, isn't it great?!" I yelled back, smiling wide. I enjoyed clubs and dancing, but music was my first love, and right now, it was calling me home. I grabbed her hand as we weaved through the crowd until I had us practically pushed against the stage.

Above us, The GorgonKnots were on fire, and the heavy bass pulsed a beat that resonated through my veins. It was risky bringing Z into a club full of Otherworlders, but Electric Delphi was a place for everyone. Besides, this band was killer. Unsurprisingly. Immortality made for an infinite amount of time to learn how to play good music.

Medusa's melodic timbre vibrated through the club, a perfect blend of beauty and rage. I got lost in the music, hands in the air, swaying to the beat with Zarena. After three more hyper-energetic songs, Zarena leaned in to yell in my ear. "I need a drink and a rest!"

I motioned my understanding as she made her way off the floor, turning to follow her. I tried not to show my disappointment—I didn't want to leave this good ass spot—but I needed to make sure she was good.

Z waved me off. "No, you stay!"

I shook my head at her. "What? No, I'm coming!" I yelled back, but she just laughed and spun me around to face the band again. I shot her an appreciative look over my shoulder, watching as she disappeared into the crowd, her red hair acting as a beacon I could follow with ease.

I threw my head back as they transitioned their original song into a cover of "Rebel Girl" by Bikini Kill that had me screaming at the top of my lungs. Energy surged and pulsed through the crowd, feeding off the band in a symbiotic loop as Medusa freed her lochs and windmilled them around. To the naked eyes, they were normal hair but to those of us in the know, the obsidian snakes weaving through were obvious.

A sudden jostle sent me stumbling sideways into something hard and tall, and . . . *Fuck me*. I looked up into the most stunning pair of gray eyes I'd ever seen. The world around me faded to nothing as they regarded me, piercing right down to my soul. I was acutely aware that the eyes belonged to a face, with a nose and lips and a chin but I couldn't wrench my gaze away from them.

Couldn't register my hands were braced against that something hard and tall, but my innate siren senses alerted me instantly that the body under my grip belonged to an immortal. His power pulsed—a quiet, steady thrum that wrapped around me.

An intoxicating scent of rosewood and clove mingled on the air between us, drawing me closer in his orbit. His eyes widened, a muscle jumped in his cheek, and it was enough to pull my gaze from his. Insane move. The rest of him was even more incredible than his eyes, and I took my time, surveying every inch. I drank him down, let my eyes travel over his body, taking in the tattooed sleeves, and the way he filled out those tight jeans, the tendrils of ink crawling up his chest and neck, peeking out from the collar of that leather jacket. He was covered in ink, even the shaved sides of his head displayed intricate skull pieces and twisted blooms. A green mohawk stood to sharp points down the center of his head. The energy between us cackled, and *Bondye*, he looked ready to fucking devour me.

I wasn't a stranger to fast and hard hookups. In fact, I *preferred* that method of pleasure. No strings, no feelings, but even by my standards, this dude was *intense*. Steadying my breaths, I inched back out of his space, dropping my hand from the lapel of his jacket, the worn leather soft against my skin.

The distance between us ached as I swayed back, but he was having none of it. A tattooed hand with MEMENTO MORI tattooed across the knuckles sank into the leather of my corset near my hip, tugging me back in his proximity. He didn't speak as he stared me down, but confidence rolled off him, dominating and patient, and Bondye, if that wasn't fucking hot enough to make me melt. I was *very* much into everything happening on this sticky, hot dance floor. Slowly, he pulled me closer. *Closer*. Until every inch of him was pressed against me, but he gave me enough time to stop him. Something told me at my slightest discomfort, he would without hesitation.

"Careful where those hands land," I teased, working to keep it casual but my voice came out far more breathy than I intended.

He studied my face as I drank in his features—the fierce cut of his chin, the green hair spiked into a mohawk. Everything about him screamed *danger*, which only served to heighten my attraction. Nothing about this could potentially be long-term, but he seemed like the kind of danger I'd be happy to be under for the evening.

"That so, love?" he drawled. *Bondye.* A British accent too? It caressed over my skin, buckling my knees. I was a goner for accents, loved the way my name sounded tumbling from rough lips, foreign lips. His gray eyes were storm clouds that caught my breath.

"That's so . . . ?" I trailed off, awaiting his response.

A small smile played on his lips. "Thanatos."

At his response an unhealthy shiver of heat rolled down my spine. *Thanatos*—I knew that name. The LOA, the Greeks, and the Norse were the most prominent pantheons residing in the N.O. Otherworlders were taught at a young age who the most powerful amongst them were, warned to avoid their attention at all costs, lest we get caught in the crossfire of one squabble or another.

But I was never one to follow the rules, self-preservation be damned, and in this moment, all I wanted was to let the immortal staring at me like lunch do his fucking worst. I shook slightly as I let his power overtake my senses, tasting it, scenting him. He smelled like darkness, like divinity, like the sweet release of death.

Thanatos, God of Death.

"I see that my reputation precedes me"—he leaned in, crowding my space, inhaling the scent at my neck before pulling back and smiling—"sweet siren."

A large hand slid up to cup my cheek, gentle and cold and powerful all at once, the size of it bigger than the entire side of my face. His gray eyes flicked between my eyes, my lips, the dusting of blue glitter glistening over my cheek like it took all his self-restraint not to drag me to the Hells right then and there.

"Maybe it does. Maybe it doesn't. Who you are doesn't matter to me." I tried to keep my voice steady, but Thanatos was tracing his thumb across my jaw. I wanted to sink to my knees and see how far he'd take this right here, in front of everyone.

I blinked twice, willing any part of my self-preservation to decide to show up, but instead, I leaned into the hand cradling me. A hand that sent thousands—if not millions—to their final resting place in the Underworld. A god who could stop my heart with a flick of his wrist. But as I stared up at him, there was no hiding how affected he was by this, and that too, made me feel powerful. Wanted.

"I think, perhaps you should go get yourself a drink," he said. Cold air rushed between us as he broke his hold, stepping away half a step. He pulled a bill from his pocket and slid it into my palm.

I stared between him and the twenty in my palm, confusion overtaking my previous horniness. "The fuck? Are you paying me to go away?" I asked, sliding my hand to my hip, feigning indifference even though the implied insult stung. I wasn't crazy. That moment was a powder keg, waiting to ignite, but he turned it off so fast I nearly got whiplash.

Thanatos folded his muscled arms across his chest, smirking with amusement. I tried not to focus on the delicious way his biceps rippled.

"Not at all, love." He shrugged, still looking me up and down. "I just want you to have a drink and give yourself time to talk yourself out of this. If after the drink you still want a ride, I'd be honored to be of service." He spun me around by the shoulders before I could reply, either to curse him out or defend myself, I hadn't decided. His body pressed against mine, cold electricity seeping through the little fabric I had on. "Find the bald bartender. He'll take care of you, love, and after he does, I will." Thanatos promised, voice dripping with dominance and yeah, just like that, I was back in. He gently nudged me toward the bar, and my feet moved, obeying his command like he'd unlocked some sort of sub space in the middle of a crowded dance floor.

I bellied up to the busy bar, the twenty clutched in my hand, still unsure what the fuck was happening. A pretty blue-haired bartender strolled up to me with a bright smile, eyeliner sharp as a blade.

"What can I get for you, darlin'?"

I leaned in, raising my voice above the loud music. "Is there a bald-headed bartender working tonight?" I asked. She cocked an eyebrow curiously, giving me a once-over before backing off the bar. "One sec, let me see if I can find him," she shouted back. I watched her walk off into the sea of barbacks and bartenders, but I lost her in the crowd of bodies when the strobes flashed.

I turned around, eyes searching for a splash of red hair in the distance. I caught Zarena's beautiful reflection in a mirror over a side booth, chatting with some guy. She looked fine, relaxed, so I let my anxiety quell. Andros hated her coming to places filled with our kind, but he was *so* overprotective of her. Z was trained to fight, and even against an Otherworlder, I knew she could hold her own. He needed to learn to lighten up and give her some damn space. After the year she'd had, she deserved to cut up a little.

On stage, The GorgonKnots wrapped their set and a DJ took over, queuing up a house remix that had the crowd moving again in no time. I resisted the urge to turn back to the bar, anxiety burning in my chest. What was I even doing? Maybe there *was* no bald bartender, and this was just a ploy to let me down gently. I could have misread the attraction. Could have mistaken that tug between us. He was a god after all, and a powerful one at that. I was barely a step above mortal—no, fuck that. He'd be lucky to spend any amount of time with me. I'm fantastic.

A throat cleared behind me, interrupting my thoughts. I turned, swallowing my tongue at the sight of the stunning man leaning over the bar, staring back at me curiously. He was taller than me, but shorter than Thanatos, with a sculpted body shown off by the open red wine blazer. No shirt. Gold chains dangled around his neck, over his chest, violet eyes flashing in the house lights. His lips tipped up in a smile, full, mischievous, as he checked me out unabashedly. I stared right the fuck back.

Okay, death god, what the Hells was this all about?

It was clear by the taste of power on the air, the thrum of electricity in his aura, this was a god all his own, with sculpted features and full lips and eyes so deeply brown that they almost bled into purple at the edges. There was a boldness to him, in the way his head tilted curiously to the side as we drank each other in.

"I heard a pretty girl was asking for me, but that description is like calling a supernova a mere light in the night sky." His words washed over me, honeyed and intoxicating, and I found myself leaning forward—just slightly—wanting to hear more. He was different than the Death God, like they were two sides of a coin—one dark and brooding, one vibrant and full of life.

"Tatiana," I offered, extending my hand. He took it, and as it had with Thanatos, sparks danced wherever his skin touched mine.

"Dionysus, but pretty girls can call me Dio." His eyes raked over me hungrily, just as Thanatos's had, and my mood instantly improved.

One way or another, I was in for a wild night.

Don't miss
the next installments
in the epic Dark Fates series

DECEMBER 1, 2026   MARCH 2, 2027

Available wherever books are sold.

But wait, there's more . . .

BLOOD & BEDLAM, a brand-new title by T.C. Kraven and the first in the NOLA After Dark series, publishes September 2026

DIVERSION
BOOKS

This September, memory is in the blood . . .

In the shadowed world beneath New Orleans's music, masks, and midnight rituals, the original vampyr reigns, keeping a fragile peace among rival clans, until he spies the one woman he lost centuries ago.

Available September 15, 2026.
Preorder now wherever books are sold!